READERS G

CONSULTANT ED

Published

Thomas P. Adler	lamed Desire–Cat on
Pascale Aebischer	
Lucie Armitt	i *Bede–The Mill on the Floss*
Simon Avery	: *The Mayor of Casterbridge–Jude Obscure*
Paul Baines	Daniel Defoe: *Robinson Crusoe–Moll Flanders*
Annika Bautz	Jane Austen: *Sense and Sensibility – Pride and Prejudice–Emma*
Matthew Beedham	The Novels of Kazuo Ishiguro
Richard Beynon	D. H. Lawrence: *The Rainbow–Women in Love*
Peter Boxall	Samuel Beckett: *Waiting for Godot–Endgame*
Claire Brennan	The Poetry of Sylvia Plath
Susan Bruce	Shakespeare: *King Lear*
Sandie Byrne	Jane Austen: *Mansfield Park*
Alison Chapman	Elizabeth Gaskell: *Mary Barton–North and South*
Peter Childs	The Fiction of Ian McEwan
Christine Clegg	Vladimir Nabokov: *Lolita*
John Coyle	James Joyce: *Ulysses–A Portrait of the Artist as a Young Man*
Martin Coyle	Shakespeare: *Richard II*
Justin D. Edwards	Postcolonial Literature
Michael Faherty	The Poetry of W. B. Yeats
Sarah Gamble	The Fiction of Angela Carter
Jodi-Anne George	*Beowulf*
Jodi-Anne George	Chaucer: The General Prologue to *The Canterbury Tales*
Jane Goldman	Virginia Woolf: *To the Lighthouse–The Waves*
Huw Griffiths	Shakespeare: *Hamlet*
Vanessa Guignery	The Fiction of Julian Barnes
Louisa Hadley	The Fiction of A. S. Byatt
Geoffrey Harvey	Thomas Hardy: *Tess of the d'Urbervilles*
Paul Hendon	The Poetry of W. H. Auden
Terry Hodgson	The Plays of Tom Stoppard for Stage, Radio, TV and Film
William Hughes	Bram Stoker: *Dracula*
Stuart Hutchinson	Mark Twain: *Tom Sawyer–Huckleberry Finn*
Stuart Hutchinson	Edith Wharton: *The House of Mirth – The Custom of the Country*
Betty Jay	E. M. Forster: *A Passage to India*
Aaron Kelly	Twentieth-Century Irish Literature
Elmer Kennedy-Andrews	The Poetry of Seamus Heaney
Elmer Kennedy-Andrews	Nathaniel Hawthorne: *The Scarlet Letter*
Daniel Lea	George Orwell: *Animal Farm–Nineteen Eighty-Four*
Rachel Lister	Alice Walker: *The Color Purple*
Sara Lodge	Charlotte Brontë: *Jane Eyre*

Philippa Lyon	Twentieth-Century War Poetry
Merja Makinen	The Novels of Jeanette Winterson
Matt McGuire	Contemporary Scottish Literature
Timothy Milnes	Wordsworth: *The Prelude*
Jago Morrison	The Fiction of Chinua Achebe
Carl Plasa	Tony Morrison: *Beloved*
Carl Plasa	Jean Rhys: *Wide Sargasso Sea*
Nicholas Potter	Shakespeare: *Antony and Cleopatra*
Nicholas Potter	Shakespeare: *Othello*
Nicholas Potter	Shakespeare's Late Plays: *Pericles, Cymbeline, The Winter's Tale, The Tempest*
Steven Price	The Plays, Screenplays and Films of David Mamet
Nicholas Seager	The Rise of the Novel
Berthold Schoene-Harwood	Mary Shelley: *Frankenstein*
Nick Selby	T. S. Eliot: *The Waste Land*
Nick Selby	Herman Melville: *Moby Dick*
Nick Selby	The Poetry of Walt Whitman
David Smale	Salman Rushdie: *Midnight's Chidren – The Satanic Verses*
Patsy Stoneman	Emily Brontë: *Wuthering Heights*
Susie Thomas	Hanif Kureishi
Nicolas Tredell	F. Scott Fitzgerald: *The Great Gatsby*
Nicolas Tredell	Joseph Conrad: *Heart of Darkness*
Nicolas Tredell	Charles Dickens: *Great Expectations*
Nicolas Tredell	William Faulkner: *The Sound and the Fury–As I Lay Dying*
Nicolas Tredell	Shakespeare: *A Midsummer Night's Dream*
Nicolas Tredell	Shakespeare: *Macbeth*
Nicolas Tredell	The Fiction of Martin Amis
Matthew Woodcock	Shakespeare: *Henry V*
Gillian Woods	Shakespeare: *Romeo and Juliet*
Angela Wright	Gothic Fiction

Forthcoming

Brian Baker	Science Fiction
Alan Gibbs	Jewish-American Literature since 1945
Sarah Haggarty & Jon Mee	Willam Blake: *Songs of Innocence and Experience*
Keith Hughes	African-American Literature
Britta Martens	The Poetry of Robert Browning
Michael Whitworth	Virginia Woolf: *Mrs Dalloway*

Readers' Guides to Essential Criticism
Series Standing Order
ISBN 1–4039–0108–2
(*outside North America only*)

You can receive future titles in this series as they are published by placing a standing order. Please contact your bookseller or, in the case of difficulty, write to us at the address below with your name and address, the title of the series and the ISBN quoted above.

Customer Services Department, Macmillan Distribution Ltd Houndmills, Basingstoke, Hampshire RG21 6XS, England

---

The Rise of the Novel

NICHOLAS SEAGER

Consultant editor: Nicolas Tredell

palgrave
macmillan

First published 2012 by
PALGRAVE MACMILLAN

Palgrave Macmillan in the UK is an imprint of Macmillan Publishers Limited, registered in England, company number 785998, of Houndmills, Basingstoke, Hampshire RG21 6XS.

Palgrave Macmillan in the US is a division of St Martin's Press LLC, 175 Fifth Avenue, New York, NY 10010.

Palgrave Macmillan is the global academic imprint of the above companies and has companies and representatives throughout the world.

Palgrave® and Macmillan® are registered trademarks in the United States, the United Kingdom, Europe and other countries.

ISBN 978–0–230–25182–3 hardback
ISBN 978–0–230–25183–0 paperback

This book is printed on paper suitable for recycling and made from fully managed and sustained forest sources. Logging, pulping and manufacturing processes are expected to conform to the environmental regulations of the country of origin.

A catalogue record for this book is available from the British Library.

A catalog record for this book is available from the Library of Congress.

10 9 8 7 6 5
21 20 19 18 17 16

Printed and bound in China

CONTENTS

ACKNOWLEDGEMENTS

My thanks to Nicolas Tredell and to the two anonymous readers, whose feedback at various stages has been tremendously helpful. The professionalism of Sonya Barker, Felicity Noble, and all at Palgrave Macmillan has made working on this project a great pleasure. I would like to thank Brean Hammond for many enlightening conversations about the eighteenth-century novel. I am grateful to my colleagues at Keele University for helping to make it such a wonderful place to teach and write. And I would like to thank my family on both sides of the Atlantic for many years of encouragement, especially Ginny Weckstein, my wife. This book is dedicated to the memory of my grandparents: Gilbert and Kathleen Seager, and James and Audrey McCormick.

Introduction

The Rise of the Novel is one of the best-known, most commonly taught, and enduringly satisfying concepts in literary criticism. Its classic formulation, in Ian Watt's seminal *The Rise of the Novel* (1957), locates this process in eighteenth-century England as the effect of a number of social and intellectual developments that resulted in the stylistic innovation of formal realism. This study will answer a number of questions. Why do we locate the rise of the novel in the eighteenth century? Why in England (or, more properly, Britain)? By when had the novel finished rising? What were the historical conditions that made the novel possible? What formal features took shape as the novel developed? And what criticisms has Watt's 'rise' model received?

Notwithstanding these criticisms, Watt still has his champions, and his thesis remains central to the debate. Reporting the later response to *The Rise of the Novel*, Lennard Davis says:

> ■ [Watt] made some really big mistakes – he thought there was 'a' novel; he thought it had a beginning; he assumed it was a narrative fiction that displaced previous narrative fictions and had a 'rise' located in metropole England. In doing so, he was naive, sexist, racist, Anglophilic, logocentric, essentialist, positivist, vulgarly materialistic, and probably homophobic. But nobody is perfect.[1] □

I hope that after reading this book Ian Watt will seem like less of a bugbear to scholars and students than Davis wittily shows he has been since 1957. I hope to achieve this, first, by carefully delineating what Watt says about the novel; second, by showing that Watt's major ideas have a history as well as a heritage. This book is an attempt to historicize fully the idea of the rise of the British novel as this concept has developed since the eighteenth century; it will be seen that this criticism precedes and goes far beyond Watt.

The discussion of criticism that follows commences with eighteenth- and nineteenth-century efforts to explain the origins of the novel and continues with twentieth- and twenty-first-century academic scholarship, which has approached the question via a variety of methodologies. I proceed from formalism and historicism through political criticisms like feminism and postcolonialism, right down to the newest kinds of critical approaches. I do not assume the reader's extensive familiarity with such theoretical approaches, nor with much more than the basics of eighteenth-century history, although I will be brief in my explanation of these rudiments. I do, however, assume some familiarity with the eighteenth-century British novel, at least the most important primary works and authors.[2]

Even the briefest outline of the emergent novel would take stock of certain major writers. This includes Aphra Behn, who published *Love-Letters Between a Nobleman and His Sister* (1684–7) and *Oroonoko* (1688), as well as other early female writers like Delarivier Manley, writing in the first quarter of the eighteenth century, and Eliza Haywood, whose novelistic career stretches from 1719 to the 1750s. The earliest household name is Daniel Defoe, author of *Robinson Crusoe* (1719) and *Moll Flanders* (1722). He was followed by Samuel Richardson, author of *Pamela* (1740–1) and *Clarissa* (1747–8), and Henry Fielding, author of *Joseph Andrews* (1742) and *Tom Jones* (1749). Tobias Smollett, Laurence Sterne, and Frances Burney are widely considered the most important novelists in the second half of the eighteenth century, leading up to Jane Austen and Sir Walter Scott at the start of the nineteenth. In addition, scholars in the past thirty years have expanded the canon to include a plethora of names with which the reader will be increasingly familiarized in the following chapters. As well as novelists who had long been deemed non-canonical (Charlotte Lennox, John Cleland, Sarah Fielding, and many more), this account extends to several more traditionally canonical works which are outliers in the story of the novel's rise – major prose fictions which may previously have seemed too early, like Philip Sidney's *Arcadia* (1590–3) and John Bunyan's *The Pilgrim's Progress* (1678–84), or ones that have not always seemed straightforwardly novelistic, like Jonathan Swift's *Gulliver's Travels* (1726), Samuel Johnson's *Rasselas* (1759), and Oliver Goldsmith's *The Vicar of Wakefield* (1766).

My focus is on accounts of *the rise of the British novel in the eighteenth century*, rather than the broader topic, *the eighteenth-century British novel*. A consequence of this is that I only discuss work on a number of later-eighteenth-century subgenres – sentimental fiction, the Gothic, and political fictions – with respect to how these have been encompassed into accounts of the novel's development. These subgenres will feature extensively, because they have been deemed important to the establishment of the genre after mid-century, but dedicated scholarship on each has been omitted.[3]

Chapter 1 discusses accounts of the rise of the novel constructed in the eighteenth and nineteenth centuries. Much has been written on what Georgian and Victorian men and women understood the novel to *be*, but little has been written on how they understood the genre to have come into *being*. This chapter supplies that need by looking at accounts of the rise of romance, the elevation of Richardson and Fielding, the process of canonization during the Romantic era, and histories of the novel in the Victorian and Edwardian periods. Chapter 2 traces the ideas behind Ian Watt's field-defining book by looking at tendencies in academic criticism in the forty years before *The Rise of the Novel.* Many of the formulations and insights associated with Watt had been lingering in the air for some time before they were so forcefully voiced as part of an integrated account in *The Rise of the Novel.* But interpreting Watt alongside contemporaneous formalist accounts of the novel also indicates the degree of his innovation. Chapter 2 will establish the terms for understanding Chapters 3 and 4: the tensions between a formalist analysis of the workings of a genre and a historicist analysis that relates genre to cultural contexts.

Chapter 3 moves through three decades of formalist criticism, from the 1950s to the 1980s. Watt's historical explanation went largely unchallenged, but some of his claims about novelistic form were modified and extended in this period. The criticism discussed in Chapter 3 analyses genre, narrative structure, and reader response, by and large discounting historical considerations. By contrast, Chapter 4 addresses historicist, ideological criticism, which prevailed during the 1980s, as the novel was assessed for its collusive participation in the transformation of social, political, and cultural life produced by capitalist economics and the political ideology of liberalism. These studies were influenced by theorists of social power and cultural formation like Karl Marx, Michel Foucault, and Mikhail Bakhtin.

Chapters 5 and 6 tackle two specific forms of historical and political criticism. Chapter 5 evaluates feminist understandings of the early novel. Why had twentieth-century scholarship managed to talk about the novel with minimal reference to female writers, especially when the novel had long been considered a 'woman's' genre? What part did the novel play in producing and disseminating patriarchal culture, particularly models of femininity that valorized domesticity? These questions and others will be addressed in Chapter 5. Chapter 6 looks at postcolonial and postnational criticism of the early novel. How did the novel represent non-European cultures and contact between Britain and its colonies? What is the relationship between the development of imperialism and the novel? This chapter also looks at the role of the novel in the rise of nationalism and recent attempts to reconceive the rise of the novel as an international phenomenon, rather than restricted to Britain.

Chapter 7 brings revisions of Watt's thesis down to the year 2000 in a number of studies that analyse the novel in relation to other competing or complementary discourses. This kind of criticism advances the historicist backlash against formalism, whereby the novel is conceived less as a genre, as a category intrinsic to itself, and more as a 'discursive field'. The work assessed in this chapter is concerned with how the novel was eventually separated from other discourses, like history and pornography, in the primordial soup of early modern prose. Next, Chapter 8 considers recent work on print culture, book history, and the history of reading practices as these have had an impact on the study of the rise of the novel. Finally, Chapters 9 and 10 focus on thematic criticism of the rise of the novel. The scholarship discussed here typically accepts the entity we call the 'novel' in the eighteenth century and assesses its engagements with analogous disciplines, ranging from economics and society to politics and medicine. The key word in many of these studies is the conjunction 'and': critics pair a contextual topic (education, family, law, and so on) with a periodized genre (the eighteenth-century novel). This kind of work is diffuse and extensive: whilst trying to be as inclusive as necessary, I focus as much as possible on studies, and parts of studies, that bring ideas to bear on the establishment of the novel. Those that hardly touch on the issue of generic change because they are writing cultural history for which literary form is immaterial receive less attention than those that tackle the question of novelistic origins.

My aim in writing this book has been to historicize changing ideas about the rise of the novel, and I would like to establish a few guiding premises for the reader. First, in the vast majority of cases, I do not propose this guide as a substitute for reading the criticism itself. Second, I do not *endorse* the understanding that the rise of the novel occurred for the first and definitive time in eighteenth-century England. The criticism I discuss at various times complicates almost every single term of this understanding – 'rise', 'novel', 'eighteenth-century', 'England', and even, insofar as they imply singularity, both instances of the definite article 'the' in 'the rise of the novel'. My account, my organization of material, my prioritizations, and my exclusions inflect this revisionist understanding in several ways. The third premise is that I have tried to supply an interpretation of rise-of-the-novel criticism that reflects on the competition between formalist and historicist understandings. This perspective will not obtrude in the exposition of individual critical works, but I will return to the tension in the Conclusion.

I will note a few things that may help the reader to navigate this book. When in the text I direct the reader to a chapter by number – for example, 'see Chapter 4' – I am referring to this guide, not to a work of criticism. Except where clarity is needful, I will give the year of publication for a literary work and the full name of an author in the first mention only. Finally, although this study proceeds chronologically for the most part, it actually organizes work by methodology, so the reader should be aware that very recent criticism appears from Chapter 5 onwards and that Chapters 9 and 10 include work published as early as 1993.

CHAPTER ONE

Eighteenth- and Nineteenth-Century Accounts of the Rise of the Novel

Writers were puzzling over the nature and provenance of fiction even as the novel was said to be rising, and the terms on which they conducted the debate continue to resonate with modern critics. This chapter addresses attempts to account for the development and progress of the English novel from the eighteenth century through the Romantic period to Victorian and Edwardian histories of fiction.

The Augustan Age, 1700–80

The word 'novel' as a label for prose fiction meant something quite different to readers at the start of the eighteenth century than to those at the end of the nineteenth. Deriving from the Italian *novella* and sharing a root with the French *nouvelle*, 'novel' in Britain before about 1750 signified a short fictional story usually involving romance, as in the lexicographer Samuel Johnson's 1755 definition: 'a small tale, generally of love'. It was widely associated with the genre of romance, as in Daniel Defoe's assertion in the preface to *Moll Flanders* (1722) that 'the World is so taken up of late with Novels and Romances, that it will be hard for a private History to be taken for Genuine'.[1] Defoe, often placed at the start of the rise of the novel, here purposefully avoids *both* these fictional labels, preferring 'history', and expresses anxiety about a newly popular (though maybe not new) genre he has since been credited with inventing. An investigation into how Georgian men and women comprehended the advance of the novel necessitates giving attention to its near kin, the romance.

Bishop Pierre-Daniel Huet's *Traitté de l'origine des romans* (1670), translated into English as *The History of Romances* in 1715, was an early effort to identify the source of romance – and to dignify this genre in neoclassical terms largely derived from Aristotle's *Poetics* (c.335 BCE).[2] Huet insists that romances, which are 'Fictions of Love' in prose or verse, have ancient pedigree, originating in the propensity of the cultures of Middle Eastern antiquity to use language figuratively, producing fables designed to preserve secret knowledge (15–16). Huet traces romance's migration from ancient Egypt, Arabia, Persia, Greece, and Rome through its decline in the Dark Ages to its post-Renaissance revival in Western Europe, culminating in 'the Excellent Degree of Art and Elegance, to which the *French* Nation is now arrived in Romances' (138). Huet's translator, Stephen Lewis, attests in 1715, like Defoe, to the proliferation of romance in early eighteenth-century England: '*Romance* has of late convey'd it self very far into the Esteem of this Nation, and is become the Principal Diversion of the Retirement of People of all Conditions' (viii). He expresses his hope 'that some *English Genius* will *dare* to Naturalize *Romance* into our Soil' (ix). Lewis's hope is not representative: the popular current was dismissive of romance and novel alike. The so-called French heroic romance, with which Huet's *History* culminates, influenced English literature mainly in the work of female writers like Aphra Behn and Eliza Haywood (both also translated continental romances). As the novel gained cultural authority during the century, these women were written out of the story of its development – which is ironic, because they, unlike Defoe, Samuel Richardson, or Henry Fielding, actually labelled their stories 'novels', in the sense intended by the Earl of Chesterfield when, in the 1740s, he called the novel 'a kind of abbreviation of a Romance' (*N&R*, p. 100).

Such distinctions between the novel and the romance, focusing on length and probability, were increasingly common and reflect the view that the novel developed from the romance – or at least that an old model of fantastical romance was giving way to a new, probable one. William Congreve draws a sharp distinction between heroic romance and novel in *Incognita* (1691), but maintains the 'devolutionary' connection between them:

■ Romances are generally composed of the Constant Loves and invincible Courages of Hero's, Heroins, Kings and Queens, Mortals of the first Rank, and so forth; where lofty Language, miraculous Contingencies and impossible Performances, elevate and surprize the Reader into a giddy Delight which leaves him flat upon the Ground whenever he gives of. [...] Novels are of a more familiar nature; Come near us, and represent to us Intrigues in practice, delight us with Accidents and odd Events, but not such as are wholly unusual or unpresidented [*sic*], such which not being so distant from our Belief bring also the pleasure nearer us. Romances give more of Wonder, Novels more Delight. (*N&R*, p. 27) □

Congreve's attempted separation of old romance and new novel, as well as foregrounding the more familiar and probable nature of the latter, suggests that the heroic romances catered for an aristocratic culture that seemed increasingly out of date (or foreign) to English culture just after the Protestant succession was bulwarked by the Glorious Revolution (1688). Associations between the progress of the novel and that of civilization increased over the next two centuries. For example, in the preface to Tobias Smollett's 1748 novel, *Roderick Random*, romance is invoked as a bastardization of ancient epic, the product of an era of 'ignorance, vanity, and superstition', whereas the novel came about when 'learning advanced, and genius received cultivation' (*N&R*, pp. 119–20). Smollett's is an early view of the novel as the product of rational, enlightened modernity.

The distinction between novel and romance was not always sharply drawn, however, partly because the terms had not yet solidified, but principally because the majority of commentators considered both pernicious, betokening a decline in cultural standards, an encroachment on probability and propriety. It was not until the time of Clara Reeve's *The Progress of Romance* (1785) that critics distinguished with consistency between novel and romance as respectively realistic and idealistic fictions. 'The Romance is an heroic fable, which treats of fabulous persons and things', explains Reeve, whereas 'the Novel is a picture of real life and manners, and of the times in which it is written'.[3] Congreve's century-old distinction had prevailed: Reeve identifies contemporaneity (a modern setting) and fidelity to reality (realism) as hallmarks of the novel that distinguish it from romances set in an indistinct, distant past and which disregard the everyday and probable. By the end of the eighteenth century, some writers expressed nostalgia for heroic romance, seeing it as the product of a golden age, inspiring chivalric manners that moralists feared had been lost in polite, commercial Georgian England. Siblings John and Anna Laetitia Aikin (later Barbauld) opined in 1773:

■ It would perhaps be better, if our romances were more like those of the old stamp, which tended to raise human nature, and inspire a certain grace and dignity of manners of which we have hardly the idea. The [romances'] high notions of honour, the wild and fanciful spirit of adventure and romantic love, elevated the mind; our novels tend to depress and enfeeble it. (*N&R*, pp. 289–90) □

What has become known as 'the rise of the novel' was still considered a negative innovation, and this is partly because it was aligned with the decline of romance. The Aikins' view was echoed by Vicesimus Knox in 1778: 'If it be true, that the present age is more corrupt than the preceding, the great multiplication of Novels has probably contributed to its degeneracy' (*N&R*, p. 304). Knox typifies the reactionary mistrust of the novel that died hard over the course of the century.

Many critics have identified the emergence of the novel with the innovations of Richardson and Fielding during the 1740s and 1750s, particularly as these both *said* they were doing something new. The publication of *Pamela* (1740–1) provoked considerable public response, ranging from praise to contempt, and necessitated Richardson's defence of his aims. He wrote to Aaron Hill: 'I thought the story, if written in an easy and natural manner, suitably to the simplicity of it, might possibly introduce a new species of writing, that might possibly turn young people into a course of reading different from the pomp and parade of romance-writing, and dismissing the improbable and marvellous, with which novels generally abound, might tend to promote the cause of religion and virtue'.[4]

Richardson understands his achievement as the morally motivated expulsion of improbable romance. Fielding's differences of outlook prompted him to lampoon Richardson and to mount his own justifications of novel-writing in *Joseph Andrews* (1742) and *Tom Jones* (1749). Though he cites literary models ranging from Homer to Cervantes, Fielding adopts a metaphor that has colonial and political overtones to arrogate originality and sovereignty to his efforts: 'As I am, in reality, the founder of a new province of writing, so I am at liberty to make what laws I please therein'.[5] The playfulness of tone does not negate the entirely earnest claim to originality. Richardson's public and private writings regarding *Clarissa* (1747–8) and *Sir Charles Grandison* (1753–4) elaborated his ideas about fiction. There were two chief differences between these pre-eminent mid-century novelists. First, whereas Richardson depicted paragons for emulation (the world as it should be), Fielding propounded a theory of morally 'mixed' characters, neither wholly good nor bad (the world as it really is). Second, whereas Richardson posed as an editor to present a series of letters between supposedly real people, Fielding embraced fictionality by utilizing a third-person narrative persona.

These moral and formal differences have provided fertile ground for those seeking the origins of the novel in the Richardson–Fielding rivalry. Allen Michie has surveyed how the contest played out in criticism from the mid-eighteenth to the mid-twentieth century.[6] The prototypes of Richardson and Fielding fuelled competing ideas not just about how prose fiction should be written but also about how it had developed. William Warburton, later Bishop of Gloucester, supplied a preface to Volume III of *Clarissa*, which expounded a 'Richardsonian' view of the progress of romance. The 'original of the first barbarous *Romances*', Warburton explains, was in a desire during the medieval period for easy entertainment, meaning they were made up of 'uncommon, extraordinary, and miraculous Adventures'. Satiety bred contempt, and the Spanish 'novel' followed: whereas everything in the romances 'was conducted by *Inchantment*; so now all was managed by *Intrigue*'. In turn, 'the avoiding these defects gave rise to the *Heroical Romances* of the *French*', which debased stories from antiquity with baleful 'modern fable and invention'. Thereafter came 'little amatory Novels, which succeeded these heavier Volumes', and 'tho' the Writers avoided the dryness of the Spanish Intrigue, and the extravagance of the French Heroism, yet, by too natural a representation of their Subject, they opened the door to a worse evil than a corruption of *Taste*; and that was, A corruption of *Heart*'. Out of this history of successive prose fictional error, Warburton concludes, came Richardson to reform fiction: 'And this was by a faithful and chaste copy of real *Life* and *Manners*' (*N&R*, p. 123). This trajectory of ancient and medieval romance progressing to sixteenth- and seventeenth-century Spanish 'amatory' and French 'heroic' romance, and on to shorter amatory novels, and, finally, to morally edifying, realistic fiction in mid-eighteenth-century England was becoming a dominant narrative.

The anonymous author (perhaps Francis Coventry) of *An Essay on the New Species of Writing founded by Mr. Fielding* (1751), gave a similar history to Warburton, but accorded Fielding prominence:

> ■ Sometime before [Fielding's] new Species of Writing appear'd, the World had been pester'd with Volumes, commonly known by the Name of Romances, or Novels, Tales, *&c*. fill'd with any thing which the wildest Imagination could suggest. [...] *France* first gave Birth to this strange Monster, and *England* was proud to import it among the rest of her Neighbour's Follies. A Deluge of Impossibility overflow'd the Press. Nothing was receiv'd with any kind of Applause, that did not appear under the Title of a Romance, or Novel; and Common Sense was kick'd out of Doors to make Room for marvellous Dullness. [...] The Disease became epidemical, but there were no Hopes of a Cure, 'till Mr. *Fielding* endeavour'd to show the World, that pure Nature could furnish out as agreeable Entertainment, as those airy non-entical Forms they had long ador'd. (*N&R*, p. 151) □

The author expresses his weariness with the formulaic plots, character types, and elevated style of old romance, which he contrasts with the pleasant naturalism of the 'new Species'. Romance is identified as women's reading and is associated with debauched French tastes. The pathological metaphor in the quotation diagnoses romance as a corrupting influence which Fielding had helped to cure.

Although the extent to which these authors wrote in direct opposition to one another can be overstated, after the middle of the eighteenth century, it was generally accepted, whether one sided with Richardson or Fielding, and despite enduring antipathy to fiction as a whole, that the new fiction (still not uniformly called the novel) superseded a romance tradition that was tired, feminine, morally reprehensible, and nationally suspect.[7] The role of Richardson and Fielding in legitimizing prose fiction, and in enabling a narrative of its rise, is hard to overstate. A 1753 letter to the periodical, *The World*, proceeds in a fairly conventional anti-novel vein, before it demands the editor to 'interpose your authority, and forbid your readers [...] even to attempt to open any novel, or romance, unlicensed by you; unless it should happen to be stamped Richardson or Fielding' (*N&R*, p. 208). The Richardson–Fielding dichotomy was, inevitably, exclusionary; whichever was given preference, 1740 became a cut-off date, relegating a lot of prose fiction to the novel's 'prehistory', reifying a romance/novel divide, and enshrining a male-dominated canon that was not systematically critiqued until the late twentieth century, as Chapter 5 will show. A good example comes from Hugh Blair's 'On Fictitious History' (1762), which briefly dwells on what he terms 'a very insignificant class of writings, known by the name of Romances and Novels'. Blair reproduces the now-familiar narrative of ancient romance to heroic romance to modern novel, and his is an early usage of the 'rise' metaphor for fiction's development, offering 'a few observations on the rise and progress of fictitious history'. In terms of the canon, in Blair's somewhat triumphalist account of old romance being trumped by new, the modern writers before Richardson and Fielding who matter are Miguel de Cervantes, author of *Don Quixote* (1605–15); Alain-René Le Sage, author of *Gil Blas* (1715–35); Pierre de Marivaux, author of *La vie de Marianne* (1731–45); and the here-unnamed author of *Robinson Crusoe* (1719), Daniel Defoe. Frances Burney's preface to her debut novel, *Evelina* (1778), adds Jean-Jacques Rousseau, author of *Julie, ou la nouvelle Héloïse* (1761), Samuel Johnson, and Tobias Smollett to Marivaux, Richardson, and Fielding in a company of important novelists. A canon was starting to take shape, and this was continued in rise-of-the-novel criticism during the Romantic period.

Romanticism, 1780–1840

Between the 1780s and 1830s, the novel gained a measure of cultural legitimacy, as an enduring narrative of its rise and of the eighteenth-century canon took hold. Histories of prose fiction became more systematic, scholarly work was written on early novelists, anthologies of novels were produced, and the periodical press that reviewed new fiction grew apace. These last two developments have been analysed for the part they played in the rise of the novel, as will be seen in Chapters 7 and 8. My aim in this section is to discuss how historians, reviewers, and anthologists understood the history of fiction at the time.

Although he follows a similar line to Hugh Blair, James Beattie provides a more tolerant and more extensive genealogy and taxonomy of prose fiction in *Dissertations Moral and Critical* (1783). Beattie aims 'to inquire into the origin and nature of the Modern Romance' and does so first by delineating the antiquity of 'Old Romance'.[8] After acknowledging classical prose writings, Beattie details the decline of learning in the Middle Ages, the ascent of feudalism, chivalry, and ideals of romantic love, and the increase of itinerant poets and storytellers, called troubadours, in medieval France, who propagated this chivalric ethos. Beattie here draws on contemporaneous medieval scholarship connecting chivalry and romance, particularly that of Richard Hurd. 'The origin of the Old Romance, which, after this long historical deduction, we are now arrived at, has been already accounted for', Beattie asserts: 'It was one of the consequences of chivalry' (559). Beattie identifies *Amadis de Gaul* (1508) as the apogee of the romances of 'knight-errantry', before the chivalric worldview and the 'Old Romance' were exploded by *Don Quixote*, which 'occasioned the death of the Old Romance, and gave birth to the New' (564). In this schema, Beattie discounts the 'intolerably tedious, and unspeakably absurd' seventeenth-century French heroic romance, 'which cannot be called either Old or New, but is a strange mixture of both' (564). The evolution we have seen in previous commentators, from French heroic romance to modern amatory novel, is expunged: writers like Behn, Manley, and Haywood, the English inheritors of this tradition, are passed over. The new romance for Beattie divides into the 'Serious', represented by Defoe, Richardson, and Rousseau, and the 'Comick', represented by Le Sage, Marivaux, Fielding, and Smollett (564). Nevertheless, Beattie ends with some familiar words of caution: 'Romances are a dangerous recreation. A few, no doubt, of the best may be friendly to good taste and good morals; but far the greater part are unskilfully written, and tend to corrupt the heart, and stimulate the passions' (573–4).

Clara Reeve, in *The Progress of Romance* (1785), is less condemnatory than Beattie: her celebration of fiction marks an important turning point in the novel's status, undoubtedly a reaction to the kind of anti-novel tirades of Vicesimus Knox and others. Ioan Williams's assessment, that Reeve's work 'is not strikingly original in the quality or manner of its critical judgments', does a disservice to its importance as a late-century statement of the rise of the novel (*N&R*, p. 298). 'I propose to trace Romance to its Origin', Reeve states, 'to follow its progress through the different periods to its declension, to shew how the modern Novel sprung up out of its ruins, to examine and compare the merits of both, and to remark upon the effects of them'.[9] Reeve's aims are taxonomical as well as genealogical: in addition to tracing origins, she wants 'to mark the distinguishing characters of the Romance and the Novel, to point out the boundaries of both' (I: vi). She presents a succession of fictitious evening dialogues between Euphrasia, a learned lady who defends romance; Hortensius, a male opponent of romance, whose prejudice must be corrected; and Sophronia, a female friend who acts as mediator.

The first six evenings' dialogues go from ancient romance to the seventeenth century. Reeve begins with the classical heritage and is more particular about the Middle Ages than Beattie. She covers the English tradition, from Geoffrey Chaucer and popular medieval romances like *Guy of Warwick* and *Bevis of Hampton*, through to Thomas Malory's *Morte D'Arthur* (1485), and on to Elizabethan romances in prose and verse, like John Lyly's *Euphues* (1578) and Edmund Spenser's *The Faerie Queene* (1590–6). Euphrasia disdains French heroic romances, refusing to 'speak of them as respectable works' (I: 17). The real interest here, however, is the movement at the start of the seventh evening, where Hortensius prompts: 'We have now, I presume, done with the Romances, and are expecting your investigation of Novels' (I: 108). As Euphrasia explains: 'The word *Novel* in all languages signifies something new. It was first used to distinguish these works from Romance, though they have lately been confounded together and are frequently mistaken for each other' (I: 110). I quoted Reeve's distinction between the two earlier in this chapter; the point to realise is that she sees the break between romance and novel as more clear-cut than any of her predecessors. The relevant heritage in the novel tradition, then, is first Italian – Giovanni Boccaccio's *Decameron* (1350–3) and Cinthio's *Hecatommithi* (1565) – and then Spanish, with Cervantes's *Exemplary Novels* (1613), and finally French, with Paul Scarron's *Le Roman comique* (1651–7), Jean Renaud de Segrais's *Zayde* (1670), and Madame de Lafayette's *La Princesse de Clèves* (1678). Reeve sees a fully fledged alternative novelistic tradition running in implicit opposition to romance during the seventeenth century, with the opposition becoming explicit in mid-eighteenth-century England.

The works of Behn, Manley, and Haywood are mentioned by Reeve, but it is mainly to decry their moral tendencies. Behn comes first in the English tradition, but she is not to be recommended. Manley is derivative and her 'works are still more exceptionable than Mrs. *Behn*'s, and as much inferior to them in point of merit' (I: 119). Haywood is reprehensible, but redeemable, because 'she repented of her faults, and employed the latter part of her life in expiating the offences of the former' (I: 120). Reeve, then, initiates a long tradition of seeing Haywood moving from the immoral amatory novella, tinged by romance, for which she gained notoriety in the 1720s, to the respectable, edifying, and realistic novel in imitation of Richardson and Fielding, which vindicates her career in the 1750s. *Robinson Crusoe* is praised, but deemed extraneous to the novel and romance traditions; the novel begins in earnest with Richardson and Fielding (Marivaux and Marie Jeanne Riccoboni are the best of the otherwise deplorable French novelists). Richardson is explicitly praised by Reeve for weaning female readers off 'the French and Spanish Romances, and the writings of Mrs. *Behn*, Mrs. *Manly*, and Mrs. *Heywood* [*sic*]' (I:138). Fielding's novels are deemed 'as much inferior to *Richardson*'s in morals and exemplary characters, as they are superior in wit and learning' (I: 139). Euphrasia sides with Richardson when discussing 'mixed characters', seeing moral problems in Fielding having depicted 'human nature as *it is*, rath[er th]an as *it ought to be*' (I: 141). The bulk of Volume II of *The Progress of Romance* discusses novels written since Richardson and Fielding, so from the 1750s to the early 1780s: 'Romances at this time were quite out of fashion, and the press groaned under the weight of Novels, which sprung up like Mushrooms every year' (II: 7). This part covers a vast range of fiction written by men, women, and anonymously, and by French and British writers. Reeve gives a strong impression that the novel had arrived and that people were more or less in agreement over what the genre was, even if particular works might occasion dispute.

Reeve attests to the influence of the reviewing industry of new fiction, deferring in her assessment of individual novels to 'those infallible judges the *Reviewers*' (II: 5). Burney also knew that the *Monthly Review*, founded by Ralph Griffiths in 1749, and the *Critical Review*, founded in 1756 by Archibald Hamilton (with Smollett as editor), could make or break literary reputations when she dedicated *Evelina* to the reviewers. The reviewers' treatment of fiction is predictably mixed, and it evinces the gradual acceptance of fiction we have seen in other late-century criticism. Some reviews also reflect on the rise of the novel. For instance, a review of Burney's *Camilla* (1796) in *The British Critic* echoes Reeve's narrative of the rise of the novel out of romance: 'To the old romance, which exhibited exalted personages, and displayed their sentiments in improbable or impossible situations, has succeeded the more reasonable, modern novel; which delineates characters drawn from actual observation, and, when ably executed, presents an accurate and captivating view of real life' (*N&R*, p. 433). As well as the romance-to-novel formulation, the reviews give a collective impression of overload. 'The rapid increase which this class of publication has acquired, and is daily acquiring, renders this part of the critic's task a work of increased difficulty', complains one: 'Our shelves are groaning with the weight of novels which demand a hearing' (*N&R*, p. 443). This perception of indiscriminate novel production, I would argue, necessitated the imposition of certain foundational prototypes, thus creating and enforcing a narrative of the rise of the novel and a canon. In 'A View of the Commencement and Progress of Romance' (1797), John Moore, a novelist in his own right, echoes that sense of being overwhelmed by the proliferation of novels at the same time that he accounts for this overload as a disintegration of certain originatory standards: 'The success of Richardson, Fielding, and Smollett, in this species of writing, produced, what great success generally does produce, a prodigious number of imitators: but by far the greatest part of them, like Hamlet's players, imitated abominably' (*N&R*, p. 440). The plethora of trash, Moore suggests, actually held back the cultural acceptance of fiction. His essay, prefaced to a new edition of Smollett, indicates how the treatment of the founding generation of novelists in Regency criticism established the canon of Richardson, Fielding, and Smollett. In turn, Hugh Murray's *The Morality of Fiction* (1805) is predictably reproving, but makes equivocal exceptions for the three Moore named, plus Burney and Moore himself.[10] The tributes at this time tend to be to individuals rather than the genre; the discourse is ethical rather than aesthetic.

The appearance of novels in anthologies at this time contributed to the legitimation of fiction. These anthologies were uniform editions printing whole novels in dozens of volumes; the most prominent were Anna Laetitia Barbauld's *The British Novelists* (1810) and *Ballantyne's Novelist's Library* (1821–4) with its critical apparatus by Walter Scott. As well as helping to establish the novel, the anthologies helped to construct an understanding of how the genre had developed. Barbauld's introductory essay, 'On the Origin and Progress of Novel Writing', leans quite heavily on Huet's *Traitté*, which her brother had recently translated.[11] Barbauld describes romance's ancient transmigration from the Middle East to Greece – 'From Persia the taste passed into the soft and luxurious Ionia' – and on to Rome, where it languished, until its revival under the Goths (378). Her history of romance in the Middle Ages is familiar, though Barbauld is more sympathetic towards seventeenth-century French 'romances de *longue haleine*' (that is, 'long-winded', referring to their bulk), placing Honoré d'Urfé's *L'Astrée* (1607–27) in the place typically accorded to *Don Quixote*, as 'the first work of entertainment of a different kind' from fantastical medieval romance (386, 385). 'The adventures were marvellous, but not impossible', states Barbauld: they were closer to reality than anything that had come before (386). She is in a minority in having anything good to say about heroic romances. Quite a few French works, some German, and even the Chinese novel, *The Pleasing History*, translated by Thomas Percy in 1761, are noted before Barbauld moves to the English context, where she mentions romances like Sidney's *Arcadia*, Roger Boyle's *Parthenissa* (1655), and 'political' romances that include Thomas More's *Utopia* (1516) and James Harrington's *Oceana* (1656) – works now rarely considered in the context of the novel. Behn, Manley, and Haywood are passed over with the usual tones of disapproval, and 'the first author amongst us who distinguished himself by natural painting, was that truly original genius De Foe' (401). After Defoe's innovations in realism:

> ■ At length, in the reign of George the Second, Richardson, Fielding, and Smollet [*sic*], appeared in quick succession; and their success raised such a demand for this kind of entertainment, that it has ever since been furnished from the press, rather as a regular and necessary supply, than as an occasional gratification. (401) □

Barbauld catalogues fiction from the second half of the century and praises novels as useless but harmless: 'The food has neither flavour nor nourishment, but at least it is not poisoned' (414). This is a rather different summation to that of Beattie less than 30 years earlier.

Barbauld's anthology, in her words, 'presents a series of some of the most approved novels, from the first regular productions of the kind to the present time' (416). It is an important moment in canon-formation. By policy, there are no translations, and copyright restrictions prevented the publishers from including some works in the series. Otherwise, Barbauld specifies public taste, her publisher's commercial demands, and her individual choice as the selection criteria. The result is that Barbauld's 50 volumes feature 29 novels by 22 novelists. Richardson, Defoe, and Fielding (in that order) comprise the first 21 volumes, with the rest distributed between a range of novelists from the second half of the century, some still widely studied today (Burney, Smollett, Johnson, Ann Radcliffe) and some less so (Frances Brooke, John Moore, John Hawkesworth). Her selection bears up Barbauld's point that Richardson, Fielding, and Smollett established the novel, making way for others. Oriental stories, the Gothic, picaresque fiction, and sentimental novels are well-represented, as are female novelists: 12 out of 29 novels are by women. Barbauld's diffuse, inclusive canon matched that of James Harrison's 23-volume *The Novelist's Magazine* (1779–89) and its imitators, which reprinted novels in serial form.

Scott's selections for *Ballantyne's* show changes in taste and priority. Most female writers included in earlier anthologies and magazine serials are omitted: just the Gothic novelists Clara Reeve, who wrote *The Old English Baron* (1777), and Ann Radcliffe, famous for *The Mysteries of Udolpho* (1794) and *The Italian* (1797), are retained. The national agenda is also apparent in Scott's selection: Cervantes and Le Sage are the only translated novelists. Though he enshrines a canon that moved from two earlier continental writers to the mid-eighteenth-century dominance of Richardson, Fielding, and Smollett, Scott was aware of earlier fictions, such as Lafayette, Bunyan, and Defoe. The last named is excluded from the anthology, but Scott had already compiled *The Novels and Miscellaneous Works of Daniel De Foe* (1810). Scott praised Richardson as 'the discoverer of a new style of writing' and 'perhaps the first in this line of fictitious narrative, who threw aside the trappings of romance', specifically those in the 'old French taste'. Likewise, he calls Fielding 'the first of British novelists'.[12] Though he probably means 'best' when he applies it to Fielding, the ambiguity inherent in Scott's designation of both Richardson and Fielding as 'first' is indicative of how evaluations of these two dominated thinking about the novel's origins.

Despite his importance in establishing a British canon of fiction, Scott appears to have seen the British novel as part of a continuous European tradition, not as an isolated national phenomenon. The same applies to John Dunlop. The eighteenth-century English novel occupies only a small section at the end of Dunlop's *History of Fiction* (1814), a work which stretches back to antiquity. For Dunlop, fiction's history cuts across temporal and geographical bounds: England is the inheritor of a tradition rather than the initiator of something new. Nonetheless, he states that 'towards the middle of the eighteenth century the number of English novels rapidly increased', which he attributes to a 'demand for something of a lighter and less exalted description' than romance: 'Accordingly, to this period may be ascribed the origin of that species of composition which, fostered by the improving taste of succeeding times, has been gradually matured into the English novel'. After dismissing Behn, Manley, and the early Haywood, Dunlop praises Haywood's later *Betsy Thoughtless* (1751) and compares it to *Evelina*, before advancing a division of eighteenth-century novels into 'the *serious*, the *comic*, and the *romantic*'. James Beattie and Hugh Murray did similar things. Richardson, Frances Sheridan, and William Godwin exemplify the 'serious'; Fielding and Smollett, the 'comic'; and the romantic is reserved for the Gothic – Horace Walpole's *The Castle of Otranto* (1764), Reeve, and Radcliffe. *Robinson Crusoe*, *Gulliver's Travels*, and Bishop Berkeley's *Gaudentio Di Lucca* (1737) are discussed separately as imaginary voyages.[13] Dunlop claims his is the first complete history of fiction, but it makes more sense to see it also as the end of a historiographical tradition, because the next relevant critic, the essayist William Hazlitt, in his lecture 'On the English Novelists' (1818), changes the nature of the enquiry into the novel's origins. The novel's pre-modern ancestry is negated in Hazlitt as it is not in Reeve, Barbauld, or Dunlop.

In terms of the canon, Hazlitt, like Scott, begins with Le Sage and Cervantes, moving to the increasingly formidable quartet of Richardson, Fielding, Smollett, and Laurence Sterne, whose stock was starting to rise. Hazlitt denies that the mid-eighteenth-century English novel was derivative or imitative of Cervantes, Le Sage, or anything else foreign: 'Fielding's novels are, in general, thoroughly his own; and they are thoroughly English'. Innovation, Englishness, and democracy are what Hazlitt contributes to the discourse on the rise of the novel. Writing in the wake of the defeat of Napoleon, he ascribes these literary developments to the Protestant establishment and representative parliamentary democracy, secured by the Hanoverian succession in 1714, a 'popular turn' in both literature and politics: 'It was found high time that the people should be represented in books as well as in parliament'.[14] Hazlitt's history exemplifies what twentieth-century historians have identified as the 'Whiggish' view of British history: Protestant, nationalist, and emphasizing the progress of liberty. Hazlitt idealizes the later part of the reign of George II, in which the emergent novel flourished, as a bucolic age of peace, progress, and freedom of opinion, unlike the reign of George III (1760–1820), marked by war and political anxiety that corresponded to a diminution in the quality of prose fiction. For Hazlitt, Burney is the best later-century novelist, though deemed inferior to her male predecessors; the atavistic Gothic novel is by-and-large deprecated; and the politicized novel of the 1790s mixes (radical) doctrine and art in ways of which the Romantic essayist disapproved. With a canon of early fiction now established, subsequent criticism had a different starting point for investigations of the rise of the novel. The next section will see how the Victorian period inherited the Romantics' aesthetic judgements, and how the male, English, mid-century, and realist (against romantic) origination of the early novel was established.

Victorians and Edwardians, 1840–1920

During the nineteenth century, the eighteenth-century novel was retroactively defined, delimited, and culturally elevated; the canons built in the Romantic period were consolidated and institutionalized. Some modern critics go so far as to describe the nineteenth-century *invention* of the eighteenth-century novel (see Chapter 7). By the end of the Victorian period, Defoe, Richardson, and Fielding were firmly ensconced as the most important early novelists, with Smollett, Sterne, and Burney credited with helping to establish the genre's status and bridging the gap to Scott and Austen. Other writers, particularly Bunyan, Swift, Johnson, and Goldsmith, were frequently credited with enabling roles. Anything else was decidedly secondary.

Rather than a book-by-book survey, I will outline general principles from histories of the novel in the nineteenth and early twentieth century, illustrating these with the criticism. Some major studies that come under view here are Hippolyte Taine's *History of English Literature*

(French, 1863–9; English, 1871), Wilbur Cross's *The Development of the English Novel* (1899), W. J. Dawson's *The Makers of English Fiction* (1905), Richard Burton's *Masters of the English Novel* (1909), George Saintsbury's *The English Novel* (1913), and W. L. Phelps's *The Advance of the English Novel* (1919). I will end with a sustained discussion of Walter Raleigh's *The English Novel* (1894), because this is an important transitional study, heralding the professionalization of literary scholarship (Raleigh was the first Oxford Professor of English Literature), and bringing together many of the ideas about the rise of the novel that critics from 1860 to 1920 address.

The narrowing of the canon that began in the Romantic period is in evidence in the Victorian era. Defoe (sometimes with Bunyan and Swift) is positioned as the imperfect progenitor, followed by the advances of Richardson and Fielding. These developments are shored up with the work of Smollett and Sterne, with little worthy of notice (Goldsmith and Burney are common exceptions) until Scott and Austen. That is the narrative of the novel's development iterated during this period. It is noticeably masculine – the work of women comes only after the pioneering strides of men; and it is narrowly English, reflected in the titles of many of these books, advertising a history of the national tradition rather than a transcultural survey like Reeve's or Dunlop's. In the hands of Victorian and Edwardian critics, 'English' becomes a remarkably accommodating designation. For Cross, a Yale professor, 'English' comprehends British and American.[15] Burton meanwhile confidently ascribes the 'birth and growth to a lusty manhood' of the 'English novel' to 'the labors of Richardson and Fielding, Smollett, Sterne and Goldsmith', ignoring Smollett's Scottishness and the Irish births of the last two.[16] The continental heritage is frequently (though not uniformly) forgotten, and the English novel is considered to have had English origins, which in turn influenced developments elsewhere. 'Certainly, the English were innovators in this field', avers Burton, 'exercising a direct and potent influence upon foreign fiction, especially that of France and Germany; it is not too much to say, that the novels of Richardson and Fielding offered Europe a type'.[17] Lafayette, Le Sage, Prévost, and Rousseau, he says, cannot be considered novelists at all, except insofar as the last, like the German novelist Johann Wolfgang von Goethe, followed Richardson's examples. Edmund Gosse likewise credits eighteenth-century England with the 'creation' of the modern novel, which is 'the exact opposite to the heroic romance', a departure from 'the rococo and coquettish work which had immediately preceded it in France'.[18] In 1871, *The Spectator* complained that 'England has hardly received the honour she deserves as the birthplace of the modern novel'.[19] That alleged neglect was decisively redressed in late nineteenth-century literary histories.

Despite odd historians reaching back to the fifteenth or even fifth century, there was an increased sense that the eighteenth-century novel marked a break from the past, rather than, as Dunlop had claimed, a continuation of ancient and medieval fictions.[20] Lord Ernle stated in 1921: 'Ancient as is their origin, modern novels are yet a new creation', and 'though Richardson and Fielding had hundreds of predecessors, they were [...] the founders of the modern novel'.[21] With this disconnection of ancient origins from modern fulfilment, there was a sharper distinction than ever between romance and novel, with the latter understood to be based on observation of the world, the workings of society, and fidelity to actual experience. There is certainly a case to be made for the Victorians commending in the past what they preferred in their own fiction, as realism is widely held to have been in its ascendancy during the nineteenth century. Taine avers that the 'anti-romantic novel' in England begins in the eighteenth century.[22] Dawson credits Defoe as 'the pioneer of an art entirely new in English literature' – realism – which Richardson and Fielding honed to produce the first great age of English fiction.[23] A representative view is Burton's, who says that although the origins of prose fiction (in the guise of romance) are medieval and Tudor, 'Richardson was the founder of the modern novel', which 'introduce[d] a more truthful representation of real life than had obtained in the romantic fiction deriving from the medieval stories'.[24]

Cross's approach is an interesting variation on this paradigm. He understands romance and realism to be oppositional ways of viewing the world, which are in alternating ascendancy: 'Romance learns from realism, and realism learns from romance. In this way literature is always moving on, and to something that can never be predicted'.[25] Novels, says Cross, were introduced to England in Elizabeth's reign, when the primitive realism of late Tudor works like Thomas Nashe's *The Unfortunate Traveller* (1594) and Thomas Deloney's *Jack of Newbury* (1597) was in dialogue with romances like Lyly's and Sidney's. Romance prevailed in the seventeenth century, until it was eclipsed by Bunyan, Defoe, and Swift – 'these three writers [...] usher in a new era for the novel' and make way for the 'eighteenth-century realists' (30). Cross goes against the grain by also fitting Manley and Haywood into this account on the side of realism: 'They represent a conscious effort to attain the real in reaction from the French romance' (20–1). The later-century revival of romance (in Gothic fiction) was palliated by Walter Scott, who, in Cross's assessment, 'combined the novel and the romance as defined by Reeve' (xv). In contrast with Cross, Saintsbury declares that the traditions of romance and novel separated two hundred years prior to Scott: Saintsbury distinguishes romance and novel on the basis that the former focuses on incident and the latter on character.[26]

Many Victorian studies begin with the eighteenth century and move from it to contemporary fiction, showing how Charles Dickens, William Makepeace Thackeray, and George Eliot are the successors of Richardson, Fielding, and Smollett. Percy Russell's statement is representative: 'It is not until we arrive at the eighteenth century that we find the true originals of the English novel as we have it now'.[27] Its popularity in the Victorian period lent a new impetus to explaining the novel's origins. The novel was fitted into a progressive historiography, which we saw taking shape in Hazlitt, characteristic of Victorian positivism, in which things in the past got better and better, tending towards the present. William Forsyth exhibits confidence in the Victorian present as an improvement on the past in all fields of enquiry, not least novelistic art.[28] In Burton's account, after Richardson and Fielding – 'the two men who founded the English novel', because 'they showed the feasibility of making the life of contemporary society interesting in prose fiction' – Smollett, Sterne, and Goldsmith helped to develop the form, leaving it as 'a perfect instrument' for Austen at the century's end.[29] Sidney Lanier, tracing an 'arc of progress' all the way from Aeschylus to George Eliot, endorses the view that Richardson, Fielding, Smollett, and Sterne are 'the classic founders of English fiction', and that the form reflects the advent of modernity along with the contemporaneous foundation of modern science (Isaac Newton) and of modern music (J. S. Bach). Lanier, however, deprecates the ethical and aesthetic worth of all the eighteenth-century fiction he discusses.[30] This is relatively extreme by now: most critics were content to condemn just late-century fiction, particularly trends like the Gothic, sentimental, and political novels. So, according to Phelps, the 40 years between Smollett's *Humphry Clinker* (1771) and Austen's *Sense and Sensibility* (1811) 'are notable for the absence of good fiction'.[31] Saintsbury gives a reasonable amount of space to those late-century writers, but he runs through them with an impatience to get to Scott's *Waverley* (1814). If, for these critics, the novel rose from Richardson to Smollett, it then sagged before Austen and Scott.

Victorian and Edwardian historians of the eighteenth-century novel, however, were on the whole becoming less moralistic and more sociological. Forsyth has little positive to say about the quality of early novels, but suggests using 'fiction as an exponent of fact' – that is to learn about the eighteenth-century culture its novels reflect, including dress, manners, the clergy, and even the state of the roads.[32] Moreover, in parallel with the rise of sociology as a field of study in the late nineteenth century, historians began to use ideas about the history of society, particularly class and national character, to account for the origins of the novel. The rhetoric is typically progressivist, fitting the novel into a story of social amelioration. Taine sees nothing short of the movement from barbarity to civilization in England effected through the moral practice of the novel, which becomes a definer of national character. The early novel is considered the form most expressive of the social goals of the middle classes, an after-ripple of Puritanism, when, following the Revolution settlement of 1688–9 and the liberation of finance from monarchical control, the religious goals of nonconformists become secondary to their social aspirations. Taine calls the emergent English novel a 'severe emanation of the middle class'.[33] These ideas about the novel are, admittedly, emergent rather than fully formed, but they get crystallized in the first half of the twentieth century, as will be shown in Chapter 2. Ideas about the middle-class English origins of the novel did not develop *ex nihilo* in the twentieth century.

Raleigh's *The English Novel* is the most influential study between Dunlop's in 1814 and Ernest Baker's in 1924 (see Chapter 2). In line with the development of national literary history that we have seen in the Victorian period, Raleigh, unlike Dunlop, views the eighteenth-century English novel in isolation from other periods and regions. Classical works 'have little enough to do with the beginnings of story-telling in English', and romance is medieval and French, so, implicitly, neither modern nor English.[34] Raleigh sees the shift from allegory to narrative realism in the Reformation and from verse to narrative prose in the Renaissance as important enabling conditions for the novel. He identifies Lyly's *Euphues* as 'the first original prose novel written in English', and sees realism being tentatively adopted by writers like Robert Greene and Thomas Lodge (29). For Raleigh, the seventeenth century saw the 'rise, decline, and fall' of heroic romance, a descendent of chivalric romance, which represents 'a resistance to realism' with a decidedly narcotic effect. 'Never for a moment, until realism began in the eighteenth century, did the writers of prose fiction in England shake off the fantasies of that opiate' (100). Fortunately, pernicious romance, politically allied with the *ancien regime* – French, Catholic, monarchical, and absolutist; not English, Protestant, democratic, and liberal – was never 'naturalised' in England. The triumph of realism was facilitated by changes in prose style, prompted by science, religious controversy, criticism, and homiletics, all of which sought to adapt writing to address a reading public, giving rise to plain style. In short, the later seventeenth century is characterized by 'a spirit of observation, of attention to detail, of stress laid upon matter of fact, of bold analysis of feelings and free argument upon institutions' (111). Precursor genres that exhibit this new spirit of investigation in the new prose style include both published material (Theophrastan character portraits, autobiographies, and periodical essays like Richard Steele and Joseph Addison's *The Spectator* [1711–14]) and unpublished material (familiar letters, personal diaries, and journals).[35] This rise of (private) reading coincides with a decline of the (public) theatre, which Raleigh says 'made way for the novel' (141). Gosse, Cross, and Dawson are amongst those who corroborate the link between the decline of the theatre and the rise of the novel.[36]

Like most critics of this era, Raleigh acknowledges important precedents for the eighteenth-century novel. Bunyan figures rather prominently for the way he overcomes allegory, with its tendency to typify experience, with realism, which aims to particularize experience. These techniques are extended by Defoe, especially in *Robinson Crusoe* (Defoe's other fictions were just seeping into the novelistic canon at this point), and imitated by Swift in *Gulliver's Travels*. Behn remains subservient to romance, as do her 'imitators', Manley and the early Haywood, though the latter is again credited with adapting to the pioneering realism of Richardson and Fielding in mid-century. As usual, Richardson and Fielding herald the novel's arrival as a work of art: aestheticism is an important aspect of Raleigh's study, as he sees these two geniuses working out problems of *technique*, an emerging concept in criticism that anticipates discussions covered in Chapters 2 and 3. For instance, Fielding, whom Raleigh favours, innovated 'the artistic conduct of a complicated plot, and, combined with this, a realism in the characters and events that should be convincing without hampering the freedom of the artist' (177). Fielding aimed 'to create an illusion of reality and not a belief in fact', which distinguishes him from writers like Defoe and, to an extent, Richardson, whose epistolary form of 'writing to the moment' encourages minute attention to detail, an intensification of Defoe's realism (178). With the novel established by the 1750s, a host of writers keep open the floodgates, most prominently Smollett and Sterne. The novel survives a brief 'revival of romance' with the Gothic, before switching to 'domestic satire' in Burney, Austen, and Edgeworth. Scott brings Raleigh's study to a close.

Conclusion

By the end of the period covered in this chapter, accounts of the rise of the novel had achieved some degree of consensus. Very broadly, the novel was new to the early eighteenth century and its novelty derived from the realist rejection of romance. This process has a number of imperfect practitioners before 1740, with Defoe the most important, but Richardson and Fielding's innovations in mid-century were consolidated by the work of Smollett and Sterne. 'Thus', says Saintsbury in a famous metaphor, 'in almost exactly the course of a technical generation – from the appearance of *Pamela* in 1740 to that of *Humphry Clinker* in 1771 – the wain [wagon] of the novel was solidly built, furnished with four main wheels to move it, and set a-going to travel through the centuries'.[37] The time just after the attachment of the sturdy four wheels (Richardson, Fielding, Smollett, and Sterne) was marked by a lack of quality, because followers of Richardson indulged the feminized genre of sentimental fiction. Indeed, Victorian historians commonly contrast the feminine Richardson and the masculine Fielding.[38] Gothic fiction was a deleterious return to romance; political fiction combined ideas and artistry in ways that seemed inappropriate to this increasingly aestheticist age. Austen and Scott begin the golden age of the novel as art, in which critics from 1870 to 1920 thought they were living. The specifically English origins of the novel had been insistently asserted, and the emergent novel was seen as an expression of democratic impulses, increasingly aligned with middle-class interests. Chapter 2 turns to the early period of academic criticism, culminating in Ian Watt's *The Rise of the Novel* (1957).

CHAPTER TWO

New Criticism to *The Rise of the Novel*, 1924–57

This chapter begins with Ernest Baker's ten-volume *History of the English Novel* (1924–39) and ends with Ian Watt's *The Rise of the Novel* (1957). In this period, a range of new ideas about the intellectual and social contexts of the rising novel, and about the formal development of fiction, were introduced. It will be shown that Watt's field-defining study is, in some respects, a synthesis of ideas about the early novel that took shape in the forty years prior to its publication. Watt's argument is here contextualized in relation to contemporaneous ideas, in particular as a reaction to formalist accounts of the emergent novel that dominated the early- to mid-twentieth century.

Baker's *History of the English Novel*

Although he also fits into a line of critics that includes Raleigh, Cross, and Saintsbury, discussed in Chapter 1, Ernest Baker advances the discussion of the novel's development because of his methodology. He begins with a definition of the novel: 'The interpretation of human life by means of a fictitious narrative in prose'.[1] Having arrogated to the novel this analytic and humanist function, Baker then retroactively applies it to individual works to see whether they fit, concluding that nothing satisfies the definition before Defoe. As well as being subjective, Baker's methodology is deductive rather than inductive, going from a general definition to particular cases, rather than surveying specimens before formulating the definition. The result is teleology – understanding past developments as inevitably leading towards and culminating in the present. With an early twentieth-century understanding of what the novel *is* and *ought to be*, Baker looks backwards for examples that corroborate that view, and finds them beginning in the early eighteenth century, though having an earlier genesis in Elizabethan experimentation.

Despite his sense that any given work is either a *novel* or *not-a-novel*, Baker does not posit the sudden creation of the form. He describes the history of English fiction as 'one multiform whole', a smooth continuity despite apparent hiatuses when either the Elizabethans or Defoe seem to be doing something new. Nonetheless:

■ The history of the modern novel begins when Defoe, in homespun narratives that decked out history with fiction or disguised fiction as matter of fact, almost as it were by accident, produced the realistic story, and was followed by Richardson and Fielding, who gave fiction an intellectual meaning and an artistic scheme. (I: 299) □

The dominant metaphor in Baker's account, as in the title of an earlier study by Stoddard, is 'evolution', which again suggests movement to a present that is held to be normative and culminatory, equating change with improvement.[2] 'The history of a literary form cannot be taken satisfactorily as beginning at the point in time when that form is evolved and complete', states Baker; the 'whole anterior process of evolution' has to be understood (I: 12). Despite spending his first volume in the medieval period, dominated by romance, Baker concludes that the Middle Ages are not part of the novel's evolution, because there is precious little *development*, due to a lack of conscious artistry and a lack of freedom of expression.

Development begins in the Elizabethan period. From the start of Elizabeth's reign in 1558, says Baker, there were two centuries to run until the time when a writer could sit down to write a novel and have a clear idea of what was expected of him. Baker thus assumes the novel's generic purity: its form is realized in the mid-eighteenth century and continued in his own era. The Elizabethan age was 'a period of doubtful successes and manifest failures, of that process of trial and error which is normal to the transition from old to new' (II: 11). Again, Baker's assumptions are teleological – works written before the idea of the novel was fixed are evaluated based on the degree to which they anticipate what came later. To adopt an imprecise analogy, one might deride the Penny Farthing for not being as fast as a motorcycle: aside from that kind of complacency called presentism, we should ask whether speed rather than appearance, affordability, or other pleasures should be the standard of judgement. Baker surveys prose fiction from Lyly's *Euphues* and Sidney's *Arcadia* to Greene, Lodge, Nashe, Deloney, and Thomas Dekker. His assessment of Thomas Forde's writing career may stand for much of Baker's coverage of the Elizabethans: Forde 'has little to do with the history of English literature, unless in an indirect way, since it might be argued that the demand for rubbish is a deterrent to those who would write better' (II: 124–5). Others fare better, though all early modern writers ultimately failed to distil the essence of the novel from the miscellaneous matter with which they worked.

Like his predecessors, Baker views the history of the modern novel as the triumph of realism over romance, something that was left unaccomplished in the Elizabethan period. Nashe's *Unfortunate Traveller* comes closest, but rather than 'the first of the anti-romances' it is 'an effort to present the romance of actuality' (II: 168). After briefly noting French heroic romances and their English imitations, Baker considers the reaction against romance brought about by the advance of prose 'plain style' under the influence of scientific discourse and the increase of personal diaries. These developments shaped Bunyan's homely narratives and English picaresque fiction, such as Richard Head and Francis Kirkman's *The English Rogue* (1665). Behn is a transitional figure, 'one brought up in the school of romance and unable to take any but a romantic view of life', but who felt the need to break away from 'the unreality of the romances' (III: 99). Manley and Haywood are deemed the best of the 'school' that followed Behn (which includes Mary Davys, Penelope Aubin, Jane Barker, and Elizabeth Singer Rowe). Notably, Baker does not suppose that the male novelists simply *depart* from their female predecessors: 'Defoe, for the most part, took a line of his own; yet he was not entirely out of their debt. Richardson and Fielding were less innovators than is usually supposed; in turning to novel-writing, they entered upon an established and thriving business, and they adopted many tricks of the trade from these humble precursors' (III: 107). The establishment of realism, however, comes with Defoe. *Robinson Crusoe*, by Baker's pre-fabricated definition, 'is the first novel in the complete modern sense' (III: 169). Defoe's achievement is accounted for by his Puritan, middle-class, manly values; his hostility to the imagination vanquished the effeminate, voluptuous residues of romance: 'Defoe's work in the reconstruction of prose fiction was to bring the novel down from the region where the plastic imagination roams at large, and fix it firmly in the solid earth' (III: 227). The realist effort was extended by Swift, who 'perfected the method by giving it more precision' (III: 238). This is noteworthy, because Swift's place in the story of the novel would fall away after Baker until the 1980s.

The age of Richardson, Fielding, Smollett, and Sterne is 'the most decisive period in the history of the English novel', termed by Baker 'intellectual realism' (IV: 5). Baker argues for the formal benefits of Richardson's epistolary technique, begun in *Pamela*, over the memoir-form of Defoe, particularly in *Clarissa*, which uses multiple perspectives, and then in *Sir Charles Grandison*, where Richardson exhibits 'mature technical dexterity' (IV: 62). Richardson's artistry prospers notwithstanding didacticism. This is truer of Fielding, who is preferred to Richardson because he completes the movement towards the employment of realism to artistic ends: 'The illusion that he achieved was unprecedented in its completeness. It was the first time that anyone had depicted the scene of life with its background and surroundings in perfect verisimilitude' (IV: 102). If *Joseph Andrews* is tentative, *Tom Jones* is the full realization of 'intellectual realism' – the attempt to capture the whole of human nature, involving the *interpretation* of experience, as well as recording it:

> ■ Defoe and Richardson had merely got together the materials, provided the stuff out of which the autonomous work of art might be made; they had not realized what further industry was demanded of the artist. Fielding took the material, and cast it into new and fully coherent shapes, without any distortion of the essential truth. He is the Shakespeare of English fiction. (IV: 191) □

Baker's *History* marks a high point in Fielding's reputation, as well as an aestheticist assessment of the early novel that prevailed in the next sixty years (see this and the next Chapter). Smollett is praised as 'a prince among story-tellers' (IV: 207). Sterne's *Tristram Shandy* (1759–67) is considered as a parody of the conventional novel, an inversion of Fielding's intellectual realism, which denies the intelligibility of reality. As parody, however, *Tristram Shandy* is a validation of the stabilization of fiction by Richardson, Fielding, and Smollett.

Baker is evidently disappointed by the novels of the later eighteenth century, particularly 'the oriental story', 'the novel of sentiment', 'the Gothic Romance', and 'the novel of doctrine' (political novels, like Godwin's). The first three are regressions to romance that distract from the progress of realism; the last dilutes artistry with polemic. Baker briefly notes Sarah Fielding, Charlotte Lennox, Francis Coventry, John Cleland, and, most fulsomely, Oliver Goldsmith, but reports a widespread 'failure to utilize the new technique' of intellectual realism after 1750 (V: 11). Burney, however, is credited with anticipating the next important age of fiction, that of Edgeworth, Austen, and Scott, before Baker gets to Victorian and Modernist novelists. Baker's condescension towards the period between Smollett and Austen is typical of the time, as evidenced by J. M. S. Tompkins's *The Popular Novel in England, 1770–1800* (1932). Tompkins justifies her examination of 'tenth-rate fiction' on the grounds of recovering tastes between mid-century and Austen. 'Popular' is a pejorative term: in the years after Smollett's death, Tompkins says, 'the two chief facts about the novel are its popularity as a form of entertainment and its inferiority as a form of art'.[3] Notwithstanding its reinforcement of Baker's value judgements, Tompkins's study remains useful for its discussion of trends in an underexplored stage of the novel's history.

Baker's aestheticist distinction between Defoe and Richardson's reportorial realism and Fielding's intellectual realism certainly anticipates Watt. The seeds of New Criticism, the dominant approach in literary studies from (roughly) the 1920s to the 1960s, are visible in Baker. New Criticism prioritized artistry and advocated formalism, because it was predicated on the view that literature acquires its meaning by virtue of its verbal organization. It encouraged a close and sensitive attention to texts, generally discounting extra-textual sources, such as biography or historical context. New Critics generally preferred lyric poetry to the novel, but those who analysed fiction focused on formal features like characterization, plot, structure, and theme, as well as techniques like paradox, irony, and ambiguity.

New Criticism

The definitive New Critical statement on the English novel is F. R. Leavis's claim that 'the great tradition' comprises Jane Austen, George Eliot, Henry James and Joseph Conrad – with D. H. Lawrence later added. Leavis pointedly discounts eighteenth-century fiction from greatness. For him, 'Fielding deserves the place of importance given him in the literary histories [...] because he leads to Jane Austen'.[4] Likewise, Richardson's 'immediately relevant historical importance is plain: he too is a major fact in the background of Jane Austen' (13). In turn, 'it was Fanny Burney who, by transposing [Richardson] into educated life, made it possible for Jane Austen to absorb what he had to teach her. Here we have one of the important lines of English literary history – Richardson – Fanny Burney – Jane Austen' (13). As such, Leavis says, Austen 'is the inaugurator of the great tradition of the English novel – and by "great tradition" I mean the tradition to which what is great in English fiction belongs' (16). Such tautology admits little by way of justification of the exclusion of earlier novelists: their significance becomes in Leavis *merely* historical and not formal. 'To be important historically is not, of course, to be necessarily one of the significant few', Leavis states (11). This 'greatness', for Leavis as for Baker, is moral, whereby the complexity of life is given due seriousness in novelistic form. Because Leavis did not believe it influenced the tradition, Defoe's *Moll Flanders* is discounted as a great novel, as it had been lauded by E. M. Forster and Virginia Woolf. Sterne's *Tristram Shandy* is disqualified because of its 'irresponsible (and nasty) trifling', a lamentable lack of seriousness (11).

Criticism in the 1950s directly responded to Leavis's dismissal of the formal and 'traditional' significance of the eighteenth-century novel. Some reacted by claiming that the novels of Defoe, Richardson, Fielding, and Sterne have formal merits. Some changed the terms of the debate to think more closely about how social forces occasioned the emergence of the novel, something that Leavis would not have denied, but which did not necessitate intense artistic appreciation of such books. On the latter side is Arnold Kettle's *Introduction to the English Novel* (1951–3). Kettle was a student of Leavis's who imbibed many of his critical principles, but added a Marxist dimension that betokened a greater concern with historical forces. 'The rise and development of the English novel, like any other phenomenon in literature, can only be understood as a part of history', Kettle insists.[5] His literary history is familiar: the novel dates to the eighteenth century. Though there are significant precursors, Kettle's definition of the novel as 'a realistic prose fiction, complete in itself and of a certain length' discounts pre-eighteenth-century works, except *Don Quixote* and *The Pilgrim's Progress* (I: 28). In Kettle's account, the decadence of aristocratic feudalism and the new Puritan, bourgeois middle class initiated a shift away from romance and towards realism, enabled by the development of a plain, descriptive style of prose and the growth of the reading public described in Q. D. Leavis's *Fiction and the Reading Public* (1932).

Kettle, like F. R. Leavis, prioritizes intertwined moral significance and formal pattern, so that the novel only truly came into being when Defoe, Richardson, Fielding, and Sterne 'attempted, not always consciously, not always successfully, to [...] achieve in their books both realism and significance, to equate life and pattern' (I: 41). This Leavisite equation amounts to a generic fusion of the picaresque, which recorded reality in a shapeless manner devoid of ethical evaluation, with the 'moral fable' (Leavis's term), which uses a story to instruct. Whereas Leavis sees the injection of artistic design into the novel beginning with Austen, Kettle makes a (limited) case for its presence in eighteenth-century writers. The concept of the moral fable is not simply sheer didacticism (art for instruction), just as Leavis's concept of artistry is not quite aestheticism (art for art's sake), because Leavis critiques authors who indulge in formal play (James Joyce, as well as Sterne) to the detriment of including an 'affirmation of life'. For Kettle, novels ideally equipoise a narrative's fable (story) and its moral through 'a controlling intelligence, a total significance' (I: 62). This is found wanting in Defoe: his need to vanquish Puritan morality for the sake of imaginative writing ensures that the story outstrips any ethical pattern; the only pattern we get is that of a man or woman's life. In Richardson, the fault rather goes the other way: despite *Pamela*'s technical innovations in realism, 'a peculiarly loathsome aspect of bourgeois puritan morality' dominates (I: 65). Fielding, in correcting Richardson's sententiousness, goes back to the other extreme, though he is the closest yet to the unity and pattern represented by great novels. Only *Tristram Shandy* remains before Kettle gets to the real business of the nineteenth century, starting with Austen's *Emma* (1816). He fits Sterne into the realist tradition in ways critics up to and including Baker had struggled to do: Sterne's novel is an 'anti-romance, a contribution towards a more realistic and satisfying literature' (I: 84). Ultimately, Kettle shines a light on eighteenth-century novels in order to validate Leavis's assessments, and to continue the equation of realism with progress.

Richard Church's *Growth of the English Novel* (1951) employs a fanciful arboreal metaphor for the maturation of the eighteenth-century novel. The novel begins in Defoe before being utilized for artistic ends by 'the four mighty limbs' of the novelistic tree: Richardson, Fielding, Smollett, and Sterne. Adopting a historical approach, Church adds little new to the discourse when running through pre-eighteenth-century factors: the rise of the mercantile class after 1688, the scientific focus on observed reality, and the increasing secularization of society. But Church, anticipating Ian Watt, crucially adds to these well-established influences on realism the empiricist epistemology of the philosopher John Locke, for whom knowledge was based on experience, not innate ideas. Whilst Church's assessments of individual novelists tally with what we have seen, his book clearly articulates the social, religious and (now) epistemological conditions that were becoming increasingly influential in accounts of the novel: the middle class, Protestantism, and empiricism.[6]

Dorothy Van Ghent's *The English Novel: Form and Function* (1953) is an important collection of formalist analyses of novels from Cervantes to Joyce. Van Ghent does not aim to account for the historical rise of the novel *per se*: she provides close readings of particular works. 'The procedure of the novel is to individualize', states Van Ghent: 'As with other art forms, what it has to say that is of collective value is said by inference from individual concrete things'.[7] Ian Watt, it will be shown, subsequently historicized this individualization, identifying social, religious, and philosophical causes unique to eighteenth-century England for the 'particularity' that Van Ghent identifies as characteristic of the novel. Van Ghent's focus is on 'form and function', whereby she understands the novel as 'one complex pattern' that has 'integral structure' and which 'embodies' profound, abstract ideas in particular actions (6). When she talks about 'the unity of the novel as a self-defining body', she reflects the New Critical tendency to reject extra-textual factors, like history. Van Ghent's selection is indebted to Leavis, but she makes greater claims for the quality of earlier novels: 'Our only adequate preparation for judging a novel evaluatively is through the analytical testing of its unity, of its characterizing qualities, and of its meaningfulness – its ability to make us more aware of the meaning of our lives' (6–7). As with Leavis, artistic form has to relate to life. If Leavis aimed to provide an essential reading list for the novel tradition, Van Ghent aimed to supplement that selection, adding *Don Quixote, The Pilgrim's Progress, Moll Flanders, Clarissa, Tom Jones,* and *Tristram Shandy,* as pre-nineteenth-century novels, attending to formal features of these works like structure, parody, paradox, realism, symbolism, and irony. As good as Van Ghent's analyses are, her work reflects the fact that formal ideals derived from Leavis's nineteenth-century canon were being uniformly applied to eighteenth-century fiction.

Walter Allen's *The English Novel* (1954) is a more traditional history than Van Ghent's 'essays in analysis', though the Leavisite assumptions are comparable: 'A novel is a totality, made up of all the words in it, and it must be judged as a totality. [...] Every novel is an extended metaphor of the author's view of life'.[8] Allen echoes Baker's view, increasingly becoming orthodox, that fiction and the novel are not synonymous: the former has existed since ancient times; the latter is a unique artistic form, 'consciously made and shaped to an aesthetic end', that arose in the eighteenth century. Realism is again the distinctive feature of the novel: 'From its very nature the novel demands a greater or less degree of realism, of fidelity to the facts of the world as men commonly see them. [...] The novelist must deal with men in a specific place at a specific time' (23). For Allen, realism has its genesis in non-fictional genres that aimed to capture reality, such as history and journalism, each invigorated in the late seventeenth century by a new flexibility, which facilitated the analysis of character in actual settings and 'the ordering and arranging of significant detail' (30). Despite Defoe's 'pioneering' efforts in producing the 'illusion of complete reality', the period from 1670 to 1740 is only 'frontier territory' (38, 31). However, 'by 1740, both in France and England, the novel was, as it were, in the air, already in existence potentially; all that was needed was someone to write it' (52). Richardson, in parallel with Marivaux in France, was the one; Fielding, Smollett, and Sterne followed. Allen helpfully mollifies some of Leavis's more critical statements, such as by claiming that 'Fielding was as superb a craftsman in his own way as Henry James', by trying to understand rather than dismiss what Leavis called Sterne's 'trifling', and by placing Austen as 'a belated eighteenth-century moralist' rather than as the first in the 'great tradition' (85).

Dissatisfaction with Leavis sharpens in Alan Dugald McKillop's important work, *The Early Masters of English Fiction* (1956), which contends that Defoe, Richardson, Fielding, Smollett, and Sterne are 'unquestionably *les cinq grands* of their field', that this field merits separate treatment from later novelistic developments, and that these writers 'represent a great tradition'.[9] McKillop is not necessarily interested in explaining the emergence of the novel, but in outlining through historical investigation and formal analysis the literary merits of eighteenth-century writers. Defoe is situated in his middle-class, Protestant milieu: his turn to fiction is explained as the 'grudging admission that feigned narrative may both teach and delight' (5). His fiction is structured as a succession of facts, circumstances or episodes, which fit into the larger aim of illustrating moral or religious lessons. His use of the autobiographical memoir, creating a 'double perspective', whereby the narrator retrospectively comments on his or her own life, creates the scope for irony, but Defoe 'is never keenly conscious of the double point of view involved when a character is talking about his own past' (31). As such, Defoe was 'an artist in spite of himself' and 'was in a sense without successors' (37, 43).

For this reason, Richardson's innovations in *Pamela* are crucial, particularly his epistolary technique, which 'gives the reader a continuous and cumulative impression of living through the experience, and thus creates a new kind of sympathy with the character whose experiences are being shared' (59). In addition, Richardson extends Defoe's realism through selectivity and artistic organization: 'His way of "writing to the moment" is not indiscriminate expansion of descriptive detail', as with Defoe, 'but a running record of significant circumstance and fluctuating feeling from the point of view of the letter-writer' (59). The subsequent multiplication of perspectives in *Clarissa* advances the technique, duplicated to the point of strain in *Sir Charles Grandison*. Richardson's novels achieved a 'new intimacy', whereby readers related to fictional characters as though they were real people, and they provided for the novel the tradition of an intelligent judgement of society later taken up by Austen. In a similar vein, Fielding's formal innovation in *Joseph Andrews* is the intrusive narrator, which enables an analysis of character and motivation. This is augmented in *Tom Jones* by 'the ordering of events in a cause-effect sequence so as to display character in action', meaning that Fielding stakes new territory for the novel's ability to characterize through plot, because he 'conceives of the novel as an elaborate structure showing the causes and effects of action' (139). This complements Fielding's moral design, because, on a simple level, characters can be condoned or condemned to the extent that they hinder or facilitate the plot arc that will see Tom redeemed and his romantic and social destinies fulfilled. This ethic is then shifted from the private individual to society in Fielding's last novel, *Amelia* (1751).

McKillop is the most fulsome critic so far in his praise of artistry in the eighteenth-century novel, especially in Richardson and Fielding: despite 'the differences between the two as artists and moralists', they stand 'not merely as worthy pioneers but as consummate masters of their craft' (146). The extent of McKillop's attention to narrative technique is unprecedented: as will be shown in Chapter 3, this subsequently became an important strand of criticism. Discussion of Smollett is still considered indispensable, but on these formalist terms, as witnessed by his omission from Kettle and Van Ghent, he suffers alongside his contemporaries, as McKillop argues that Smollett is less interested in technique. For example, the shift from first- to third-person narration between *Roderick Random* and *Peregrine Pickle* (1751) is hard to rationalize in terms of Smollett's aims, and in *Humphry Clinker* 'Smollett is not much concerned with epistolary machinery' (173). Nonetheless, in terms of the definition proffered in *Ferdinand Count Fathom* (1753) of the novel as a large picture containing many characters and unified by a plan, his fictions make formal sense as satirical modifications of the picaresque. On the other hand, McKillop's praise for Sterne's 'artistic eye' is the culmination of the late-Victorian and Modernist turnabout in this writer's critical fortunes, which Leavis's dismissal had put into question. McKillop shows that 'planlessness' is part of Sterne's plan, and that in fact 'design is carried to excess' (193, 210). Reversing the tendency to see *Tristram Shandy* as a parody of the conventional novel, as Baker had done, McKillop contends that Sterne's project is an extension of the examination of cause and effect, experimentation with narrative technique, and the articulation of an inner coherence of vision through artistic form, all of which fits the larger project of the eighteenth-century novel. McKillop interestingly assumes a collective agenda rather than individual acts of innovation when he speaks of 'the general enterprise of the eighteenth-century novelists', and he ends *The Early Masters* with an attempt to unite the enterprises of these five writers. We no longer have isolated spurts of multidirectional activity; we have a cohesive collective effort to exalt a new form.

Northrop Frye and the novel

New Criticism focused on artistry, usually the Leavisite balance between aesthetic form and moral vision; it privileged a select number of works, analysing their uses of language; and it understood genres as having histories independent of other kinds of history. Because New Criticism promoted the autonomy of the individual work with its own aesthetic unity and significance, largely free from historical forces, the canon of the emerging novel is by this point as narrow as ever. The early novel could be understood with minimal reference to pre-eighteenth-century prose fiction, 'minor' novelists, non-'English' literature, or the broader literary background. A mode of formalism that is related to, though distinct from, New Criticism is the archetypal criticism of Northrop Frye's *Anatomy of Criticism* (1957).

One way in which Frye is distinct from New Critics is his movement away from the coherence of individual works and towards a typology of modes in which recurrent archetypal motifs and patterns correspond to a universal ethos. Frye does not treat the novel as a distinct form; he is closer to earlier historians, like Dunlop (see Chapter 1), who place the modern mimetic novel within a broader progression of prose fiction.[10] However, Frye is not especially concerned with how modes behave in history. History is marginalized in Frye's theory, with the exception of literary history, as texts can only be interpreted in relation to other texts with which they bear an affinity, something he says is missed by histories of fiction that privilege the novel. As Frye later characterized this 'inadequate' procedure with disapproval: 'The critical method suggested by realism begins by detaching the literary work being studied from its context in literature. After that, the work may be discussed in relation to its historical, social, biographical, and other nonliterary affinities'.[11] In Frye, literary works are not occasioned by historical developments, but are made up of other literary works. Literature remains divorced from history in Frye's system: literary history provides a substitute for history itself. Working from history to texts is clearly wrongheaded for Frye, making this kind of formalism more anti-historical than the merely ahistorical New Criticism.

According to Frye, fictions 'may be classified, not morally, but by the hero's power of action, which may be greater than ours, less, or roughly the same' (33). This entails five modes.

1. In *myth*, the hero is superior in *kind* to other men and their environment, typically a God.
2. In *romance* the hero is superior in *degree* to other men and his own environment: human, but capable of marvellous actions in a world where ordinary laws of probability are suspended.
3. In the *high mimetic* mode, the hero is superior in degree to other men, but not to his natural environment, so his behaviour conforms to probability; this mode is typical of epic and tragedy.
4. Where the hero is not superior to other men or his environment, we are in the *low mimetic* mode of the novel.
5. Finally, if the hero is inferior to us, the mode is *ironic*.

These modes are not discrete; rather, 'the forms of prose fiction are mixed, like racial strains in human beings, not separable like the sexes' (305). Nor are they (explicitly) evaluative – Frye rejects the axiology inherent in New Criticism – but they provide a 'diagrammatic' organization of fictional modes.

Frye maps his modes onto history. 'Looking over this table', Frye remarks, 'we can see that European fiction, during the last fifteen centuries, has steadily moved its center of gravity down the list' (34). From classical *myth* to medieval *romance*, this 'center' moved to the *high mimetic* in the Renaissance, under 'the cult of the prince and the courtier', manifesting itself in 'the genres of drama, particularly tragedy, and national epic', as in Shakespeare and Milton. Thereafter:

> ■ A new kind of middle-class culture introduces the low mimetic, which predominates in English literature from Defoe's time to the end of the nineteenth century. In French literature it begins and ends about fifty years earlier. During the last hundred years [i.e. before 1957], most serious fiction has tended increasingly to be ironic in mode. (34–5) □

For Frye, prose fiction since Defoe is not collapsible into the rubric 'novel'; the novel is not fundamentally different from prose fiction that precedes it; and the English tradition is not unique. Despite that nod to the middle class and his assertion that high mimetic waned in tandem with the declining authority of the aristocracy, Frye does not see forces of history impelling this devolution of modes: the historical movement down the list is incidental. And, as J. Paul Hunter argues, Frye's brand of formalism tends to privilege modes with universalist values, such as romance, and to deprecate a form like the novel that tends to resist classical structural norms and to concentrate on 'the particular, the circumstantial, and the individualized'.[12] This is where Ian Watt comes in.

Watt's *The Rise of the Novel*

Whereas Frye looked to decentre the novel from the criticism of prose fiction, to rescue the romance from being judged as an inferior because less realistic type of novel, and to deny the importance of historical circumstances to generic change, we see diametrically opposed principles in Ian Watt's *The Rise of the Novel*, also published in 1957.[13] Watt's is the single most important book written on this subject and its relevance has not dissipated, despite claims to the contrary. Watt's thesis is to some degree the culmination of arguments about the early novel's social and intellectual contexts and its formal evolution that had been developing in the first half of the twentieth century. However, Watt rejects ahistorical impulses in the study of genre which characterized the work of his contemporaries, and restates the novel's centrality as a form of prose fiction, and its newness in the eighteenth century as the literary product of specific social developments in England.

A general overview of Watt's book will be given before outlines of individual chapters. Watt sees the novel as the pre-eminent form of modernity, entirely distinct from older forms of prose fiction. The novel arose due to certain social, historical, and intellectual conditions in early eighteenth-century England, particularly the emergence of an increasingly literate reading public with leisure time, which they chose to spend reading stories about people more or less like themselves. The defining formal characteristic of the novel is realism, the attempt to approximate reality closely through language, an innovation influenced by empiricist philosophy. This taste for true-to-life stories is characteristic of the emergent middle class, which is a product of nascent capitalism, the restriction of monarchical power, the abatement of traditional aristocratic authority, and the secularizing and democratizing impulses of Protestantism. Individualism is the common factor in these sociocultural developments, and novels quickly began to depict individuals (as opposed to 'type' figures) who make sense of the world through their own experiences (in accordance with philosophical empiricism), make their own money (as under capitalism), and work out their own spiritual salvation (in line with Protestantism). Defoe, Richardson, and Fielding are the writers who begin the novel.

It is not just because it reflects the historical rise of individualism that the novel is distinct from past forms, but because of how it presents the world. Watt avers that 'the novel's realism does not reside in the kind of life it presents, but in the way it presents it' (11). Realism is a question of form, rather than content, and so is labelled 'formal realism', a convention which is 'the lowest common denominator of the novel genre as a whole' (34). Watt contends that formal realism marks 'a break with the old-fashioned romances' betokened by the novel's rejection of the universal themes promoted by neoclassical literature in favour of 'realistic particularity' (10, 17). In contrast to Frye, who thought that all stories were variations on a few archetypal narratives, Watt argues that the novel eschews 'traditional plots' that aim for universal truths, and instead presents 'particular individuals having particular experiences at particular times and at particular places' (31). Characters, action, and setting in the novel are specific to a recognizable social milieu. This is evident in naming: the early novelists broke with tradition because they named their characters in ways that indicated they were to be understood as 'particular individuals in the contemporary social environment' (19). Rather than Britomart, Lysander, or Christian, for example, characters in novels are named Moll Flanders, Pamela Andrews, or Tom Jones. Realism affects time and setting, because 'the characters of the novel can only be individualised if they are set in a background of particularised time and place' (21). A 'modern sense of time' was brought about in the wider culture by the mechanization of timepieces and the increased objectivity of historical study: it resulted in 'a sense of personal identity subsisting through duration and yet being changed by the flow of experience' (24). For Watt, the novel was uniquely capable of representing this modern experience of temporality. A number of features mark the novel's difference from the 'timeless' stories of allegory and romance, including chronological consistency (we can tally Crusoe's time on his island), temporal specificity (Clarissa's death is pinpointed to 6.40 p.m. on Thursday, 7 September), and historical setting (the 1745 Jacobite Rebellion occurs in the background of *Tom Jones*). The treatment of spatial setting is equally particular in the novel, which presents stories occurring in what appear to be actual physical environments.

The realism thus defined by Watt is a nineteenth-century critical standard applied retroactively to the eighteenth century. Despite characterizing eighteenth-century French fiction (from Lafayette to Laclos) as 'too stylish to be authentic', Watt purports to be tracing in England the emergence of the standard eventually to be achieved by the nineteenth-century French realists and naturalists, such as Honoré de Balzac and Emile Zola (30). Watt does not see formal realism as new *per se* to the eighteenth century. It 'was not discovered by Defoe and Richardson; they only applied it much more completely than had been done before' (33). That is to say, earlier stories may well evince particularity of time or place, or individualize characters in a realistic manner. The difference in the novel is of degree rather than of kind: Defoe and Richardson's independence of literary conventions made it possible for them to make formal realism an objective rather than just a tool of their narratives, as had previous writers. Watt states that the new literary realism correlates with 'philosophical realism', though he is careful not to state a direct causal relationship between philosophical context and literary form. Philosophical realism comprehends the sceptical tradition initiated by René Descartes and the empiricism of John Locke and George Berkeley, in the late seventeenth and early eighteenth century, which represented a new epistemology predicated on mistrusting knowledge that comes from outside of individual experience. Because the novel is influenced by Locke's prescription that the purpose of words is 'to convey the knowledge of things', Watt states that 'the function of language is much more largely referential in the novel than in other literary forms' (102, 30). This means that novels use language in denotative and descriptive ways to represent particular things and people.

Watt follows some of his predecessors, like Raleigh and Q. D. Leavis, in identifying the reading public as crucial for the ascent of the novel. Though he accepts that the evidence is not conclusive, Watt contends that considerable increases in literacy and purchasing power occurred during the later seventeenth and early eighteenth century. The emergent middle class was the main beneficiary of these economic changes, and the novel was closer to their economic capacity than other, older and better established, forms of literature. However, the novel was not yet a popular form. Watt acknowledges the small proportion of the publishing industry taken up with fiction; it is not until later in the century that circulating libraries 'led to the most notable increase in the reading public for fiction which occurred during the century' (43). Watt does, however, argue that social reorganization supplied the fiction market, notably the increase in free time as a result of economic specialization and the increase in feminine leisure. A trickle-down effect meant that people below the middling sort were affected, like apprentices and household servants. In Watt's view, the content of early novels depicting economic individualists who make good catered for the escapist aspirations of such readers, who did not carry the traditional literary standards of their social betters or adhere to the rigid social hierarchy that those tastes buttressed. As the fictional marketplace grew under the auspices of booksellers, the professionalization of authorship took hold, and traditional literary patronage declined. Commercially motivated writers like Defoe and Richardson – with a similar independence from literary tradition and an inside knowledge of book production – supplied this new reading public. The rise of the novel was the result.

Watt moves to the single most important social factor in his account of the rise of the novel, individualism, brought about by 'the rise of modern industrial capitalism and the spread of Protestantism' (60). At this point Watt draws on the sociological work of R. H. Tawney, *Religion and the Rise of Capitalism* (1926), arguing that the Glorious Revolution (1688) put paid to monarchical absolutism, increased political democracy, freed trade from royal monopolies, and brought about economic specialization. Under this new economic order, social relations were based not on collective units like family, church, guild, or township, but on the individual. The political philosophy of liberalism, formulated in Locke's *Two Treatises of Government* (1689), consolidated the enfranchisement of citizens by theorizing indefeasible individual rights. Religion moved much the same way, because Protestantism placed the responsibility for salvation more on the self, and less on priestly mediators, enabling 'democratic individualism' (80). Using Max Weber's *The Protestant Ethic and the Spirit of Capitalism* (1905), Watt argues that these social developments helped to enshrine 'the novel's general premise that the individual's daily life is of sufficient importance and interest to be the proper subject of literature' (74).

The novelistic representative of individualism is Robinson Crusoe, whose motivations are 'the dynamic tendency of capitalism itself' (65). Defoe's castaway novel reflects the new social order, endorsing mobility and meritocracy, the subordination of sedentary social and familial ties to the pursuit of personal wealth, and 'an absolute equivalence between individual effort and individual reward' (72). Religion is a secondary consideration due to 'the profound secularisation of [Defoe's] outlook, a secularisation which was a marked feature of his age', explaining the discrepancy between Crusoe's religious professions and his actions. Crusoe's religion conforms to his socioeconomic ambitions: it is not that Defoe's religious justifications for his hero's actions are not sincere, but that they are not full-sighted. In formal terms, '*Robinson Crusoe* initiates that aspect of the novel's treatment of experience which [...] outdoes other literary forms in bringing us close to the inward moral being of the individual', combined with 'the objective representation of the world of everyday reality' (75, 80). Individualism, then, lends the novel intense subjectivity but also objectivity. However, for Watt, *Crusoe* is an inaugural but not an exemplary novel, because it is a fantasy of 'absolute economic, social and intellectual freedom for the individual', and so belongs with western myths of modern individualism like *Don Quixote*, *Faust*, and *Don Juan*, rather than with the novel (86). Whereas *Crusoe* stands as a *myth* of individualism, the novel proceeded to address the *reality* of the individual's relationship to society.

Moll Flanders illustrates for Watt Defoe's focus on economic individualism, but also his formal limitations. Watt elaborates on Defoe's realism, which is fuelled by the author's desire to convince readers of the story's truth through a plain style and a referential correspondence between words and things. Watt accounts for this, as had Baker and Kettle, through the rise of plain prose style typical of the Royal Society's publications, Protestant preaching practices, political journalism, and commercial writing, all of which aimed to communicate directly and clearly. Defoe's aim was 'to bring the language of literature much closer to the speech habits and the comprehension of the ordinary reader' (101). In historical terms, Defoe's are the first narratives which feature all the components of formal realism. However, they are formally fallible because 'they make formal realism an end rather than a means, subordinating any coherent ulterior significance to the illusion that the text represents the authentic lucubrations of an historical person' (117). In short, Defoe presents action in a consecutive rather than aesthetically or ethically coherent manner, writing, Watt supposes, at a speed that occluded artistic considerations about technique.

Watt contends that economic considerations are paramount for Defoe and for Moll; therefore, religious instruction, professed as the goal in the preface, is not upheld by the narrative. It is not quite that Defoe was incapable of fusing moral vision and artistic form: it is, firstly, that this was not his true objective and, secondly, that he did not see religious sincerity and selfish economic activity as ethically opposed. On the question of irony, Watt differentiates between intention and effect, concluding that we cannot attribute deliberate artistry to Defoe. Though we may see irony in the discrepancy between how Moll acts and her pious protestations, Defoe did not. Defoe's role in the rise of the novel is that of facilitator rather than founder, because 'the novel could be considered established only when realistic narrative was organised into a plot which, while retaining Defoe's lifelikeness, also had an intrinsic coherence; when the novelist's eye was focussed on character and personal relationships as essential elements in the total structure, and not merely as subordinate instruments for furthering the verisimilitude of the actions described; and when all these were related to a controlling moral intention' (131). For Watt, Richardson took the further step of organizing his material with this moral and artistic purpose, and he is the first true novelist.

Richardson's advance, then, is attributed to his success in dealing with formal problems which Defoe had left unresolved. However, Watt's discussion of *Pamela* is mainly sociological, not formal, accounting for the coterminous rise of the novel with the rise of the conjugal family, bourgeois social prerogatives, and individualism. Watt asserts that, in eighteenth-century England, 'the code of romantic love began to accommodate itself to religious, social and psychological reality', and the result was the novel of courtship and marriage (136). Despite women's wider removal from economic individualism at this time, legislation like the Marriage Act (1753) gave them greater marital choice and cemented the contractarian conception of marriage that had been mounting. Developments in the cultural conception of marriage were also tied in with the increased importance of private property, as the chastity of a bride ensured the legitimate transmission of property. As will be seen in Chapter 5, Watt is idealistic about how these social changes empowered women. However, anticipating some arguments that stem from gender history which we will also see in Chapter 5, Watt perceives increasingly dichotomous sexual identities taking hold in *Pamela*, as 'the conception of sex we find in Richardson embodies a more complete and comprehensive separation between the male and female roles than had previously existed' (162). As well as advancing psychological verisimilitude in fiction, Richardson's novel is also interpreted by Watt as a middle-class attack on traditional aristocratic privilege.

In his discussion of private experience and fiction, Watt argues that the rise of the novel reflected new perspectives on subjectivity, the consequence of reorganizations of urban and domestic space and new uses of print. Specifically, along with a new emphasis on the individual's ethical responsibility, the transformation of London into a modern city finally removed the traditional sense of community that is residual in Defoe. Notwithstanding ongoing hostility to urbanization, not least in Richardson, 'the world of the novel is essentially the world of the modern city', Watt surmises; 'both present a picture of life in which the individual is immersed in private and personal relationships because a larger communion with nature or society is no longer available' (185). Consequences of urban growth included suburbs and private areas within domestic space, as locks started to be put on doors and women had closets where they could be alone – to write and read. Familiar letter writing increased, enabled by the establishment of a cheap and efficient postal service, and this became the very stuff of Richardson's fiction. If communal relationships were dissolving, new relationships between readers and fictional characters were forming, because Richardson's epistolary technique, whereby a character exhaustively communicates their immediate mental state to a correspondent, enabled a much deeper identification between reader and character. For Watt, as for Baker before him, Richardson's employment of epistolary form gave him an advantage over Defoe's autobiographical memoir, because 'it makes us feel that we are in contact not with literature but with the raw materials of life itself as they are momentarily reflected in the minds of the protagonists' (193). What Watt terms the 'privacy [...] of print' also encouraged the reader's participation in the novel's action and their identification with characters (199). He even imagines readers relatively new to mechanized type (print on page) surrendering their awareness of illusion due to habituation with print technology. The readerly identification fostered by the novel's presentation of inner life catered for middle-class escapism and exploited aspirations to social advancement.

Watt's discussion of *Clarissa* suggests a new 'literary maturity' for the novel, which becomes in Richardson's hands 'a literary structure in which narrative mode, plot, characters and moral theme were organised into a unified whole' (208). In *Clarissa*, Richardson – unlike Defoe, a conscious innovator – solved the formal and moral problems inherent in the singular perspective of *Moll Flanders* and *Pamela*. The multiple correspondents in *Clarissa* permit the reader an objectivity lacking in those earlier novels, but without compromising interiority: we get 'complete' characterization, ensuring that no-one in *Clarissa* seems less than a real being. Richardson overcomes limitations of didacticism, which preferred characters to be representatives of vice or virtue, in order to present a moral drama with psychological depth, remedying the ethical oversights of *Pamela* (is the heroine sincere or duplicitous?) by ensuring that, in *Clarissa*, 'we can never assume that any statement should be taken as the complete and literal truth' (229). The heroine is not always aware of her own feelings and has a limited outlook, but other perspectives are presented, so that the reader is aware of the author's objective treatment of character. This psychological depth ensures that *Clarissa* is ethical and aesthetic rather than merely moral and didactic. In historical terms, Watt interprets *Clarissa* as a bourgeois solution to the clash between Cavalier and Puritan sexual ideologies: that is, between Lovelace's libertinism and Clarissa's sexual reserve. And Watt also thinks, in Freudian terms, about the historical establishment of sexual roles, whereby the sadistic and sexual male is opposed to the masochistic and asexual female. The point is that Richardson displayed insight into the subconscious and unconscious drives behind these roles, and rendered these in realistic fictional form.

Turning to Fielding, Watt strikes a defensive note, because in *Joseph Andrews* Fielding presents the view that the novel is not 'the unique literary expression of modern society', but rather 'a continuation of a very old and honoured narrative tradition' – specifically, epic (239). Watt concludes, however, that the epic influence on Fielding was inconsiderable and unimportant for the development of the novel. The novel in the hands of Defoe and Richardson, Watt surmises, fits into 'a long-standing movement in Christian and middle-class apologetics against the glamour of the pagan and warrior virtues' celebrated in epic (244). Bellicose, aristocratic, and martial forms of honour (epic) were being replaced by internal and spiritual ones, nullifying distinctions of class and gender (novels). Moreover, epic excludes those expectations about everyday life that comprise the novel. The preface to *Joseph Andrews* appears to align this work with epic, but 'Fielding's attempts to bring his novel into line with classical doctrine could not be supported either by existing literary parallel or theoretical precedent' (250). In short, his practice did not match his professions, because Fielding gives more verisimilitude than is present in epic, betokening 'a somewhat ambiguous attitude to the epic model' that ultimately justifies Watt in interpreting *Joseph Andrews* as 'a parody of epic procedures' (254). By the time of *Amelia*, Fielding was invoking epic by analogy, rather than identification; in *The Journal of a Voyage to Lisbon* (1755), he critiques epic's infidelity to everyday experience; and in *Tom Jones* he identified his role not with the epic poet but with the 'historian or biographer' whose aim is to give a particularized and faithful account of his time (257). Ultimately, then, Watt resists Fielding's epic claims, which aim to lend the new form older pedigree.

Watt accounts for the different artistic ends of Richardson and Fielding in terms of their different social outlooks. These differences are illustrated by Watt through an adept comparison of similar scenes in *Tom Jones* and *Clarissa*, Sophia Western and Clarissa Harlowe each resisting paternal injunctions to marry Blifil and Solmes, respectively. On the one hand, Richardson supplies 'detailed description of individual states of mind, a description which requires a minute particularity in the presentation of character' (261). On the other hand, Fielding's equivalent scene aims for comedy rather than psychological plausibility: his approach to character is 'external', Richardson's 'internal' (272). Plot takes priority over character in Fielding, whereas the reverse is true in Richardson, so that plot is an external stimulant of character rather than shaped by character. These formal differences correspond to opposing outlooks. Fielding viewed human nature as static, so that moral development is not really possible and personal relationships are relatively unimportant determinants of personality. To reflect this outlook, Fielding advanced the novel by adding 'realism of assessment' to Defoe's and Richardson's 'realism of presentation' (288). By this Watt means that Richardsonian form entails detailed presentation without explicit objective commentary. Fielding's aim, by contrast, was analytic: 'He is not interested in the exact configuration of motives in any particular person's mind at any particular time but only in those features of the individual which are necessary to assign him to his moral and social species' (272). Aside from actually attempting to stem rather than embrace individualism, Fielding thought narrative presentation without assessment morally dangerous; he tried to occlude the reader's immersion in illusion by using intrusive narrators that foreground rather than conceal invention. Watt sees a bifurcation of the novel tradition in the Richardson-Fielding rivalry: the Aristotelian prioritization of plot over character carries forwards from Fielding to Smollett and Dickens; its inverse, character over plot, goes from Richardson, Sterne, and Austen to Proust and Joyce.

Ultimately, Watt states that 'Fielding's technique was too eclectic to become a permanent element in the tradition of the novel' (288). Accordingly, Watt expresses his preference for Richardson, formal realism, and the investigation of individuated character and personality in the novel. Fielding's technique is deemed 'deficient' because it was unable to convey 'larger moral significance through character and action alone, and could only supply it by means of a somewhat intrusive patterning of the plot and by direct editorial commentary' (287). Watt suggests that first Sterne and then Austen try to reconcile Richardson's 'realism of presentation' with Fielding's 'realism of assessment'. By equating narrative with consciousness in an ultimately parodic manner, Sterne retains Richardson's psychological closeness whilst keeping Fielding's manipulative intrusions. Austen finishes this process, in effect completing the rise of the novel:

■ She was able to combine into a harmonious unity the advantages both of realism of presentation and realism of assessment, of the internal and of the external approaches to character; her novels have authenticity without

> diffuseness or trickery, wisdom of social comment without a garrulous essayist, and a sense of the social order which is not achieved at the expense of the individuality and autonomy of the characters. (297) □

Long after Austen took this step, Joyce's *Ulysses* (1922) was, Watt says, 'the climax of the novel's development' (296). France caught up in novelistic art only when she caught up politically, which means not until after the Revolution (1789) empowered the middle class a full century after the equivalent process in England, and produced Balzac, Stendhal, and the Naturalist School, who all benefited from their English predecessors. Watt says that the formal elements being negotiated by Defoe, Richardson, and Fielding – realism of presentation and realism of assessment – encapsulate the entire later tradition, which reshuffled these approaches.

Conclusion

Watt pieced together so many of the several ideas that had been floated by his predecessors that he has rendered most of them obsolete. Modern critics typically start with Watt, but it is worth acknowledging the provenances of his findings. We have seen that the teleology for which Watt was subsequently criticized (see Chapter 3) was the product of a deductive, essentialist, and progressive approach to genre well represented by Baker. The view of realism displacing romance enshrined in Watt has a long history that has been tracked in Chapters 1 and 2. We have seen that commentators from Baker to Kettle credited Defoe with the rough-hewn innovation of realist technique subsequently given intellectual, ethical, and artistic shape by Richardson and Fielding. What Baker called intellectual realism is similar to Watt's realism of assessment, although, unlike Baker, Watt privileged the presentational realism associated with Richardson. The psychological verisimilitude Watt credits to Richardson's resolution of formal shortcomings in Defoe is anticipated by Allen's and McKillop's accounts. Both Allen, when he talks about the specificity of time and place given in fiction, and Van Ghent, who notes the novel's propensity for particularization and individualization, introduce ideas that Watt developed. In terms of context, the rising middle class's role in dictating literary form had been mooted since the nineteenth century and critics slightly earlier than Watt, such as Kettle, Church, and McKillop, had linked this with Protestantism and empiricism as conditions conducive to the novel's rise. Nevertheless, the originality of Watt's contribution should not be understated, not least his ability to synthesize diffuse historical and generic claims about the novel that had been accruing for the past century. And Watt, of course, reversed the predominantly formalist tendency of mid-twentieth-century criticism. This was to prove temporary. The following chapter examines how the rise-of-the-novel narrative was modified during the dominance of formalism in the quarter-century after Watt.

CHAPTER THREE

Restructuring the Rise of the Novel, 1958–85

This chapter surveys rise-of-the-novel criticism in the immediate wake of Watt, who set the terms on which the discussion would be conducted for decades and who became the figure everyone had to deal with. A wider turn to the rhetoric and poetics of fiction informed analysis of the early novel at this time, as literary criticism concentrated on narrative structure, technique, and genre, rather than historical contexts, producing a considerable amount of formalist supplementation to Watt's sociohistorical approach. We might say that scholars broadly accepted Watt's historical points but sought to clarify aspects of his account of the formal properties of the emergent novel. After outlining early responses to Watt, this chapter considers approaches to the novel through genre, plot, characterization, reader response, and narrative technique. The process of canonization I traced in Chapters 1 and 2 left Defoe, Richardson, Fielding, Smollett, and Sterne as the novelists before Austen who mattered. This narrow canon and the formalist tendency to focus on particular works mean that the treatment of individual authors and novels became important in understandings of the rise of the novel in this period.

Early responses to Watt

Watt's claim that the novel represented a new literary form was promptly challenged. Frye continued to view the modern novel as 'a realistic displacement of romance' that 'had few structural features peculiar to itself', critiquing 'common critical assumptions about fiction which have been fostered by the prestige of a displaced and realistic tradition'.[1] In *The Epic Strain in the English Novel* (1958), E. M. W. Tillyard contends that the novel is not a genre: that label is reserved for tragedy, comedy, epithalamium, dirge, satire, and epic. These classical *genres* have 'strains' that run through multiple *forms,* including drama and novel.

Tillyard traces the 'epic strain' in fiction since 1700, which comprises four features: (i) a choric quality that expresses the feelings of a group; (ii) a speaker able to speak for a multitude; (iii) 'heroic' treatment of the subject; and (iv) 'dense' language and 'intense energy and application'.[2] Tillyard contends that *Robinson Crusoe* initiated the epic strain in the British novel, continued in Walter Scott, Joseph Conrad, and Arnold Bennett, whereas Henry Fielding, George Eliot, and James Joyce stake epic claims that ultimately fall short.

Watt had argued that the decline of universalist literary standards and the rise of narrative particularization produced the novel, partly following the Marxist, György Lukács, whose landmark study, *The Theory of the Novel* (1916), had defined the genre as a displacement of epic. By contrast, Tillyard claims that *Crusoe* 'heads the small list of those English novels which [...] embody, to a larger or smaller degree, the qualities that mark the epic as an autonomous literary kind', suggesting that *Crusoe* reaches towards the universal (25). Whereas *Crusoe* is a mythic expression of modern individualism for Watt, Tillyard asserts that it is 'an epic, but an epic having some of the limitations of the middle-class ethos whose choric expression it was' (50). Like Watt, Tillyard downplays Fielding's epic claim, not because, as Watt said, Fielding did not really mean it, but because he did not quite achieve it, as *Tom Jones* 'fails of epic effect' (58). Tillyard explicitly challenges Watt on two counts (197–8). First, he denies the novel's break with traditional plots and techniques is as violent as Watt claims, arguing that the supposedly new, 'realistic' sense of time and place, though rarer, is discernible in earlier literature. But Watt does not in fact claim formal realism as an eighteenth-century invention: he only says that Defoe and Richardson used this technique more purposefully than anything that came before. Second, Tillyard contends that the features Watt offers as characteristic of the novel are typical of early eighteenth-century culture more generally. However, Watt argues that a modern sense of time and place is a *precondition* for the novel as well as a *characteristic* of it: presumably he would say that this *influenced* drama and poetry, but *occasioned* the novel. Tillyard was writing just one year after Watt and is perhaps too close to be full-sighted, but his study indicates one direction the formalist response would take.

Like Frye and Tillyard, Robert Scholes and Robert Kellogg, in *The Nature of Narrative* (1966), aim to decentre the novel from the study of narrative, resisting the view of 'the novel as the final product of an ameliorative evolution, as the perfected form which earlier kinds of narrative – sacred myth, folktale, epic, romance, legend, allegory, confession, satire – were all striving, with varying degrees of success, to become'.[3] Scholes and Kellogg counter the teleology of rise-of-the-novel criticism: 'The tendency to apply the standards of nineteenth-century realism to all fiction naturally has disadvantages for our understanding of every other kind of narrative' (6). By contrast, they observe that the novel 'represents only a couple of centuries in the continuous narrative tradition of the Western world which can be traced back five thousand years' (9). The target of these comments is Erich Auerbach's *Mimesis: The Representation of Reality in Western Literature* (1946), an important influence on Watt, which considered the entire history of narrative through the paradigm of realism.

The charge of 'teleological bias' was levelled directly at Watt by J. Paul Hunter, John Richetti, and English Showalter. In *The Reluctant Pilgrim* (1966), Hunter states that the 'rise' metaphor 'barely disguise[s] the assumption that the novel is organic, moving more or less predictably toward a realization of perfect form'.[4] For Richetti, in *Popular Fiction Before Richardson* (1969), 'what is involved is nothing less than a gratuitous imposition of the social and philosophical norms (summed up in such terms as bourgeois democracy and pragmatism) and the narrative effects (summed up in the term realism) we value most upon a body of writing which was at least partly unaware of, if not hostile to, them'.[5] Showalter's concern with French developments, in *The Evolution of the French Novel* (1972), leads him to reject Watt's view that the novel was the result of specifically English social developments, was pioneered by a number of English writers, and was characterized by realism's self-conscious break with romance. Richetti questions Watt's neglect of fictions by women immediately before Richardson; Showalter highlights Watt's neglect of French fiction: both of these subvert the 'rise' narrative. Following David Hirsch, who argues that Watt's conception of realism is based on a misreading of the empiricist philosophers, Showalter charges that Watt subjectively declares certain works to be realistic and therefore novelistic, whereas realism was only one amongst many 'minor' fictional modes in this period. The consequence is that Watt produces 'anachronistic misinterpretations'.[6]

Wayne Booth's *The Rhetoric of Fiction* (1961) also faults Watt's focus on realism, his 'all-pervasive assumption [...] that "realism of presentation" is a good thing in itself'. In countering the 'dogma' that 'novels should be realistic', Booth argues that Watt's criteria lead him to elevate Richardson over Fielding, because the latter's 'realism of assessment' diminishes the authenticity Watt privileges.[7] Watt himself addresses the widely-held view that Fielding is under-appreciated in *The Rise of the Novel* in a 1968 response to his book's early reception. He says that the imbalance in the treatment of the two kinds of realism is attributable to cuts, which shed his book of further chapters on Fielding, Smollett, and Sterne.[8] Fielding was not the only writer to whom critics thought Watt had done an injustice. A debate raged about whether irony in *Moll Flanders* is consciously intended by Defoe or (as Watt claimed) an inadvertent by-product of careless composition. Watt ceded little ground in his 1967 survey of this debate, admitting a degree of irony, but denying its place in the encompassing structure of Defoe's novel. *Moll Flanders* remained for Watt a work *containing* irony, but not a work *of* irony.[9] This debate was significant for the larger perspective of the novel, because at stake was the precise place of Defoe as either a pioneer of narrative art and hence the inventor of the novel, or a hack who unwittingly discovered techniques that he was neither motivated nor competent enough to exploit. The argument reflects a wider movement towards concerns of novelistic structure, premised on fiction having distinct formal features. Language, structure, narrative, and genre were the terms on which the rise of the novel was to be evaluated in the 1960s and 1970s.

Structure and shape

Less preoccupied in the wake of Watt to seek literary-historical explanations for novelistic origins, critics in the 1960s looked for structural unity in novels through authorial moral vision. In *The Appropriate Form* (1964), Barbara Hardy makes 'a good story', 'the lively representation of reality', and the 'working-out of a moral problem' desiderata for the novel. The only eighteenth-century novelist Hardy discusses in depth is Defoe, whom she classifies as an ethical dogmatist who used fiction to embody an ideology – specifically, providentialism.[10] In this respect, Hardy demurs from Watt's reading of *Crusoe* as an essay in secular individualism. Also looking for aesthetic unity in Defoe's ideational consistency, and also departing from Watt, is Maximillian Novak, whose *Economics and the Fiction of Daniel Defoe* (1962) debunks Crusoe's capitalist credentials, instead identifying Defoe as a proponent of an older, more conservative economic system: mercantilism. Then, in *Defoe and the Nature of Man* (1963), Novak identifies Defoe as a writer giving fictional form to philosophical ideas about the law of nature, asserting that Defoe's novels 'may be regarded as a series of moral fables presented in a vivid and realistic manner'. Novak's work implies that the novel came into being when Defoe used fiction as a vehicle for ideas.[11]

Contemporaneous criticism of Fielding follows a similar trajectory, focusing on authorial moral and ideological organization of fiction, partly reacting to Watt's perceived downgrading of this author. In *The Moral Basis of Fielding's Art* (1959), Martin Battestin contends that Fielding's 'art of the novel' consisted of *Joseph Andrews*'s dramatization of Latitudinarianism, a theological movement which promoted moral rectitude rather than doctrinal purity.[12] In *Fielding's Art of Fiction* (1961), Maurice Johnson, with a similarly ethical and intentionalist methodology, describes Fielding progressing from the art of parody in *Shamela* (1741) to the art of comic romance in *Joseph Andrews*, and on to the art of the novel in *Tom Jones*, a career culminating in *Amelia*, which aims to bring moral precepts down to real life.[13] In *Henry Fielding: The Tentative Realist* (1967), Michael Irwin finds that Fielding's experimental realism subordinates aesthetic considerations to didactic ones in aiming to supply practical morality to readers in a period of religious division.[14] Andrew Wright's *Henry Fielding: Mask and Feast* (1965) and Glenn Hatfield's *Henry Fielding and the Language of Irony* (1968) inch the formalist debate from ethical to more strictly aesthetic questions, drawing attention to rhetoric, linguistic play, and irony, and making these features central to Fielding's conception of the novel form.[15] Robert Alter's *Fielding and the Nature of the Novel* (1968) also works from assumptions of artistic innovation, discussing style, character, and 'architectonic' structure in Fielding's novels.[16] And Homer Goldberg's *The Art of 'Joseph Andrews'* (1969) considers that work as the realization of the form of the novel, 'a planned system of actions with its own internal probabilities and ethical and emotional coherence', which advances several continental prototypes, namely Cervantes, Scarron, Le Sage, and Marivaux.[17]

This survey of 1960s Fielding scholarship indicates the ethical direction that formalist criticism took. Likewise, in *Fiction and the Shape of Belief* (1966), Sheldon Sacks addresses how an author's moral beliefs are embodied in fiction. He identifies three 'mutually exclusive' types of prose fiction.[18] 'Satire', illustrated by *Gulliver's Travels*, propounds a negative morality and does not concern itself with probability or consistency of character; a satire is 'a work organized so that it ridicules objects external to the fictional world created in it' (26). 'Apologue', typified by *Rasselas*, lays no stress on plot, probability, or character, and its moral purpose can be easily encapsulated – the futility of pursuing earthly happiness in *Rasselas*, for example – because an apologue is 'a work organized as a fictional example of the truth of a formulable statement' (26). The third type, the 'represented action', approximates to the novel and is explicated briefly through *Pamela* before Sacks moves to an extended study of *Joseph Andrews*, *Tom Jones*, and *Amelia* as 'represented actions'. 'In any work which belongs to this class', Sacks explains, 'characters about whose fates we are made to care are introduced in unstable relationships which are then further complicated until the complications are finally resolved by the complete removal of the represented instability' (15). The resolutions may be comic or tragic, where things respectively turn out well or badly, or else 'serious', where 'the final stabilization of relationships may result either happily or unhappily for the characters with whom we are most in sympathy' (22). The important thing is that the reader draws conclusions from the events, so that the represented action makes moral and artistic ends coterminous: 'The shape of belief in actions cannot be the pattern of ridiculed objects peculiar to satire or the exemplified thematic statement of apologue. [...] If his novel is coherent, then the writer's relevant beliefs, like all other qualitative parts, must be subordinate to the artistic end which informs the work' (61).

Sacks does not evaluatively rank the three fictional types – satire, apologue, and represented action. They each have their formal purpose. He explicates the 'controlling ethical statements' in Fielding's novels, showing that the use of narrator, techniques of characterization, and narrative structure are the means by which Fielding directs the reader's ethical response to action. The rise of the novel can thus be dated to the time when Richardson and Fielding 'chose to embody sincere moral purposes in forms of prose fiction of such a nature that the achievement of their moral purposes becomes absolutely consequent on the effectiveness with which they accomplished an artistic end' (247). Sacks notes the tendency to assume that the didactic Richardson was a moralist who accidentally pioneered the novel and that the craftsman Fielding was a novelist who incidentally moralized. However, each can be considered a proponent of the 'represented action', because their moral design exceeds the basic presentation of precept and example, typical of apologue. Because *Moll Flanders* is not organized as an 'action' in this way, the novel begins with Richardson and Fielding, not Defoe (267).

Robert Donovan's *The Shaping Vision* (1966) provides readings of major novelists in terms of how their moral aims determined the shape or structure of their fictions. Donovan upholds Watt's conception of the novel as a new form in the eighteenth century, and also reacts to Leavis's deprecation of the artistic quality of early novels. Like Sacks, Donovan emphasizes authorial control: 'every novel represents, as it stands, the full realization of its author's design', because 'the artist's vision is itself the shaping instrument'.[19] Expressly rejecting historical concerns, Donovan supplies structural interpretations of individual novels that seek each work's formal logic. He shows that the dual perspective created in *Moll Flanders* by the retroactive first-person narrative, which makes Moll both subject and object of the narration, ensures that conscious irony, famously denied by Watt, is present in Defoe's work. Richardson's vision in *Pamela* is 'social' (the middle class ameliorating the aristocracy) rather than personal (concerned with characters' private lives), and the action of the novel can be explained in terms of the author's class concerns. The 'unifying perspective and inner form' of *Joseph Andrews* lies in its status as a parody of *Pamela*, wherein Fielding exposes and tests the moral outlook propounded by Richardson. The 'vision' of *Tristram Shandy* is Sterne's desire to expose the discrepancy between moral theory and execution, between words and the things represented, and this accounts for the novel's self-reflexivity. The multiple epistolary form of *Humphry Clinker* creates layers of irony, which give it an internal novelistic unity, not an 'external' unity that would assign it coherence in terms of non-novelistic genres (travelogue, satire, or political treatise) or with reference to the history of ideas.

Donovan, then, moves away from looking for artistic purpose in ethics and ideas, and towards a more aestheticist concentration on 'inner form'. Douglas Brooks also reflects this switch in *Number and Pattern in the Eighteenth-Century Novel* (1973). Brooks contends that a Renaissance tradition of numerology, which saw nature as a reflection of cosmic patterns, persisted during the period of the rise of the novel, and lends formal unity to the fiction of Defoe, Fielding, Smollett, and Sterne. Brooks states: 'By the term "numerology", as it is used in modern literary criticism, is meant (i) the structural exploitation in the literary artifact of symbolic numbers and (ii) any kind of arithmetical patterning'.[20] Though scepticism about the validity of numerology was increasing by the eighteenth century, Brooks says that readers remained familiar with and affectionate towards finding numerical structures with biblical or symbolical significances in literature. Readers traced chiastic, symmetrical, or repetitive patterns, by which authors sought to enhance their thematic and moral purposes and to imply by analogy that divine Providence orders the universe. To give a few examples, discussing Fielding's fiction, Brooks counts page, chapter, and volume numbers, as well as revealing the symbolic use of numbers, to argue that 'the structure of *Tom Jones* is in accord with Augustan aesthetic and theological proportional theory' (108). After experimenting with iconographical numerology in his earlier fictions, Smollett's final novel is a culmination of the practice: '*Humphry Clinker* is the last work to be written in the main stream of that numerological tradition which certain eighteenth-century authors inherited from Renaissance humanism. Structurally and thematically it is a finely-wrought and moving monument to the ideals of English Augustanism' (158). Brooks's exposition of recurrent images and themes, of narrative patterning, and of characterization, suggests that early novelists were more concerned with orderly structuring than previous criticism had admitted. Though Richardson is not analysed by Brooks, a similar shift is noticeable in studies that start with the assumption that he is a conscious artist.[21] Of course, the body of criticism in the 1960s and 70s that assesses the artistry of the big five eighteenth-century novelists follows McKillop's *Early Masters* as much as it does Watt's *Rise*.

The 'intergeneric' rise of the novel

A considerable amount of scholarship between 1965 and 1985 looked at how the novel developed from anterior genres or alongside parallel genres, as well as how it borrowed techniques from other modes of writing. First up, Robert Adams Day's *Told in Letters* (1966) surveys epistolary fiction before Richardson, estimating that between 1660 and 1740 'over two hundred works in five hundred editions' were told in letters: 'Some of the most popular tales of the day were letter fiction; several of these were widely imitated, and a few were of remarkable literary merit, at least for their time and their kind'.[22] Though cautious about asserting the quality of this 'subliterature', Day looks to 'indicate "missing links" in the English novel's evolution', so that 'Richardson's work may be viewed historically as the culmination of a process or development rather than as a literary eruption' (5, 9). Richardson's achievement is decidedly downgraded by Day, as 'all the elements of the genre which he brought to maturity were present in English fiction and had already been developed to a degree which he certainly reached but did not often surpass' (190–1). Day acknowledges the influence of French epistolary fiction; he addresses the contribution of non-fictional letter writing to the novel; and he discusses the technical features of narrative relayed partly or wholly through correspondence. The epistolary mode permits greater subjectivity, multiplying points of view, and achieving immediacy, intimacy, and psychological drama. In approximating the vocal quality of a soliloquy and in reading like blank verse, fictional letters, Day contends, were influenced by drama, and anticipate the intensive subjectivity of the Modernist stream of consciousness.

In his important and enduringly relevant book, *Popular Fiction Before Richardson*, Richetti studies 'recurrent narrative patterns' in the first forty years of the century that formed the 'ideological matrix' from which Richardson and Fielding's realistic novels emerged.[23] Richetti examines five proto-novelistic subgenres: rogue and whore biographies, travel narratives and pirate stories, scandal chronicles, amatory novellas, and pietistic romances. He contends that such stories – by the twentieth century consigned to oblivion, irrelevance, or ethical disapproval – were 'entertainment machines and fantasy inducers', read for 'escapist' purposes in the period, providing 'fantasies which allow pleasurable identification and projection' (263, 5). Though in literary terms these fictions amount to 'a compost heap' out of which the novel flowered, Richetti claims these forms helped to clarify ideological dilemmas for non-elite readers by depicting 'the embattled individual in a hostile and vicious world' (21). In manifold ways, popular fiction plays out this self/world paradigm, which articulates the historical tension between a traditional religious worldview and a newer secular ethos that prioritized individual survival and prosperity.

In Richetti's account, criminal biographies not only participate in the rise of the novel because they advance realism, but also because their narrative pattern of sin, repentance, and divine judgement replicates society's punishment of self-assertive individualism: the criminal's career 'evokes the desire for secular freedom and economic self-determination which is a real part of the outlook of the age; but this latent social aggression is, at the same time, a source of guilt and anxiety which must be severely and decisively punished' (34–5). The confessional element in popular criminal biography, the 'best' examples of which are Defoe's *Moll Flanders* and *Colonel Jack* (1722), injects a homiletic tone, meaning that the criminal is 'a mythical figure of great significance: an embodiment of the secular energies of the age which chafe under the traditional system of social and moral limitations and their religious foundations' (59). Voyage literature exhibits the same 'novelistic dialectic of the secular and religious' (91), as the wide world is at once conquerable by the dynamic, piratical individual, and the site of this individual's spiritual regeneration.

Richetti turns from criminal adventure fiction to modes that were typically female-authored – the scandal chronicles of Manley, Haywood's amatory novellas, and pietistic romances by Penelope Aubin, Jane Barker, and Elizabeth Singer Rowe. Although Richetti brings less traditional works into view, he characterizes this material as 'unreadable' and 'morally indefensible', valuable only for its ideological significance, as the secular-religious dialectic is again played out, particularly in 'the mythology of persecuted innocence' these forms exploit (166). Scandalous allegories of sexual predation in high places, written by Manley and Haywood, articulate 'latent social antagonism' towards aristocratic corruption and 'reflect that basic ideological split between [...] the secular and religious views of experience which characterizes the early eighteenth century' (148). The amatory novella, exemplified by Haywood's *Love in Excess* (1719–20), is a 'vulgarization' of the French heroic romance and, through 'erotic and pathetic "intensity"', an extension of the 'persecuted innocence' theme (172, 193). Whilst Manley and Haywood were writing erotic fictions, however, 'pious' women writers used romance conventions in the service of Christian instruction. In works like *The Life of Madam de Beaumont* and *The Strange Adventures of the Count de Vinevil* (both 1721), Aubin applies the theme of 'innocence tested' to the literature of travel and adventure, in order to seduce her readers into virtue through what Richetti labels 'Christian "realism"', which claims moral rather than literal truth (219). Rowe uses the self/world dialectic in *Friendship in Death* (1728) to counter atheism by pitting a heroic believer against a faithless world. Richetti claims that the ideological conflicts he traces in these narrative patterns are also present in Defoe and Richardson, who made 'realism and psychological verisimilitude serve the ideological needs we have found their now-obscure contemporaries attending to', so that these techniques 'were new and superior means towards older ideological ends' (265). Defoe and Richardson's formal innovations ultimately elevate them above their peers in their rendering the 'novelistic dialectic' between expansive individualism and social constriction.

Jerry Beasley's *Novels of the 1740s* (1982) complements Richetti's focus on popular fiction in the century's first four decades by assessing the breakthrough works of Richardson, Fielding, and Smollett in relation to the 'some three hundred works of fiction' published in the 1740s, when 'the English novel as we know it today was born and nurtured through its infancy'.[24] Beasley describes the majority of these novels as 'tenth-rate pulp, artistically depraved and morally shallow', but insists they provided fertile ground for the three named writers (2). He discusses fictions that replicate contemporary history in the form of espionage stories, secret histories, and voyages; fictional biographies of pious paragons and low-life rogues; picaresque and Quixotic novels; and works in the tradition of continental novellas, particularly by Haywood, Jane Collier, and Sarah Fielding. Although they transcend such limited forms, Beasley argues that the decade's important novels are indebted to such modes, so that *Clarissa* is like secret history because it reveals libertine machinations, *Amelia* owes a debt to military memoirs, and *Roderick Random* and *Jonathan Wild* (1743) extend the picaresque and rogue biography. Beasley, countering Watt's preference for Richardson, elevates Fielding: 'Of all the fiction writers so busily at work in the early years of the eighteenth century, only the author of *Joseph Andrews* and *Tom Jones* seriously undertook to articulate any aesthetic of the novel, or to identify and defend prose fiction as a new literary form' (184). Basically retaining Watt's distinction between realisms of presentation (Richardson) and assessment (Fielding), Beasley privileges the declared artistry of Fielding, with *Tom Jones* as 'the triumphant achievement of its author's genius' (208).

Single-author studies of Defoe, Richardson, and Fielding emphasized their indebtedness to prior literary forms. For instance, Margaret Anne Doody's *A Natural Passion* (1974) explains how Richardson developed the formal and ideological preoccupations of earlier female-authored fictions: 'It is quite evident that all three of Richardson's novels are not an innovation but a development, by an artistic genius, of a minor tradition established by the writers of love-stories told in the feminine voice'.[25] Doody considers how Richardson adapts dramatic, didactic, and religious modes to create a tragic novel in *Clarissa* and a 'domestic comedy' in *Sir Charles Grandison*. Mark Kinkead-Weekes and Ira Konigsberg develop the point made by Day that Richardson's novels are indebted to the dramatic tradition. In *Samuel Richardson: Dramatic Novelist* (1973), Kinkead-Weekes sees Richardson's advances in epistolary form as 'dramatic' because the removal of an authorial filter provides greater immediacy. By presenting direct voices in the manner of 'writing to the moment', Richardson reveals things about his characters that they do not know, thereby advancing the technical possibilities for characterization in fiction.[26] In *Samuel Richardson and the Dramatic Novel* (1968), Konigsberg considers more direct and particular dramatic influences, indicating Richardson's familiarity with a number of playwrights and asserting that 'Richardson brought to the English novel subject matter and techniques developed in the drama, and that it was the resulting integration of these dramatic elements with fiction that is responsible for the subsequent course of the English novel'.[27] Reasserting the more traditional view, which I noted in Chapter 1, that the rise of the novel and the decline of drama are related, Laura Brown's *English Dramatic Form* (1981) argues that the realistic novel was the logical genre to succeed drama in representing 'moral action'.[28]

In response to Watt's characterization of the novel as the expression of secular modernity, other scholars reassessed the significance of religious forms of writing on the rise of the novel, most notably with respect to Defoe. G. A. Starr demonstrates the influence on Defoe of spiritual autobiography – the Protestant custom of recording one's experiences to look for signs of divine grace and shaping a life into a providential pattern pivoting around conversion.[29] In a similar vein, J. Paul Hunter adduces a number of Puritan narrative forms, which 'provided Defoe with a framing vision for *Robinson Crusoe*', including 'guide' books, providential literature, spiritual biography, and allegory.[30] The novel was increasingly looking like a genre that not only took off from other forms, but which retained features from them.

Taking a broader view, Ronald Paulson's valuable study, *Satire and the Novel* (1967), connects the rise of the novel with the decline of the Augustan heyday of satire – the age of Dryden, Swift and Pope.[31] The novel represented new values, 'middle-class, matter-of-fact, and realistic', which were antithetical to satire's conservative universalism. The 'legalistic' view of character that allows satire to make absolute moral pronouncements based on representative actions was challenged by an 'organic' view of character wherein the novel encouraged readers to delay judgement while motives and causes are assessed. The satirist's critique of society, usually focused on a villain, gives way to the novelist's championship of the individual, usually focused on a hero. And the satirist's belief in objective truth is qualified by the subjective epistemology of Locke enshrined in novels.

As may be seen from this précis, Paulson accepts many of Watt's terms, but re-evaluates the contribution of Fielding and 'realism of assessment'. In Paulson's account, Fielding turned to the novel from a career as a satirical dramatist and pamphleteer when he objected to *Pamela*'s strategy of immersing its readers in action in ways that occlude critical judgement. Influenced by the Earl of Shaftesbury's reconceptualization of laughter as affirmative and therapeutic rather than derisive and misanthropic, Fielding shifted the function of the satirist away from that of a prosecuting attorney and towards that of an impartial judge. Like William Hogarth's paintings, Fielding's novels aimed to 'replace the fantasy of traditional, emblematic, and Augustan satire with a more restrained delineation, closer to experience, and reliant on "character", rather than "caricature", on the variety rather than the exaggeration of expression' (108). Paulson describes in *Joseph Andrews* and *Tom Jones* a number of techniques through which the novel reforms satire. These include a 'touchstone' structure, which ethically evaluates characters based on their behaviour towards a stable moral norm (the protagonist); an objective commentator, which fixes the reader's judgement of character; the principle that motive, rather than consequence, determines the moral meaning of action; and the view that truth is not self-evident, but rather something to be found out.

It is not simply that the novel was in competition with satire and prevailed, but that the novel successfully absorbed satire into its workings, the two genres proving mutually enabling: 'After 1730 Fielding, Smollett, and Sterne were the only first-rate satiric temperaments to emerge in England, and all three turned to the novel' (9). Whereas Fielding fuses satire and novel, Smollett's modification of the picaresque produces novels *about* satire. In *Roderick Random*, a protagonist dissociated from the corrupt world is endowed with the satirical vision to judge society. *Peregrine Pickle* questions the efficacy of destructive satire, inviting the reader's negative judgement of misanthropic social critics. *Humphry Clinker* completes the process by qualifying the negative satirist (Bramble) with more affirmative social attitudes (Clinker and Melford). In Smollett's last novel, 'the evil object has become simply the reflection of a point of view – a symptom of sickness or isolation or a sense of fun' (208).

Smollett's 'satirist satirized' *motif* is paralleled in *Clarissa* and in Sarah Fielding's *David Simple* (1744), as the absorption of satire into the novel is achieved in sentimental fiction, although this process is anticipated by the blend of political satire and melodrama in early-century scandal chronicles, like Manley's 1709 work, *The New Atalantis*. Though Sterne returns to Augustan themes and aims to satirize the conventional novel, he also palliates satire in novelistic ways, modifying its severity. Paulson surmises that, 'as it was absorbed by the novel, the satiric judgment was complicated (Fielding) or emotionalized (Smollett) or softened (Sterne)' (310). Paulson argues that the subsequent rise of the novel of manners completes the novel's accommodation of satire. Charlotte Lennox's *The Female Quixote* (1752), *Sir Charles Grandison*, *The Vicar of Wakefield*, and *Evelina* are 'transitional novels', which severally provided the ironic perspective, criticism of courtship, and detached objectivity based on moral propriety that paved the way for Austen. In *Pride and Prejudice* (1813), 'satire has been successfully sublimated', making Austen's novels a 'destination' for 'satiric accommodation' (291, 306). For Paulson, Austen provided a means whereby realism could be moral, elaborating Watt's view that Austen combined the realisms of presentation and assessment pioneered (respectively) by Richardson and Fielding.

Paulson mentions the picaresque as a satirical form and Robert Alter, Alexander Blackburn, and Walter Reed each show the formative influence of this earlier continental mode on the eighteenth-century British novel. Alter's *Rogue's Progress* (1964) acknowledges the persistence of the picaresque, showing how its formal features (first-person narrative, episodic structure, and an itinerant, isolated hero) influenced the eighteenth-century English novel.[32] In *The Myth of the Picaro* (1979), Blackburn rejects Alter's 'genre' approach and pursues an 'archetypal' or 'mythic' approach indebted to Frye, finding that 'classic' picaresque from sixteenth- and seventeenth-century Spain meets 'dialectical' picaresque in eighteenth- and nineteenth-century France and Britain. Picaresque becomes a 'submerged element' in the 'realistic' novel of manners and retains 'symbolic' purport in the nineteenth- and twentieth-century novel.[33] Balancing 'picaresque' and 'quixotic' modes, Reed's *Exemplary History of the Novel* (1981) argues that 'the novel first emerged as a significant literary phenomenon in [sixteenth-century] Spain', but is a 'multinational' genre, which 'arises and rearises in different regional cultures at different times'.[34] The novel, for Reed, is a modernizing genre that 'opposes the forms of everyday life, social and psychological, to the conventional forms of literature, classical or popular, inherited from the past' (4). Reed argues that the 'picaresque' and the 'quixotic' modes, initiated in turn by *Lazarillo de Tormes* (1554) and *Don Quixote*, adopt contrasting approaches to the novel's confrontation with literary tradition, becoming alternative models for subsequent texts. The eighteenth-century English novel was an outgrowth of this 'ongoing Continental debate' (119). Defoe and Fielding use picaresque and quixotic, respectively, to challenge Augustan neoclassicism. *Pamela* and *Clarissa* meanwhile are 'radical transformations of romance', leaving Richardson extraneous to the 'dialectic' of picaresque and quixotic (135, 263).

Approaches to the novel through genre informed criticism of Fielding in this period. Henry Knight Miller and James Lynch argue for Fielding's debt to romance.[35] J. Paul Hunter, in *Occasional Form* (1975), shows that Fielding occupies a liminal position between Augustanism and modernity, reaching for epic form through contemporary homiletic and didactic genres. He achieved this in *Tom Jones*, which stands as an 'epic of modern consciousness'.[36] In *Narrative Form in Fiction and History* (1970), Leo Braudy argues that the novel and modern history developed in tandem, because, in the hands of David Hume, Fielding, and Edward Gibbon, history and fiction were equally concerned with 'the establishment of a specific social milieu and an examination of the relations of individuals and institutions within that society'.[37] Braudy explains that these writers all 'use a prose narrative to treat problems of the individual in society, problems of the human character in time and history' (5). They believe that their work 'benefits society by helping to expand individual perception and sympathy'; they evince scepticism about 'any systematic explanation that claims absolute truth and perpetual relevance'; and they convey 'the impression of artistic power' in their narratives (11–13). From this mutually enabling arrangement, history and the novel move apart later in the century, as 'the factual world of historical interpretation and the fictive world of the novel gradually achieved more distinct identities' (4–5). The relationship between history and fiction is picked up in several studies discussed in Chapter 7.

Two other, purportedly factual, genres related to the novel are autobiography and travel writing. In *Travel Literature and the Evolution of the Novel* (1983), Percy Adams acknowledges the influence on the 'amorphous' form of the novel of genres as diverse as epic, picaresque, history, journalism, and religious genres, but posits that factual and pseudo-factual travel narratives are a decisive influence. His wide-ranging survey of this tradition argues that the obfuscation of fact and fiction prevalent in travel literature infiltrated the novel, and the novel's propensity to record detail in realistic ways was inherited from voyage literature. Stock-in-trade devices of early novels, like first-person narration, epistolary form, and autobiographical memoir, all derive from travel writing; structural features of the novel, like action, character and language, confirm for Adams that the novel evolved from travelogues.[38]

Other critics sought to explain the connections between autobiographical writing and the novel. Patricia Meyer Spacks, in *Imagining a Self* (1976), argues that the novel and autobiography developed in parallel in the eighteenth century, facing similar formal problems in articulating identity during an age of sceptical philosophy. These problems include memory's relationship to imagination and invention, the balance of consistency and changeability that will convince and instruct, and accounting for self and action in mutual terms. Tackling these issues gives novels organizational complexity: 'Novelist and autobiographer must find the causality that produces plot: this, therefore that; this and this and this, therefore me; and, deeper still, the laws of motivation that generate psychic action: the answer to the question, Why this and that?'[39] Spacks reads *Robinson Crusoe* and William Cowper's posthumous *Memoir* (1816) as expanded spiritual autobiographies, and she argues that *Tristram Shandy* and Edward Gibbon's fragmentary *Autobiographies* (1796) share experimental formal goals. Spacks posits that new strategies for writing the self for an audience manifest in *Pamela* and Colley Cibber's *Life* (1740), and assesses *Tom Jones* and James Boswell's *London Journal* (written 1762–3; published 1950) as masculine stories of development. She considers the construction of and constrictions on female identity in fiction and memoirs, and evaluates strategies of self-articulation in Burney's journals and novels. The emergent novel and life-writing provided models for one another, because this period saw unprecedented acts of self-assertion in print.

Reader response, character, and narrative technique

The previous section considered the 'intergeneric' rise of the novel – the relationship of the novel to previous and parallel genres, literary and non-literary, fictional and factual. J. Paul Hunter's *Before Novels* (1990) resumes this line of enquiry, as we will see in Chapter 7. This section, however, looks at how critics in the 1970s and 80s analysed technique in the developing novel.

Frederick Karl offers *The Adversary Literature* (1974) as a 'study in genre', that is, the internal workings of the new novel. He by and large follows Watt on sociohistorical matters and on the novel's realism, but the idea of genre that emerges is the novel as a highly self-conscious form, representing subversive, 'adversary' cultural interests: 'In several ways we can see eighteenth-century fiction as a growing power for subversion of a particular kind, the subversion that leads to a different kind of social morality, not necessarily better or more stable, but one based on self-knowledge, self-evaluation, and self assertion'.[40] Traditional aesthetic and social values were under attack and the novel led the charge. In terms of narrative technique, the 'protean self' of Defoe's novels is matched in the discrepancy between the self who retrospectively and dispassionately narrates and the self who acts. The sexual and social transgressions of Richardson's novels are lent force by epistolarity, which Karl compares to Modernist techniques of interior monologue and stream of consciousness as ways of keeping character and consciousness, rather than plot, before the reader. *Tom Jones* is the highpoint of the eighteenth-century novel, because Fielding unified technical aims and moral instruction: 'When Fielding's need turned to moralizing, his fiction turned closer to the novel' (152). Fielding is credited by Karl with the 'reshaping of narrative, character, plot, theme, and language' in the service of realism, subversively demonstrating that moral systems inhibit human nature (147).

Two books in the 1970s approached the emergent novel through reader-response theory (*Rezeptionsästhetik*), which treats literary works as rhetorical effects by foregrounding the reader's role in the creation of meaning. In *The Created Self* (1970), John Preston analyses the ways in which early novels rhetorically 'create' a reader, who is 'addressed' by the narrative, be that *Moll Flanders* trying to coerce the reader into a sympathetic view of her actions, Fielding's garrulous cosying-up to the reader in *Tom Jones*, the modelling of the writer-reader relationship in the epistolary form of *Clarissa*, or Sterne's invitation to the reader to help fill in the deliberate gaps in *Tristram Shandy*.[41]

Wolfgang Iser's interest in readership in *The Implied Reader* (1972) is more historical, less rhetorical, than Preston's, delineating a stage in 'the history of reading', and considering generic change through time. Iser accepts Watt's historical analysis of the reading public, but extends the idea of the reader's involvement: 'What was presented in the novel led to a specific effect: namely, to involve the reader in the world of the novel and so help him to understand it – and ultimately his own world – more clearly'.[42] Iser traces the process in the development of the novel whereby the reader gets gradually less direct guidance from the text. At the beginning is Bunyan, whose *The Pilgrim's Progress* instructs the reader in interpreting emblematic signs either by allowing her to judge occurrences with a knowledge superior to the characters or making her share in the characters' uncertainty. *Tom Jones* is innovatory because it demands a more participatory reader, who 'realizes' the text by filling in gaps between the world presented in fiction and the world she knows, creating the effect of realism. Richardson is the predictable fall guy as, after Fielding, 'the novel is no longer confined to the presentation of exemplary models, à la Richardson, inviting emulation; instead the text offers itself as an instrument by means of which the reader can make a number of discoveries for himself that will lead him to a reliable sense of orientation' (45). Fielding, then, removes Richardsonian didacticism paradoxically by supplying more explicit guidance to the reader. Like Karl, Iser sees Fielding's involvement of the reader as a manifestation of 'an historical trend of the eighteenth century – namely, the revaluation of empirical reality as against the universal claims of normative systems' (55). The ultimate triumph of the aesthetic over the didactic in eighteenth-century fiction comes with *Humphry Clinker*, as 'the traditional forms of the novel, developed during the eighteenth century, undergo a definite transformation in Smollett's last work' (59). Smollett combines the genres his three novelistic forbears had perfected: travelogue (Defoe), epistolary (Richardson), and picaresque (Fielding). On their own, each of these forms gives empirical reality a certain meaning, because they describe and classify; in bringing them together, Smollett moves from representing a preconceived reality to merely suggesting it for the reader. He achieves this by having multiple narrators give their perception of events, people, and places, so that the reader has to mediate. Along with Sterne, Iser contends, Smollett marks the end of the 'traditional eighteenth-century novel' (78).

Moving from the reader to character, Paula Backscheider's *A Being More Intense* (1984) argues that Bunyan, Swift, and Defoe developed new characterization techniques that created a 'more intense', 'real', and 'familiar' 'social being', which contributed to 'the birth and shape of the novel'.[43] This is the moment when 'what happens within a character begins to be at least as important as what happens to him' (xviii). Backscheider widens the range of texts customarily considered in rise-of-the-novel criticism, because this crucial phase in the history of characterization was wrought by Bunyan's *The Holy War* (1682), Swift's *A Tale of a Tub* (1704), and Defoe's pamphlets, as much as it was by *The Pilgrim's Progress, Gulliver's Travels,* and *Robinson Crusoe*. Backscheider is cautious about labelling even these latter works 'novels': none wholly satisfies our sense of what a novel should be, yet all have 'indisputably novelistic elements', particularly their 'concentration on character as complex, individual and mutable' (66). For her sense of the 'novelistic', Backscheider uses Sacks's 'represented action'; for her understanding of character, she uses Lukács's notion of novelistic heroes as 'seekers' displaced from the communal integrity of epic by the dissonance of modernity and Erich Kahler's work, in *The Inward Turn of Narrative* (1973), on the early modern development of the representation of consciousness. Backscheider concludes: 'One of the most characteristic qualities of the novel begins in these works, the internalization of theme. As the novel develops, plot becomes less important and the narrator gradually fades; the novel is consumed by the individual, the protagonist' (173). The consequence of this 'internalization of theme' is the creation of 'supraindividuals', more individuated than allegorical or epic characters, but whose experiences illumine the human condition, approaching the epic in cultural authority, and addressing secular and not just religious themes.

Arnold Weinstein's *Fictions of the Self, 1550–1800* (1981) also focuses on character and selfhood, though he takes a pan-European approach and handles a longer period of development. As we will see in Chapter 6, a view of the rise of the novel confined to the eighteenth century often seems tenable only with a parochially English perspective, a point also made by Ioan Williams in *The Idea of the Novel in Europe, 1600–1800* (1978). Weinstein shows the continuity of eighteenth-century English novels with previous French, Spanish, and German works. He sees the acts of 'self-affirmation and self-realization' as the primary concern of prose narrative from *Lazarillo de Tormes* to *Tristram Shandy*, a concern that necessitates new techniques of characterization.[44] 'From my point of view, character is always center-stage', Weinstein states: 'Every text studied here depicts the appetite for selfhood, the desire not merely for survival, but also for integrity and even consistency' (14). Weinstein discerns four movements in the fictional representation of the self. The first is the 'marginal self' depicted in continental picaresque and Baroque fiction, up to *La Princesse de Clèves*, where protagonists struggle against constraints on individualism. Next come 'orphan tales' – *Moll Flanders*, *La Vie de Marianne*, and *Joseph Andrews* – which celebrate the triumphant self. This 'idyllic interlude' in selfhood is succeeded by fictions that 'reveal the conflict between self-as-authority and society' (15). This group comprises Abbé Prévost's *Manon Lescaut* (1731), *Clarissa*, Choderlos de Laclos's *Les Liaisons dangereuses* (1782), and Goethe's *The Sorrows of Young Werther* (1774). The final set – Denis Diderot's *Le Neveu de Rameau* (1805), *Tristram Shandy*, and Rousseau's autobiographical *Confessions* (1782–9) – comprises solipsistic fictions of subjectivity, which internalize the self. As Weinstein condenses his argument, the evolution of the novel 'takes the self from marginal to flourishing to defiant on to internalized', which is also a movement from the 'mimetic' (representational) to the 'generative' (solipsistic) mode (16–17).

In *Narrative Technique in the English Novel* (1985), Ira Konigsberg charts developing narrative technique in the eighteenth-century novel. This is one of the last studies to use the Defoe–Richardson–Fielding–Smollett–Sterne–Austen canon without qualification. Konigsberg clarifies and amplifies ideas about the novel's formal development by focusing on *how the story is told*, finding that 'these writers extended earlier literary techniques and created new ones to establish narrative methods basic to future novelists'.[45] Fiction was responsive to developments in perceptional psychology: 'The novel was largely the creation of the sensibility and metaphysical direction of an age – an age coming to believe that reality was inside the individual and the universe was an extension of the inner world' (10). The novel moves from the representation of exterior reality to the dramatization of interior subjectivity as it develops between Defoe and Austen. Its development is accretive: each writer adds to his or her predecessors some new approach that 'extends the reader's capacity and broadens the future possibilities of the form' (15).

Konigsberg's author-focused chapters are insightful. Defoe's contribution was to render reality in a more concrete manner than in previous literature through a single character's experience. Richardson's epistolary form involves both character and reader in narrated events to a greater degree than Defoe's memoir-novels. *Clarissa* presents complicated relationships *between* characters, 'creat[ing] for the reader a sense of specific and continuing locales, of action taking place within an actual physical context', and slowing down the pace of the novel to enhance the reader's involvement in a self-contained, autonomous illusion of reality (85). In turn, Fielding advances fictional form by 'minimiz[ing] the authenticity of the mode of telling', making him 'the first of our novelists to emphasize his work as created art and to exploit the nonmimetic elements of the novel form itself' (100). Fielding supplies ironic assessments of character that involve the reader in judging situations and persons, and an architectural structure that surpasses bare chronology. Building on this by parodying it, 'Sterne writes a novel about the way in which the writer creates his vision and the way in which the reader recreates that vision in his own mind, how he perceives what he thinks the writer is depicting by reading his language' (164). *Tristram Shandy* presents the workings of its eponymous narrator's mind, which shows the external world to be a projection of the consciousness. Smollett advances this in *Humphry Clinker* with a 'parallactic' narrative, which uses multiple perspectives on reality: 'In order to see the world with some fullness and accuracy, we must view it from a number of individual perceptions – we must see it with parallactic vision' (193). Finally, in Austen, Konigsberg states, 'we see the culmination of this early development and a paradigm for future writers in the genre', as *Pride and Prejudice* 'synthesizes and brings to fruition the various techniques developed in the genre during the eighteenth century' (213). Austen's development of free indirect discourse, a mode of narrative that merges a character's voice with that of the objective narration, retains an ironic distance from character but enables intimate interior involvement with them, as well as accounting for the way individual perception shapes reality.

Conclusion

The next chapter explains a turn away from formalist questions of technical development to historical questions of generic origins. For purposes of contrast, therefore, I will conclude this chapter with the psychoanalytic approach to the novel's origins advanced by Marthe Robert's *Origins of the Novel* (French, 1972; English, 1980). Robert maps psychoanalytic theory onto the familiar story of the novel's rejection of romance, transposing Sigmund Freud's account of the 'Family Romance' onto literary history in order to describe the novel as an Oedipal infant seeking to victor over what came before it. Freud's Family Romance is the two-stage process that frees an individual from his parents. In the first (asexual) stage, after a halcyon period of parental adoration that is narcissistic, the infant recognizes his parents' fallibility when he starts to feel slighted, resulting in the childish fantasy of being an adopted child and the hope of replacing his parents with better ones. This is the 'foundling' narrative and it expresses itself in plots of fantasy, the denial of reality. In the second (sexual) stage, the child gains knowledge of his origins: the 'facts of life' render his maternity certain, but paternity uncertain, leading to a revengeful fantasy in which the child considers himself an illegitimate hero, the mother unfaithful, and the father, though wronged, the sole guarantor of legitimacy. This is the 'bastard' narrative and it expresses itself through realism, the acceptance of reality. To take some examples from our period, the social elevation achieved through discovered parentage (in Fielding and Smollett) or the rebellion against parental authority (in Defoe and Richardson), would be considered as contingent social displacements of these universal psychosexual patterns: they are set in particular social contexts, but they encode these essential, universal developmental truths.

However, for Robert, it is not just that some novels' plots draw on the Oedipal pattern, such as by justifying murder, revolt, and usurpation against authorities that are (displaced) parental symbols. Rather, it is that the novel genre itself can be 'psychologized' in these same terms:

> ■ During the whole of its history the novel has derived the violence of its desires and its irrepressible freedom from the Family Romance; in this respect it can be said that this primal romance reveals, beneath the historical and individual accidents from which each particular work derives, more than simply the psychological origins of the genre; it is the genre, with all its inexhaustible possibilities and congenital childishness, the false, frivolous, grandiose, mean, subversive, and gossipy genre of which each of us is indeed the issue [...] and which, moreover, recreates for each of us a remnant of our primal love and primal reality.[46] □

The universalist tendencies of Robert's study, its focus on psychological essentials that apply in all times and places, are manifest here. The novel genre confirms the ubiquity of the transhistorical Oedipal complex: sociohistorical factors are not *determinants* of genre, but *accidents* of genre.

As the 1980s progressed, the 'interior' approach to the novel's formal development typified by Konigsberg – seeing fiction's evolution through successive responses to formal problems – became less popular. And the universalist approach to generic development free from historical contingency, which Robert exemplifies, came under increasing attack, particularly in studies (replicating Robert's title) by Lennard Davis and Michael McKeon. Politicized criticism dominated the 1980s and 1990s, particularly in historicism, feminism, and postcolonialism, which (respectively) occupy the following three chapters.

CHAPTER FOUR

Cultural History and the Rise of the Novel, 1980–9

This chapter surveys rise-of-the-novel criticism in the 1980s, a predominantly historicist period of literary scholarship which set about explaining how texts are the products of social and cultural forces. New, historically grounded, explanations of the novel's emergence appeared. Tellingly, however, this chapter begins and ends with restatements of the enduring significance of Ian Watt's *The Rise of the Novel*.

Daniel Schwarz recruits Watt to the historicist cause in a 1983 essay, demonstrating his enduring relevance as literary studies moved to contextual approaches. Schwarz assesses Watt as a 'response to the New Critical orthodoxy of the day' with its 'insistence upon the autonomy of the text', against which Watt 'insists that ideas and novels do not exist "independently of each other"' and 'demonstrates that biographical, sociological, and historical knowledge explain the forms of works of art and are necessary for understanding their meaning'.[1] The studies discussed in Chapter 3 generally (though not uniformly) accepted the historical part of Watt's account and sought to correct or elaborate on aspects of his literary-formal explanation. By contrast, the studies discussed in this chapter expand, further particularize, and (sometimes) reject Watt's historical account.

Foucault, social power, and the novel

The application to the emergent novel of Michel Foucault's work on social power marked both a shift away from questions of form and genre to those of ideology and history, and a reversal of a longstanding humanist tendency to see literature as generally edifying. In the accounts of Lennard Davis, John Bender, and Nancy Armstrong, literature is complicit in producing the bureaucratic modern state and its insidious means of social control through surveillance, discipline, and discursive practices that circulate ideology and condition subjects who internalize power in ways that obviate the need for its external enforcement. For Armstrong and Bender, the novel facilitated the ideological work of two of the modern state's key props, the domestic sphere and the penitentiary.

The first scholar to apply Foucault's work to the emergent novel, however, was Lennard Davis in an important study called *Factual Fictions* (1983). In the 1996 re-issue, Davis states his central claims:

> ■ These are that novel and journalism are intricately connected, perhaps more interconnected than the novel and romance; that cultural attitudes toward fact and fiction shifted during the early modern period; that this shift was influenced by an increasing legal pressure to distinguish levels of proof, veracity, and evidence; that the rise of print culture created new categories of textuality that provoked problems in distinguishing levels of veracity; that there was an interconnection between criminality and fictionality which novels had to try to refute; and finally that the culture enforced this new relation between fact and fiction by isolating narrative forms – news, novels, history – based on their presumed relation to veracity.[2] □

Davis argues that degrees of factuality and fictionality were *not* used to distinguish genres in early modern England, but that, in response to the rise of news reportage in the seventeenth century, it became a legal necessity for political authorities to differentiate between factual and fictitious writing. The novel emerged at the historical moment, in the early eighteenth century, when authors were compelled to specify the degree of veracity in printed texts.

Countering the assumptions of many studies discussed in Chapter 3, Davis denies that the novel constituted a reaction to any other fictional form, such as romance. Romance and the novel have fundamentally different approaches to the representation of reality: romance presents the world idealistically (as it should be), whereas the novel depicts the world in a reportorial, realistic manner (as it actually is). As such, journalism – focused on presenting in plain prose the here-and-now in a professedly truthful manner to middle-class readers – is where Davis locates the origins of the novel: not romance, which is focused on a distant past, is professedly fictional, and upholds neoclassical decorum for aristocratic readers. *Don Quixote* and heroic romances are, for Davis, red herrings in the search for the origins of the novel: romances do not present uncertainty as to whether they are fact or fiction, which is characteristic of the new form, because they flourished *before* fact and fiction were at issue in genre (24). Davis distances himself from Watt in his methodology: where Watt had argued that cultural conditions influenced narrative in an 'osmotic' way, gradually permeating the shape of the novel, Davis contends that discursive acts of power controlled through the law determine generic formation. Novelistic discourse is (in Foucault's sense) 'the ensemble of written texts that constitute the novel (and in so doing define, limit, and describe it)'. This ensemble by no means involves only novels and literary criticism; it also includes 'parliamentary statutes, newspapers, advertisements, printer's records, handbills, letters, and so on' (7). Non-novelistic texts and institutional acts of power combine to delimit the novel as a fictional discourse.

Davis argues that, in the medieval period, the law was hazy about the question of veracity: for instance, a statement was deemed libellous if it damaged a person's reputation, regardless of its truth or falsity. As printed material proliferated amidst seventeenth-century political crises, the state required legal mechanisms that would allow the prosecution of printers who criticized the government. The lapse of the Licensing Act in 1695 ostensibly liberated the press, because it put paid to pre-publication censorship. However, tighter libel laws and taxation bolstered state control of print, which was needful as print commanded more and more authority. Thereafter, in contrast to the 'cultural indifference to fact and fiction' in the previous period, the first quarter of the eighteenth century witnessed an unprecedented drive to differentiate fact from fiction (100). Novelists, many of whom also wrote journalism, presented fictions as true stories, making the novel 'an ambiguous form – a factual fiction which denied its fictionality' (36). This disavowal of fictionality, wherein writers from Behn and Manley to Defoe and Richardson claimed their novels were true stories, was necessitated by a 'double discourse' that associated fictionality with criminality. The attacks on their truth-claims levelled against Defoe and Richardson forced them gradually to embrace fiction, and it is with Fielding that we get imaginative narrative that proclaims its fictionality. The origins of the novel, for Davis, lie in the 'division of fact and fiction, news and novel, the movement from untroubled fictionality of Cervantes to the inherent ambivalence of Defoe, Richardson, Fielding, and later writers' (223).

A central concept in Foucauldian analysis is ideology, a culture's dominant set of ideas and social practices which have the effect of upholding ruling-class interests. For Davis, 'the novel is [...] a discourse for reinforcing particular ideologies, and its coming into being must be seen as tied to particular power relations' (9). Here, and in his more general *Resisting Novels: Ideology and Fiction* (1987), Davis contends that novels are ideological in just this sense: they produce states of consciousness in individual readers that help maintain the hegemonic power of the few. Rather than a manifestation of an ideology which they just *reflect*, such as bourgeois values (as Watt argues), novels actively *produce* ideology. Davis, following Foucault, sees novelistic ideology as especially invidious, because unlike power relations that predate the advent of print, modern ideology is invisible, occurring as common sense and appearing universal. Novels are *like* ideology inasmuch as they seem both true and false, real and imaginary.[3]

John Bender's original and insightful *Imagining the Penitentiary* (1987) also focuses on the ways in which novels produce consciousness to enforce power relations. Drawing critically on Foucault's *Discipline and Punish* (1975), which describes the theories behind the development of penitentiaries, Bender conceives of the novel as a vehicle of social change, an ideological form that aims at transparency through realistic representation, removing the distance between itself and everyday practices. Bender argues that the rise of the novel enabled and paralleled penal reform: the eighteenth century saw the movement from the use of prison as the 'liminal' place in which criminals were detained prior to judgement and punishment (execution or transportation) to new penitentiaries, which used incarceration itself to punish and rehabilitate. Fictional depictions of prisons between 1719 and 1779 helped to sanction the conception and construction of actual penitentiaries in late eighteenth-century England: 'Fabrications in narrative of the power of confinement to shape personality contributed to a process of cultural representation whereby prisons were themselves reconceived and ultimately reinvented'.[4] Novels and penitentiaries are analogous 'cultural systems', because each assumes that narrative can reconstruct personality (11). Penitentiaries assume a novelistic idea of character, seeking to alter motivation and to reconstruct the fictions of personal identity that underlie consciousness.

The historical pillars around which Bender operates are James Oglethorpe's 'gaol committee' of 1729, which aimed to alleviate the unpleasantness of 'liminal' prisons, and the full-scale introduction of penitentiaries in the 1780s, epitomized by Jeremy Bentham's Panopticon designs (1787–91), which became Foucault's metaphor for the pervasive system of surveillance that maintains order in the modern state. 'Randomness was one of the rules in the old prisons', Bender explains: 'the squalor, the disease, the possibility of escape, the periodic jail deliveries voted by Parliament; the chance that your creditors might relent, the courts miscarry, the judges commute death to transportation, your patrons gain a reprieve, your friends revive your corpse after hanging' (27). By contrast, the new penitentiaries – enforcing solitude, silence, penitential reflection, cleanliness, and labour – 'banished chance and fortune [...] in favor of human planning and certitude imagined in material terms' (34). Prison 'was reformed into a programmatic course of events with the end of shaping personality according to controlled principles' (35). The philosophical justifications for this came from the sceptical empiricism of David Hume and the materialist utilitarianism of Bentham, thinkers who 'located reality in the instantaneous present of impressions and stressed the constructed, "fictional", aspect of concepts such as self, character, justice, law, nature, final causation, any stable or self-evident notion of which they refused to accept' (35). Hume and Bentham saw the individual self as the product of an array of circumstances; the novel also showed that personality is the product of events. If human motives can be accounted for by causality, as novels implied, they can be re-shaped to social ends by controlled circumstances within the penitentiary.

Defoe reflects these changes in conceptions of personality and social practice especially clearly. His fictions 'contradict the cultural predicates of the liminal prison and shape the penitentiary idea' (63). *Robinson Crusoe* is 'a prospective allegory of the move from the old, fever-ridden jails to the clean, healthy, contemplative solitude of the penitentiaries' (55). Crusoe moves through stages that reflect a desirable transition in penal practice: the effect of his confinement is mental reformation, as errant personality is reconstituted as self-consciousness by solitary reflection, and life is comprehended as a story, whose every detail is significant in accounting for malfeasance. A similar transition is undergone by Moll Flanders in Newgate, the archetype of the 'liminal' prison. Instead of the randomness of the old prisons, Moll achieves 'a reformation according to a narrative sequence of rewards and punishments over time', a key aspect of the 'penitentiary idea' (50). In *A Journal of the Plague Year* (1722), the penitentiary idea is extended to how urban space is constructed in ways that atomize individuals, validate solitary survival, and sanction confinement for the purpose of mental reformation.[5] Bender argues 'that novelistic conventions of transparency, completeness, and representational reliability [...] subsume an assent to regularized authority' (72). Consent about what constitutes realism endorses authority.

Bender discusses John Gay's *The Beggar's Opera* (1728) and William Hogarth's prints, non-novelistic texts that use proto-novelistic, realistic narration to expose the inadequacies of the old prisons, in conjunction with Oglethorpe. With Fielding (novelist, civil magistrate, and founder of the first organized police force, the Bow Street Runners), Bender notes connections between the evidentiary reportage of crime and the devices of the novel – both try to construct a realistic narrative. Fielding's development of omniscient narrative is important here:

■ Fielding's inventive magistracy in Bow Street, no less than his novelistic innovation, signals a major stage in the emergence of structures of feeling that enable the narrative penitentiary because he takes the step from consciousness contrived as a narrative of the material world to the inclusion of omniscient, inquiring authority in that world. (145) □

Jonathan Wild and *Amelia*, often overlooked alongside Fielding's better known novels, furnish Bender's examples, especially the benevolent

Dr. Harrison in *Amelia*, a character who takes over the omniscient function of the narrator in ways that validate impersonal supervision in the penitentiary. Bender ends with Adam Smith's theory of sympathy, prison architecture, and paintings by Thomas Rowlandson and Joseph Wright of Derby – all to the effect that isolation became aestheticized as a desirable social system.

Nancy Armstrong's influential and demanding *Desire and Domestic Fiction* (1987) also applies Foucault's theories to the eighteenth- and nineteenth-century novel. She draws on Foucault's *The History of Sexuality* (1976–84), which is about the ideological work of discourses of gendered sexuality. Armstrong argues that the novel was instrumental in establishing a new form of desire that promoted the construction of the domestic woman.[6] Like Watt, Armstrong sees the rise of the novel as bound up with middle-class individualism, but she sees the new individual promoted by novels as female. In a period when 'gender came to mark the most important difference among individuals, [...] psychological differences made men political and women domestic rather than the other way around, and both therefore acquired identity on the basis of personal qualities that had formerly determined female nature alone' (4). Fictions with female protagonists, depicting courtship, marriage, and domesticity, neutralize class struggle by substituting for it ostensibly apolitical gender conflict: 'Especially when acted out as the options of a female protagonist, social competition could be sexualized and therefore suppressed even while it was being experienced' (51). In the service of bourgeois hegemony, the novel disentangled sexual relationships from the language of politics in order to mask socioeconomic interests by presenting them as psychological and consigning them to the feminine realm.

Armstrong follows Foucault in arguing that in this period the bourgeoisie's battle for dominance over the aristocracy took the form of a struggle to displace power from physical force to discursive force, 'a moment in political history when power became knowledge and worked mainly through discourse to create a subject ideally suited to inhabit a modern institutional culture' (190). The middle-class's success over the aristocracy resulted in a form of governance by consent and contract rather than by coercion and punishment: 'The history of domination over the subject's material body seems to come to an end as the state begins to *control* individuals through strategies of discourse rather than by means of physical violence' (16). Armstrong reversed the tendency of feminist criticism to identify instances of female victimhood in the past, instead arguing that the middle-class woman was empowered through novelistic representation, as 'the modern individual was first and foremost a woman' (8). This individual operates on a psychological, subjective level that divorces her from economics, politics, and class conflict. By the nineteenth century, men too 'were products of desire and producers of domestic life' (4) – that is, they were feminized.

In terms of genre, whereas Davis looked to news journalism, Armstrong shows that the novel borrowed formal strategies from, and extended the political agendas of, conduct manuals for women, didactic tracts prescribing 'proper' female behaviour that were popular reading in the seventeenth and eighteenth centuries. The later parts of *Pamela*, for example, replicate the instructional strategies of conduct literature. In terms of the fictional canon, Armstrong is highly selective. Fielding is mentioned only in relation to how he read Richardson. Defoe appears as a writer of feminine conduct books rather than a novelist and, 'inasmuch as his masculine form of heroism could not be reproduced by other authors, we cannot say *Crusoe* inaugurated the tradition of the novel as we know it' (29). Through a perspective that stresses courtship and marriage, *Pamela* becomes the prototypical novel, the only one before Austen discussed at length, as Richardson's 'story of relentless sexual pursuit and the triumph of female virtue proved infinitely reproducible' (29). Ideology is produced through iteration, and the novel elides politics rather than stimulating political debate: therefore *Pamela*, not *Crusoe*, dictated the direction the novel would take. The bourgeois Pamela's virtuous resistance and eventual reformation of her seducer recodes the aristocratic association of women's desirability with wealth and status. From Richardson's fictionalization of the conduct book and Austen's prototype of the courtship novel in *Emma*, Armstrong moves to what she calls the rise of female authority in Victorian fictions by women: Charlotte Brontë and George Eliot.

It should be acknowledged that Foucauldian analysis has not been unanimously embraced. William Warner, for instance, discerns a contradiction in seeing power as mystified by social practice yet transparent enough to be critiqued.[7] McKeon, we shall see, objects to its apparent determinism. The studies discussed in the following section historicize the early novel by elucidating the range of its cultural contexts, but from vantages focused less on power and control.

Social, political, religious, philosophical, and sexual discourses

W. Austin Flanders's *Structures of Experience* (1984) follows the studies by Watt and Richetti (see Chapters 2 and 3, respectively) which addressed conflict between the individual and society, claiming it is the tension between 'personal experience and the act of writing which underlay the emergence of the novel'.[8] There are three parts to Flanders's study.

The first chapter chronicles 'the advent of liberalism and the isolation of the self', treading familiar contextual ground in the rise of individualism: the fragmentation of society, the dissolution of traditional state, church, and familial authority, and new challenges to religious, political, and epistemological orthodoxies. The second chapter addresses form, charting the progression from retrospective first-person narratives (Defoe) through epistolary stories (Richardson) and on to Fielding's third-person biographical form, a cycle that culminates with Sterne's frustration of the autobiographical mode. As well as these canonical mainstays, Flanders considers Gothic and less canonical novels. In the final four chapters, he discusses four sociocultural themes in the early novel – the family, female experience, deviancy and crime, and urban experience. Flanders contends that the conflict of self and society is apparent in the early novel's representation of all these forms of life.

Leopold Damrosch's *God's Plot and Man's Stories* (1985) builds on Watt to explain the secularization of eighteenth-century society, of which the novel is both symptom and agent.[9] He traces the mounting dissonance between an authoritative Christian providentialism and its particular articulations in narratives from Milton to Fielding. Human life was widely considered as a narrative invented by God, but interpreted by people; and whereas novels recount what happens to particular people at particular times, providence purports to explain what always happens. Therefore, the novel was especially well-suited to stage the tensions in the central doctrines of Puritanism: novelists psychologized and tested religious tenets in mimetic stories. In the period after the English Civil Wars, Damrosch argues, the absolute authority of the Bible was being diluted, strict doctrine was being replaced by ethical theology, and Puritanism was morphing into nonconformity – from dogmatic sects seeking to change the world to a social class seeking toleration and social prestige. It is not simply, as was commonly argued, that Puritans distrusted art as lies, but rather there was a tension between their desire for plainness and sincerity and for emblematic, allegorical significance that made fiction necessary: 'On the one hand art is a falsification of unmediated experience, but on the other hand experience itself can only be understood in categories like those employed by art' (68). The difficulty for Puritans lay with authorial manipulation of events, a usurpation of God's role. The mimetic attention to detail and pretension of veracity in the early novel masks this anxiety – but not completely.

In this account *Paradise Lost* (1667–74) 'falls midway along the line that Lukács traces from epic to novel' (78). Milton's attempt to justify divine providence shifts focus from *why* mankind fell to *how*: that is, Milton uses narrative as a sleight of hand to affirm orthodoxy by constructing a causal story to explicate doctrine. With *The Pilgrim's Progress* Bunyan 'develop[s] a mode of allegorical narrative that points forward toward the novel even while it resists many of the implications of its form' (121). It is less true that mimetic realism is straining to escape from allegorical and didactic bonds, and more accurate to say that there is a productive tension from the coexistence of the two modes: 'It might be said that the eighteenth-century novel emerges not from the simple transformation of allegory into circumstantial narrative, but rather from the jolting that occurs when the two modes run uneasily in harness together' (171).

Robinson Crusoe, despite Defoe's intention to 'dramatize the conversion of the Protestant self', in fact 'reflects the progressive desacralizing of the world that was implicit in Protestantism' (187, 192). Defoe's turn to the novel does not just reflect an increasingly secular world: he opposed Puritan objections to fiction as lies 'not only because he thought Puritan faith compatible with fiction, but also because he was moved to test Puritan faith *through* fiction' (204). The process of imaginative creation is free from the anterior text of the Bible for the first time. In turn, *Clarissa* is, at one level, a highly Puritan novel, celebrating the power of passivity, the renunciation of the world, and the fulfilment of an exemplary function. However, in elevating the assertive self, in privileging mimesis over allegoresis, and in absenting God from the action, Richardson participates in the secular progress of the novel. Fielding completes the process, brazenly embracing the comparison of divine and literary creation: 'An omniscient and affectionate narrator acts as the disposing deity of a fictional universe, instructing the reader, by means of a plot whose coherence is only gradually revealed, to understand the operations of a Providence that subsumes all of the apparent accidents of chance or Fortune' (263). Subsequently, says Damrosch, the novel developed along the lines of mimetic realism, meaning that it stopped asking the theological questions that were instrumental in its emergence.

In a similar manner, Stuart Sim's *Negotiations with Paradox* (1990) contends that the modern novel developed out of ideological wrestling with the contradictions of Puritan soteriology (ideas about final destination), particularly the doctrine of double predestination. This is the belief that salvation is reserved for the few 'elect' and that damnation is assigned to the 'reprobate' remainder, not by the kind of life lived, but at the start of time by God. The apparent paradox of individual free will shaping a journey to either salvation or damnation, the end of which is predetermined by divine decree, means that *a priori* 'discourse knowledge' (dogma) conflicted with observational knowledge (experience). This, Sim says, led Bunyan (to some degree) and Defoe (to a greater degree) to challenge Puritan ideology through fiction.[10] The anxiety induced by the paradox of reprobation (the damned are responsible for their destiny, despite it having been decided before the Creation) intensified the individual sense of self which became prominent in the novel.

Sim contrasts the approaches of the two writers: 'Where Bunyan swiftly moves to shore up his own ideology when contradictions come on the scene, Defoe is more prone to highlight the problems of dealing with such contradictions and to pursue them through to their often unpalatable conclusions' (5). Where Bunyan exploits Calvinist paradoxes for narrative ends in *The Pilgrim's Progress, The Life and Death of Mr. Badman* (1680), and *The Holy War,* Defoe exposes those paradoxes and actively interrogates Puritan ideology. Where Starr and Hunter, discussed in Chapter 3, interpreted Defoe's novels as basically conventional spiritual autobiographies, Sim interprets them as subversive ones. With *Moll Flanders* and *Roxana* (1724), Sim says that Defoe extends his critique of spiritual paradox to social questions: capitalism, liberalism, and the status of women. Defoe is an analyst rather than a proponent of both Calvinism and capitalism, who 'interweaves spiritual and economic considerations' in a manner that is increasingly secular and increasingly novelistic (156).

Going from religious to sexual discourses, Robert Erickson's challenging but rewarding *Mother Midnight* (1986) sets the rise of the novel alongside intersecting developments in obstetrics, the growth of prostitution, women's roles in the weaving and cloth trades, and high infant mortality. In particular, he foregrounds the figure of 'Mother Midnight', the ambiguous and culturally overdetermined personage who acts as midwife, procuress, bawd, and witch-like symbol of fate. Erickson addresses this 'fate' in *Moll Flanders, Pamela, Clarissa,* and *Tristram Shandy,* 'as experienced in the context of seventeenth- and eighteenth-century representations and discussions of the midwife, the witch, the "cunning woman," the bawd, and the traditional figure of fate as spinner and sewer of men and women'.[11] Just as Armstrong relates the novel to feminine conduct literature, Erickson relates it to seventeenth-century midwife manuals to demonstrate the rising cultural authority of Mother Midnight, and her appearance at the transitional moments of birth, procreation, and death in the emergent novel.

Moll Flanders's governess is the archetypal Mother Midnight in eighteenth-century fiction: she is a 'professional secret keeper', the architect of Moll's 'ill-fate', and 'a figure of "impenetrable" darkness' with 'almost godlike ambivalence and omniscience' (53, 55). Noting the figurative analogy between midwifery and thievery, Erickson contends that Moll returns to a symbolic childhood and is educated anew under Mother Midnight, before her eventual establishment in America is facilitated by the maternal figure who continues to operate at home. Erickson barely mentions Freud and never mentions Foucault, but it may be said that his study is an attempt to historicize sexual and medical discourses in the manner of Foucault, building on psychoanalytic criticism that interprets narrative as symbolizing sexual development.

For instance, Erickson interprets *Clarissa* as a protracted psychosexual drama of gestation, parturition, and weaning, which shows how cultural concepts of birth and maternity were tied up with those of fate. The rake, Lovelace, acts as 'a master midwife of human affairs', who delivers the eponymous heroine up to the bawd, Sinclair, and to her eventual fate, rape and death (139). Erickson labels *Clarissa* 'a tragic epic poem in prose', hence an inversion of Fielding's description of *Joseph Andrews* as a 'comic epic-poem in prose'. Finally, *Tristram Shandy* is a 'midwife book', a translation of sexual reproduction into writing, that brings together the themes of childbirth, fate, and death, incorporating the terminology of midwife manuals, staging birth within the action, and reflecting new cultural discourses about gestation.

Next come two books on philosophy and the novel. In *Scepticism, Society and the Eighteenth-Century Novel* (1987), Eve Tavor argues that the novel developed in dialogue with sceptical philosophy: the writings of John Locke, Bernard Mandeville, and David Hume. Defoe is interpreted as a Lockean acolyte, following in his novels the philosopher's epistemological and political theories to bring about middle-class, bourgeois ideology. Richardson's *Clarissa* challenges Mandeville's famous equation of private vices with public benefits, the idea that individual greed benefits society. *Tom Jones* is an 'epistemological satire', which draws on Hume's *Treatise on Human Nature* (1739–40) in order to demonstrate the shaky foundations of knowledge and belief.[12] Sterne reverses the traditional association of fiction and scepticism, as *Tristram Shandy* is an 'anti-sceptic' novel, which inaugurates 'a new positivism and a new belief', attacking scepticism by parodying it. Sterne therefore sets the agenda for the more optimistic nineteenth-century novel.

Moving from epistemology to political philosophy, Carol Kay's *Political Constructions* (1988) brackets discussion of three canonical novelists – Defoe, Richardson, and Sterne – with discussion of three important thinkers on government – Thomas Hobbes, David Hume, and Edmund Burke.[13] Towards the start of the period, Defoe is most like Hobbes, inasmuch as *Crusoe* and *Moll* are dramatizations of the transition from a barbaric 'state of nature' to individualism under societal laws. The eighteenth-century 'moral sense' philosophers, particularly Francis Hutcheson and Hume, soften Hobbes's assessment of human nature by emphasizing voluntary compliance with society's rules. In turn, Richardson's *Pamela* celebrates political consent, whereby words regiment behaviour, but this is problematized in *Clarissa*, which is alert, like Hume, to the artificial nature of social agreement. Sterne's *Tristram Shandy* and *A Sentimental Journey* (1768) are less 'didactic' than Defoe's contractarian and Richardson's consensual fictions: the social conditions that bred fear in Hobbes and Defoe occasion complaisance and apolitical aesthetic play in Sterne. The influence of Hobbes was waning, Kay asserts, indicated by Burke's political writing, which retains Hobbesian notions of the wickedness of human nature but argues that individuals will be induced to comply with state power through veneration and sympathetic identification, not through compliance induced by fear. The novel, according to Kay, helped to 'domesticate' and palliate Hobbes's concept of political sovereignty over the course of the century.

In line with other studies discussed in this chapter, Kay challenges the assumption that the novel developed along strictly formal lines and independently of politics, leading to her refusal to essentialize the genre and separate it from other discourses, particularly other prose forms. The novel is not to be treated as fundamentally different from political treatises by Hobbes, Hume, and Burke. However, Kay, like most in this section, demurs from the view of the novel as a form of ideological imprisonment, as expressed by the Foucauldian critics. Kay considers the novel a 'political construction' that *participates in debates* over the nature of individual obligation to state apparatuses. Like Damrosch, Sim, and Erickson, Kay ascribes to the novel a greater degree of ideational autonomy – freedom from structures of power – than Bender or Armstrong. The emergent novel's status as a potentially subversive rather than an inevitably repressive form continues in the next section.

Bakhtin, dialogism, and the novel

The belated discovery by the Anglophone world of the literary theory of Mikhail Bakhtin, a Russian critic writing under Stalin, had a profound effect on the direction of novel criticism during the 1980s. His works which proved most influential in criticism of the early novel were *Rabelais and His World* (Russian, 1965; English, 1984) and four essays published collectively as *The Dialogic Imagination* (English, 1981). Bakhtin was struck by the fact that 'of all the major genres only the novel is younger than writing and the book', and that the novel is the genre that is still developing, both in terms of form and canon, in contrast to a 'completed' genre like epic.[14] Bakhtin developed a theory of the novel that was at once a formalist and a historical explanation of its rise.

When comparing epic and novel, Bakhtin is in implicit dialogue with Lukács, who saw the novel as the expression of dissonant modernity wherein the individual is estranged from the world, unlike in epic. Bakhtin contrasts the 'dead language' of epic, expressive of a hierarchical and repressive social organization, with the 'openness' of the novel. For Bakhtin, the novel is fundamentally 'polyphonic' (multi-voiced) or dialogic, rather than monologic (single-voiced). Bakhtin describes the novel's 'parodic stylization of other genres', suggesting that because the novel is in touch with the contemporary and dynamic present – unlike the 'absolute past' of epic – it infectiously 'novelizes' other genres (5). In fact, the novel is a composite of other genres, which parodies them, and which exposes their conventional use of language. As for the historical explanation, Bakhtin's historical scope extends back to Ancient Greece, the late Middle Ages, and the Renaissance, which produced François Rabelais's *Gargantua and Pantagruel* (1532–52), the defining work of fictional 'carnivalesque' and 'grotesque realism'. Bakhtin argues that the novel, understood as parodic 'low' culture winning out over the stultifying 'high' culture, became dominant at each of these historical moments, and in the late eighteenth century, it 'reigns supreme' (5). Bakhtin speaks of a 'prehistory of novelistic discourse', rather than simply charting a 'rise'. Bakhtin identifies as crucial to the formation of novelistic polyglossia (the hybrid nature of language) the rupture in European civilization produced by its coming into contact with a wider world, and the disruption of hermetic 'national languages' that had, as long as they were uncontaminated, sustained an 'epic' outlook. Bakhtin was attractive to new historicist critics in the 1980s because he viewed literary language, particularly that of the novel, not as an ahistorical entity, but as a dynamic and diverse encapsulation of competing dialects, meaning that the novel encloses different discourses and, thus, stages the clash of various social perspectives at particular historical moments.

In *Masquerade and Civilization* (1986), Terry Castle deftly applies Bakhtin's notion of the 'carnivalesque' to describe 'the carnivalization of eighteenth-century English fiction'.[15] Castle focuses on the discourse of the 'masked ball', or masquerade, an assembly where paying guests were anonymized by costume: the masquerade's 'popularization as a form of public commercial entertainment' provoked widespread hostility, an anti-masquerade campaign that Castle surveys comprehensively (113). What gave masquerade its 'radically unsettling aspect in the contemporary imagination' was the blurring or subversion of traditional ideological distinctions of gender and of class (55). Masquerades were potentially socially levelling and they provided women, as well as men, with sexual outlets, two 'sociological violations' that drew attacks on the foreignness of masquerade and its part in the wider 'commercialization and secularization' of culture (12). Narratives of inadvertent homosexuality, of unwitting prostitution, and of post-masquerade rape were all part of a reactionary rhetoric that assisted in reifying concepts of sexual deviance, as bestiality, transvestism, and necrophilia were implied in the popular costumes of animals, cross-dress, and corpses. The masquerade is a 'master trope of destabilization', which consists of 'pleasure, women, sex, the unknown [...], a comic imbroglio involving mistaken identity and transvestism, erotic and political intrigue, deceit, commotion, and badinage' (117, 111).

Masquerades promptly made their way into contemporary novels, which Castle notes was hardly surprising given the 'narrative potential' of masquerades and given that each was a product of novelty-seeking cultural demands (114). Masquerade scenes feature prominently in eighteenth-century fiction, from early 'masquerade novels' (Defoe's *Roxana* and Haywood's fictions) through Smollettian picaresque and the domestic fictions of Richardson and Fielding, and on to society novels (Burney) and politicized 1790s fictions (Elizabeth Inchbald). Castle finds that novels often repeat on the surface the anti-masquerade sentiments of the wider culture, but because, as Bakhtin suggests, narrative is not held to dogmatic statement, these novelists display 'ambivalence' about the 'didactic project' of condemning masquerade as immoral (126). Castle, working with Bakhtin's understanding of discourse, not Foucault's, provides a contrast to the ideological readings discussed earlier in this chapter. For Bakhtin, the novel expressed liberating linguistic energies that were potentially revolutionary. The novelistic deployment of the masquerade threatens patriarchal structures, including female subordination, normative sexual relations, traditional class arrangements, 'unitary notions of the self', and moral stability, because characters act 'uncharacteristically' during masquerade (4).

Castle contends that the carnivalesque produced 'polyphonic' forms and analyses four novels which, she says, destabilize formal norms (127). Richardson's neglected sequel, popularly called *Pamela II* (1741), initially enacts a 'decarnivalization' of *Pamela*, because the original novel inverted gender and class norms through the heroine's sexual resistance and social mobility. By contrast, in the sequel, Pamela becomes an 'ideologue' for the status quo, as *Pamela II* eschews narrative and novelty in favour of didacticism – that is, until a masquerade temporarily 'recarnivalizes' the novel. Ultimately, however, Richardson works to 'domesticate' the 'ideological and formal paradoxes' of the masquerade in order to contain instability (173–4). Turning to Fielding, Castle notes that it is strange that a writer so hostile to masquerades in his non-fiction reflects 'ambivalence' in his novels. The masquerade trope in *Amelia* overturns didacticism for 'narrative possibility', supplying 'characterological complication' by ethically compromising the eponymous paragon (237). These energies are not conscious: they embody a 'cultural ambivalence' rather than Fielding's 'private ambivalence', but show 'the masquerade's adulterating influence on the fictional world – and the mysterious power of the figure to insinuate, in the place of moral certainty, a tropology of ambiguity and complexity' (242). The gender subversion that had so far remained implicit and unconscious was made explicit in Burney's *Cecilia* (1782), which, Castle argues, uses the carnivalesque as 'a way of articulating a subterranean will to power' which is utopian and feminist (256). Ultimately, however, Burney's carnivalesque is a closed system that is overridden by patriarchy. *Cecilia* is seen 'not as a sentimental patriarchal comedy, but as a more diffident, even poignant account of female co-optation', which betokens 'Burney's ideological retreat from her initial vision of female authority' and a negation of the masquerade world with its 'feminocentric values' (270, 276). In comparison, the libertarian impulse of Inchbald's *A Simple Story* (1791), written amidst the proto-feminism of the 1790s, proffers 'a carnivalized fictional landscape' and 'the most self-consciously politicized invocation of the carnivalesque in eighteenth-century literature', which quells male prohibition and violence, licensing female pleasure and expression (293, 309).

At precisely this historical moment, Castle argues, the masquerade very suddenly disappeared from the cultural landscape. Notwithstanding some nineteenth-century allusions that register as anachronism, masquerade's 'abrupt, virtually total eclipse by the end of the century' is understood as 'a symptom of larger cross-cultural changes, in particular the reform of popular culture that climaxed in Europe in the middle and late eighteenth century' (98, 99–100). Though she brings forward the historical shifts he discerned, Castle follows Bakhtin in listing, at the heart of this change, industrialization, urbanization, capitalist expansion, increased literacy, the fragmentation of traditional communities, and the rise of class consciousness. In short, this is what the historian Derek Jarrett, quoted by Castle, calls the progress from political 'turbulence to regimentation' and from 'an age of neglect to one of supervision', with the ascent of bourgeois ideology (100). Watt had, of course, related the rise of the novel to the rationalist metaphysics of the eighteenth century. Castle's account of the co-existence alongside this bourgeois philosophy of an atavistic 'carnivalesque' complicates the matter. In place of a coherent cultural picture, typical of the studies I surveyed in Chapter 2, she perceives conflict and contestation in which individual works are not holistic unities (as in the New Critical tradition), but rather are articulations of disorder and disunity, expressive of their cultural contexts. Where Watt saw stability, new historicists saw instability, as we shall see in turning to Michael McKeon's work.

McKeon's *Origins of the English Novel*

Michael McKeon's *The Origins of the English Novel, 1600–1740* (1987) is the most ambitious and difficult study of its topic.[16] It is perhaps also the most satisfying explanatory account. Adopting a dialectic historical method, McKeon traces the long 'prehistory' of the English novel's full-fledged emergence in the mid-eighteenth century. Dialectical method understands historical categories in triadic formations, whereby an idea (thesis) is countered by its direct opposite (antithesis), but compromise produces a third (synthesis), which resolves the conflict but is itself then subject to a new antithesis. McKeon contends that the novel arose to 'mediate' two parallel, dialectically constituted, cultural crises in the early modern period. One was an epistemological question: How best to tell the truth in narrative? The other was an ethical question: What constitutes virtue? McKeon recaps this in his 2002 introduction:

> ■ On the level of narrative epistemology, the traditional idealism of romance is criticized by a standard of naive empiricism, which is itself challenged by a more extreme mode of skepticism that turns against naive empiricism its own weapons, demystifying it by the same epistemological standards that naive empiricism employs against romance. On the level of socio-ethical ideology, the aristocratic belief that birth determines worth is de-essentialized by the progressive belief that worth is determined by internal merit and rewarded by external success, a position in turn challenged by the conservative view that the 'new aristocracy' championed by progressivism is no less arbitrary and unjust than the old. (xvii) □

The two questions are collectively answered by competing interest groups in twin, schematic, dialectical movements. How best to tell the truth in narrative? 'Romance idealism' was challenged by 'naive empiricism', which in turn was subject to the critique of 'extreme skepticism'. We will see that these terms equate to types of narrative. What constitutes virtue? 'Aristocratic ideology' was confronted by 'progressive ideology', which is then attacked by 'conservative ideology'. These three political viewpoints are buttressed by their respective narrative equivalents (romance, empiricism, and scepticism): ways of telling stories correlate with social outlooks, ways of knowing the world.

McKeon's account immediately appears abstract, but that transpires to be part of the point. Both the 'novel' – and the six categories that comprise the two dialectical processes that bring it into being – 'must be understood as what Marx calls a "simple abstraction," a deceptively monolithic category that encloses a complex historical process' (20). Simple abstractions are a bit like umbrella-terms: they are operational, contingent, and provisional categories that adumbrate diversity. By this is meant that misleadingly simple terms (like 'novel', 'romance', 'aristocracy', and 'conservative') necessarily encompass a great deal of divergence from whatever is *essentially* novelistic, aristocratic, and so on; but the terms themselves remain helpful, because they 'make conflict – and its mediation – accessible by simplifying and institutionalizing its terms' (268). This semantic use of abstraction (to simplify) enacts in miniature what McKeon sees the abstract category we now call 'the novel' doing in this historical period: it explains (cultural) conflict. Abstractions, McKeon later cautioned, are 'ideological constructs that regard themselves as teleological culminations and self-sufficient completions of a lesser evolution'.[17] In other words, proponents of 'aristocratic', 'progressive', or 'conservative' ideology *abstracted* their ideas from the continuum of history, thereby denying the historical contingency of their own values, which to them appeared universal.

McKeon distances himself from Watt's alignment of middle-class ideology and epistemological empiricism together producing the realist novel. Watt is commended for understanding genre in history, whereas Northrop Frye is charged with evacuating history from the formation of genre. But Watt sees only part of the dialectic, as he struggles to accommodate the persistence of romance and critiques of individualism, therefore failing to account for Fielding's scepticism and conservatism (9–10). Equally, McKeon believes that Bakhtin's model – the 'novelization' of other genres – accounts for *only* Fielding of Watt's trio, because it fails to accommodate 'naive empiricism', realistic representation, and bourgeois ideology (13–14, 118). As McKeon puts it, 'the emergent novel undertakes not a straightforward defence of class (let alone of the middle class) but an experimental inquiry into the ethical implications of contemporary social change' (xxiii). Rather than a kind of propaganda tool for one class, then, the novel mediated between competing interests to make social change comprehensible. McKeon depicts a 'field of possibility' in narrative, whereby the novel was never tied to one side of either of the epistemological or the socioethical dialectics it mediates (xix). This is a looser understanding of the relationship of literature to power structures than we see in criticism that, in McKeon's words, 'relies on a model of ideology that attributes to literature the basic function of reinforcing a "dominant" or "hegemonic" socio-cultural norm, conceiving literature as a regulatory system of "containment" that only in unusual cases can be mobilized in the "counterhegemonic" direction of "resistance"' (xxiii). Here, McKeon has his eye on Foucault: instead he proposes that 'containment' and 'resistance' be treated dialectically in ideological formation. In adopting a Marxian dialectical model of literary history, McKeon traces the gradual stabilization of the novel as a cultural instrument that arose to resolve those analogous questions about truth and virtue.[18]

McKeon begins the 'questions of truth' with the 'destabilization of generic categories', particularly the decline of 'romance idealism' (26). After the Middle Ages and Renaissance, romance came under attack due to a confluence of factors. The seventeenth-century historical revolution elevated 'empirical attitudes in the study of history' (43). The growing authority of print 'contributes to and reinforces an "objective" standard of truth', concerned with whether and how something happened (46). These are the challenges levelled at 'romance' by 'naive empiricism', which claimed for itself historical veracity, as, for example, in the reportage of news. However, just as empiricism, purporting 'to document the authentic truth', attacked romance's falsifications, in turn, 'the extreme skepticism of the opposing party demystifies this claim as mere "romance"' (48). For instance, eyewitness memoirs and secret histories, genres that appeal to the empirically verifiable, were attacked as 'romances', invalidated as a means to truth by precisely what made them an effective attack on romance – their appeal to subjectivity.

This epistemological 'double reversal' came about as a result of the historicist revolution and the scientific movement (63). Natural history emerged, first in the work of Francis Bacon, who pioneered modern scientific method, and then the Royal Society (founded in 1662), as a mode of factual narration that tended towards the separation of science and religion (75). This separation is because Holy Scripture's status as historical record became vulnerable, as writers increasingly challenged the biblical account, whereas 'natural history' claimed incontrovertible empirical authority. The historicism of the epistemological revolution, the dependence on corroborated truths, expedited secularization. This affected 'histories of the individual', biographically arranged narratives which increasingly demonstrated 'a formal tension between what might be called the individual life and the overarching pattern', akin to what Damrosch labelled 'god's plot and man's stories' (90). McKeon traces the movements from saints' lives to spiritual biographies, from picaresque to criminal biography, and from Christian pilgrimage to scientific travel. In each of the latter cases, self-examination does not proceed from 'the truth of a great Author but from the principles of a materialist epistemology' (104). This is the attack levelled at romance idealism by naive empiricism. Subsequently, extreme skepticism emerged in opposition to naive empiricism with 'a far more radical conclusion, the unavailability of narrative truth as such' (119). Its product was realism, which took up older threads of probability and verisimilitude, and 'validates artistic creation for being not history but history-like' (120). Realism, then, was a reaction to, rather than simply an endorsement of, empiricism. To recap the epistemological dialectic in McKeon's words: 'The empiricism of "true history" opposes the discredited idealism of romance, but it thereby generates a countervailing, extreme skepticism, which in turn discredits true history as a species of naive empiricism or "new romance"' (88).

The parallel social dialectic encompasses 'questions of virtue'. Here, 'aristocratic ideology' was destabilized by an attack from 'progressive ideology', which was itself attacked by 'conservative ideology'. These three ideologies map analogically onto, respectively, 'romance idealism', 'naive empiricism', and 'extreme skepticism' from the 'questions of truth'.

So, for instance, aristocratic honour, justified solely through hereditary birthright, was shown to be an untenable fiction by progressive ideology, which agitated for greater meritocracy. By analogy, romance fictions, which commentators as far back as James Beattie in 1783 recognized upheld an aristocratic worldview (see Chapter 1), were attacked as fiction by pretended 'true histories' that validated empiricism in service of a progressive social agenda. Rather than a rise of the middle class, which historians have variously located as early as the fifteenth century or as late as the nineteenth, McKeon argues for the rise of 'class orientation', in which 'class criteria gradually "replace" status criteria', as 'financial income and occupational identity' erode more traditional status markers (163–4). Progressive ideology was in turn negated by conservative ideology 'in an intersecting pattern of political, religious, and socioeconomic debates whose language and preoccupations suffuse much of the early novel itself'. The novel succeeds over other genres because it 'gives form to the fluidity of crisis by organizing it into a conflict of competing interpretations' (174). The novel localized the large historical upheavals through which early modern men and women lived.

McKeon traces this social process through seventeenth-century challenges to political absolutism, a new emphasis on private individuals like Oliver Cromwell, and the liberation of economics from state control. This last produced capitalism, largely thanks to Protestantism, because its doctrine of grace was a levelling force against the aristocratic, 'prescriptive' conception of honour. As McKeon states, 'the progressive critique of aristocratic ideology demystifies prescribed honor as an imaginary value, explaining virtue as a quality that is not prescribed by status but demonstrated by achievement' (212). The subsequent conservative backlash shared this 'anti-aristocratic animus against prescription', but within limits: McKeon sees conservatism 'not as the negation of capitalist ideology but as the expression of a wish to halt the implacable juggernaut of capitalist reform at a stage that preserved, at least for property owners of a certain political and social persuasion, the best of both worlds' (209). McKeon proceeds to discuss texts that mediated the progressive-conservative binary, noting the novel's especial aptitude for making social change comprehensible, because 'narrative imposed solutions upon problems of social categorization by locating them in time. Stories transformed the static conflict of incompatible social identities into a potentially intelligible relation of events on a continuum of change' (220). On the progressive side was Thomas Deloney's *Jack of Newbury* (1597), a vindication of free trade and free religion. On the conservative was *Thomas of Reading* (1600), a 'story of upward mobility gone sour' and hence a circumscription of individualism (234). Rogue narratives by Mary Carleton and Francis Kirkman, and love stories by

Manley, Haywood, Behn, and Congreve, also took positions in this cultural conflict.[19]

Having delineated severally the questions of truth and virtue, McKeon then argues that, although the epistemological and socioethical debates 'are pursued by contemporaries as distinct questions', in fact they 'begin to seem not so much distinct problems as versions or transformations of each other', as 'epistemological choices have ideological significance' (266). The conflation of these questions 'is the founding premise of the novel genre, whose work it is to engage intellectual and social crisis through a simultaneous and comprehensive mediation' (266). In other words, the novel was the medium through which 'transgeneric questions of truth and virtue' are resolved (269). In the final section, McKeon analyses three pairs of prose fictions: *Don Quixote* and *The Pilgrim's Progress*, *Robinson Crusoe* and *Gulliver's Travels*, and *Pamela* and *Joseph Andrews*. McKeon pledges not to provide comprehensive readings, but rather 'to accentuate those features of great works – which are themselves traditionally accorded a central role in the origins of the novel – that confirm the utility of the argument and the evidence that have gone before' (267). The particular texts are plugged into the social history. In asserting that the novel is dialectically constituted, McKeon's emphasis is on process rather than precedence: no first novel is identified, though the category was stabilized by 1750.

Don Quixote seems rather isolated, coming much earlier than the other novels and from a different country. McKeon suggests that the parallel epistemological and social crises occurred earlier in Spain, but were less protracted and less profound than in England. In his textual analyses, McKeon shows that dialectical method is not simply a schematic approach to history, because each part of the triad contains or implies the others. So, for example, 'the text of *Don Quixote* encloses a development from the self-criticism of romance, to the naive empiricism of "true history," to a final orientation of extreme skepticism; and in a correlative movement, from an early and progressive ideology to a late and conservative one' (273). Cervantes's parody of chivalric romance and of aristocratic privilege hereby condenses the entire dialectic. Bunyan's 'literalization of allegory' is understood as a rejection of romance through Christianity and empiricism; and on the social level, the career of Christian in *The Pilgrim's Progress* 'manages to transvalue feudal service and its ethos in a way that does not simply degenerate into individualistic self-interest and capitalist self-service' (314, 312). Defoe's *Robinson Crusoe* naturalizes capitalist self-interest by equating social with spiritual mobility. Defoe's empiricism and progressive ideology was dialectically countered by Swift's scepticism and conservatism in *Gulliver's Travels*, which contests that empiricism is as flawed a way of knowing the world as idealism, and that new measures of status entail as much injustice as aristocratic privilege. Thus McKeon suggests that *Gulliver*, opposed as it is to the energies of the emergent novel, nevertheless plays a dialectic role in its establishment.

The dialectic culminates in Richardson and Fielding. *Pamela* is a backlash against romance, but also the breaking point of fiction's claim to be 'true history'. It critiques aristocratic *droit de seigneur*, the traditional privileges of the nobility, but in a way that makes mobility based on intrinsic merit dependent on a higher social order that confers as well as rewards honour. Richardson's solution to 'status inconsistency', a discrepancy between intrinsic merit and outward rank, is hypergamous marriage (that to a person of a superior class), which removes Pamela from class conflict to bourgeois domesticity, and mediates status inconsistency with gender stability (patriarchy). As McKeon concludes: 'What is most remarkable about *Pamela*'s utopian achievement is precisely the image it provides of real empowerment under conditions that seem somehow to be unaltered. [...] By this means social change takes on the face of a seamless continuity' (380–1). This is the essence of the novel's role in eighteenth-century culture. Fielding, by contrast, embodies the 'extreme skepticism' of 'conservative ideology'. In *Jonathan Wild*:

> ■ The critique of the old, romancing histories is supplemented by a critique of the 'new romance' of naive empiricism, and its modernized methods of imposing on the credulity of the reader [...] Like his epistemology, Fielding's ideology is the issue of a double critique: first of aristocratic ideology by progressive, then of progressive ideology by conservative. (383, 385) □

Fielding's strategy for propounding this scepticism and conservatism was 'a fiction so palpable, so "evident to the senses," that its power to deceive even a "willing" audience becomes neutralized' (393). This is self-conscious third-person narration, typified by *Joseph Andrews*, which marked a major step in the establishment of the novel as an aesthetic mode, apparently free from sociohistorical questions. In the wake of the 'formal breakthrough of the 1740s [...] the young genre settles down to a more deliberate and studied recapitulation of the same ground, this time for the next two centuries' (419). In other words, the social and epistemological questions that generated the novel subsequently became its subject matter, as the novel forsook 'moral and social pedagogy' for the realm of 'aesthetic pleasure' (408).

McKeon's *Origins* was recognized as a remarkable achievement, though it was challenged almost immediately. William Warner labels its dialectic method teleological – McKeon reads the past as inevitably tending to the present, giving each minute aspect of history a part in a fatalistic progression from religiosity to secularization, from feudalism to capitalism, and from romance to realism.[20] Alistair Duckworth remarks that social and epistemological crisis appear to be endemic in culture, not just early modern culture.[21] Homer Obed Brown suggests that McKeon's dialectical scheme is 'mechanical' and that the stability of the term 'novel' by 1750 is overstated.[22] Feminist critics, as will be seen in Chapter 5, felt that McKeon ultimately affirmed a narrowly male canon.

From a more traditionally formalist perspective, Ralph Rader, in 'The Emergence of the Novel in England' (1993), challenged McKeon's historicist method, denying the instrumental importance of social history in generic formation.[23] Taking an essentialist view of the novel genre ('we need first to say what the novel is as a form, a thing in itself'), Rader reaffirms 'the traditional assertion that Richardson's *Pamela* was the first unequivocal novel', because it 'had manifest posterity, but no ancestors' (69, 71, 75). By Rader's definition, 'a novel is a work which offers the reader a focal illusion of characters acting autonomously as if in the world of real experience within a subsidiary awareness of an underlying constructive authorial purpose which gives their story an implicit significance and affective force which real world experience does not have' (72). Rader thus clarifies, in opposition to historicism, the premises of formalism: the novel is a realistic story, constructed by a controlling authorial design of which the reader is aware, and which has something moral to say, meaning that it is not quite like the randomness of real life. Works of fiction either achieve this or not: for Rader, nothing before *Pamela* does. Rader's bases here are Aristotelian; McKeon's reply contends that such an argument is a product of post-eighteenth-century standards of aesthetic autonomy, implicitly Coleridge's recasting of Aristotle: 'The foundation of Rader's *method* (the separability of form from history) is a tacit but logical consequence of the utter conviction with which he embraces his *thesis* (the coextension of the novel and the aesthetic effect)'. Against Rader's impressionistic and tautological claim that *Pamela* is first because, unlike anything earlier, it *feels like a novel,* McKeon says that an aesthetic effect like realism has to be accounted for not as an 'instantaneous manifestation', which suddenly appears in 1740, but rather for its 'protracted and contradictory emergence'.[24] This debate is significant because it indicates the relative strength of the historicist approach by the early 1990s, and as will be seen in the remainder of this book, the formalist position has since been in abeyance.

Conclusion

This chapter has analysed a body of criticism that collectively contends that the rise of the novel was brought about by the social needs it serves rather than unique formal features it possesses. I conclude with two essays that restate, in the wake of McKeon, the importance of Watt in the rise-of-the-novel debate reawakened by 1980s historicism. In 'The Heirs of Ian Watt' (1991–2), Robert Folkenflik notes that the main critique of Watt from Marxian, Foucauldian, and Bakhtinian approaches concentrates on his 'reflection model of the relation of society to the novel', that is, the idea that social developments are simply mirrored in literature, which is replaced by the new historicist insistence that literature is both the document *and* the agent of social change.[25] Folkenflik calls for a widened canon, and this will resonate in the remainder of this book: most significantly, the neglect of female novelists was gradually being redressed. John Richetti, however, in 'The Legacy of Ian Watt's *The Rise of the Novel*' (1992), notes that Watt's canon was itself revisionist, reacting against the 'great tradition' propounded by Leavis (see Chapter 2). Richetti commends Watt's discrimination, arguing that, amongst writers of fiction in the first half of the century, Watt picked correctly, and had commendably *not* treated all texts as though they were artistically equal or of an equivalent sociocultural importance. Richetti contends that critics of the emergence of the novel who tie it in with social power are 'essentially indebted to [Watt's] enduring example'.[26] As well as supplying pre-emptive correctives to his 'heirs', Watt prioritized historical particularity, as opposed to searching for totalizing explanations for origins. Furthermore, for Richetti, Watt balances traditional formalist and historical evaluations, as opposed to the historicist reaction against formalism in 1980s criticism. Richetti maintains that, as of 1992, thirty-five years of criticism had usefully extended Watt without superseding him. Folkenflik and Richetti's reflections disabuse anyone who might think Watt had been rendered obsolete by this point. Chapter 7 will address reconsiderations of the rise of the novel in the 1990s, but in Chapter 5 I will retrace my steps by turning to feminist criticism.

CHAPTER FIVE

Feminism and the Rise of the Novel

Feminist literary criticism, which first gained ground in the 1970s and 1980s, now informs a major strand of eighteenth-century novel studies. The work surveyed in this chapter has achieved several things. It has recovered and accounted for the aesthetic and historical significance of a large corpus of female-authored novels before Jane Austen. It has helped to explain the processes of canon formation by which these novels came to be excluded. It has appraised the representations of women in canonical fiction. And it has provided critiques of the gendered ideologies of the early novel, particularly its collusion in the cultural disenfranchisement of women, such as through its promotion of the private, 'domestic' sphere of cloistered femininity as a separate realm from the male 'public' sphere of political and economic activity. This chapter begins with the recovery efforts of the 1980s, moving to a section on romance and realism that reflects on the gendering of genre, then to studies that have elucidated the early novel's gendered ideologies, and finally to competing accounts of the novel's relationship to domesticity.

Women reading and writing fiction

Brian Corman's recent *Women Novelists Before Jane Austen* (2009) gives a history of women's novels in critics' canons of early fiction, extending from the eighteenth century to the 1950s, showing the criteria by which women's contributions to the novel's rise were (usually) excluded.[1] In the 1950s, Watt acknowledged the numerical superiority of female novelists, but located the rise of the novel in the contributions of three men: Defoe, Richardson, and Fielding. McKillop's addition of Smollett and Sterne basically consolidated the canon. Earlier studies of female-authored novels were written by Joyce Horner (during the Suffragette movement of the 1920s) and by B. G. MacCarthy (during the Second World War when women's roles diversified to include traditionally male responsibilities).[2] The claims of these scholars for women's contribution to the novel were relatively modest. MacCarthy surveys quite broadly and is not generally dismissive, but she takes realism, initiated by Defoe and finessed by Richardson and Fielding, as a norm and gauge for the women's novels she surveys. Hence, MacCarthy finds a lot of early eighteenth-century fiction (Behn, Manley and Haywood) noxious and much of the later sentimental fiction mediocre, at best a market stimulus necessary for the advance of 'masculine' realism. The feminist movement of the 1960s and 70s recovered female contributions, though in major studies women's writing before Austen was more often acknowledged than it was analysed. Burney is arguably an exception, serving as she did more generally as a stepping stone from Richardson to Austen. Ellen Moers gives writers before Burney only passing attention; Elaine Showalter sees women's novels beginning 'about 1750'; and Eva Figes, in her view that the novel was a form begun by men and taken over by women around 1800, replicates the dismissal she criticizes.[3] The reversal of this neglect of eighteenth-century female novelists was undertaken in the 1980s by Dale Spender's *Mothers of the Novel* (1986), Jane Spencer's *The Rise of the Woman Novelist* (1986), and Janet Todd's *The Sign of Angelica* (1989).

These studies set out with the principle that, as Spencer puts it, 'women's role in the novel's rise has been underestimated [...] as far as possible edited out of the historical account, in a familiar move to belittle and suppress women's achievements'.[4] The most authoritative instance of this exclusion is Watt. Todd states that 'patriarchal literary history, exemplified in Ian Watt's *Rise of the Novel*, has largely written women out of its story of eighteenth-century fiction – of Defoe, Richardson, Fielding, Sterne and Smollett'.[5] Spender sees the male bias of the canon as a conspiracy perpetrated to deny 'that it was women and not men who made the greater contribution to the development of the novel'.[6] She contends that this female origin is denied because 'women writers are the bearers of women's traditions that were vitally important to women in their own time', and she avers that 'women were the mothers of the novel and that any other version of its origin is but a myth of male creation' (6). Spender makes claims for the aesthetic (as well as historical) significance of over 100 women who wrote over 500 novels during the 'long' eighteenth century (1680s–1830s). She supplies near-comprehensive (albeit error-strewn) inventories of these works.[7] Particular writers are selected for individual assessment, starting with Behn, Manley, and Haywood, in whose work 'we witness [...] the rise of the novel' (83). Spender's final chapters are devoted to individually introducing and outlining the writing careers of Sarah Fielding, Charlotte Lennox, Elizabeth Inchbald, Charlotte Smith, Ann Radcliffe, Mary Wollstonecraft, Mary Hays, Frances Burney, Maria Edgeworth, Lady Morgan, Amelia Opie, and Mary Brunton. These names form a partial cast-list for this chapter.

Less introductory than Spender's biographical and bibliographical book, Spencer's *The Rise of the Woman Novelist* argues that 'in the eighteenth century [the novel] was an important medium for the articulation of women's concerns, and its rise was centrally bound up with the growth of a female literary voice acceptable within patriarchal society'.[8] Resisting the temptation to see instances of female writing in the past as *de facto* positive acts of liberation, Spencer argues that 'the terms on which women writers were accepted worked in some ways to suppress feminist opposition' (xi). Women chose to write novels because it was a profitable activity open to them despite a new ideology of femininity that increasingly confined them to a private, domestic space. However, their writing was tolerated partly because domesticity became its subject. 'By the beginning of the eighteenth century', Spencer explains, 'a path was open for the woman writer, but it was full of pitfalls' (32). In short, the 'terms of acceptance' set out by a patriarchal order for female writers dictated the kinds of fictionalized 'self-portraits' available to early-century women novelists as well as the kinds of femininity viable in later-century works. As the century progressed, the mode of sexually liberated female wit typified by Behn, Manley, and Haywood was sharply rejected. Instead, women's novels stressed chastity and modesty, modelled on Richardson's 'exemplary morality', and working in support of the ideology of gendered separate spheres (89–90). This was geared towards gaining male acceptance and is well illustrated by the careers of Sarah Fielding and Frances Burney.

The rise in popularity and prestige of novels by women, Spencer shows, masked the deterioration in their actual social position. Three possible fictive responses were available to the woman novelist operating within such strictures: protest, conformity, and escape (107). The protest strategy manifests in rebarbative stories of seduction, which 'could reveal the contradictions at the heart of the bourgeois ideology of femininity' (112). Spencer tracks this from Manley and Haywood's attack on the double standard 'that overlooked promiscuity in men but severely punished women for any breach of chastity' through to the more conservative sentimental seduction plots of mid-century, which promoted virtue: 'not only chastity, but by implication, submissiveness and self-abnegation' (127). Spencer states that by the time of Inchbald, Hays, and Wollstonecraft's late-century fictions, which were actually written with proto-feminist agendas, 'women novelists were beginning a new feminist revision of the seduction tale' (127).

The 'central women's tradition', however, is conformist, enacting a didactic reformation of a heroine. Novels ranging from Mary Davys's *The Reform'd Coquet* (1724) and Haywood's *Betsy Thoughtless* to Burney's *Evelina* and *Camilla* indicate how pervasive was the motif of a heroine cajoled out of mistaken notions in the service of patriarchy. In fact, this is the tradition inherited by the nineteenth century, particularly Austen, who adopts 'the convention of the lover-mentor', depicting male suitors who 'school' heroines out of errant wilfulness (168). Despite the apparently progressive assumption here that women are capable of moral growth, as the stasis of virtue or villainy gives way to 'the dynamics of character change', this narrative arc buttresses patriarchal mores, because women are made tractable (141).

Finally, Spencer considers escapist fictions, romances that 'offered escape from male-dominated reality through a fantasy of female power' (184). Though the fantasy of imaginative escape is satirized in Lennox's *The Female Quixote*, making it finally a reformed heroine story, Spencer shows that escapism prevails in Sophia Lee's *The Recess* (1785) and Ann Radcliffe's *The Romance of the Forest* (1791). These Gothic fictions 'presented a fantasy of female power', but, despite allowing a space for women's hopes and desires, this fantasy is ultimately a 'false panacea' (201, 209–10). Spencer thus argues that the rise of the woman novelist was an agent in the decline of female enfranchisement.

The progress of female-authored fiction traced by Janet Todd shows similarities to and differences from Spencer's. Todd does not just challenge Watt's exclusion of women; she challenges his main metaphor, the *rise* of the novel: 'Literature is not progressive; there is not really a *rise* of the male or of the female novel, although several women at the end of the period, like Clara Reeve or Anna Laetitia Barbauld, assessed fiction in this way'.[9] Todd divides her study into three chronological stages:

> ■ The first dealing with the Restoration and early eighteenth century, a period of considerable frankness in writing when the status of female fiction remained dubious; the second dealing with the mid-eighteenth century, when sentimentalism and the cult of sensibility flourished, giving a new respectable image and restricted subject matter to the woman writer; and thirdly the last two decades, in which there is in part a reaction to this restriction and in part a conscious and public embracing of it. (3) □

Todd's title, *The Sign of Angelica*, refers to Angelica Bianca, the self-portrait of A. B., Aphra Behn, in Behn's play, *The Rover* (1681), a prostitute who advertises her services by boldly displaying a sign depicting herself. Todd argues that this self-consciously *constructed* version of femininity was gradually replaced by a sentimental, domestic femininity that *denied* its own social contingency and increasingly came to seem natural, not constructed. She follows a dominant principle of feminism: gender roles are socially learned and culturally enforced (including in literature), rather than biologically determined by sex.

Part 1 of Todd's book traces the move from seventeenth-century romance to the scandalous narratives of the early eighteenth century, which seem to reject female inferiority. In part 2, Todd shows that 'in the middle of the eighteenth century, women entered literature in strength', but 'what women created in the mid-eighteenth century was not simply writing but *feminine* writing' (125). The novel 'had become a feminine genre', associated with professional female authorship, leisured female readership, and the fine feelings and sympathy promoted by sensibility (139). In part 3, Todd moves to the end of the century when new proto-feminist ideas that stemmed from the French Revolution (1789) informed the novels of 'revolutionary' writers like Wollstonecraft and Hays, although Burney's *Camilla* illustrates the simultaneous employment of 'moral authorship and authority' for conservative ends by a female novelist. Despite the regrettable narrowing of subjects available to women writers by the end of the century, Todd concludes that the 'central position' of female fiction showed progress. Indeed, the broad range of pre-Austen novels discussed by Spencer and Todd is augmented by *Fetter'd or Free* (1986), a collection of 23 essays that address women's fiction from 1670 to 1815. These essays place authors within social and economic relations of the times, and try to answer the question of whether they were allowed a voice only to endorse patriarchy or able to transcend patriarchy to develop proto-feminist forms of self-expression and critiques of gender relations.[10] The essays' conclusions are varied.

Ruth Perry, in her groundbreaking *Women, Letters, and the Novel* (1980), studies how women consumed fiction. She broadly accepts Watt's historical markers for the novel's emergence: middle-class Protestantism, capitalism, and urbanization all tending towards individualism.[11] She, however, considers the novel's role in the developments in gender relations wrought by these social changes. Middle-class women's lives were increasingly domestic, because capitalism separated work and home, designating the latter feminine:

> ■ Novels developed at a time when literate women – the sort that figured in such books – were dispossessed of all meaningful activity save marrying and breeding, and when even these activities were to be done only in socially acceptable patterns. [...] In this changing society, novels embellished and perpetuated the myths of romantic love needed to strengthen the new economic imbalances between men and women and necessary to make the lives of the dispossessed seem fulfilled. (x) □

Women's solitary reading of epistolary fiction and their writing letters made the imagination more important than lived reality, supplying consolatory experiences for disenfranchised women. 'The epistolary novel was the perfect vehicle for stories of romantic love', Perry states, 'because its very format demanded a subject matter in which emotional states were most prominent' (138). Epistolary novels with 'isolated' heroines, then, fill leisure time by suspending attention from reality for women denied emotional satisfaction in their real lives. Perry sees the novel as a prop of bourgeois patriarchy, a stance, we shall see, common to much feminist scholarship.

Terry Lovell's *Consuming Fictions* (1987) also focuses on the consumption of fiction from a perspective that fuses Marxist and feminist methodologies. She takes Watt to task for establishing the novel as a realistic and bourgeois form in ways that obscure gender, and proposes to 'focus on the place of women and of a highly differentiated gender order, in the production, reproduction and transmission of a class culture'.[12] What role do female consumers play in the novel's replication of middle-class ideology? Lovell notes the 'commoditisation' of literature in the eighteenth century as patronage was replaced with production for an anonymous market. Because 'the novel came into existence as a commodity', it had to establish its literary 'use value' in contradistinction to its capitalist 'exchange value' (28). It achieved this by valorizing realism as an *aesthetic* quality, thus denying any relationship to the market. This was accomplished in Victorian realism, when the novel finally became respectable literature – only after it had been stigmatized as a commercial and effeminate genre in the Romantic period, particularly in the non-realist fantasy of the Gothic mode, which was ambivalent about capitalist bourgeois rationality.

Lovell advances the view that, although the novel's origins lie in the respectable realism of Richardson and Fielding, it was predominantly considered 'entertainment' rather than 'literature' until the mid-nineteenth century. As such, it was impelled to critique capitalism as well as to endorse it, so 'Watt overemphasized the extent to which the novel unproblematically reproduced the values of market capitalism' (29). Because of the novel's marginal status, 'its ability to contribute to the maintenance of bourgeois hegemony through the literary celebration and exploration of the classical bourgeois virtues [...] was slight' (73). Watt confuses his aesthetic categories (leading him to accept realism as normative) with his sociological ones: his interest in production and consumption should have led him to acknowledge the place of women writers and readers. Acknowledging the presence of women writers in the canon after the eighteenth century, Lovell argues that it is the addressee rather than the author that determines the acceptability of a novel: female-authored books that addressed women only were neglected, but those with a more 'general' appeal, normalizing a male reader regardless of who might actually read, were acceptable. Most importantly, Lovell states that 'at every point in the history of the English novel women have played a distinct and crucial role in its production, consumption and transmission' (159–60).

The 1980s, then, saw a considerable feminist revision of the socio-historical bases used to account for the rise of the novel. The canon was shaken to such a degree that Judith Kegan Gardiner claimed a long-neglected epistolary novel by Behn as the 'first English novel'.[13] As another gauge of this sea-change, Burney's novels were the subject of a number of feminist re-evaluations during the 1980s and 90s that have elevated her to canonical status.[14] The following section discusses studies that address the social realities of female experience at the moment of the novel's origins and the relationship of romance to realistic representation.

Gendering genre

If the eighteenth-century novel is to be considered a realistic genre, to what extent is its depiction of women's lives historically accurate? In *Women's Lives and the Eighteenth-Century English Novel* (1991), Elizabeth Bergen Brophy answers this question with reference to seven novelists – Richardson, Fielding, and five women (Sarah Fielding, Lennox, Sarah Scott, Reeve, and Burney). These all wrote in the dominant tradition of 'responsible realism': fiction about everyday reality that has a moral purpose. Brophy compares novels with a trove of primary evidence from social history, particularly the diaries of real women, in order to gauge how accurately novels reflect the experiences of daughters, mothers, wives, spinsters, and widows. She generally finds that fiction reinforced patriarchal ideology: daughterly obedience, wifely duty, and companionate marriage are the goals for women in society and in fiction.[15]

By contrast, Mona Scheuermann's *Her Bread to Earn* (1993) rejects totalizing accounts of the representation of women in early fiction, arguing that 'women are depicted as strong, capable, and responsible members of society in a surprising variety of works', and that 'many of the most positive depictions, as well as the most nasty, appear in the works of male novelists'.[16] Scheuermann's textual analyses of women's financial dealings in fiction reveal that they are not always victims and not always 'sheltered from the world beyond their families', as 'novelists from Defoe to Austen depict women engaged with society rather than cloistered from it' (248, 251). Scheuermann does note 'the apparent contradiction between the gloomy legal truths and the life-images in the novels' (9). Her main focus, however, is on textual representation rather than social history, and there she finds Defoe's heroines remarkably capable of supporting themselves in adverse conditions, a motif still strong in radical fictions by men and women towards the end of the century, despite the more restrictive mid-century portrayals of women in Richardson and Fielding. Scheuermann argues that 'the images of women in eighteenth-century English novels are essentially positive', even if this did not reflect social reality (251).

I will move now from the historical truths of female existence as represented in novels deemed realistic to the competing genre of romance. Watt and McKeon (see Chapters 2 and 4, respectively) posit a sharp break between romance and novel, opposing the archetypalism of Frye (see Chapter 2), who sees the mimetic novel as a realistic displacement of romance. Margaret Anne Doody (see Chapter 7) will propose doing away with the word 'romance' altogether, as it is one and the same with the novel. Deborah Ross, in *The Excellence of Falsehood* (1991), argues that, in the romance-versus-realism debate that dominated the eighteenth-century discourse on the novel, women constantly found themselves on the 'wrong' side: that is, romance. Ross contends that, despite masculine censure, female novelists found aspects of seventeenth-century French heroic romances appealing, particularly their elevation of the heroine. Women writers depended on elements of romance to suggest the complexities of women's social positions; they did this by fusing romance and realism. So, despite Watt and McKeon's claims, Ross argues that 'the novel never has fully separated itself from romance'.[17]

Ross describes four stages in female novelists' use of romance. First, Behn and Manley bathetically contrast idealized romance with sordid reality as a feminist strategy of social critique that produces tragic love stories (39–40). In mid-century, Lennox and Haywood reshuffle the combination of romance and realism to promote virtue in deference to male strictures on feminine fiction, providing 'practical demonstrations of how good, ordinary women can attain true love' (84). *The Female Quixote* typifies the 'realist manifesto' of 'anti-romance', now tending towards comedy, not tragedy (94–5). However, Lennox is ambivalent about romance, because her novel does offer women liberation; the co-existence of romance and realism results in a contradictory morality. Later in the century, Burney's courtship and Radcliffe's Gothic novels retain romance in order to critique patriarchy, as the heroines suffer the pains of romantic adventure without the reward of romantic ending. Finally, Austen supplies the 'romantic denouement', because she achieves harmony between romance and realism, bringing 'women's romantic desires closer to what the real world might be willing to offer them', as heroines successfully adjust their romantic desires to the social order (165). Austen's formal innovation of 'multidirectional irony', which enabled subtle social critique, was developed from the blend of romance and realism in previous women novelists (207). That is, female writers were unwilling to fully swallow what they were nonetheless promoting as proper feminine behaviour.

Less positive than Ross about the enduring association of women and romance, Laurie Langbauer's *Women and Romance* (1990) argues that romance has been derided and excluded by novel criticism precisely because of its perceived femininity.[18] Genre in the eighteenth- and nineteenth-century English novel relies on and reinforces gender division, and later 'realist' accounts of the novel scapegoat romance. Langbauer says that in Watt's analysis, for instance, romance 'becomes the bedrock against which the novel takes its meaning and establishes its identity by establishing its difference' (17). Since the eighteenth century, the novel has basically denied its own past in romance, deeming unreality a formal weakness associated with female readerships. Binaries of genre enable those of gender: elevating realism over romance propagates 'unexamined gender assumptions', equivalent to man's arrogation of superiority (34). At the moment of the novel's emergence, the heroine of Lennox's *The Female Quixote*, Arabella, torn between a 'romantic' outlook that empowers her and a 'realistic' one that domesticates and disempowers her, parallels Lennox's dilemma between romance and novel. By the end of the century, these terms were even more polarized. Even a 'progressive' novelist like Wollstonecraft proves complicit in the gendering of genre because she assumes 'the structural parallel between romance and women', prior to even more stark essentialism in the Victorian period (91).

The early 1990s also saw attention turn to the eighteenth century's particular form of the romance: the courtship novel. Katherine Green's *The Courtship Novel, 1740–1820* (1991) argues that the historical transition from predominantly arranged marriages to 'companionate marriages', in which young women exercised some choice, necessitated a new literary form: 'Courtship novels, which were written by women and for women – and thus may in some measure be said to have feminized the English novel [and] appropriated domestic fiction to feminist purposes'.[19] Green asserts that heroines by this period are chosen by and choose a suitor based on affection, rather than status. Applying the social historian, Lawrence Stone's, concept of 'affective individualism' (see Chapter 9), Green states that novels representing the experiences of ordinary women were part of 'a broader social imperative to legitimize women's self-actualization as affective individuals' (14). The courtship novel, then, was a feminized space, rather than a form of social control, as Nancy Armstrong had influentially argued (see Chapter 4). To place class above gender, as Armstrong does, Green says, 'is both to undervalue the dynamic relationship between female writers and readers and to impose an anachronistic mistrust of the domestic on one's reading of eighteenth-century texts' (158). As the novel moved away from seduction and betrayal (pre-1740) to courtship and marriage, women published more successfully because they encouraged readers to sympathize with a heroine. The commodified depiction of heroines is a 'counterideological' form of protest. Ultimately, the courtship novel served a 'progressive, feminist' cause, aiming 'to disturb established ideas about how dutiful daughters and prudent young women should comport themselves during their courtships' (160–1).

Ruth Bernard Yeazell meanwhile calls 'narratives of female resistance and female choice' *Fictions of Modesty* – the title of her 1991 book.[20] She analyses fictional and non-fictional injunctions to female modesty in the eighteenth and nineteenth centuries, including novels from Richardson's *Pamela* to Elizabeth Gaskell's *Wives and Daughters* (1864–6), conduct books, philosophy, and works of natural science. Yeazell argues that modesty itself is a fiction, a precariously constructed female sexual ideal reinforced in the English novel, in which 'modesty triumphs everywhere' (x). Novels make a story out of conventional femininity, engendering and eroticizing desire in the process. Female modesty was not intended to inhibit sexual activity, but to increase it by deferral: plot in the courtship novel delays its resolution (marriage) because female modesty delays consummation and fuels both male desire and readerly desire. Richardson's *Pamela* is a predictable prototype. Cleland's *Memoirs of a Woman of Pleasure* (1748–9), commonly known now as *Fanny Hill,* is read, contrary to expectation given its sexually explicit content, as a 'fiction of modesty', because the heroine remains diffident and naive despite her prolific sexual activity, retaining a 'virgin heart' for her first lover (102). Burney's Evelina is caught in 'the almost impossible double bind' of having to enter society to be courted whilst avoiding self-display, but triumphs through remaining modest (130). These eighteenth-century novels demonstrate the cultural undesirability of female experience; though teleologically directed towards marriage, they focus on the 'narrative middle' of female experience, after sexual awakening but before marital disposal.

Also addressing desire and fiction, Patricia Meyer Spacks, in *Desire and Truth* (1990), examines the power of plotting to shape social truth.[21] She seeks to extend the insights of psychoanalytical theories about how narrative exploits readerly desire and Nancy Armstrong's argument about how novels produce appropriately desiring subjects. Spacks, however, opposes the ideological criticism of Armstrong, arguing that plot in the eighteenth-century novel does not just express dominant power relations; it can also reshape dominant ideas, for good or bad. So, for instance, *The Female Quixote* is an archetypal instance of the suppression of desire on terms laid out in Samuel Johnson's criticism, in order to produce an 'ethically sound novel' (31). In literary historical terms, Spacks sees a progression from Richardson, Fielding, and Cleland's novels about power relations, which depict sexual struggle and idealize female changelessness, to a rejection of such plotting after 1760, first in the sentimental novel, then the Gothic, and finally the political fictions of the 1790s. Later-century novelists 'reject power and elevate affiliation as the central principle of plot' (144). There was a shift among male writers after 1760 from the phallic power struggles of mid-century to stories of harmonious relationships and familial obligation. Finally, Austen and Scott 'demonstrate rich fictional possibilities, both structural and substantive, in double awareness of power and community as simultaneous if conflicting human impulses' (237). It is not simply that the nineteenth-century novel advanced from plot to character or that it 'resolved the problems of fictional structure with which the eighteenth-century struggled' (238). Spacks explains how eighteenth-century novels were constructed to represent and shape reality through exploitation of narrative desire.

Rather than the post-1740 *courtship* novels that Yeazell, Green, and Spacks argue help to *establish* the form, Ros Ballaster, in *Seductive Forms* (1992), addresses *seduction* narratives, 'amatory fiction' by Behn, Manley, and Haywood, that helped *initiate* it before Richardson. Ballaster argues that Richetti's analysis of this material as 'popular' (see Chapter 3) judges it too negatively and identifies its ideological significance too simplistically.[22] Watt's 'realist teleology and valorization of Richardsonian domestic or sentimental fiction' (see Chapter 2) has, for Ballaster, unjustly obscured this body of women's writing (10). Armstrong, because she starts with *Pamela*, omits an earlier stage in the relationship of political and gender ideology (see Chapter 4). McKeon's method (see Chapter 4) is embraced, as Ballaster subjects early women's novels to 'epistemological and formal questions of genre and its formation', but the 'generalized conflict between bourgeois and aristocratic ideologies' McKeon plots is 'more relevant to a later period', because amatory fiction has to be read in the context of 'the specific party political distinctions of Whig and Tory' (11). Richetti reads Behn, Manley, and Haywood's gender representations as 'about' secularization, and McKeon reads them as 'about' social change over centuries – both diachronic readings that make literary texts sociological documents. In response, Ballaster aims to provide 'a synchronic analysis of a particular historical moment in the making of the English novel', reading sexual strategies not as cover for ideological ones, but intertwined with them (29).

The English novel, in Ballaster's account, turns out to have French origins. Resisting 'realist teleology' that looks forward from Defoe and Richardson, Ballaster looks back to the 'feminocentric' traditions of prose fiction of seventeenth-century France. She outlines what the heroic romance, the *petite histoire* (or *nouvelle*), the *chronique scandaleuse* (or *roman à clef*), and love-letter fiction offered to English women writers from the 1680s onwards.[23] Behn, Manley, and Haywood generated 'imitations and transformations of French models in order to produce an indigenous British amatory tradition peculiarly attuned to the ideologies of gender in contemporary (party) political discourse' (42). Amatory fictions, then, are complex, direct interventions in the sexual and political discourses following the political crises of the 1680s: the emergence of parties, the 1688 Revolution, Queen Anne's Tory government, and the Whig ascendancy under Robert Walpole. Each writer resists masculine constructions of gender. Behn does so through subverting gendered expectations of narrative voice. Manley allegorizes female reading and writing, thereby mixing normally 'discrete discursive categories', like personal and public, fact and fiction, erotic and pathetic, in order to show their instability and artificiality (151). Haywood exposes female oppression and compensates women with the pleasure of fiction. All three, all Tories, are situated in their precise political moments: Behn as a defender of Stuart absolutism, Manley as an opponent of Whiggery, and Haywood against Walpole. These women forged 'a specifically female writing identity for themselves', precisely by engaging with party politics (30). The story ends with Richardson's pioneering domestic, sentimental fiction and the parallel shift away from party political struggle to generalized class conflict which ushered in a new ideology of virtuous, domestic women, a process that Haywood anticipates. This transformation assigned women new kinds of cultural authority, but restricted women's ability to undermine fictions of gender identity in the ways they had done earlier in the century.

Towards the end of *Seductive Forms*, Ballaster addresses links between masquerade and amatory fiction, building on Castle's attention to this motif in fiction after 1740 (see Chapter 4). Mary Anne Schofield and Elizabeth Craft-Fairchild each tackle 'masquerade fiction' as a culturally specific manifestation of women's romance in the eighteenth century. As well as featuring actual masquerades in their plots, female-authored novels in Schofield's estimation adopt rhetorical strategies of disguise, indirection, and artifice to embody states of mind and resistance to patriarchy. In *Masking and Unmasking the Female Mind* (1990), Schofield argues that 'novelists use the cover story of their romance plots to mask their own feminist, aggressive intentions and to unmask the facile and fatuous fictions they are supposed to be writing as members of the weaker sex'. Ostensibly didactic novels that offer 'a fashionable tale of love and romance' actually challenge 'masculine plots'.[24] Schofield's optimism about the feminist potential of masquerade fiction is not matched by Craft-Fairchild, who, in *Masquerade and Gender* (1993), tells a story about how masquerade, which had threatened to subvert patriarchy in the early eighteenth century (Behn and Haywood), becomes the oppressive 'condition of femininity' by the turn of the nineteenth (Inchbald and Burney). Masquerade embodies 'women's repression of desire and their role-playing to conform to a repressive domestic ideal'.[25] Craft-Fairchild argues that Castle takes conservative commentators like Henry Fielding at their word in seeing masquerade as subversive. Adopting 'a feminism that hopes to address women's complicity in creating and maintaining the ideology that controls them', Craft-Fairchild rebuts Schofield by insisting that every text both constructs and deconstructs gender norms, and so 'leaves the foundational terms of representation intact' (24, 11). Incipient feminism, then, is ultimately contained in this form.

Finally here, Josephine Donovan's *Women and the Rise of the Novel, 1405–1726* (1999) reasserts the novel's break with romance, which had been largely denied in feminist studies, stating that women's 'contribution to the rise of the realist novel has not yet been recognized'.[26] She sees women writers, beginning in fifteenth- and sixteenth-century France, then seventeenth-century Spain, and finally Restoration and eighteenth-century England, aiming for 'familiar realism'. Bakhtin's view of the novel as an everyday, familiar genre that enables a destabilization of traditional authority through its dialogic form (see Chapter 4) informs Donovan's view of the novel as an anti-authoritarian site of protest against female subordination (x). She combines Marxist and feminist methodologies, first invoking Lukács's 'standpoint theory', from *History and Class Consciousness* (1923), by which a critical consciousness emerges in groups that are objectified by capitalism. Donovan extends this from social class to gender in order to argue that women were adequately placed to critique patriarchal capitalism that treated them as commodities. Next, she applies Lucien Goldmann's Marxist view of the novel, given in *Towards a Sociology of the Novel* (1963), as a dialectical response to capitalism. Goldmann saw capitalism promoting production for exchange and profit, thereby marginalizing production for direct use, and giving rise to alienation: the novel, Goldmann states, critiques this process by presenting a hero who must find authentic values and oppose the objectification of capitalism. Integrating Bakhtin, Lukács, and Goldmann, Donovan argues:

> ■ Women's base in use-value production [...] provided a critical, ironic standpoint from which to judge the machinations of the exchange system. This viewpoint was, I contend, an important basis for the irony seen in their early literary production, and it contributed to the dialogical consciousness Bakhtin posited as essential to the rise of the novel. (17) □

Because capitalism shuffled women into production connected with use – that is, domestic work – they were well placed to critique the new economic arrangements and their own marginalization; they did this by adopting realism as a critically ironic attack on romance, thereby creating the modern novel.

Donovan offers the 'framed-novelle' as 'the dominant genre in prose fiction in the late medieval and early modern period, until it was superseded by the novel' (29). Donovan here follows the Russian Formalist Viktor Shklovsky, who argued in his *Theory of Prose* (1925) that medieval collections of discrete short stories gradually developed a common 'frame' to link the stories and then eventually these episodes became unified as a single story. Framed stories thus evolved into the modern novel. Because it is associated with women and originated in France, Donovan surmises, this genre has been overlooked by Anglocentric and androcentric critics. Key texts in this tradition are: Christine de Pizan's *Le Livre de la cité des dames* (1405–7), the anonymous *Les Évangiles des quenouilles* (c. 1466–74), Jeanne Flore's *Les Comptes amoureux* (1531), Marguerite de Navarre's *L'Heptaméron* (1558), María de Zayas y Sotomayor's *Novelas Amorosas y ejemplares* (1637), and Margaret Cavendish's *Sociable Letters* (1664). The 'framed-novelle' is an inherently dialogic form in Bakhtin's sense, because a number of short stories exist in dialogue with one another and with the voice that frames and presents them. This form allows for a narrative critique of 'theoretism'; general maxims about women that may come from the narrative frame are challenged in the particular stories, making this form a potent feminist critique. The culmination of Donovan's literary genealogy comes with Manley's *New Atalantis*, Davys's *The Reform'd Coquet*, and Barker's *A Patch-Work Screen for the Ladies* (1723); she credits to these authors the invention of 'feminist critical realism' (113). Donovan makes anti-romance as crucial as romance in the feminine tradition, though she also suggests that critical realism was promptly eclipsed by sentimental, domestic modes after the 1720s. Ultimately, she may have outlined a heritage that the novel subsequently rejects.

Gendered ideology and the rise of the novel

Feminist criticism of the rise of the novel necessarily includes critiques of the gendered ideologies of novels that were central to that rise. In this line of criticism, an important flashpoint is the critical debate over interpretation of Richardson's *Clarissa*, and specifically the heroine's rape by the rake, Lovelace. The debate was sparked by the high-theory, deconstructionist interpretation of William Warner, which reads the text, against the grain of Richardson's expressed intentions, as championing the charismatic Lovelace over the pious Clarissa in the 'struggle for interpretation' of this story.[27] Terry Castle responded by reclaiming Richardson's stated intent, saying that the hermeneutic struggle and the rape each model the historical condition of women under patriarchy.[28] Virtually simultaneously, Terry Eagleton sought a combination of Marxist and feminist approaches to elucidate Clarissa's ultimately doomed resistance to patriarchy and Richardson's promotion of bourgeois ideology against dominant aristocratic values, represented respectively by the victim and the rapist. Eagleton provides an excoriating attack on critical methods like Warner's that divorce rape from material history and make it 'stand for' textual interpretation.[29] In a review of two decades of *Clarissa* scholarship prior to Warner, Sue Warrick Doederlein suggests that academic criticism has replicated and endorsed Lovelace's own 'detachment from that crucial event' and characterizes this academic discourse as tantamount to 'gang rape', reproducing by not adequately critiquing the gender values that make rape a tool of patriarchy.[30] This is what Castle and Eagleton aimed to redress. In 1987, Frances Ferguson rounded off the Warner-Castle-Eagleton debate with a sensible compromise between materialist-historical and textual-interpretive aims by conducting a historical investigation into the complexities of the eighteenth-century law of rape to argue that 'Richardson rewrites the rape story to create the psychological novel'.[31] Formal innovation is clearly sometimes reliant on dubious gender politics.[32]

The works of canonical male novelists remained an important focus of gender criticism in the 1990s.[33] Madeleine Kahn's *Narrative Transvestism* (1994) addresses the fact that many of 'the first canonical novels [...] were written by men in the person of women'.[34] As 'narrative transvestites', Defoe and Richardson 'absent' themselves from their fictions by adopting female voices: 'This narrative projection of the male self into an imagined female voice and experience was an integral part of the emerging novel's radical and destabilizing investigation of how an individual creates an identity and, as our society if not our biology requires, a gendered identity' (6–7). The novel form fits into the history of the formation of an individualized selfhood produced by binary gendering, and operates through 'suggestive transgression' to test the limits of gender categories (80). Kahn applies twentieth-century psychoanalytic concepts of male-to-female transvestism to these authors, and the social history of how gender categories were enforced in the eighteenth century to two novels, *Roxana* and *Clarissa*. She argues that 'narrative transvestism' allowed the male novelist 'to explore his society's experimental transgression of boundaries even while it afforded him some distance from and control over the risks he was taking' (45). In *Roxana* and *Clarissa*, 'the self continually shifts its identity from male to female and back again to claim the attributes of both and the limitations of neither' (26). This is because 'the male must continually redefine the female to assert his identity as not-female', and so the cross-dressed novel 'provides a model by which men can learn to read women, and women can learn to allow themselves to be read' (47, 149). By investigating new constructions of masculinity and femininity, novels ultimately shore up gender division and hierarchy.

Like Kahn, Helene Moglen, in *The Trauma of Gender* (2001), uses psychoanalysis in her examination of novels by Defoe, Richardson, Sterne, and Horace Walpole. She argues that 'as surely as it marked a response to developing class relations, the novel came into being as a response to the sex-gender system that emerged in England in the seventeenth and eighteenth centuries'.[35] For Moglen, the early novel was 'bimodal', combining realism with fantasy. This duality enabled the novel to manage the strains on individual subjectivity imposed by social changes in gender configurations, which essentialized gender difference through economic, political, and scientific discourses and practices from the mid-seventeenth to mid-eighteenth century. The realistic strain worked to naturalize social difference through a single, overarching perspective that stressed psychic wholeness and organized desire in conformity with patriarchal, bourgeois social goals. It manifests in sons' narratives that involve an attempt to achieve autonomy and to replace the father (*Bildungsroman* and picaresque), and in daughters' narratives of courtship, marriage, and maternity, which perpetuate patriarchy. The fantastic strain, however, sexualizes rather than represses women, shows the instability of subjectivity, exposes the masculine repression of women, and critiques bourgeois, capitalist ideology. It comes into its own with the Gothic novel at the end of the century, but always threatens to 'interpenetrate' realistic texts, as the modes are 'mutually constitutive' (12). The fantastic strain appears (submerged) in the realist tradition of Defoe, Richardson, and Sterne: in the psychic turmoil following the return of Roxana's daughter, in Clarissa's post-rape madness, and in Tristram Shandy's castration anxiety. The fantastic strands of these narratives are fragmentary, neither dominant nor sustained, and thus disrupt without finally threatening the hegemonic values of realist texts. The misogyny of realistic fiction is not simply masculine hatred of women, but articulations of loss occasioned by the trauma caused by the cultural assignment of a single gender to each individual.

The rise of the domestic novel

Since Armstrong's *Desire and Domestic Fiction*, it has been common to read the novel as a discourse of gendered subjectivity. Armstrong contended that the novel sought to disentangle sexual relations from political power in order to mask socioeconomic interests by representing them as psychological and identifying that consciousness with apolitical women. Earlier sections of this chapter have been concerned with the novel's production of gendered identity and the prescription of domesticity as women's proper place. This section addresses studies that take up, extend, and challenge Armstrong's thesis.

In *Dangerous Intimacies* (1997), Lisa Moore reads the early novel's homophobic treatment of female same-sex desire as a 'legitimation of the rise to power of bourgeois identity as a cultural norm' prescribing virtuous female domesticity and heterosexual love.[36] Despite the potentially 'disruptive aspects' of its representing female-female intimacy, the novel, from Cleland and Sarah Scott in the mid-eighteenth century to Edgeworth and Austen at the start of the nineteenth, is 'the representational site of the virtuous bourgeois woman' (8, 13). Moore addresses the novel's bifurcated discourse, which divided 'romantic friendship' from 'sapphism'. The former is female companionship and the latter is sex between women; one was idealized and the other was a site of cultural anxiety. These two models continued to exhibit a 'dangerous intimacy' in the period, so that the novel had to do the cultural work of severing them. It could do so, because it dramatized varieties of friendship and love between women; and it did do so by moving female friendship from the physical to the psychological. The all-female support community of Scott's *Millenium Hall* (1762) promotes domestic virtue and bourgeois solidarity, rather than a lesbian alternative to heterosexuality. *Fanny Hill* presents homosexual activity as merely preparatory for more fulfilling heterosexual sex. Edgeworth's *Belinda* (1801) evinces 'anxiety over the possibility of sapphic sexuality', because a virtuous heroine is threatened with seduction by a sapphic figure (98). It solves this in part by foisting lesbianism onto a 'racial other', indicating how racial, sexual, and class identity were mutually consolidated. Finally, Austen's Emma must learn self-restraint by rejecting homosocial bonds as the price paid for her ascent to 'female domestic power', achieved when she embraces heterosexual desire (20). The novel, in Moore's account, models femininity as domestic, sexually diffident, and maternal.

Eve Tavor Bannet takes a different tack in her study of 'Enlightenment feminisms and the novel', *The Domestic Revolution* (2000). Rather than analysing fiction as a disciplinary system, she contends that it served an instructional purpose for women coping with the domestic revolution that introduced and subsequently naturalized gendered separate spheres. The family and the domestic realm, Bannet suggests, were 'not yet conceived as secondary to the real business of society or to the serious concerns of men', as they would be under nineteenth- and twentieth-century liberalism.[37] Because the state was generally regarded as analogous to, rather than separate from, the family, philosophical debates about these spheres mutually informed each other. Bannet identifies two models of Enlightenment feminism, which she labels 'Egalitarian' and 'Matriarch' (3). In their response to Locke's challenge to the analogy of state and family, the 1753 Marriage Act, and Rousseau's prescriptive definitions of femininity, these two (unofficial) groupings debated gender relations, and did so by writing didactic fiction for women. In brief, Egalitarians believed gender hierarchy to be a damaging social construct; they promoted equality and denied women's innate domesticity and inferiority. Matriarchs, on the other hand, believed in women's inherently superior sense, and that the patriarchal system had subordinated them through force, but that displaying domestic 'feminine virtues' could help women wrest back control. These two antithetical stances were taken up in fiction that was 'philosophy teaching by example', as 'public' women (novelists) taught 'private' women (readers) through illustrative narration how to govern the family. Egalitarian novelists, like Burney, Hays, and Wollstonecraft, are idealistic, hence less effectual in providing ordinary women with means of empowerment than Matriarchs, like Sarah Scott, Haywood, and Edgeworth. Though the latter promote feminine propriety that seems to reinforce women's subordination, they do so as posture rather than prescription, a tactic for winning authority rather than a collusion with patriarchy.

Helen Thompson's densely-written, but originally argued book, *Ingenuous Subjection* (2005) also looks to rebut theorists, like Armstrong, 'who argue that the domestic novel facilitates the ideological fiction of a private sphere divested of any trace of power'.[38] She argues that the domestic novel marshals a latent critique of male dominance by inscribing what she calls 'ingenuous subjection' – that is, wives' ambivalent and knowing compliance with patriarchal forces as a means of highlighting the arbitrary and artificial nature of that dominance. The early feminist critique of Locke's late seventeenth-century contractarian political philosophy is crucial. Carole Pateman's *The Sexual Contract* (1988) had shown that Locke dismantled *political* patriarchy (monarchical absolutism), but left *gendered* patriarchy in place. In contrast to Locke, Thomas Hobbes had denied *a priori* sexual difference based on physiology. Thompson argues that Hobbes's work enabled first Mary Astell and then a number of eighteenth-century female novelists to explore the difference between *woman* (implying equality of individuals regardless of sex) and *wife* (implying subordination based solely on sex).

The domestic novel, according to Thompson, functioned partly to remind women that their subordinate place in patriarchy was based on social organization and not on nature. It explored the paradox that liberalism notionally ascribed freedom to individuals, but actually insisted that wives were subordinate to their husbands. From Davys's *The Reform'd Coquet*, Defoe's *Roxana*, and Richardson's *Pamela*, Thompson traces 'ingenuous subjection' through novels by Haywood, Lennox, Frances Sheridan, and Wollstonecraft, alongside conduct books and political philosophy. Thompson does not say simply that women gain power through compliance, let alone that the novelists intend as much, but that 'what defines the eighteenth-century novel's representation of women's compliance *as* political is a standard of contractarian virtue which, registered by the persons of women as well as the persons of men, exposes the arbitrariness of Lockean husbands' power' (16). Thompson thus critiques the gender blindness of the pre-eminent historian of the public/private split in early modern culture, Jürgen Habermas, whose seminal *The Structural Transformation of the Public Sphere* (1962) had focused on the bourgeois male sphere of rational discussion that he said first emerged in early eighteenth-century England. Habermas had remarked on the coeval role of the 'intimate sphere of the conjugal family' in the production of bourgeois consciousness and even offered 'the mediocre *Pamela*' as the prototype of the domestic novel, which modelled and enabled relations between 'private' individuals.[39] In Thompson's account, drawing on other feminist criticisms of Habermas, this account of the public sphere is an idealization that ignores actual exclusions, namely women's.

Also advancing on Habermas by fleshing out the import of the 'intimate' sphere is Michael McKeon's monumental *The Secret History of Domesticity* (2005). This book traces the long history of the 'separation out' of the public and the private, categories that are *tacitly* understood in traditional, pre-modern society as *distinct*, but *explicitly* understood in modernity as *different*. This separation, entailing the abstraction of 'public' and 'private' as epistemological categories, McKeon contends, influenced all areas of cultural life in the seventeenth and eighteenth centuries, producing domesticity and its concomitant fictional form, the domestic novel. At the political (and most 'public') level, the separation entails the 'devolution of absolutism' from the sovereignty of the monarch in the absolutist state to the private autonomy of individuals – from political subjecthood to ethical subjectivity. It comprehends what McKeon calls 'virtual publics': the post-Reformation movement from religion as public observation of ritual to personal conviction kept private; the accelerated 'publication of the private' after the seventeenth-century print revolution; the emergence of public opinion as the sum of individual, private perspectives on issues that affect all; the capitalization of production that severed political economy from the production of goods in the household; and the acceleration of the sexual division of labour, which designated the domestic realm feminine and private, the political sphere masculine and public. At the domestic (or 'private') level, this period witnessed the privatization of marriage, the family, and the household, paralleled by the emergence of a new understanding of sexual difference and individual subjectivity.[40] The novel is a crucial agent in domestication.

The cultural history McKeon handles is, I hope, partly familiar from his own earlier work and the concerns of feminist scholars discussed above. Crucially, and in contrast to Armstrong, McKeon does not see domesticity as a mask for political concerns, but rather as the culmination of a process of making politics legible in terms of the domestic, so that domestic novels do not appear apolitical for strategic reasons, but rather absorb, incorporate, and internalize the political within a story that focuses on personal matters. With respect to narrative form and prose fiction, McKeon tracks developments from the end of the sixteenth to the early nineteenth century. Allegorical political romances like Philip Sidney's *Arcadia* and John Barclay's *Argenis* (1621) narrate early modern public crisis: for example, Sidney represents Queen Elizabeth's prospective marriage as a pastoral romance. After the Restoration and amidst the political turmoil of the Stuart dynasty's diminishing authority, Behn's *Love-Letters Between a Nobleman and His Sister* and *romans a clèf* like Manley's *New Atalantis* make public scandal into private romance, an important step on the way 'toward the narration of private life' characteristic of domestic fiction (547). Haywood's progression from politically charged satires to stories of private individuals illustrates the privatization or 'domestication' of experience. Arriving at Richardson, McKeon places *Pamela* as the endpoint of this process of separation and abstraction of public and private. The modern division between public and private constitutes 'the generic division of knowledge that gives British culture the domestic novel' (327). A long process of domestication is replaced by domesticity.

McKeon's book covers much more than generic development and his concerns are not strictly feminist. Indeed, Helen Thompson has since argued that '*Secret History* aggravates the incoherence of the role marriage plays in Habermas's theory', arguing in line with her own *Ingenuous Subjection* that absolutism does not devolve equally on both partners in a marriage. Hence, Thompson claims that McKeon 'evokes a domesticity whose culmination is sealed by its occlusion of the conjugal sphere's native political grievances'.[41] I will have cause to return to some of these questions in the first section of Chapter 9, but the next chapter covers postcolonial and postnational criticism.

CHAPTER SIX

Postcolonialism, Postnationalism, and the Rise of the Novel

Postcolonial criticism's interest in historical literature endeavours to track its complicity in imperial ideology, and the attention postcolonialists have given to the rise of the novel is exemplary in this regard. In addition, critics have addressed the emergent novel's role in propagating both racial and national ideology. The Englishness of the novel, a construction I traced in Chapters 1 and 2, has been challenged by critics who locate the rise of the novel in international cultural exchange.

Imperial ideology and the novel

When postcolonial literary criticism proliferated in the 1980s, certain novels were subjected to criticism that revealed their support for imperialist ideology, perhaps most notably *Robinson Crusoe*. Martin Green traces the genealogy of the adventure novel from Defoe onwards, in which 'dreams of adventure' in fiction cover up 'deeds of empire' in historical fact: popular writers entertain with novels in ways that endorse imperial expansion. Green argues that '*Robinson Crusoe* is a central mythic expression of the modern system, of its call to young men to go out to expand [the] empire'.[1] Peter Hulme places *Crusoe* in a history of narrative encounters between Europeans and Caribbeans. The realism identified by Watt is complicit in *Crusoe*'s mythologization of empire, the ideological construction of the Caribbean as rich pickings in Defoe's 'colonial romance'.[2] The eminent postcolonial theorist, Edward Said, identifies the realistic novel as an agent of imperialism, a connection he sees beginning with Defoe, but continued in the nineteenth-century realist tradition of Austen, Charlotte Brontë, Dickens, and Conrad.[3]

Firdous Azim's *The Colonial Rise of the Novel* (1993) identifies the rising novel as an 'imperial genre'.[4] Azim aims 'to show how the world of the novel is tied to the historical task of colonial, commercial and cultural expansion' (7). She begins with a similar philosophical context to Watt, namely Lockean epistemology: the novel's 'main formal property' was 'the central narrating subject', and its ideological task, in line with the Enlightenment, 'was an attempt to define the subject as homogeneous and consistent' (10). Because it professed to use language in a referential way, assuming that the object of discourse (what a novel is about) and the real world are equivalent, the novel was a tool of European imperialism:

> ■ The birth of the novel coincided with the European colonial project; it partook of and was part of a discursive field concerned with the construction of a universal and homogeneous subject. This subject was held together by the annihilation of other subject-positions. (30) □

Using Said's concept of discourse (indebted to Foucault) and Gayatri Chakravorty Spivak's theories about colonial subject positions (subalterns), Azim argues that novelistic discourse predicates the subjective positions of colonizer and colonized, making the novel 'an imperialist project, based on the forceful eradication and obliteration of the Other' (37). In short, the novel endorsed the universality of the coherent subject, mainly by silencing other groups: women, lower class people, and persons of colour.

Like several feminists, Azim locates *Oroonoko* at the novel's origins, but she challenges feminist understandings, contending that Behn's novel 'does not further the feminist project of establishing the novel as a woman-to-woman discourse'; rather, 'the female first-person authorial voice interjects into the textual terrain merely to highlight racial divisions, which, rather than gender differentiation, is the primary concern of the novel' (59). Behn's narrator, in Azim's interpretation, progressively withdraws from sympathetic identification with the wronged African slave, ultimately affirming a shared identity with Europeans that excludes this exotic 'Other'. Defoe's *Roxana* is important for the novel's movement from colonial adventure (*Oroonoko* and *Robinson Crusoe*) 'into the more domestic and homely domain'. Azim traces 'the shift in the novelistic terrain from a romanticised land to an idealisation of femininity and identity within a more domestic, European setting' (62). She argues that proto-feminism, from Astell in the 1690s to Wollstonecraft in the 1790s, mounted arguments for gender *equality* based on racial *inequality*: comparing women's status to black or oriental slaves' solidified and hierachized racial identity. Equally, the novel 'creates its narrative structures by placing the narrating subject in positions where its desired sovereignty and autonomy are created in conjunction and opposition to these other sites' – that is, sites where there are slaves (66). In *Roxana*, Azim argues, an ideal identity is forged in opposition to 'Others' that include those of a lower status and foreign slaves, which for Azim shows the intersections of race, class, and gender at the moment of the novel's emergence. Her argument is extended in important ways in a 1996 article by Mike Marais, which argues that the 'epistemological underpinnings' of the early novel collude with colonialism, because the development of realism, most famously in *Robinson Crusoe*, perpetuates an empiricist understanding of knowledge that imposes a dichotomy between subject and object, the individual and the world to be conquered.[5]

Azim skips more than a century from Defoe to Brontë: the gap is filled by other critics who set the emergent novel within larger imperial concerns. Laura Brown and Felicity Nussbaum each interrogate intersecting discourses of race, imperialism, and gender in the eighteenth century, including in the novel. In *The Ends of Empire* (1993), Brown takes in Behn's *Oroonoko*, Defoe's *Captain Singleton* (1720) and *Roxana*, and Swift's *Gulliver's Travels* in her examination of how incipient commercialization and colonialism are rendered in literary representations of female corruption, victimization, and sexuality.[6] Nussbaum's *Torrid Zones* (1995) discusses novels such as *Roxana*, *Pamela*, *Fanny Hill*, *The Female Quixote*, *Millenium Hall*, and Phebe Gibbes's *Hartley House, Calcutta* (1789). She traces the imaginative and discursive connections in eighteenth-century culture between the tropical 'torrid zones' of imperial conquest and the female anatomical 'torrid zones' of misogynistic understanding. Nussbaum shows that the emergent ideology of domestic womanhood depended rhetorically on contrasting representations of exotic 'Other' women of empire. For example, Nussbaum juxtaposes *Pamela* with accounts of African travel, showing that polygamy, sometimes proposed as a solution to problems of English sexual relations, was rejected in Richardson's novel in the name of European superiority to African customs.[7]

Also addressing links between the domestic (woman) and imperial (colonies), Maaja Stewart's *Domestic Realities and Imperial Fictions* (1993) assesses Austen's novels' 'deep responsiveness to economic and cultural shifts occurring during the years of revolutions, trade wars, imperial adventurings, and slavery'.[8] Stewart contends that conflicts between older and younger brothers in Austen's novels play out a conflict of values between the traditional landed estate and new money gained by mercantile and colonial activity. Colonel Brandon's sojourn in India, Captain Wentworth's naval career, and Sir Thomas Bertram's trip to Antigua illustrate the argument. In a similar strain to Nancy Armstrong (see Chapter 4), Stewart suggests that the early novel's production of a feminized domestic subjectivity is a political act that masks its political function. In Austen's case, heroines like Anne Eliot and Fanny Price provide cultural reassurance that the values of the hereditary estate will endure in a mercantile and imperialist age.

As well as Austen in the early nineteenth century, Defoe has remained central to the debate about the early novel's imperial agenda.

In a 2003 essay, Brett McInelly reiterates *Robinson Crusoe*'s complicity in empire-building. Notably, he argues that 'British colonial history made the genre of the novel possible', rather than vice versa. The novel's focus on individual character 'defused insecurities' about empire: 'Imperialism contributed significantly to the construction of the focal point of the novel's attention, namely, the individual (British) subject'.[9] But this familiar argument is turned on its head by Robert Markley in *The Far East and the English Imagination* (2006). Markley notes that Defoe's sequel, *The Farther Adventures of Robinson Crusoe* (1719), which witnesses the demise of Crusoe's island colony and the hero's travels in Asia, is usually omitted from accounts of the novel's rise. Markley punningly argues that *Farther Adventures* 'reorients the values and assumptions which traditionally have defined *Robinson Crusoe* and the realist "rise" of the novel', because here Defoe fails to 'bridge the gaps and resolve the inconsistencies within the Eurocentric ideologies of selfhood, economic individualism, and colonialist appropriation'.[10] Markley thus shows how ambivalent the archetypal colonialist novelist, Defoe, actually is about empire in light of European feelings of inferiority in relation to China.

Nation, race, and the rise of the novel

In the last fifteen years, critics have considered the colonial work done by the emergent novel in constructing racial ideologies, in imagining exotic locales of imperial desire, and in consolidating nationalism. Roxann Wheeler, in *The Complexion of Race* (2000), fits the novel's concern with colonialism into her argument that skin colour emerged as a marker of racial identity only in the late eighteenth century. Before then, cultural factors like religion, clothing, cannibalism, marital customs, and economic organization designated racial difference, rather than physical distinctions. These 'other forms of racialization' are illustrated by *Robinson Crusoe* and *Captain Singleton*, in which Defoe both 'establishes and undermines racial differences'.[11] Wheeler then argues that mid-century 'inter-marriage' novels by William Chetwoode, James Annesley, and Henry Brooke play host to the co-presence of race as religiocultural difference and the emergent ideology of skin colour, which she shows takes greater hold by the century's final quarter.

Srinivas Aravamudan's *Tropicopolitans* (1999) is also a cultural history that addresses novels, rather than a genre study. The neologism Tropicopolitan is 'a name for the colonized subject who exists as both fictive construct of colonial tropology *and* actual resident of tropical space, object of representation *and* agent of resistance'.[12] Novels participate in the cultural work of colonialism and in resistance, as Aravamudan analyses the colonialist ideology of Behn's *Oroonoko* and Defoe's mercantile adventure stories. The implications for genre of this work are pursued further by Aravamudan in a 2005 essay, which argues that 'the voluntary parochialization of the vast fiction and nonfictional archive [...] into the artificial unity of a so-called eighteenth-century English or British novel is a nationalist and xenophobic project'. He recuperates 'the particular genre of the surveillance chronicle in the period from 1684–1724', a form of fiction that is concerned with intercultural exchange, the prototype of which is Giovanni Paolo Marana's *Letters Writ by a Turkish Spy* (1684–94), an epistolary story about a Muslim living in Paris, which was a Europe-wide hit. The 'intercultural translations of the tropes of exploration, speculation, and circumspection' illustrated by this narrative and its imitations destabilize the parochially *English* origins of the novel, which 'recuperates fiction for the nation'.[13] The nationalism Aravamudan identifies here will be further explored later in this chapter.

Novels build nations. That is part of the ambitious claim of Benedict Anderson's *Imagined Communities* (1983, 1991). Anderson describes the *imaginative* component of nationalism, a sense of belonging based on mental affinity rather than actual contact with all other members of the state. This concept of nation is particular to the last few centuries, Anderson argues, and it is sustained in part by writing, particularly the newspaper and the novel, two products of the capitalization of print, the move to vernacular languages, and mass literacy.[14] The activity of perusing a newspaper or thumbing through a novel, Anderson argues, fosters a sense of belonging because one *imagines* other members of the nation doing likewise at the same time. This imagined simultaneity of experience is enabled not just by the activity of novel reading but also by the *form* of the novel: as something is happening in one place, the reader has to suppose other things are happening in others. Anderson writes:

> ■ The historical appearance of the novel-as-popular-commodity and the rise of nation-ness were intimately related. Both nation and novel were spawned by the simultaneity made possible by clock-derived, man-made 'homogeneous empty time', and thereafter, of Society understood as a bounded intrahistorical entity. All this opened the way for human beings to imagine large, cross-generation, sharply delineated communities, composed of people mostly unknown to one another; and to understand these communities as gliding endlessly towards a limitless future. The novelty of the novel as a literary form lay in its capacity to represent synchronically this bounded, intrahistorical society-with-a-future.[15] □

This requires some unpacking, particularly Anderson's points about temporality. In talking about 'simultaneity', Anderson reflects on the way that newspaper-reading, an activity synchronously performed by different members of a nation, united them and supplied shared goals. He extends this to the novel by suggesting that its narrative structure allowed for the reader to imagine things happening 'meanwhile' in relation to the action being narrated. An analogous imaginative 'meanwhile' – elsewhere, but within the same world – is necessary for a conception of national homogeneity. Finally, readers of novels are invited to imagine a limitless future, as things could carry on after the ending, which is analogous to the conception of the modern nation.

Anderson is not strictly interested in the ways that particular novels produce national identity – for example, the way in which *Robinson Crusoe* is the avatar of Anglo-Saxon Protestantism, how Fielding's novels envision a roast-beefy England, the advocacy of a unified Britain in *Humphry Clinker*, or the representations of Englishness in Austen's novels. Rather, as Jonathan Culler notes, Anderson considers the novel as supplying a 'condition of possibility' for the origin and spread of nationalism, rather than 'as a force in shaping or legitimating the nation'.[16] The latter idea, however, is taken up by Patrick Parrinder in *Nation and Novel* (2006), which explores 'how the novel has represented the cultural nation of England'.[17] This 'cultural nation' is distinct from the 'political nation' of Great Britain created by the Union of the Scottish with the English and Welsh parliament in 1707, or the United Kingdom after Ireland's incorporation in 1801. In fact, Parrinder starts as early as Malory's *Morte D'Arthur* (1485), a work that now rarely features in histories of the novel. The Arthurian legend, along with other national myths like Robin Hood and Dick Whittington, Parrinder says, has been figuratively replayed in English novels. He infers that the novel's agenda is less the inner life of the individual and more the racial consciousness of a nation. Though *Nation and Novel* is a broad survey of the novel rather than an account of its origins, Parrinder connects the developments of national consciousness during the course of the sixteenth century and the emergence of the novel in the seventeenth. The novel, in this account, is a 'national allegory': the gradual product of particularly Protestant ideas about nationhood from the Reformation to the Restoration, and its rise is tied in with the parallel rises of the concepts of a national literature and a national character (27). The ascent of the novel depended on a sizeable community of readers who spoke the same language and shared roughly the same cultural assumptions.

Other critics have charted the emergent novel's role in what Janet Sorensen calls 'internal colonialism', the incorporation of 'peripheries' (Scotland and Ireland) into Britain. In such accounts, the novel is a 'national form', which forged national identity 'in the period of a coterminous "rise" of nations and novels in Britain in the eighteenth and early nineteenth centuries'.[18] In *Acts of Union* (1998), a study of the literary treatment of the 1707 Union of the English and Scottish parliaments, Leith Davis argues that the novel 'functioned to represent the contradictions of British national identity during' the years following the 1745 Jacobite Uprising.[19] Davis contends that the novel was particularly suited to papering over cracks in British identity made visible by armed support for the banished House of Stuart, which came to a head in 1745. The Jacobite Rebellion forms a backdrop to the action of Fielding's *Tom Jones*, is recent memory in Smollett's fiction, and is the subject of Scott's *Waverley* – novels by authors with pro-union agendas from both sides of the border.

The American rise of the novel

It is conceivable that Watt derived his famous title from Alexander Cowie's *The Rise of the American Novel* (1948).[20] Cowie's study was updated by Cathy N. Davidson's *Revolution and the Word* (1986), a study of American fiction immediately after Independence (1776), which considers the novel as a 'political and cultural forum' for the establishment of a new nation. In this account, experimental fictional form and experimental political organization go hand in hand: the novel contributes to emerging national identity by supplying 'literary versions of emerging definitions of America'.[21] The novel was a relative latecomer to America due to the absence in colonial times of a large reading public, the slow development of printing, and the absence of a book market. Accounts of post-Revolutionary American fiction often identify William Hill Brown's *The Power of Sympathy* (1789) as the first novel written in America by an American citizen.

William Spengeman's 1984 essay subverts this genealogy by labelling *Oroonoko* 'the earliest American novel'.[22] Despite being written by an Englishwoman and being set in Africa and Surinam, Spengeman insists that a more expansive definition of America is required for the period before 1776. It is not just that *Oroonoko* is set in 'British America', but that Behn 'employed a narrative form that had been devised specifically to register those changes, in the shape and meaning of the world and in the concepts of human identity and history, that were prompted by the discovery, exploration, and settlement of America' (407–8). Spengeman's claim, that *Oroonoko* 'anticipate[s] the whole subsequent history of English fiction', is literary and formal, rather than simply geographical (390). Identifying an 'ambiguity of tone that enhances the novelistic effects', he claims that Behn found 'a new way of writing fiction' directly contingent on New World encounter, so that the features that distinguish the novel from other genres 'have an apparent source in the narrative form through which America made its way into the English language' (403, 410).

Whereas Davidson posits the influence on American fiction of Richardson's sentimental prototype, *Pamela*, Nancy Armstrong and Leonard Tennenhouse, in 'The American Origins of the English Novel' (1992), contend that a North American genre – the captivity narrative – was the model for Richardson. They question 'the English origins of the English novel' by addressing stories of English people held captive by Native Americans, such as the tremendously popular *True History of the Captivity and Restauration of Mrs. Mary Rowlandson* (1682).[23] 'Once created', they explain, 'the appetite for narratives of this particular kind never diminished with the rising popularity of fiction on both sides of the Atlantic' (392–3). Armstrong and Tennenhouse note that 'Rowlandson anticipated *Crusoe* in representing the English in the New World as an abducted body', but also that the captivity narrative is 'the prototype of the sentimental fiction identified with Richardson' (393, 403). The novel, then, is not an exclusively 'European genre', but 'one that simultaneously recorded and recoded the colonial experience' (386). The key moment in *Pamela* is the heroine's captivity in her aristocratic master's estate: 'Were it not for the fact that Pamela is locked away in the heart of an older agrarian England, the terms of her captivity would certainly have reminded scholars before now of Rowlandson and all other women captured by Indians' (397). Developing the argument from Armstrong's *Desire and Domestic Fiction* (see Chapter 4), they argue that 'both narratives [...] identify the virtues of the English with the virtues of an ordinary Englishwoman' (398). Stories like Rowlandson's perform colonial work, placing English women as victims of heathenism, 'predispos[ing] us *not* to think of the English as intruders who were decimating the native population and driving it from its homeland' (394). In *The Imaginary Puritan* (1992), Armstrong and Tennenhouse fit this transatlantic account of the novel's origins into a bigger argument about historical developments that brought about modernity: the rise of the middle class and capitalism, the power of print culture in fostering national identity, and alterations in the family, all of which produced the nationalized and individualized 'self'.[24] Armstrong has revisited her argument about individualism in *How Novels Think* (2006), as will be seen in Chapter 9.

Other critics have recently looked for the emergence of the novel in transatlantic cultural exchange. In a 2003 article, Ed White reaches back even further in American history than Armstrong and Tennenhouse or Spengeman, identifying Captain John Smith, of Pocahontas fame, as a 'colonial novelist'. White identifies 'a specific colonial moment for a particular formal innovation', claiming that the 'initial intimate contact with Indian societies inspired and demanded the unifying framework of the novel'. Smith's *The Generall Historie of Virginia* (1624) and *The True Travels, Adventures, and Observations of Captaine John Smith* (1630) participate in what Bakhtin calls 'novelization', a 'multigeneric' response to the multifaceted nature of modernity wrought, in this case, by colonial contact.[25] Elizabeth Maddock Dillon, in a 2005 essay, argues that novels from Britain that represent America and those from the newly formed United States contribute to globalization, as 'the novel participates in articulating the contractual episteme of a world market – both in terms of its possibilities and its limits'. Dillon contends that 'the insistently domestic and familial content of the early novel – in its very emphasis *formulating* the domestic – speaks to the social, economic, and cultural effects of colonialism rather than the particularity of national identity'.[26] In its combination of domestic content and internationalism, Dillon posits, the novel paradoxically facilitates both colonial expansion and nationalist contraction.

The most ambitious, if sometimes rather far-fetched, transatlantic account of the novel's emergence to date is Laura Doyle's *Freedom's Empire* (2008), which identifies the novel as the product of 'Atlantic modernity' stemming from political debates of the 1640s.[27] Doyle counters race-blind attitudes to 'freedom' that she says dominated rise-of-the-novel criticism up to Watt. She shows that 'race first takes shape as a *revolutionary* formation in seventeenth-century England' in the form of 'a uniquely Saxonist legacy of freedom' (2–3). Whilst seventeenth-century Protestant England reconceived its liberal heritage in terms of the (non-Roman, non-Norman) Anglo Saxon past, it was simultaneously participating in a transatlantic slave trade, revealing an 'interproduction of freedom and bondage' (3). British and American novels from the seventeenth to the twentieth century are 'stories of racial destiny': the archetypal novel is a 'liberty plot' with 'racial subtexts' (15–16). This begins with stories that narrate transatlantic crossings (Behn and Defoe) and those that produce a 'nativist discourse' of liberty as a Briton's birthright (Haywood and Richardson) in a world where slavery is other people's birthright (43). Doyle asserts that 'the Anglo-Saxon race's entry into a "state" of liberty is from the beginning associated with an Atlantic crossing and trauma of exile', explaining why in the novel's long history 'the troubled entry into modernity, race, and freedom takes the form of a cataclysmic crossing of the Atlantic Ocean' (4–5).

The racial ideology of freedom was first developed in historical discourse – the conjunction of 'Protestantism, privatization, print, and mercantile colonialism' – before being enshrined in national histories and the novel (21). In Enlightenment historiography after the Civil Wars, 'history is a freedom struggle', a fight to get from bondage to liberty (58). Historians of England like James Harrington, David Hume, and Catherine Macaulay develop this understanding, later adopted by early US national histories, which connect American independence with the Saxon 'freedom plot' of the English Revolution. In turn, 'novels and histories become partners in the project of narrativizing racial liberty, of institutionalizing it as a mode of story' (59). Novels and histories share the narrative potential for promulgating racial ideology, because 'the private, interior event of reading could newly emplace Anglo-Atlantic subjects in a public, racial history' (68). Anglophone novels encode allegories of the English Revolution to disseminate this racial notion of freedom. In *Oroonoko*, Behn 'renarrate[s] the story of England's revolutionary past' to 'fashion a *romance* of history', and 'in this way she begins the work of the Atlantic novel' (103, 115). *Clarissa* is a 'national allegory' of the Civil Wars, as its heroine is 'pressed between the competitive brother of the commonwealth and the open force of the monarchy' – that is, her father's authority (136). Richardson tracks an 'emergent consensus organized around an idea of native liberty', as 'Clarissa embodies a new Protestant nobility, middle-class, modest, and theoretically free' (138–9).

The emergent novel's recurring 'plot of sexual ruin' is also connected to Anglo-Saxon racial destiny (47). Doyle identifies a 'swoon moment', a character fainting and awakening in an altered state, which 'encodes the seventeenth-century Anglo-Atlantic experience of migration, civil war, kidnapping, forced overseas labor, and radical public challenges to class and gender assumptions' (7). This swoon marks a moment of undoing or betrayal. It is developed in an ostensibly sexual context in Haywood, where endangered heroines pass out, and a colonial context in Behn and Defoe, where characters awaken into slavery or slave-driving, but it is given epic importance in *Clarissa*, whose heroine is raped when unconscious. The early novel's concern with rape is part of a broader cultural concern with consent. The Atlantic may be literally absent from many fictions, but the innovation in the depiction of interiority and consent that comprise 'the English-language novel's rape plot has geopolitical sources in Atlantic modernity' (118). In essence, in Doyle's account, the novel emerges as a narrative form capable of sustaining a contradictory ideology of freedom predicated on legitimating slavery.

The international rise of the novel

Recent critics have attempted to place the rise of the novel in the contexts of maritime history and international exchange. First up, *Remapping the Rise of the European Novel* (2007) is a collection of essays that engage with the parochial nature of its primary intertext, Watt's *Rise of the Novel*, which had limited its concerns to eighteenth-century England. The essays variously seek to antedate the novel's rise from the eighteenth century, to claim the importance of non-English traditions, and to show that the sixteenth, seventeenth, or nineteenth century is more crucial for other European traditions, from France, Spain, and Germany to Italy, Russia, and Greece. As Andrew Hadfield says, 'the rise of the novel in Europe was a contingent and discontinuous process'.[28] These essays disabuse readers of the view that eighteenth-century England can be isolated or should be privileged in accounting for the rise of the novel. To give two pertinent examples: first, Diana de Armas Wilson contends that 'the European novel enjoyed multiple rises before the eighteenth century, that it rose with especial vigour in huge polyglot domains of empire, and that its rise was linked to explorations of non-European worlds'.[29] She argues this by comparing *Robinson Crusoe* with Heliodorus' *Aethiopica* (c. 225–250 CE) and Cervantes's *Persiles y Sigismunda* (1617). Second, Kate Williams analyses the liberality with which French novels were translated into English as a way of stressing the importance of intercultural exchange to the progress of the novel.[30] The developments in non-literal translation Williams described are addressed by Mary Helen McMurran's *The Spread of Novels* (2010).

McMurran recasts the rise of the novel as part of a shift in the practice of translation. Before the eighteenth century, translation involved amplification, omission, and adaptation: the original work was used more as a source than as an authoritative text. There was frequently uncertainty or indifference about whether a work was translated. Some translations purported to be original, others were falsely labelled translations as a publisher's ploy, authors and translators were not always distinguished or they remained anonymous, and sometimes works were unwittingly retranslated into their original language. Moreover, translation was not considered specialized work, but derided as hack writing, or treated as a leisured, non-professional activity. Readers were often multilingual, which obviated the need for fidelity. And French and English were not considered fundamentally different languages – they were 'analog languages': vernaculars, to be differentiated from the 'transportive languages', Latin and Greek. McMurran argues that, enabled by the laxity of copyright law, there was a thriving trade in cross-Channel exchange, which made prose fiction 'a melting pot rather than a series of nation-to-nation trades', in which 'the novel consolidated as a genre because it was a stranger nowhere, a circulatory phenomenon that linked languages and regions'.[31]

However, McMurran sees a change occurring in the mid-eighteenth century. Readers before then accepted fictions as mobile, fluid, multilingual affairs, 'but the shift in translating from a premodern, thick system of transmission to modern literary exchange between nations brought about the consolidation of fictions into the form we refer to as the novel'

(20). A new belief in the incommensurability of different languages and a new awareness of national identity occasioned this shift: 'Around the 1740s, fiction translating in particular began to reflect English and French discourses about the nation' leading commentators 'to distinguish novels more frequently based on their national origin' (114). *Pamela* reflects, first, the new nationalism, because it is purposely differentiated from French literature; and, second, a new view of translation, because Richardson ensured that the French version was faithful, so that the author's message was retained. Paradoxically, at the very moment novels were held to be representative of a single national culture, a new idea of the novel's universality developed. Richardson's second novel laid claim to universal, human values that transcended nation: 'The *Clarissa* event unleashed both the acceptance of the English novel in a new nationalized novel system and a form of cosmopolitanizing in which the literary form captured the universal "human heart"' (123). The Abbé Prévost's abridged translation of *Clarissa* was seen as a 'mutilation': presumably no one would have cared earlier in the century. Denis Diderot's *Eloge de Richardson* (1762), elevating its subject to a status that transcends nationality, suggests that the forces of universal appeal and national embodiment have been in competition throughout the history of the novel.

McMurran's claim that the novel emerged from 'a complex cultural discourse of nation-based cosmopolitanism peculiar to the mid-eighteenth-century cross-Channel area' (100) is supported by the essays collected in *The Literary Channel* (2002). These essays situate the 'inter-national invention of the novel' in Anglo-French exchanges during a period of 'cultural transnationalism' that 'predated the modern nation's emergence as an imagined community'. Doing so reveals the novel's part in 'the construction of a sentimental code of universal humanity that transcends the worldly interests of nation'.[32] The essays show that in the period, up to about 1760, 'the subject of the novel was less nation than normative humanness without markers of exclusive national identity', such as in the sentimental 'subgenre', which depicted 'the interior, emotional qualities that demarcate a distinctive shared humanity' (18). After 1760, fiction on both sides of the Channel was engaged in the cultural work of shoring up national boundaries and was increasingly conceptualized as a national form.

Margaret Cohen also challenges accounts of the novel based on impermeable national boundaries in *The Novel and the Sea* (2010), foregrounding 'the specific impact of maritime history on the novel' in 'the global age of sail'.[33] She claims that 'sea adventure fiction' is a neglected mode which depicts action rather than psychology, work rather than education or love, and homosocial masculine community rather than heterosexual, private sociability. The genre is kick-started with *Robinson Crusoe*, which advanced 'a new poetics of adventure' that existed 'in competition with the success of the maritime book' (7). That is, *Crusoe* adapts techniques from nonfictional sea voyage literature, including a plain prose style, a predilection for accounting, and a propensity for 'remarkable occurrences', extreme events at sea that structure episodic adventure fiction. 'Defoe's association of his writing with the maritime print corpus was a bid for popularity and prestige', Cohen explains (60). The novel derived its status, as Adams had argued (see Chapter 3), from its affiliation with factual maritime writing.

Cohen contends that '*Robinson Crusoe* initiated a wave of maritime adventure fiction across the 1720s to 1740s in Great Britain and France', a genre she dubs the 'maritime picaresque', due to its focus on itinerant, marginalized individuals (88). As well as Defoe's *Captain Singleton* and *A New Voyage round the World* (1725), Cohen discusses Rufus Chetwood's *Voyages and Adventures of Captain Robert Boyle* (1726), Charles Johnson's *A General History of the Pyrates* (1724–8), Prévost's *La Jeuness du Commandeur* (1741) and *Les Voyages de Captaine Lade* (1744), and Smollett's *Roderick Random*. Cohen then notes the relative absence of sea adventure in fiction from 1748 to 1824. She explains this hiatus in a number of ways. First, glancing at Benedict Anderson, she asserts that 'these years coincide with the moment when the novel was engaged in unifying the nation as an imagined community in the English and French traditions', which entailed 'the novel's pervasive association at this time with feminized sociability' (102, 103). Second, Cohen posits that adventure fiction faced stiff market competition from voyage literature during the great age of discovery dominated by Captain Cook. Finally, the Romantic reconceptualization of the sea as a sublime, threatening, awe-inspiring terrain for the isolated individual kept it out of polite fiction. Although developments in the novel's focus and in the aesthetic use of the ocean occasioned 'hydrophasia', or a forgetting of the sea, James Fenimore Cooper, looking back at the maritime picaresque of Smollett, revitalized sea adventure fiction with *The Pilot* (1824), and its importance to the novel continued in the nineteenth century.

Conclusion

Postcolonial and postnational criticism has played an important role in revealing the imperial, nationalistic, and racial ideologies that shaped the emerging novel. It has challenged the association of the novel with Englishness that has dominated rise-of-the-novel criticism since the nineteenth century when histories of fiction were first written in terms of isolable national traditions. The next chapter backtracks slightly, turning to revisionist studies of the novel's development written during the 1990s.

CHAPTER SEVEN

Rethinking the Rise of the Novel, 1990–2000

The 1990s and the new millennium produced a considerable amount of revisionist scholarship that sought to complicate the enduringly authoritative account of the novel's rise offered by Ian Watt. With the launch of *Eighteenth-Century Fiction* in 1988, the subject gained a dedicated journal. In the previous two chapters, I surveyed feminist and postcolonial work which overlaps chronologically and sometimes methodologically with the accounts discussed here. Collectively, the work in this chapter approaches the early novel less as a cohesive literary form and more as a contested historical discourse – in the period itself and in later reconstructions. The chapter finishes with the special issue of *Eighteenth-Century Fiction*, called *Reconsidering the Rise of the Novel* (2000).

Formalism and historicism

J. Paul Hunter's *Before Novels* (1990) is one of the most readable and wide-ranging treatments of the early novel. He makes an important methodological case for cultural historicism, reading texts as contingent products of particular cultural moments and rejecting essentialist approaches to genre. Hunter aims 'to restate the case for the novel as a distinct and definable literary form that exists in time, that emerges and develops in a particular context (although not, shazam, full-blown at a certain moment), and that has a particular place in the history of cultural phenomena'.[1] He rejects ahistorical theoretical trends, from New Criticism to structuralism, that disregard context. Acknowledging criticism levelled at Watt for ignoring developments elsewhere, Hunter expressly limits his investigation to England, stating that 'the crucial *formative* influences on the species are historical, cultural, and particular, and [...] these need to be sorted out in detail for each national strand before moving too quickly to the intertwinings' (xxii). *Before Novels* thus illuminates the historical conditions that provided fertile ground for the emergence of the novel in England. Hunter analyses what he calls the novel's 'pre-texts': 'the materials that readers read before there were novels to read – materials that were often non-narrative, non-fictional, and non-literary in the accepted modern sense' (xvi).

The cultural desire for novelty resulted in three waves of 'novelistic' production. The first, in the 1690s, was trans-generic, not just involving prose fiction (16). One of its main suppliers was John Dunton, founder of *The Athenian Mercury* (1690–7), a populist periodical that published 'strange and surprising' stories that pretended to be new and true, and advised its readers on everyday topics. This prefigures the concentrated spurt of novels in the 1720s, with Defoe and others, and then the more self-conscious innovations of the 1740s, with Richardson and Fielding. Against Watt's singular and linear rise, Hunter proposes a twin rise. Though the term 'novel' had neither stability nor cultural respectability until well into the next century, by the time Clara Reeve wrote *The Progress of Romance* (1785) certain aspects of novels were generally accepted (see Chapter 1). Hunter lists ten features that constitute a 'working definition' of the novel (23–5):

1. Contemporaneity.
2. Credibility and probability.
3. Familiarity.
4. Rejection of traditional plots.
5. Tradition-free language.
6. Individualism and subjectivity.
7. Empathy and vicariousness.
8. Coherence and unity of design.
9. Inclusivity, digressiveness, and fragmentation.
10. Self-consciousness about innovation and novelty.

The list moves between the kind of life the novel depicts (the believable, here-and-now of everyday experience), how it is presented (in ordinary language which foregrounds individual perception), and how readers engaged with this material (sympathetically, to learn about the world, and, increasingly, aesthetically, albeit with formal expectations alien to us).

From formal properties, Hunter moves to social contexts. The first is readership: revisiting the evidence for an increase in literacy, Hunter concludes (notwithstanding scanty evidence) that 'literacy in the English-speaking world grew rapidly between 1600 and 1800' (65). Correlation of increased literacy with the novel's growth is not evidence of a causal connection, because steep rises in literacy do not simply align with novelistic production, but Hunter does infer that readerly demand is crucial to shifts in literary form. Readers 'create texts by communicating, though not necessarily consciously or directly, their needs and desires to those in a position to make books' (xix). Like Watt, Hunter emphasizes capitalism, developments in print technology, urbanization, and the individualizing tendencies of Protestantism as important factors in providing a field of possibility for the novel. The following synopsis reveals a validation and expansion of Watt: 'The early novel's insistent attention to daily life in contemporary circumstances among more-or-less ordinary human beings who communicate in informal language signals a whole range of powerful attractions for eighteenth-century readers' (91). Novels supplied entertainment and instruction to readers newly interested in the here-and-now and sought to help those readers answer, like Dunton, practical questions about everyday existence. These novel desires and desires for novels successfully weathered the backlash from conservative cultural commentators. The novel, in Hunter's account, is also a product of an increasingly urban population: London is central to many novels, with its starker social inequality, faster pace of life, commercialism, alienation, and waning sense of community. The break with tradition at this time is indicated as much by the disappearance of fairy tales as it is by the emergence of the novel: the cultural needs once met by oral fairy tales were gradually being satisfied by printed fictions. This is symptomatic of an aggressive distrust of past culture, which is consonant with a fascination for novelty, plus the movement away from communal reading customs and towards silent, private reading. The taste for novelty and for stories relevant to experience led to particular and probable stories which eschewed the supernatural and distant.

Before Novels recovers the wide range of things people read prior to the novel's rise. This includes journalism: as well as newspapers, pamphlets, and criminal biographies, there were occasional meditations, which extracted meaning from everyday objects, and Books of Wonders, that dealt in strange happenings. All these forms of journalism were concerned with the present moment, all fuelled and satisfied the cultural desire for novelty, and all validated empiricism through documentary, eyewitness reportage that helped readers interpret the world. These readers wanted and expected such guidance, and Hunter 'describe[s] how the concerns and methods of didacticism came to affect the novel formally, structurally, ideologically, and phenomenologically' (247). The novel took its materials from religious treatises, sermons, conduct books, and a 'guide' tradition, which provided practical instruction for regular men, women, and children on issues ranging from cookery and housekeeping, to trade and conversation, all the way to discerning the likelihood of one's eternal salvation. Hunter posits that the didactic books' injunctions to self-examination and combination of precepts and narrative illustrations directly informed the novel. Finally, Hunter addresses historical modes, starting with 'private' forms such as spiritual autobiographies and memoirs, as 'attitudes began to soften about the uses of privacy and about the propriety of making personal history public if it could conceivably have edifying effects' (316). As well as often adopting the same form, 'the novel reaps from autobiography a capacity for introspection, self-awareness, and subjectivity' (329). Meanwhile, genres with a more objective than subjective, public than private, dimension, like history, biography, and travel books, influence the novel's concern with 'broader human issues of place and time' (355). Hunter's *Before Novels* is certainly the most capacious or holistic approach to the rise of the novel through cultural history.

Margaret Anne Doody's review of *Before Novels* illustrates some methodological differences between formalism and historicism. Doody objects that Hunter 'is very desirous that the eighteenth-century English novel be considered a new genre, without predecessors, and he is anxious to eliminate that bad old world of romance from our view'. Her own approach would include earlier continental literature, an acknowledgement that realism is not a defining feature, and attention to the 'multiplex forms' of fiction, which would reveal 'that the English had a much less central position' in its history. Doody concludes by stating that 'talk of the cultural moment conceals beneath its historicism a claim to power'.[2] From a formalist vantage, she sees historicism as a nationalistic and androcentric project. The principal claim of Doody's subsequent book, *The True Story of the Novel* (1996), is that 'the Novel as a form of literature in the West has a continuous history of about two thousand years'.[3] Doody dismisses 'parochial' accounts that locate the novel's rise in eighteenth-century England.

Doody's definition of the novel is minimalist and hence capacious – 'a work is a novel if it is fictional, if it is in prose, and if it is of a certain length' – which includes ancient narratives, medieval romances, and early modern prose fictions (16). The popular critical division of romance and novel for Doody is facile. She explains how and why pre-modern literature came to be left out of the narrative of the novel's rise, identifying two important seventeenth-century historians of romance, Salmasius and Huet (see Chapter 1), who believed that romances derived from the Mediterranean basin in antiquity. Doody suggests that this ancient and international genesis was increasingly rejected as national agendas took hold, a process accelerated in eighteenth-century England. The print revolution and the greater visibility of women writing and reading novels caused a backlash that debased the novel by feminizing it: 'To pretend that the novel is primarily directed towards females (including those of both middle and upper classes) is reassuring, for women (unlike youthful male aristocrats) are theoretically disabled from bringing concepts into social currency' (278). Doody does not buy into the narrative of privatization and domestication propounded by Armstrong (see Chapter 4). She thinks this is 'a true enough description of something wished for by cultural regulators', but not what actually happened (278).

Nonetheless, the eighteenth century attempted to enervate the novel, to deny its power by limiting it to the quotidian, the prosaic, and the contemporary. By this time, 'the Novel or Romance needs much more defense than it used to require' (281). It increasingly started to define itself against the past, and realism became the norm due to restrictive authoritative pressures: 'We may sense in the increasing pressure to produce novels that are lifelike, probable, verisimilar, an effort to tie the Novel down, to clip its wings so that it will not be guilty of the extravagances of moral imagining' (285–6). With this 'prescriptive realism' came a 'great forgetting' of the novel's ancestry. It is not that, as Watt claimed, realism was new to this period, but that it became dominant, and Doody sees 'the Rise of Realism [...] as a political event, and a direct – if delayed – effect of Huet's establishment of the international history of the Novel' (287). She locates the rise of realism not in Defoe's formal innovation, but in Charlotte Lennox's apparent rejection of romance for realism in the denouement of *The Female Quixote*. Realism has mainly dominated the novel since the mid-eighteenth century and has written its own partisan history, which Doody believes Watt, McKeon, and Hunter are guilty of perpetuating.

The methodological differences between Hunter and Doody are those between a cultural historian and an archetypal formalist. To this extent, this debate replays the conflict between the approaches of Frye and Watt in 1957, discussed in Chapter 2. Hunter engages directly with Frye and archetypalism as part of his insistence that particular historical and cultural questions are more a propos than expansive formal ones. In what serves as a riposte *avant la lettre* to Doody, Hunter states that 'making all prose fiction, from all ages and places, into the novel is not a serious way of dealing with either formal or historical issues'.[4] Doody constructs a timeless continuum, downplaying the influence of social history on genre, disregarding distinctions between prose fiction forms, and assessing the 'deep rhetoric' of the novel that manifests in a number of recurrent motifs, or tropes, from antiquity to now (304). It is an account in which the novel has no history and can negate historical difference. By contrast, the majority of criticism of the early novel has, since 1990, been primarily historicist, though also evincing scepticism, like Doody, about the novel's partisan history, its retroactive construction as a stable discourse, and its tactical self-definition against other forms, raising a number of problems with Ian Watt's *The Rise of the Novel*.

Historiography

William Ray's *Story and History* (1990) is a comparatist account of French and English fiction, which considers the novel's role in the rise of 'a genuine historical consciousness'.[5] Ray examines the interactions between 'personal story' (novel) and 'public account' (history), arguing that 'the French and English traditions both lead to a vision of social reality as the product of a competitive economy of collective narration' (51). The early phase of the novel – Lafayette and Defoe – reflects an antagonistic relationship of the individual to the social, but with Marivaux and Richardson, 'individualism is recast in terms of a communal discourse' and personal narration yields to the shared narration of history (105). By the time of Fielding, protagonists are learning social responsibility, and in Rousseau the novel consolidates its 'position as a mode of learning about the contemporary world' (266). Sterne, Diderot, and Laclos show history to be an inescapable force, integral to the definition of individuals, which is markedly different from Defoe, where self and world are separate. Ray reflects on the disappearance of personal narration from the nineteenth-century novel, which reflects not just historic preferences, but also the novel's 'cloak of innocence', by which it claims to be representing rather than shaping reality (316). What Ray ultimately establishes through extended close readings is that the rise of individualism is met by the formation of the social, which results in the novel transforming conceptions of history.

Rather than history *per se*, Everett Zimmerman's *The Boundaries of Fiction* (1996) addresses 'fiction's responsiveness to developments in historiography', that is, the writing of history.[6] Zimmerman argues that 'the novel constitutes itself from its interactions with history': 'It is constituted as a new kind of writing through its differentiation of itself from conventional assumptions about poetry or imaginative literature and through its accommodations to assumptions about history' (222). The novel opportunistically imitates history's objection to imaginative writing, but also muscles in on history's realm. History in one form or another is precisely what writers like Defoe, Richardson, and Fielding claim they are writing, of course. And though the novel does not take history as its subject explicitly until Scott, Defoe fictionalized the 1665 plague, *Tom Jones* is organized around the 1745 Jacobite uprising, and the events of the Nine Years' War (1688–97) are behind the battle re-enactments in *Tristram Shandy*. The novel's relationship to history-writing is combative: fiction provides 'a critique of historical studies as a way of making a place for itself' (4). Not simply feigning authenticity, 'eighteenth-century novels explore the basis of narrative authority, raising questions about the evaluation of evidence contained in writing' (11). The new novel was regarded as a threat to genuine history – the 'truth' – because it substituted a more stimulating though less accurate representation of reality. As such, 'the novel exposed the limits of the verifiable and the inevitability of a narrative perspective (even in history) that is rooted in time, place, and individuality, not in abstract truth and universality' (21). The novel discredited history's rival claim to authority by claiming an affinity with history.

Zimmerman invokes the postmodern understanding of history, derived from philosopher Paul Ricoeur, as an *emplotment* of *traces*: 'traces' are physical remnants of the past, most obviously documents; 'emplotment' refers to the construction of narrative. Because history is an emplotment of traces, it is fictive – partial, selective, biased. The eighteenth-century novel exploits these qualities of history to argue its own greater truth, a claim made most fully by Godwin in 'Of History and Romance' (1797). The novel is part of what Zimmerman characterizes as 'skeptical historiography' – a new demand for verifiability that infected both sacred and secular history. He borrows the term 'figura' from theorist Erich Auerbach; it refers to a providential worldview that sees history in terms of 'the biblical master narrative' (62). In line with some contemporary challenges to the historicity of scripture, culminating in Hume's denial of miracles and revelation, the novel reflects the shift from 'figura' to 'trace'. The eighteenth century increasingly viewed the Bible less as a master narrative giving doctrinal certainty and more as a collection of historical documents, the truths of which were improbable when tested against experience. The 'figural view of history', which is intact in Bunyan's *The Pilgrim's Progress*, is fractured by the time of Defoe (88). Crusoe's journal, struggling to reconcile experience with providential order, exemplifies what Zimmerman means by 'trace'; *A Journal of the Plague Year*, similarly constructed out of the documents of the past, registers an inability to fit history into a figural order of significance. Zimmerman, then, follows the line of scholarship that sees new secular, empirical epistemology producing the novel.

In Zimmerman's account, Swift's *A Tale of a Tub* is a progenitor of the novel, attacking forms of textual and historical scholarship (later picked up in fiction) in response to 'the battle of the books', a historiographical debate over the competing merits of 'ancient' and 'modern' learning. Whereas Swift was an 'Ancient', wary of modern historical compilation, Richardson was a 'Modern': he posed as the historian-collector behind an archival collection of putatively authentic documents, his novel *Clarissa*. Next, Zimmerman considers the dissolution of providential plotting by comparing *Tom Jones* and *Caleb Williams* (1794). Zimmerman focuses on Fielding's mediation of a divine plan through the plotting of a historian, which draws attention to the limitations of historiography. Fifty years later, Godwin rejects Fielding's figural narrative, explaining *human* institutions in human terms: '*Caleb Williams* finds that the sweeping narrative concatenation of a book like *Tom Jones* is itself misleading because of its failure fully to acknowledge the powerful institutions that govern even its consensual truths' (177). *Tristram Shandy* and Henry Mackenzie's *The Man of Feeling* (1771) thematize the problematic construction of the past out of material traces, in order to advance the novel's critique of historiography. For example: 'Like the Bible revealed by textual criticism, the interpolated tales of *Tristram Shandy* disintegrate into damaged texts, poor translations, and dubious proveniences' (199). Zimmerman concludes with Walter Scott, who marks the shift from 'historicized fiction', which adopts techniques from history-writing, to the historical novel, which takes history as its subject. Scott, then, repairs the 'boundary' between fiction and history at the moment when the novel moves to the aesthetic.

Although like Zimmerman he states that 'the novel was a fictional form that could do the work of history', Robert Mayer, in *History and the Early English Novel* (1997), takes a different tack, arguing that seventeenth-century historiography was a constitutive part of novelistic discourse.[7] He outlines what he calls 'Baconian historiography', historical practices connected to the early seventeenth-century writer Francis Bacon. Mayer analyses Baconian historiography's various manifestations in the seventeenth century, which constituted the discursive matrix of what was subsequently called the novel. Baconian historiography 'featured a taste for the marvelous, a polemical cast, a utilitarian faith, a dependence upon personal memory and gossip, and a willingness to tolerate dubious material for practical purposes, all of which led to the allowance of fiction as a means of historical representation' (4). Early eighteenth-century readers would have accepted novelists' claims to be giving them 'matters of fact': the novel was part of a historical discourse that tolerated fiction.

What, then, were the features of Baconian historiography? Mayer shows that history was a means of persuasion, despite its theoretical commitment to impartiality. It entailed a new scientific approach to the past through the compilation of documents. It sanctioned fiction, seeing invention as no breach of faith, justifying fiction as instructive, and identifying only the intention to deceive as mendacious. It acknowledged that a lack of certainty is legitimate in history, but privileged the authority of the participant. And it accepted that history should be used to dictate action in the present. Mayer traces these aspects in the sceptical yet tolerant treatment of myths, like those of Brut and Arthur, which were retained in authoritative histories until well into the eighteenth century, which indicates the persistence of tradition and tolerance for fiction in history. In *The History of Myddle* (1700–9), Mayer discerns the application of antiquarian methods to an anecdotal, communal, and utilitarian kind of history. In the highly personal histories of the English Civil Wars written by the Earl of Clarendon, Richard Baxter, and Lucy Hutchinson, Mayer shows that a partial (biased *and* incomplete) perspective posed less of a problem for early readers than for modern historians. Likewise, secret histories, which exposed the scandalous private lives of public figures, fused fact and fiction and were transparently partisan. History catered to the demand for 'knowing strange things', the taste for the strange and surprising. By contrast, over the course of the eighteenth century, in the age of Enlightenment historiography typified by Hume, Robertson, and Smollett, 'history ostensibly became a far more disinterested form of intellectual inquiry', as fiction, rhetoric, and polemic were banished (139).

For Mayer, Defoe is 'the central figure in the emergence of the novel', and in many respects Mayer has been reading backwards from Defoe in order to establish the *horizon of expectations* of Defoe's earliest readers (182). This term comes from the reception theorist, Hans Robert Jauss, who argued that meaning is produced in the dialogue between the author's text and the reader's expectations. Jauss argues that particular works could transform readers' expectations, thereby creating a new horizon. Mayer's point is that in Defoe's career we see the fictive element of Baconian historiography hiving off into something new: 'The novel in England was constituted upon a dialogue between the fictional and the historical within a new discourse that asserted the power of fiction to do the work of history' (140). It is not simply that Defoe was the first novelist, but that he was what Foucault would call an 'initiator of discursive practice', because his works challenged readers to rethink the boundaries between fiction and history (159). Defoe's fictions were written within the discursive possibilities of history – specifically, Baconian historiography. However, because 'Defoe's historical practice forces the fact-fiction dilemma upon the reader' in an unprecedented way, these narratives initiated a new discourse, novelistic discourse, into which they were then retroactively incorporated in the nineteenth century, at which time Defoe was 'read into the discourse of the novel' (160, 156). However, Mayer surmises that the novel, from its origins to postmodernism, 'has militated against the view that fictionality and historicity are mutually exclusive' (234). The novel emerged from history-writing, but history remains a constitutive part of the novel.

More recently, Frank Palmeri's *Satire, History, Novel* (2003) establishes a 'genealogical' model of generic change in which emergent forms challenge, appropriate, and disavow earlier ones. Palmeri claims: 'In the second half of the eighteenth century novelistic and historical forms of narrative came to occupy dominant positions comparable to the one occupied by satiric narrative in the first decades of the century – partly by defining themselves in opposition to satire, but also by appropriating satiric elements'.[8] Palmeri thus extends the work of Paulson (see Chapter 3). He suggests that this transition occurs at variable rates in Britain compared to France and Germany due to the earlier appearance of the Habermasian public sphere in Britain (see Chapter 5). Palmeri accounts for generic change through two successive 'paradigm shifts' (a term coined by the scientist, Thomas Kuhn, describing the change from one dominant worldview to another). First, a 'skeptical and paradoxical' seventeenth-century cultural paradigm yields to a more assured, moderate one in the eighteenth century, before the onset of an organic one by the turn of the nineteenth century: respectively, these paradigms resemble the traditional labels Renaissance, Enlightenment, and Romanticism. The generic displacement of satire is traced through wide-ranging examples of narrative in a number of genres: satiric almanac, historical memoir-novel, philosophical history, historical novel, conjectural history, and *Bildungsroman*. Whereas Zimmerman and Mayer place history and novel in competition, Palmeri sees them acting in concert to displace satire.

With a different perspective on the interaction of novel and history, Karen O'Brien's 2005 essay argues that these evolved in parallel but separate ways, reacting to each other. The novel first distances itself from historical modes, but then conforms to historical practices when it is better established. Against Mayer, O'Brien argues that historicity and fictionality were fairly well understood as distinct when fictions were claiming to be fact. After the novel had preponderantly distanced itself from history, history borrowed strategies from fiction to move away from certain classical conventions towards 'affective' ones, encouraging readers' identification with (historical) characters in similar ways to novels. In turn, the novel rediscovers history, appropriating the historiographical attempt to show the development of manners, in order to legitimate itself, and thereby developing a greater historical sense.[9]

The rise of novelistic discourse

Joseph Bartolomeo's *A New Species of Criticism* (1994) surveys eighteenth-century writing about the novel – in treatises, periodical reviews, and novels themselves – because 'moving the discourse to the foreground will demonstrate the constitutive cultural role it played, its success in forging a place for the genre in literary and popular culture'.[10] He finds the most prominent characteristic of eighteenth-century novelistic discourse is a resistance to closure, as the novel remained an amorphous, malleable form until the nineteenth century. Early-century prefaces to novels, from Congreve to Defoe, and including many female authors, vary between claiming artistic respectability, moral purpose, or actual truth. Bartolomeo finds that Defoe's prefaces take the discourse on the novel further than his contemporaries, because they evolve from simple truth claims to 'a reader-oriented aesthetic' and claims for conscious artistry (44). Prefaces are less defensive later in the century as fiction becomes more acceptable, meaning they could be used in parodic ways or as a forum for espousing a poetics of fiction. Following the mid-century contest between Richardson and Fielding, morality, probability, and originality were taken up as novelistic desiderata in the periodical press, which started to review new novels in the 1740s and 50s. Predominantly harsh assessments were 'a self-conscious attempt on the part of the reviewers to stratify the genre and its audience, in order to establish and maintain authority over an elite class of readers' (114). Novels were deemed too numerous, a corruption of standards, or a predominantly female genre until late in the century. Reviews did, however, offer advice which helped to shape the novel: they contributed to the sense in the later part of the century that the novel was splitting into subgenres (Gothic, sentimental, oriental), and they increasingly validated the artistry of prose fiction and normalized realism as its highest standard. Bartolomeo ultimately calls the eighteenth-century discourse on the novel a critical heteroglossia, drawing on Bakhtin's concept of the novel's dialogic form: certain prescriptions and predilections were important, but the debate on the novel never became monologic.

As we saw in Chapter 1, critical commentary on fiction from the late eighteenth-century onwards generally privileges Richardson and Fielding as originators of the novel. In *Licensing Entertainment* (1998), William Warner sets about explaining why this is the case. He argues that the 'elevation' of the novel was not an effort to install a new literary form, but rather an attempt to reform reading practices in response to the onset of a market-driven 'media culture'.[11] Defoe, Richardson, and Fielding were reacting to the 'novels of amorous intrigue' written by Behn, Manley, and Haywood, and trying to dignify the novel by differentiating their efforts from these predecessors. Warner centralizes the dynamic novelistic genre of amatory fiction that proliferated in an expanding market for print entertainment. He reveals how it was later erased from the literary record because of its incompatibility with the serious status to which the novel aspired. And he shows how first Defoe and then, more systematically, Richardson and Fielding were engaged in an attempt 'to absorb and overwrite the novels of Behn, Manley, and Haywood' (277). Thus, Warner reframes the Richardson-Fielding rivalry in terms of a common project to elevate novel reading, one which basically succeeded as the novel gained what the philosopher Pierre Bourdieu calls 'cultural capital'.

Warner traces a long process of canonization, running from the eighteenth-century 'anti-novel discourse' to Ian Watt, whereby 'the novel' was discursively delimited to make it English, edifying, and realistic. By contrast, the 'novels of amorous intrigue' appeared sexually immoral, French, and unrealistic. People mistrusted novels in the early eighteenth century because they exemplified market conditions: anonymity, social mobility, commercial motivations, exploitation of desire, and obliviousness to moral effects. The cultural response was to stereotype the novel-reader as female. If the defence of fiction around 1720 is that novels are true and are morally edifying (Defoe), the claim around 1750 is that novels have cultural value (Richardson and Fielding). Subsequently, discourse on the novel treats it as a form for transmitting valuable social knowledge. Its scandalous origin in amatory fiction is increasingly occluded in discussions from Reeve (1785) and Dunlop (1814) to Raleigh (1894), and Saintsbury (1913), all of whom I discussed in Chapter 1. As well as imputing moral seriousness to the novel, by the nineteenth century historians were thinking in nationalistic terms, trying to identify the *English* origins of the *English* novel, and finding these in Protestantism, empiricism, and middle-class morality. Frenchified romances like Behn's, Manley's, and Haywood's were written out of the history of the novel's development. Certain formal aspects of certain works were labelled 'realistic', and then this was made a precondition for all novels.

Warner recovers these neglected prose fictions by analysing Behn's *Love-Letters Between a Nobleman and His Sister*, Manley's *New Atalantis*, and Haywood's *Love in Excess*. The trajectory of amatory fiction proceeds from Behn's importation of the conventions of French romance to Manley's use of fantasy for satirical political purposes and Haywood's making it a successful, saleable formula. Behn turned from stage-writing to print publication because the latter was less heavily regulated; her novelistic entertainments were 'licensed by the market'. Warner counters the feminist assumption (see Chapter 5, especially Ballaster's *Seductive Forms*) that amatory fiction represents a gendered discourse that presupposes a female readership; the evidence is that men and women alike read these books, notwithstanding the cultural effort to trivialize them as feminine. An important aspect of Warner's approach is his reading novels as mini-allegories of the developments of reading he is describing, so that Behn's Silvia personifies the novel on the market, Manley's stories of seduction stage the seduction of the reader, and Haywood thematizes the absorptive reading that her fictions encourage. This continues when he turns to the backlash against amatory fiction and absorptive reading in Defoe, Richardson, and Fielding.

Defoe's *Roxana* is interpreted as a parodic version of amatory fiction, 'shaped to produce an ethical alternative to prevailing patterns of reading for entertainment' (150). Defoe writes in direct dialogue with his female forebears, partly to inject morality into licentious stories, but equally to exploit their appeal, which compromises Defoe's didactic efficacy. Amatory fiction would be overcome not by repudiation but by assimilation, and that is Richardson's job. *Pamela* is an allegory of reformed reading, which stages in Mr. B's conversion after reading Pamela's letters the same thing it aims to effect in readers. Though Richardson tried to make entertainment appear the goal when it was really the means to edification, *Pamela* was read as a salacious book, most memorably by Fielding. Warner argues that *Joseph Andrews* is a critique of both absorptive reading and Richardsonian didacticism. Fielding presented his novels as entertainment and as artifice; he tries to diminish the arbitrary control of the author and to make readers think for themselves, becoming critics in the process. *Joseph Andrews* encodes a lesson in how novels should be read, which illustrates the principle that the novel was generated by the tastes of its readers, not by generic imperatives or individual authors' innovations.

Taking a similar line to Warner, Bradford Mudge, in *The Whore's Story* (2000), argues that pornography and the novel emerged together as competing discourses 'that were "invented" together at the beginning of the eighteenth century'.[12] However, these discourses were not fully separated until later in the century when, provoked by a proliferating market for print, middle-class moralists renegotiated the boundaries of legitimate pleasure, separating writing into high and low, and designating literature 'high' and pornography 'low'. The novel joined the ranks of literature: Behn, Manley, and Cleland were jettisoned to safeguard the moral authority of reformist works like Richardson's and Fielding's. Like Warner, Mudge posits that a retroactive process of morally motivated generic differentiation gave rise to the novel. Moreover, prohibitions on certain kinds of reading matter exploited gendered cultural discourse, as the cultural threats of prostitution, masquerades, and financial gain were discursively aligned with certain books to designate them pornographic. In particular, the definition of good and bad books was linked to a related debate about good and bad women: texts could be classified based on the kinds of women who inhabited their pages.

Mudge premises that 'pornography simply did not exist as a recognizable category' before about 1750 (27–8). The function of sexually explicit art, as Behn and Manley's books indicate, was not solely to arouse. Defoe is part of the bourgeois effort to impose a standard of ideal femininity, but his effort to distinguish good from bad desire fails for Mudge, as for Warner, because the pleasure of the narration undermines his moral intent. The perceived 'feminization' of the novel led to two responses: 'First, cultural commentators openly declaimed against women's novels as undesirable by-products of a new literary marketplace; second, male authors attempted to redefine the romance novel to make it at once more realistic and more moral' (70). In contrast to the 'chaos of the early eighteenth-century marketplace', in which the amatory novella was just one of many forms of erotica, Richardsonian domestic fiction banished the whore and celebrated the virgin (183). Novelists for the next century laboured to reify the novel as literature, not pornography. The new separation, meanwhile, gave pornography a safe haven, and it grew 'increasingly accustomed to [its] own marginal position in the scheme of things' (251). Its dissociation from the novel enabled pornography's proliferation.

Warner and Mudge both take the focus away from intrinsic formal qualities of particular novels, emphasizing instead the ways in which later axiological taxonomies have constructed the rise of the novel. This is extended in the work of Homer Obed Brown and Clifford Siskin. In *The Institutions of the English Novel* (1997), Brown makes the arresting claim that 'the eighteenth-century novel was invented at the beginning of the nineteenth century'.[13] He asserts:

> ■ The fictions of Defoe, Richardson, and Fielding, it could be argued, only became 'the novel' by means of retrospective histories that made them seem inaugural and exemplary at once. [...] What we now call 'the novel' didn't appear visibly as a recognized single 'genre' until the early nineteenth century, when the essentially heterogeneous fictional prose narratives of the preceding century were grouped together institutionally under that name. (ix, xvii–xviii) □

Rather than 'invention', Brown prefers to think about the *institution* of the novel: both in the sense of its 'beginning' and its authoritative status. He pluralizes *institutions*, because there were multiple actions and processes by which the novel became an authoritative monolith, with Defoe, Richardson, and Fielding each representing 'a different, incomplete beginning', prior to 'the early nineteenth-century institution of the novel' that consolidated their endeavours (7). 'Institution' signifies the retroactive establishment and legitimation of the novel in the Romantic period, well after Watt's threesome were dead. Walter Scott, Brown shows, was the key figure in this process, both for the novels he wrote and what he wrote about his predecessors.

Brown faults Watt for seeking to recuperate the eighteenth-century novel by nineteenth-century standards (realism), and he rebuts McKeon's contention that the novel (or, for that matter, romance) was institutionally and terminologically stable by 1750 (xiii). For instance, Scott's historical novels privileged romance in an institutional act of both novelistic form and national identity: 'For Scott, the role of the novel is that of the romance and the epic before it: the foundation of a nation and a national identity that represents Britain's "natural" heterogeneity' (14). After rather diffuse chapters on letters and gossip, on disguise in Defoe, on history in *Tom Jones*, on the sermon in *Tristram Shandy*, and on the Waverley Novels (some of which had been individually published many years earlier), Brown looks at Defoe's canonization as a novelist in the nineteenth century, which he says is 'paradigmatic of institutional histories of the novel' (175). Defoe was not considered a novelist until Scott wrote about him as such; even then he was not considered a major novelist and was often written about as a hoaxer or liar rather than as an artist. Defoe became a major novelist and artist only when critical priorities shifted in the 1950s and 60s, and his inclusion has entailed exclusions that delimit the 'novel' category. Brown thus destabilizes what we think of as novelistic by showing the contingencies of the novel's construction.

In a similar vein, Clifford Siskin's *The Work of Writing* (1999) argues for a Romantic-period rise of the novel – both in *quantitative* terms, because the publication of new fictions proliferated towards the end of the eighteenth century, and in *generic* terms, because the novel only gained the status of 'literature' in the early nineteenth century.[14] Siskin argues that the periodical press, the professionalization of criticism, and new ideas about creative authorship discursively enabled *literature* to shift from a synonym for 'writing' to a hierarchical aesthetic category. Periodicals fostered desire for prose fiction (through reviews) and they dispersed fiction (novels in magazines). Siskin describes 'a two-tier market – one in which the popularity of one product [periodicals] supports rather than cannibalizes the sales of the other [novels]', the effect of which is the 'increasing consolidation of the cultural power of the novel' (168–9). Siskin terms the 'discourse of and about novels' *novelism* (173). He notes four things about novelism. First, it entails a shift in the understanding of literary production from imitation to innovation, or literary creation. Second, Fielding and Richardson are elevated whilst their predecessors and immediate successors are denigrated: the novel is not so much thought to have steadily *risen* as to have suddenly *arisen*, before flatlining after 1750. Third, the discourse of the novel is bound up with that of the nation: the novel quickly becomes the *English* novel. Fourth, the English novel is part of the re-organization of knowledge into disciplines: Siskin is most immediately concerned with the emergence of Literature, as novelism is hived off from 'scientificity' (188).

Warner, Brown, and Siskin each treat the novel less as an alienable category (genre) and more as an organization, retroactively constructed, of certain material into a system or institution, maintained and disciplined by a discourse that does not just represent the novel but constitutes it. Before I discuss the novel's place in print culture in Chapter 8, the next section details several essay collections which consolidate some of the changes in thinking about the emergent novel derived from historicism, feminism, and postcolonialism.

Reconsidering the rise of the novel

Student-friendly essay collections can provide a helpful gauge of dominant thinking about a topic, which is certainly the case with *The Columbia History of the British Novel* (1994) and *The Cambridge Companion to the Eighteenth-Century Novel* (1996).[15] In terms of the canon, Defoe, Richardson, Fielding, Sterne, and Burney have single-author chapters in both works; Swift and Smollett gain individual treatment in *Cambridge* and are connected by the satiric tradition in *Columbia*. As well as McKillop's *cinq grands*, Burney is now well ensconced thanks to the endeavours of feminism, and other essays in these collections address early-century amatory novelists and later-century women writers. Swift's return to the conversation indicates that the distinction between satire and novel was giving way, as were most purist approaches to genre. Accordingly, attention is also given to later-century subgenres – Gothic fiction, sentimental novels, and 1790s political fiction. This is an indicative field for the historicist studies I will discuss in Chapters 9 and 10. A special issue of *Eighteenth-Century Fiction* (2000) meanwhile features 18 essays that collectively reconsider the rise of the novel. The editor, David Blewett, correctly remarks that 'the shadow cast by Watt's *The Rise of the Novel* is so long that general studies of the early novel are still written in its shade'.[16]

The collection aims to shed further light on the intellectual moment of *The Rise of the Novel*. Watt's own account of its genesis in a 1978 lecture is posthumously published here. In that piece, Watt thinks of his book as a synthesis of two influences: the Leavises' historical, empirical, and moral criticism (on the one hand), and the continental sociological traditions of Marxism and phenomenology (on the other).[17] The former influence is interesting because Novak indicates how much of a departure Watt's *Rise* represents from Leavis's *Great Tradition* (see Chapter 2).[18] Carnochan also relates Watt to previous novel theorists, arguing that Watt extended prevailing aestheticist priorities by relating the novel to sociohistorical developments.[19] McKeon, meanwhile, argues that Watt wrote within a tradition of 'grand theory' novel scholarship that included Lukács, Bakhtin, and José Ortega y Gasset, author of *Meditations on Quixote* (1914). But McKeon differentiates Watt from these because Watt posits the novel as a sharp break from premodern narrative (epic or romance), rather than a transformation.[20] Davis meanwhile believes that Watt was part of a process in mid-twentieth-century criticism whereby the novel was gaining academic respectability.[21] Hunter expands this to suggest that eighteenth-century studies as a whole were gaining greater academic attention, partly due to the importance of the novel.[22]

Watt's emphasis on realism as the 'lowest common denominator' of the novel is approved by Byrd and Seidel, who each suggest it helps to explain the novel form beyond the period of Watt's coverage.[23] Richetti and Novak both defend Watt's canon against forms of cultural criticism that eschew questions of 'value'. Novak decries Warner's apparent desire to replace the Defoe – Richardson – Fielding trajectory with one of Behn – Manley – Haywood – Richardson – Fielding. 'Good as they are', Novak states, 'the three women writers named above were simply never writers of world significance. Defoe was'.[24] Richetti, also against Warner's levelling tendencies, invokes Bakhtin's criterion of novelistic dialogism in order to affirm 'the generic originality and intellectual/aesthetic power (of various kinds, to be sure) of the line that begins with Defoe and flourishes in Richardson, Fielding, Smollett, Sterne, and Burney and that is not fully achieved by other eighteenth-century novelists'.[25] An answer of sorts comes in Todd's essay on Behn's *Love-Letters*, accounting for its neglect in studies of the novel by showing that its use of epistolary form is more bound up with Restoration politics than the privatized 'transcript of subjectivity' valorized in novel criticism that privileges Richardson.[26] Also attending to oversights about women writers, in this case Mary Davys, J. A. Downie uses bibliometric data to deny Watt's contention that the novel is new and rises from the early eighteenth century: he shows that the word 'novel' dates from the mid-sixteenth century and that readers were comfortable with prose fiction well before the eighteenth.[27] Watt's thesis is qualified in parts, but still dictates the debate.

Conclusion

The perspectives that I have discussed in this chapter put the traditional 'rise', complicated but finally endorsed in the studies discussed in Chapter 4 and even up to Hunter's *Before Novels*, under intense scrutiny. Heralding this change, Robert Hume talks about the 'pernicious influence of evolutionary views of the novel', the 'organicist assumptions' that entail a Darwinian search for *origins* or which plot an *ascent*, in the manner of Watt and McKeon. Hume attacks '*ex post facto* attempts to find logic, order, reason, and teleology in a chaotic jumble of particulars' and 'den[ies] the feasibility of generic history as it has long been known and practiced'.[28] The kinds of historical approach

I will discuss in Chapters 9 and 10, I suggest, have evinced a similar scepticism about literary history, or have avoided literary history in favour of a thematic brand of historicism that pairs a contextual topic (often arbitrarily) with a periodized genre: in our case, the eighteenth-century novel. This is notwithstanding the doubts of scholars from Mayer and Brown to Siskin and Warner that such a thing as *the eighteenth-century novel* exists. Next, however, I turn to approaches to the early novel through eighteenth-century print culture, which have become important in the past twenty years.

CHAPTER EIGHT

Print Culture and the Rise of the Novel, 1990–2010

This chapter examines the impact on the study of the emergent novel of recent work informed by book history, the economics of literary production, and the history of reading. It asks how the emergent novel fits into eighteenth-century print culture, how and by whom early novels were produced and read, and what significance should be accorded to fiction's physical and typographical form in accounting for the novel's rise. This work builds on studies I have surveyed in previous chapters, and the reader of those chapters will realise how longstanding is the connection between the novel and developments in print technology. Ian Watt posited that the novel's rise was coincident with that of a middle-class reading public (see Chapter 2). Terry Lovell subsequently shifted Watt's focus on production to consumption of fiction (see Chapter 5). Lennard Davis argued for the formative influence on the novel of the deregulation of print, and Michael McKeon, following Elizabeth Eisenstein's groundbreaking *The Printing Press as an Agent of Change* (1979), set the novel's emergence in the larger revolution in print technologies (see Chapter 4). William Warner analysed the novel's emergence in the history of the advent of entertainment media (see Chapter 7), and feminist scholarship gauged the extent of women's access to print culture and the rise of the professional female writer (see Chapter 5). J. Paul Hunter supplied the pre-eminent analysis of reading practices and the emerging novel (see Chapter 7).

The quantitative rise of the novel

It is beyond the scope of this chapter to give a history of the publishing trade in the eighteenth century; a certain amount can be pieced together from my discussion of rise-of-the-novel criticism, but the reader may benefit from consulting a concise history like John Feather's.[1] Four bibliometric checklists collectively cover, as comprehensively as possible, all known novels published in the period from 1700 to 1800. William McBurney, covering the first four decades, characterizes this as a period of undirected fictional production, whilst Jerry Beasley sees a quite sudden proliferation of fiction and a greater sense of purpose in the 1740s.[2] Raven characterizes the 1750s and 60s as 'a period of marked if sometimes halting growth', but labels the century's final three decades the period when the novel 'comes of age'.[3] Data from these checklists is collated in Figure 8.1, though it should be noted that the compilers use slightly different criteria for inclusion.

J. A. Downie uses this kind of data to challenge Watt, who had argued that the novel arose in conjunction with the middle-class reading public. Downie denies the adequacy of the evidence for the developments Watt describes and proposes a new focus, away from the role of authors and readers, and towards the publishers and booksellers. He notes that only a handful of new fictions were published each year before *Pamela*, with publishers preferring reprints of proven sellers to new titles, and that growths in the printing industry affected other areas than fiction, namely the newspaper. Only after 1770, by which time Richardson, Fielding, Sterne, and Smollett were all dead, did the publishing industry manifest the kind of scale that made a middle-class readership a force in determining literary production. Downie emphasizes that the novel is a construction and an artefact, something made, rather than a natural phenomenon, as is implied in organic metaphors like 'rise'

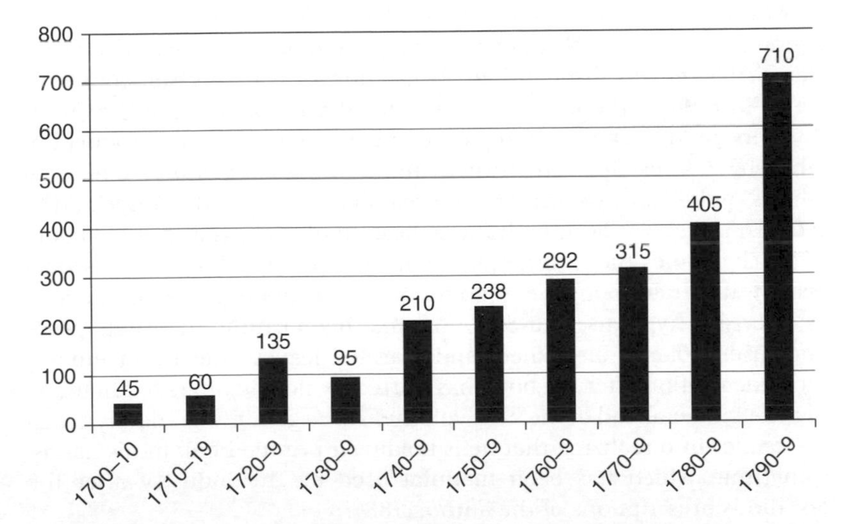

Figure 8.1: New novel production in Britain, 1700–99, by decade (includes first English edition of translated works). Data collated from checklists compiled by McBurney, Beasley, Raven, and Raven and Forster.

or 'origins'.[4] The novel, it must be remembered, although it was rising in quantity throughout the century, accounted for only a small part of published material.

Print technology and the novel

In 1936, Walter Benjamin distinguished the 'novel' from the 'story' based on the former's 'essential dependence on the book', which meant that 'the dissemination of the novel became possible only with the invention of printing'.[5] The connections between print technology and the rise of the novel has been further explored by a number of critics. In *Textual Communication* (1991), Maurice Couturier supplies a 'print-based theory' of fiction to support his claim that 'it was the printing press which gave birth to the modern novel'.[6] Couturier here builds on Walter Ong's assertion that 'the print world gave birth to the novel', because 'the novelist was engaged more specifically [than the dramatist] with a text and less with auditors, imagined or real'.[7] Couturier outlines developments in the print industry that paved the way for the novel: the growing book trade, relaxed publishing laws, and an expanded readership. He foregrounds the commercial enterprise of the bookseller-publisher, the development of circulating libraries, the decline in state regulation of print, the increasing professionalization of writing, and the growing reading public.

Couturier next turns to the physical and typographical form of early fiction. Describing features like title pages and prefatory text, Couturier claims that novels display their 'bookishness' in highly self-conscious ways. Moreover, the authorial poses of early novelists from Cervantes to Defoe and Richardson replicate the process of book production, whereby manuscripts are turned into print, as the authors pose as editors, publishers, or printers of a real document. In this respect, 'the modern novel was born with the reification of the text as printed book' (77). The games that Sterne plays with the physical format of *Tristram Shandy* illustrate Couturier's point. Sterne exploits typography, such as asterisks, hyphens, and dots, to make his meaning; he omits pages and inserts blank, blackened, and marbled leaves; and he includes a mock dedication after the book has started, which he offers to sell to the highest bidder ahead of the next volume. These gambits 'gradually coach the reader into realizing that he is holding a printed book in his hands, something which has been manufactured by the industry after the fastidious prescriptions of the author' (88).

Couturier identifies *three* births of the novel, sorting the genre into third-person narration (Cervantes to Fielding), memoir (Defoe to Smollett), and epistolary (Richardson). All three forms are antagonistic towards oral storytelling. Third-person narration has ancient roots, but Couturier suggests that, in the hands of Cervantes and Fielding, the *printed* novel sustains a subversive metafictional relationship to these older *oral* methods (104). The development of first-person picaresque is coincident with the rise of print, and it too stages a 'struggle between oral and typographic language' (120). Epistolary fiction creates layers of narration – novelist, editor, writer, addressee, publisher, and reader – designed to emphasize its status as print. Couturier says that the eighteenth-century novel 'corresponded to a new publishing formula' and was 'manufactured in such a way as to make it more eminently transportable and readable by isolated readers' (52) as 'a small and comparatively cheap book meant for entertainment which could be read silently at home' (139).

Richardson and Sterne are the two eighteenth-century novelists who have attracted most attention from analysts of print culture. Stephanie Fysh, in *The Work(s) of Samuel Richardson* (1997), contends that Richardson's careers as printer and novelist made him uniquely interested in controlling the physical and textual aspects of his novels, their reception, and his ownership of their intellectual property.[8] In *Sterne, the Moderns, and the Novel* (2002), Thomas Keymer argues that *Tristram Shandy*, through its 'innovative use of print technology' is 'a parody of the realist novel' that nevertheless had a 'galvanizing effect on the novel genre – its formal conventions, its commercial presence, its status as a cultural force'.[9] Keymer situates *Tristram* in a larger history of experimental 1750s fiction, such as John Kidgell's enigmatic *The Card* (1755) and the anonymous *Life and Memoirs of Mr. Ephraim Tristram Bates* (1756), flagging up commercial pressures that led authors to innovate with the form of the book, in order to distinguish their products from the multitude of books on the market. The serialized publication of *Tristram* entails 'contingency, malleability, elasticity, improvisation' (87), a guarantee of Sterne's formal innovation and that *Tristram* was up-to-the-minute with the literary and political culture of the 1760s.

Keymer glances forward to George Eliot's *Middlemarch* (1871–2) to illustrate points about Sterne and serialization. Leah Price, in *The Anthology and the Rise of the Novel* (2000), also takes the story up to Eliot, arguing that the anthology is a product of print culture that developed in tandem with the novel. To this end, Price shows that the process of abridging, summarizing, and anthologizing Richardson began almost immediately, largely due to the 'sheer bulk' of his novels, and that the author was himself at the heart of this process.[10] Amidst a cultural climate that read Richardson for the sentiment, not for the story (as Samuel Johnson once put it), the extrapolation of edifying maxims was favoured over what Clara Reeve called the 'dry story'. Collections of excerpted moral apothegms salvaged what was worthwhile from dispensable narrative, setting aside plot and epistolary form for extrapolated passages. Such anthologies were encouraged not just by Richardson's textual apparatus (like indexes), but also licensed by the format of Richardson's novels, which are themselves presented as selective collections of documents (letters) – that is, as anthologies.

Price contends that the defeat of perpetual copyright in 1774 enabled collections of reprinted novels, helping to consolidate the genre. In addressing what other critics (Siskin and Brown: see Chapter 7) called the Romantic rise of the novel, Price shows how Walter Scott was abridged, both with respect to his novels and Lockhart's biography; that Radcliffe's chapter headnotes are verse fragments that would have been familiar to readers from anthologies; and that Shakespeare was 'novelized' through expurgation by Charles and Mary Lamb. Finally, Price suggests that the popularity of Alexander Main's anthologized excerpts from George Eliot, published in 1872, helped to establish the novel's cultural identity and authority – just as those from Richardson had a century earlier. This is paradoxical, because Main's anthology devalues narrative, changes words, and presents characters' statements as Eliot's own: it seems to undermine, not reinforce, her own very serious attempt to elevate the novel. However, Main insisted that Eliot had 'for ever sanctified the Novel by making it the *vehicle* of the grandest and most uncompromising moral truth' (107). Eliot came round: *Daniel Deronda* (1876) and *Theophrastus Such* (1879) were more 'epigrammatic' than her earlier novels, because they 'were both written in the expectation of being excerpted' (106). Anthologies, then, purported to educate where the novel was accused of either corrupting (in Richardson's day) or merely entertaining (in Eliot's). 'The novel' Price states, 'could not have become respectable without the tokenism embodied in the anthology' (7).

In her original and incisive *Graphic Design, Print Culture, and the Eighteenth-Century Novel* (2003), Janine Barchas argues for the interpretive importance of early novels' paratextual features: aspects of books that are not the main text. Barchas sheds light on authors' and publishers' efforts to manipulate meaning and sell their products through book design.[11] Faced with a sceptical target audience, novel producers used frontispieces, title pages, images, and even musical scores, as well as punctuation and other typographical features, to help define and elevate the fledgling genre. Barchas thus 'aims to contextualize the manner in which the novel genre's original audience read and experienced the new species of writing', reminding us that these paratexts are often omitted from modern, standardized reprints (11). Indeed, modern editions add their own paratexts, so that we read *Moll Flanders* with the author's name and 'World's Classics' printed on the cover, for example.

Barchas argues that 'the novel first borrows the printed trappings of authority, then, as it grows more confident, it subverts and mocks that authority, eventually shedding its own graphic plagiarism' (18). Starting in the 1750s, 'the novel begins a slow striptease of its graphic attire' – its author portraits, cacophonous title pages, and graphic embellishments (18). The early novel increasingly experimented with the 'printedness' of the printed book before it settled down to comparative uniformity in the nineteenth century.

Frontispieces are decorative illustrations, often with a motto, at the beginning of a book. In its early days, the novel used the frontispiece to support its claim to authenticity, as Defoe's frontispieces enforce the fiction that the protagonist is the writer. However, parody of this strategy came almost immediately, such as in Swift's use of the 'author' portrait to undercut Gulliver's narrative authority. By mid-century, the frontispiece was being employed in multiple ways: mockingly, as in the depiction of the canine 'author' of Francis Coventry's *Pompey the Little* (1751); to illustrate 'the novel's self-conscious mid-century materiality', as in Kidgell's *The Card* (50); or to shift the genre's focus from individual to community, as in Scott's *Millenium Hall*. Barchas next considers the verbose and 'crowded' title pages of early novels as 'a telltale sign of an experimental genre' (65). The novel slowly found its feet through the unstable generic identifications used in long titles ('Life', 'Adventures', 'Memoirs', 'Voyages'), which is evidence of an 'identity crisis', temporarily solved by mid-century when many novelists settled on 'History'. Title pages were a way of marketing novels, of dignifying the genre, and of controlling readers' expectations.

Barchas also argues that the novel used typographical features, from asterisks to chapter divisions, to convey a sense of narrative time and to control reading time. The novel's propensity for lists is part of its claim to authority. For instance, '*Robinson Crusoe* reinforces the inventory-keeping that is the hallmark [of] contemporary scientific observation' (179). This culminates in the 100-page index to *Sir Charles Grandison* with which Richardson repackages the genre as respectable, a 'formal move to place the novel on the same shelf as other indexed books, and, by extension, to lend it an authoritative, referential status' (213). Barchas interprets the inclusion of a musical score in *Clarissa* as a similar attempt to elevate the novel by implying a high level of cultural literacy. And she interprets dashes in Sarah Fielding's *David Simple* as an embodiment of a gendered, non-verbal world inhabited by female characters, subsequently undermined by her brother Henry's editing in a later edition. This illustrates Barchas's claim that editing and reprinting alters meaning. Her book is amply illustrated, demonstrating the visual and material diversity of early novels, to which the work surveyed here attests.[12]

Authorship, the marketplace, and the Rise of the Novel

Brean Hammond's study of the professionalization of authorship, *Professional Imaginative Writing* (1997), foregrounds the importance of emerging forces of commercialism for the rise of the novel, focusing on the market competition between Haywood and Defoe.[13] Hammond historicizes the process that Bakhtin called 'novelization', 'a hybridization that breaks down traditionally observed generic boundaries', and 'makes stories relevant, realistic, narrative, and domestic' (250, 8). Even cultural conservatives, ideologically opposed to novelization, participate in the novel's triumph, as Hammond sees the mock-epic and periodical essay contributing to the rise of the novel. A prime example is Swift, whose *Gulliver's Travels* 'is ideologically opposed to the set of attitudes and beliefs that was fuelling the development of the novel', but who is involved just like Defoe and Haywood in a marketplace competing for readers of fictional stories (271). Hammond parallels Warner (see Chapter 7) in characterizing the novel – starting with Defoe, culminating in Fielding – as 'a high-cultural repudiation of the narrative energies going into romantic novellas' like Haywood's (286).

Siskin's 'novelism' – 'the habitual subordination of writing to the novel' that obtains in the later eighteenth century (see Chapter 7) – is the eventual destination of Hammond's 'novelization'. George Justice, in *The Manufacturers of Literature* (2002), labels this 'novel culture'. 'The novel comes about', says Justice, 'through the cooperation of various agents in pursuit of economic and cultural self-interest: authors, editors, publishers, printers, reviewers, and readers'.[14] Justice focuses on 'second-generation novelists' of the 1770s, arguing that the rise of the novel is 'a fiction created by writers like [Frances] Brooke and Burney to advance the commercial and artistic aims of their writings' (149). Both writers place their works in a genealogy of 'good' novels to distinguish them from the competition, and in the process help shape a story of the novel's rise. In addition, 'book reviews and advertisements aided and abetted this novel culture through criticism and publicity' (167). A pertinent example is Burney's dedication of *Evelina* to the *Monthly Review* and *Critical Review*, a ploy that acknowledges the power of professional novel-reviewing. In *The Fame Machine* (1996), Frank Donoghue notes the marked difference between Fielding's derisive address to professional critics in *Tom Jones* and Burney's deferential dedication in *Evelina*.[15] The difference indicates the rapidity with which novelists accommodated themselves to reviews, which mediated their relationship with the public. Sterne heeded reviewers' preferences for sentimentalism; Smollett derived a mode of authoritative social criticism from his review work that shaped his late novels. Donoghue does not go quite so far as to say that the novel's authority derived from the reviews, but does argue that these were important cultivators of taste and demand.

Donoghue only briefly addresses female literary careers, such as Burney's. In *Nobody's Story* (1994), Catherine Gallagher considers 'how women writers integrated the changing concept of woman into their authorial personae, how they connected it to the discourse of marketplace exchange, and how prevalent notions of authorship were altered in the process'.[16] She considers the authorial strategies of five 'representative' women novelists – Behn, Manley, Lennox, Burney, and Edgeworth – as they produce the 'rhetorical effect' of vanishing, being replaced by 'author-selves', a 'fictional Nobody, a proper name explicitly without a physical referent in the real world' (xv). Self-presentational strategies that omit the self result from the experience of authorship as dispossession and alienation in the marketplace as it moved from seventeenth-century patronage to eighteenth-century professionalism. Gallagher's approach here is Marxist: she identifies books as commodities in Marx's sense of physical objects with abstract value generated by exchange. This new conception of literary production affected male and female writers, but the latter emphasized dispossession due to the vantage lent by their gender. The development of female authorial dispossession, Gallagher explains, was formative in establishing the presentation of fiction *as* fiction and the desirability of reading such books, resulting in the cultural dominance of the novel and its investment in feminine consciousness.

Gallagher shows that the discourse of female authorship was rendered in economic terms and that the novel's development paralleled the rise of a market economy. She explores the material conditions of production, payment, and distribution of novels. Accordingly, the 'case study' chapters address 'five different stages of authorship in the marketplace' (xiv). First, Behn moves between metaphors of prostitution and monarchy in her evolving conception of authorship, feminizing the question of authorial property and forging a 'novel authorial identity' for the marketplace, as she moved from drama to prose fiction and from patronage to professionalization (17). Manley's career is placed in the 'unprecedented politicization of authorship' during Queen Anne's reign, wherein Manley makes her political points by equating femininity and fictionality (94). Rather than presenting fiction as fact, Manley presents fact as fiction, allegorizing real people in stories, exploiting readers' desires for scandal, and indicating the increasingly public aspect of politics.

Lennox inhabits the moment when this public, political sphere was hived off from a private, female, domestic realm (see Chapter 5), which is coincident with the separation of 'men of letters' from political hacks, a development that initiated intellectual property rights. The Lennox chapter contains Gallagher's most explicit statements on the rise of the novel. She posits that the rise of fiction as a 'discursive category', distinct from lying, occurred in the mid-eighteenth century (163). Stories and characters by this point did not need an actual referent (as they did in Manley's political allegories) making the novel literally *nobody's story*, a fiction about a nonexistent character: 'There was no sudden novelistic revolution that purged English narrative of somebody and replaced him or her with nobody. Nevertheless, in the middle decades of the century, fictional nobodies became the more popular and respectable protagonists' (165). Gallagher thus locates realism in the fact that fiction is taken for granted, not suppressed; she adduces Hume's idea of sympathy as a kind of fiction to account for people's willingness to identify with made-up characters. Lennox, however, exemplifies women's authorial dispossession, as she proved unable to capitalize financially on her work.

As well as authors and characters, 'Nobody' suggests the impersonality of fiction's readership in Gallagher's discussion of Burney. *Evelina* is *by* 'Nobody' (published anonymously), *about* 'Nobody' (the characters are made-up), and *addressed to* 'nobody in particular' or 'everybody equally' (an impersonal and diversified mass readership). Aware of the market, Burney conceived of her writing career as a protracted debt for early success, and thematizes this in her stories, as does Edgeworth. Edgeworth wrote when 'the novel was associated with prodigality, waste, and the loss of private property'; she both aimed to redeem fiction and to divest it of didacticism (279). Edgeworth thus completes Gallagher's account of how fictionality emerged in the literary marketplace through the contribution of women writers' authorial strategies.

Thomas Keymer and Peter Sabor approach the literary market through a bestseller in *'Pamela' in the Marketplace* (2005), an analysis of the brouhaha caused by Richardson's novel. The controversy, they say, was 'a milestone in literary history', sparking an unprecedented surge in fiction and indicating 'the emergence of a thriving, dynamic, and fully commercialized marketplace for print': it is 'a defining moment in the history of print and consumer culture as well as that of a genre'.[17] Keymer and Sabor survey the range of fictional responses – hostile, friendly, and somewhere in between. They analyse Richardson's marketing tactics, suggesting that '*Pamela*'s success lay as much in commercial strategy as in literary achievement' (22). Richardson tried to rig the market: his hand is discernable in much of the reaction to *Pamela*, such as his soliciting praise from his literary friends, his encouraging clergymen to extol the novel from the pulpit, his likely manipulation of magazine commendations, and his hints about a real-life original for Pamela. All of this promoted the book, but Richardson may also have sponsored attacks on *Pamela*, including *Pamela Censured* (1741), one of the works that enabled Richardson's own sequel. High-minded literary intentions sit comfortably alongside the profit instinct. For instance, Keymer and Sabor reconstruct the life and career of John Kelly, author of *Pamela's Conduct in High Life* (1741), the publication of which Richardson opportunistically exploited. The story of the novel's emergence in this account extends beyond the canonical – that is, beyond Richardson; beyond Fielding, who launched his novelistic career by parodying *Pamela*; beyond Haywood, who rejuvenated hers with *Anti-Pamela* (1741); and beyond Cleland, whose *Fanny Hill* exploits the pornographic potential of Richardson to become 'the most commercially successful' novel to compete in the *Pamela* controversy (104). For Keymer and Sabor, it is Kelly who personifies 'novelization', 'a shift in the balance of literary power away from a traditional manuscript culture characterized by elite patronage, generic conservatism and classical erudition, and towards the vulgarly commercialized, market-led, innovative or hybridizing print culture of the modern age' (75).

The history of reading

In Chapter 3, I looked at reader-response criticism by Preston and Iser. Augmenting this work, which typically conceives of the reader as a rhetorical construction predicated by the text, scholars have attempted to reconstruct the history of reading at the moment of the novel's rise. This involves gathering statistical and anecdotal data about actual novel readers (rather than imagined ideal readers) in order to understand their sociological make-up: how many people could read? to what level of 'competency'? how was the reading public organized by gender? by class? Mayer, for example, uses Pierre Bourdieu's work on taste to substantiate Watt's claim about the novel's middle-class appeal, showing how the novel appealed to the middling sort by its length, subject, style, and morality.[18] Historians have addressed *how* novels were read (aloud or silently? publicly or privately? professionally or for leisure? extensively, with a few texts, or intensively, with many texts?).[19] Spacks, for instance, in *Privacy* (2003), balances her account of individual, private novel reading with attention to communal, collective customs.[20] Historians of reading also aim to account for the cultural discourse *about* reading – for example, whether people thought reading was a dangerous recreation or morally profitable – and what kind of institutional and cultural regulations were imposed. Warner, for instance, examines eighteenth-century paintings depicting readers to argue that novels were perceived as a threat to Enlightenment ideals of reading as educative.[21] Novels participate in these discourses, because they have things to say about reading. Hunter's *Before Novels* is the most systematic investigation to date of reading practices, literacy, and the sociological make-up of the reading public in relation to eighteenth-century fiction; the reader is advised to read the first section of Chapter 7 before proceeding with this one.

In *Richardson's 'Clarissa' and the Eighteenth-Century Reader* (1992), Tom Keymer uses contemporary responses to *Clarissa* to construct its readers' experiences and horizons of expectation. From Richardson's correspondence with his (mainly female) readers and other printed reactions, Keymer ascertains that *Clarissa* attempts to develop and exercise the readers' faculty of judgement, helping them to educate themselves and to act ethically in practical and spiritual cases. Keymer shows how didactic tactics shifted the emphasis to the reader: 'It is by an active encounter with difficulties, and not by the passive reception of lessons, that Richardson's reader may learn'.[22] In this respect, Richardson fulfils Samuel Johnson's dictum that fiction supplies 'mock encounters', allowing readers to practice ethical choices ahead of real-life scenarios. These moral effects are enabled by Richardson's formal choices: 'The narration of events by the protagonists themselves, the simultaneity of narrative and event posited by the epistolary form, and the famous particularity and prolixity of Richardson's writing all combine to close the gap between the world of the novel and that of the reader's own experience' (200-1). But Keymer shows how resistant readers lacking in 'literary competence' could be when faced with a new, experimental genre: they rejected Richardson's overtures about the moral necessity of Clarissa's death and offered alternative endings. Keymer's empirical approach to reading, historically explaining Richardson's aims, tacitly rejects Warner's deconstructionist claims about textual instability and the reader's attempt to wrest control from the author in *Clarissa* (see Chapter 5).

Ellen Gardiner's *Regulating Readers* (1999) is similarly concerned with how the novel teaches an instructional type of reading, as she traces 'the rise of the novel-as-criticism', examining 'how fiction helped to shape professional critical practices and to define the role and function of the professional critic in the eighteenth century'.[23] Gardiner tracks the newly installed role of the professional literary critic as this is defined by eighteenth-century novelists. In Richardson and Fielding, Gardiner finds an extension of the patrician effort of Addison and Steele's *Spectator* to limit 'access and experience of culture', privileging masculine over female judgement (22). *Clarissa* 'reproduces an ideology that seeks to exclude women from critical practice', and *Tom Jones* attempts to 'exclude women from the profession of literary criticism' (62, 81). This occurs on the level of action: Clarissa is a gullible and irresponsible reader, so interpretation that appropriately moralizes events falls to the editor, Belford, Richardson's self-portrait. Turning to female novelists,

Gardiner finds that Lennox's *The Female Quixote* endorses the masculine programme through its transformation of immoral romance into morally responsible fiction, its relegation of women's reading to passive consumption, and its promotion of male criticism in the heroine's reformation. However, Haywood rejects *The Spectator*'s critical elitism and in *The Female Spectator* (1744–6) she uses the pretext of training women to fulfil the duties of wife, daughter and mother as a ruse, instead 'train[ing] women to participate in the public world of the culture industry' (31). Following this lead, Sarah Fielding and Jane Collier's *The Cry* (1754) and Austen's *Mansfield Park* (1814) resist the subjugation of feminine critical authority: through Fanny Price, Austen 'depicts criticism as a viable activity and profession for women' (148). Gardiner thus sees novels taking sides in gender debates over professional reading and conceives of the genre as self-serving, dictating the terms on which it is to be read and judged, making novelists literary critics.

Elspeth Jajdelska's *Silent Reading and the Birth of the Narrator* (2007) argues that a shift took place over the course of the late seventeenth and early eighteenth century from reading as speaking aloud to an audience to silent reading, 'hearing' an internal voice.[24] This transition affected prose style and genre in a number of ways, and one consequence is 'the birth of the narrator' central to the rise of the novel. Jajdelska thus develops Hunter's findings about 'silent reading in private spaces', saying that 'many features of the new genre of the novel crystallized in the early eighteenth century, at the same time as fluent silent reading may first have reached critical mass' (168, 192). Jajdelska makes her case by comparing punctuation and relative clauses, each denoting pauses, in the (by our standards) rambling and untidy prose of Ralph Thoresby's letters and the elegant, tidy essays of Joseph Addison. She contends that there is a shift in the early eighteenth century in how writers 'modelled' readers – pauses are more appropriate in silent reading. In addition, the empirical data Jajdelska presents suggests that fluent, silent reading was enabled by increasing book ownership, rising literacy, an increase in reading for pleasure, and more children reading in engaged (varied, frequent, and recreational) ways.

Jajdelska differentiates between early novels using a 'Storyteller' and those using a 'Narrator'. The former, exemplified by Defoe, tends towards 'dramatic monologue', favouring long passages with few pauses, performative prose, and rapid switches in temporal and spatial focalization. Jajdelska looks at stylistic revisions of earlier prose fictions (*Gulliver's Travels* and *Pamela*) that she argues try to improve clarity for the new silent reader by making the narrative voice more consistent. And finally, she contends that, 'as the century progressed, a new generation of writers began to write for readers as hearers [the internal monologue of silent reading] by creating Narrators from scratch' (187).

The Female Quixote illustrates the novel oriented towards a silent reader. Jajdelska explains the rise of novelistic discourse, in which we accept that there will be a voice with a 'notional location in time or space' mediating between the reader and the action, as a consequence of the rise of silent reading (167). Of course, in modern parlance, Defoe's fictions have 'narrators', but Jajdelska differentiates later narration, whether first- or third-person, which assumes that someone will be reading it in their head, not performing it vocally.

In a 2007 essay, Susan Whyman also attends to the reading practices of private individuals, defining 'epistolary literacy' as an emergent skill for middle-class ladies, fostered and exploited by Richardson.[25] Whyman analyses the correspondence of one of Richardson's readers, Jane Johnson, who writes about her experiences of reading epistolary fiction, illustrating the impact it had on the social and literary habits of provincial, middle-class Englishwomen. Johnson makes a valuable addition to the retinue of readers detailed by Keymer, especially as 'she reads *Clarissa* in a way that Richardson has encouraged', using the ethical quandaries it raises to understand her own life (597). Johnson even wrote her own Richardsonian fiction. Whyman does away with the notion that novel-reading is 'passive' to show us 'how a provincial woman without formal education can use a story to develop ideas about power, class, gender, and political economy' (600). The influence is a 'two-way street': Richardson's formal and thematic choices are equally informed by the fact that women of this background comprised a sizeable market for fiction (606). The rise of the novel, Whyman suggests, is part of a communication shift wrought by the advent of epistolarity.

David Allan, in *Commonplace Books and Reading in Georgian England* (2010), suggests that the rise of the novel and the decline of the commonplace book are 'conjoined narratives'. A commonplace book is a personal record of reading. Georgian men and women transcribed literary extracts into them or recorded their thoughts on what they were reading. Allan's research indicates a sudden decline of 'commonplacing' after the first quarter of the nineteenth century. He explains this in terms of material conditions, such as the fact that books became much cheaper and so personal ownership discouraged note-taking; but he also conjectures that the decline is due to the reading techniques encouraged by prose fiction, which 'increasingly threatened note-taking practices'. The almost total absence of the novel from commonplace books suggests not just the novel's low status before the nineteenth century, but also that novels are 'unhelpful, if not downright hostile, to the kinds of reading experience that commonplacing was assumed to sustain'.[26] Contemporaries thought novels provided the instant gratification of narrative pleasure, not the rational education and moral edification to be achieved through selection, transcription, and reflection, which commonplacing encouraged. Allan, then, indicates how the advent of fiction altered reading practices, which complements work on how changes in reading enabled the rise of the novel.

In *Reading Fictions* (2008), Kate Loveman 'situate[s] the "rise of the novel" within a broader history of reading' by showing that, during the Restoration and early eighteenth century, 'an abiding concern with deception – its pleasures and its dangers – structured relations between authors and readers'.[27] Loveman traces 'the social, political and religious imperatives which leant prestige to a wary, even suspicious, approach to texts' (15–16), arguing that readers feared excessive credulity in a culture where print was endemically distrusted. The ability to read sceptically and to assess the reliability of narrative was deemed essential, because political texts sought to 'rail', 'wheedle', 'bubble', 'delude', 'joke', 'ridicule', 'banter', 'sham', 'bite', and 'bamboozle' readers. All of these verbs were invented between 1653 and 1703 and carried connotations of social stigma, as credulous reading was associated with disenfranchised groups like Catholics, women, children, and the 'vulgar'. Civic participation demanded sceptical literacy, because the Exclusion Crisis (1678–81) and the Glorious Revolution (1688) occasioned a proliferation of published matter in a variety of genres that gave contradictory information. Readers had to assess degrees of reliability and authenticity. Loveman downplays the emphasis on solitary, silent reading found in several works discussed here, stressing a social dimension to reading. For instance, sociability in coffee-house and club culture was facilitated by a feigned willingness to believe tall tales, as civility proscribed expressing disbelief and encouraged participation in fiction. This is the horizon of expectations for early novelistic narrative. Therefore, Defoe, Swift, Richardson, and Fielding 'were involved in efforts to anticipate and respond to readers' sceptical, and often explicitly political, critiques of their fictions as shams' (127).

Defoe and Swift had good form here: they each had careers in political journalism before writing fiction. Defoe's ironic attack on religious nonconformity in *The Shortest Way with the Dissenters* (1702) was taken at face-value by Anglican Tories. Under the pseudonym Isaac Bickerstaff, Swift parodically predicted and reported the death of the astrologer John Partridge. These 'shams' and 'bites' set the stage for *Robinson Crusoe* and *Gulliver's Travels*, which did not transform generic expectations so much as conform to popular reading habits. Charles Gildon's lampoon of *Crusoe*, which rebutted its claim to be true, was an exercise in 'playful pedantry', in discerning factual inconsistencies in order to display readerly discernment (141). After Gildon's attack, Defoe uses unreliable narration in *Moll Flanders* and *Roxana* as a strategy for displacing the reader's attention to deception from the author to the characters. Swift, meanwhile, invites readers to understand *Gulliver's Travels* as 'a skilled elaboration of the conventions of shamming coffee-house wit' (166), which frequently took the form of recounting a fantastical voyage. Turning to *Pamela* and *Shamela*, Loveman counters Davis's claim that fact and fiction were still in a gradual process of rupture and Warner's argument that *Pamela* innovated a new practice of reading that placed an interpretive burden on the reader (see Chapters 4 and 7, respectively). She draws on Richardson's correspondence with *Pamela*'s readers to describe 'the language of polite pretence' that she says characterized that novel's reception (181). The real shift that took place with *Pamela* was an affective involvement in fictitious stories, which contrasts earlier readers' guardedness about being duped: 'It was becoming more acceptable not only to assume authorial benevolence but also to be seen to subsume oneself emotionally and intellectually in the author's worldview' (178). However, this sentimental readerly response was not unanimously accepted: Fielding labelled *Pamela* a sham, and his cousin, Lady Mary Wortley Montagu, veered between sceptical rallying and emotional involvement in her reading of Richardson. Loveman thus deftly traces developments in readers' receptivity to fiction.

Conclusion

The criticism discussed in this chapter has done important work by locating the emergence of the novel in print culture, by accounting for fictional form in ways that include typography and physical format, and by historicizing readers' experiences of fiction. In the final two chapters, I will turn to scholarship that relates the eighteenth-century novel to a number of social and intellectual contexts that have influenced the development of the form.

CHAPTER NINE

Thematic Criticism of the Rise of the Novel (I): Family, Law, Sex, and Society

This chapter and the following discuss criticism of the rise of the novel since the mid-1990s. This work is predominantly historicist, and I have labelled it thematic, because typically a historical topic is analysed in relation to the novel. Some studies make more of an issue of generic development than others, and these will be accorded more space. Thematic contextual criticism often operates with a selective smattering of texts, which can appear arbitrary and on whose supposedly representative status large generalizations about the novel's development and eighteenth-century culture are sometimes based. The guiding assumption of much of this criticism is that literature is both an agent and a reflection of social change, participating in extra literary discursive formations. In this chapter, I will cover work on the emergent novel in relation to family, law, sex, and society.

The family, sex, and marriage

My section heading adopts the titular formula of Lawrence Stone's *The Family, Sex, and Marriage in England 1500–1800* (1977). Stone's influential account of the development of the 'closed domesticated nuclear' family informs several of the studies discussed here, which address kinship, conjugal relations, and sexual practices in the eighteenth-century novel.

T. G. A. Nelson's *Children, Parents, and the Rise of the Novel* (1995) argues that 'the child became an important and continuous theme of English fiction' throughout the eighteenth century, 'though its chief function is often to serve as a focus for discussions of the feelings of adults for children rather than to permit an exploration of children's feelings about themselves'. The novel only tentatively explores 'the inwardness of childhood, a topic fraught with difficulty and embarrassment', and therefore tends to linger over the topic only to reflect on adult conduct.[1] So, for example, 'in *Joseph Andrews* [...] affection for children is one of the clearest marks of difference between good and bad characters' (120). Ultimately, novels broach without solving the question of whether parents' urge to love and nurture children outweighs their urge to reject or neglect them. Taking a different tack, in *The Politics of Motherhood* (1996), Toni Bowers examines new ideas about motherhood that came to be understood as 'natural' in the eighteenth century, arguing that a new maternal ideology was constructed in the narratives of Defoe, Haywood, and Richardson.[2]

Christopher Flint's *Family Fictions* (1998) argues that the new form of the novel 'consciously manipulated social attitudes concerning the family'.[3] Against the thesis of Nancy Armstrong (see Chapter 4), who links the emergent novel to middle-class empowerment through its dissemination of a new female ideal, Flint argues that the novel's representation of domestic relations is defensive, reacting to the perceived dissolution of family structures as much as offering new models. Flint contends that novels do the cultural work of 'refin[ing] both individual autonomy and a sense of contractual obligation that would ensure autonomy' (17). Novels thus shape selves into individuals and family members. Flint proposes three approaches that novels adopt towards the nuclear family on the levels of narrative treatment and ideological argument: 'marginalization', 'legitimation', and 'disavowal'. Although they are loose and overlapping strategies, these correlate to a three-staged literary history of eighteenth-century fiction. Flint's two examples of early narratives that marginalize the domestic family are Behn's *The Fair Jilt* (1688) and Defoe's *Robinson Crusoe*, each of which foreground the individual rather than family ties; but whereas 'Behn's scandal narratives embrace the family in order to reject it, Defoe's fiction rejects the family the better to embrace it' (130). In mid-century, *Pamela* and *Betsy Thoughtless* legitimate family order more directly: the individualistic scandal and adventure themes of Behn and Defoe give way to narratives moving towards domestic felicity in ways that 'reinforce the ideological preeminence of marriage in bourgeois culture', and which enhance 'patriarchal empowerment' (245, 205). Flint finds that after 1760 narratives disavow this domestic model by casting patriarchs as tyrants, showing the domestic family to be dysfunctional, disorderly, or exploitative, and resisting the tidy formal resolutions of domestic fiction. *Tristram Shandy*, *The Castle of Otranto*, and Wollstonecraft's *Maria* (1798) exemplify this stage. For instance, 'Sterne's fiction exposes the stubborn paternalism that is sublimated in both eighteenth-century family instruction and realistic narrative' (278). Reading these novels against didactic and philosophical contexts, Flint offers an important perspective on the ways in which the family was imaginatively rendered in the rising novel and the impact on the form of fiction occasioned by the novel's engagement with debates about the family.

Richard Barney's *Plots of Enlightenment* (1999) is also concerned with the novel's role in socialization, calling it 'a genre distinctly qualified to edify readers via the fictionalized maturation of its protagonists'.[4] Barney traces the early history of the *Bildungsroman*, the novel of education, showing that 'educational theory during the late seventeenth and early eighteenth centuries formed an indispensable source for the English novel's narrative form and its often contradictory representation of individuals' social identity' (2). The 'pedagogical agenda' of the novel is derived from a body of theory of which Locke's *Thoughts on Education* (1693) is representative. Locke's promotion of 'supervisory pedagogy', a pattern whereby an instructor observes the subject and intervenes when behaviour requires correction, is replicated in *Robinson Crusoe*'s narrative strategies. In *The Female Quixote* and *Betsy Thoughtless* it helps to orchestrate bourgeois femininity through the domestication of education. The '*Observation, Intervention, and Resolution*' educative model allows the novel to 'negotiate a provisional alliance between individual autonomy and social discipline', producing 'improvisational subjectivity', whereby individuals act in ways that are apparently free, but remain aware of constraints (13, 16). As such, Barney extends the Foucauldian analyses offered by Armstrong and Bender (see Chapter 4), identifying the novel of education as 'a concrete form of political practice' that controls readers under the pretext of 'being morally uplifting and instructive' to them (201, 107).

A number of books focus on fatherhood. In *Impotent Fathers* (1998), Brian McCrea relates the emergent novel to a 'demographic crisis' in the English gentry and aristocracy between 1650 and 1740, as around half of landowners failed to produce male heirs and death rates meant that many fathers were not around to supervise their oldest son's marriage.[5] The consequent scenarios, entailing problems of property transmission, are familiar to us from the period's novels: Mr. B's unsupervised courtship in *Pamela* and the orphaned heiress's marital dilemmas in *Cecilia*, for instance. The novel helps to formulate the cultural response to this crisis of patriarchal authority. McCrea critiques the 'totalizing' feminist view of patriarchy as that which 'marginalizes and oppresses the female' by arguing that 'novels by Burney and Lennox, as well as by Fielding and Smollett, begin in the absence rather than the presence of paternal authority' (18). These absences should be read quite literally: there was a real shortage. As a result, patrilineal succession became a 'legal fiction': first-cousin marriage was sanctioned, ancestral names were changed, and inheritances passed through the female line (as in *Tom Jones*). These historical matters are represented in literary fiction in plots involving orphanhood, marriage, and inheritance. Novels by Defoe, Smollett, and Fielding register the anxiety about demographic crisis and assist in the cultural work of redefining how inheritance could happen.

In the later-century, Richardson, Burney, Lennox and Inchbald depict 'patriarchs who are absent, impaired, or dead', indicating the lasting effects of social crisis (28). By the 1750s, the novel 'no longer needed to prop up an impaired patriarchy', but the issues raised by this initial function enabled it to turn to an exploration of characters' inner lives (191). McCrea's historical explanation of the novel's function is perhaps a subset of the social and ethical questions McKeon argues the novel helps to mediate (see Chapter 4).

Also attending to patriarchy, Caroline Gonda's *Reading Daughters' Fictions, 1709–1834* (1996) looks at father–daughter relationships in the early novel through a feminist lens:

> ■ At a time when moralist and novelist alike were preoccupied with the image of a vulnerable and corruptible young woman reader, and with the dire effects novel-reading could have on her, fictional representations of daughters' relationships with their fathers offered a moral framework for her.[6] □

The novel's 'ideological function' is 'to reiterate the socially sanctioned patterns of a woman's life' – daughterly obedience and heterosexual marriage – whereas contemporary rhetoric suggested that novels corrupted and created undutiful daughters (37). In the line of domestic, courtship fiction, Richardson and Burney enforce the lesson that a father's neglect of his duty does not absolve the daughter from hers. In early-century amatory fiction and Romantic-era Gothic, incest is a potential threat to patriarchal power that implies the fragmentation of the family, and which must therefore be contained. In a similar vein to Gonda, though more optimistic about the novel's potential as a site of resistance, Eleanor Wikborg's *The Lover as Father Figure* (2002) analyses patriarchal strictures and the defiant textual strategies that female novelists adopt. Wikborg emphasizes the novel's exploration of father-daughter incest. This is usually indirect or non-literal, as the lover adopts a tutelary or guardian role typical of a father. Analysing female-authored fiction from Behn to Austen, Wikborg argues that this conflation of the roles of lover and father is a subversive strategy that exposes contradictions in patriarchal ideology and allows courtship novels to serve as conduct guides for both men and women.[7]

Ellen Pollak's *Incest and the English Novel, 1684–1814* (2003) is self-professedly *not* 'a totalizing account of the development of the early English novel': Pollak's interests are cultural rather than literary-historical.[8] Nevertheless, her placement of the novel as the culmination of a long debate and an 'ongoing narrative tradition' about what constitutes incest contributes to an important historical argument about what ingredients went into the new form (11). This extends from the debates about Henry VIII's divorcing his sister-in-law to kickstart the English

Reformation in the 1530s through to eighteenth-century works that used Genesis to argue that natural law allowed incest and that restricting it infringed on masculine prerogative. Pollak links the proliferation of cultural discourse about incest in religious, legal, popular print, and novelistic material to the class, kinship, and political struggles that resulted in a modern gender system. She resists, first, the tendency to downplay the cultural significance of incest before the Romantic period (when, the story goes, its surfacing in the Gothic heralds the hidden desires of modern sexuality), and, second, the universalizing tendencies of psychoanalytic and anthropological approaches, which deny historical contingency, typically because they see incest from a perspective that normalizes the nuclear family. With a feminist and historicist methodology, Pollak argues that the eighteenth century was the period in which the incest taboo was made to appear natural rather than cultural, and that the novel played its part in this development.

Against the cultural myth that sees incest as transgressive and liberatory for women, Pollak shows that both incitements to and prohibitions against incest uphold the patriarchal assumption that women are sexual property to be circulated amongst men, because incest stories force readers 'to see the world from the point of view of masculine power' (52). Behn's narratives about incest indicate their heroines' 'specular status in reciprocal relations between men' and Manley's are 'sites of homosocial struggle in which guardians violate paternal trust by usurping the posthumous rights of fathers over daughters' (74, 92). As such, the heroine is empowered only by withdrawing from such relations. By contrast, male-authored novels (Defoe, Fielding and Sterne) are 'occasions for consolidating and naturalizing the contradictory logic' of patriarchal ideology and 'legitimate the operation of masculine privilege' (21, 58). In *Moll Flanders*, for example, the heroine's economic agency is expelled by her acceptance of affective kinship and her horror at incest. In accepting a lower place in the gender hierarchy, Moll consolidates patriarchal assumptions. Accepting the incest taboo also encodes English superiority over colonized Others: this cultural logic is completed in *Mansfield Park*, in which the legitimation of close-kindred marriage maintains strict boundaries between English and African populations.

Finally in this section, Ruth Perry's *Novel Relations* (2004) takes a similarly feminist and cultural historicist approach in her survey of familial relationships in fiction from Richardson's *Clarissa* to Austen's *Persuasion* (1818). She draws on a wide range of secondary historical sources and readings of many novels to support her central thesis: during the second half of the eighteenth century, the primary basis for kinship shifted from consanguineal ties (blood relations based on lineage) to conjugal and affinal ones (marital and parental bonds in the nuclear family). Whereas this shift enabled young men, who could make their way in a world freed from constraints of lineage, it afflicted young women, because they were increasingly dispossessed. The novel 'functioned to explore and work through the changing kinship arrangements which regulated domestic life and intergenerational relationships in a world rapidly being transformed by market forces, urban anonymity, and the spread of literacy'.[9] The changes in kinship are coeval with the shift from a status-based to a class-based society, from agrarianism to industrialized capitalism, from the family as unit of production to one of consumption, and from community to individual. Perry devotes chapters to women's relationships with their fathers, sisters, brothers, guardians, husbands, and aunts, with the last becoming important as motherly substitutes following the 'erasure of maternity' in terms of legal rights (341). She describes 'the great disinheritance': the legal and psychological losses experienced by girls in their families of birth, as heritable property and affection were withdrawn from daughters. The sexualization of young women in the later part of the century was undertaken partly at least by novels, and the training took the form of instilling sexual honesty. Novels both supported the shift towards conjugal kinship and expressed regret and nostalgia for the passing consanguineal system. Perry's engagement with Lawrence Stone indicates how this field of study has changed: in place of the 'companionate marriages' of 'affective individualism' Stone champions, Perry describes marriage as 'privatized' and 'sexualized', which disenfranchises rather than empowers women.

Law, property, and criminality

John Zomchick's *Family and the Law in Eighteenth-Century Fiction* (1993) provides a convenient bridge from the concerns of the previous section to this one. He traces the novel's complicity in the establishment of what he calls the 'juridical subject', an 'internally coherent and self-regulating' individual who acts with freedom and responsibility, but having internalized social codes as private conscience.[10] This instilment of ethics in the period was necessary due to new individualistic behaviour encouraged by capitalism; against this the 'eroticized family' offers respite from the hostile relations of civil society (19). In the family, behaviour is, in appearance at least, non-coercive, mutual, and reasonable; it is a haven from the public sphere, as Habermas conceived it. In the merger of private conscience and public law, the 'juridical subject' is predicated first as a private individual in a civil society built on competition, and second as a member of the family where relations are based on cooperation. Novels provide characters who function as exemplars: 'As the novelists of eighteenth-century England create the juridical subjects in their fictions, they contribute to the creation of the modern, secular subject of rights whose ethical nature is both product and producer of the peculiar traditions of English law' (2). The novel's job is to narrativize the subject's relation to society: protagonists who submit to the law are rewarded with domestic happiness; those who fail face 'exile, death, or transcendence' (20). Zomchick builds on some of the ideological work I discussed in Chapter 4, which follows Foucault in seeing social power displaced from violence to ideology, especially as he argues that 'the internalization of juridical discourse collapses the distance between power and personal choice', because 'instead of being governed by the will of another, the individual appears self-governing' (30).

Clarissa, *Amelia*, *Roderick Random*, and *The Vicar of Wakefield* 'end by generally affirming society's juridical structures and recommending, as it were, the subject appropriate to such structures' (177). These novels discipline readers into civility. Clarissa and Lovelace are negative examples, the former failing to negotiate the competing claims of autonomy and obligation, the latter manifesting an 'anarchic version of individualism' that eschews civil ties, whereas civic order is recuperated instead in Belford's reformation as a model juridical subject (81). In *Roderick Random* and *Amelia*, heroes who curb their impulses and 'internalize socially advantageous constraints' are rewarded with worldly success and a contented family life (106). *The Vicar of Wakefield* is a 'family fable' and 'political fiction' that gives law, embodied in the benevolent magistrate, supreme authority (155, 170). At either end of Zomchick's account are two outliers. *Roxana* 'describes the moment before sexuality and economy are relegated to separate spheres', staging a conflict between affective needs and possessive aspirations when juridical subjectivity was as yet imperfectly formed (40). At the end of the century, *Caleb Williams* is a critique of the 'juridical narrative paradigm', wherein the law persecutes rather than protects, domestic retreat is denied, and the protagonist alienated (178).

Wolfram Schmidgen's *Eighteenth-Century Fiction and the Law of Property* (2002) is also suspicious of the ideological effects of the novel. Schmidgen 'examines how the eighteenth-century novel, along with legal, economic, and aesthetic texts, represents the relationship between persons and things'.[11] He argues that eighteenth-century England was a 'transitional' culture, moving from traditional communal relationships based on a system of landed property characteristic of feudalism, to modernity, based on a commodity fetishism that dissociates the material object from its origin, characteristic of industrial capitalism. This is discernible in novels' descriptions of things with respect to persons. In the fiction of the first half of the century, 'communal forms embed persons and things in concrete social, economic, and cultural contexts, preventing their emergence as separate objects that could begin to cultivate exclusive relationships and bounded identities and thus escape the condition of groundedness' (134). That is, people are anchored by their relationship to the manor house, and the boundaries between persons and things are fluid, so that the items the artisan Crusoe makes are extensions of his person which retain a 'determinate' meaning and an identifiable origin. This 'interconnectedness' gradually disappears in the second half of the century (185). In *Tom Jones*, the manor house dominates as a guarantor of traditional value, but alienation from the collective is anticipated in the Man of the Hill's narrative. Schmidgen reads later-century novels – sentimental, Gothic, and historical fiction – in relation to Adam Smith's transformation of prevalent economic ideas from stable value (mercantilism) to the circulation of objects (capitalism). The development is uneven and gradual rather than a simple rupture, and its manifestation in fiction produces 'hybrids' rather than clear-cut cases. Defoe and Fielding anticipate subsequent developments, and Radcliffe and Scott regret the passing of 'communal' order. Unlike Watt and other Marxians, Schmidgen does not see the novel as unfailingly modern and capitalist, because it also engages with 'pre-modern realities' (64).

In *Engendering Legitimacy* (2006), Susan Paterson Glover, like Schmidgen, examines novels in relation to property law, in particular 'the ways by which experimentation in prose fiction, [...] begins to offer a re-vision of that enmeshing of law, land, property, and political power, imagining a new ground for authorial and political legitimacy'.[12] The legal status of women is crucial here: by marital law they had limited rights to property; however, their bodies ensured the legitimate transmission of property from father to son and legitimate political succession. Glover explains that questions of ownership, contractual evidence, and natal and political legitimacy are prevalent in the early novel. Notwithstanding his traditional Tory view that male ownership of land confers the right to govern, Swift's fictions are inflected by the author's own feelings of disinheritance, conjoined with that of the Irish nation. Defoe's masculine vision of individual property rights in *Crusoe* marginalizes women, and his heroines are punished for behaving like possessive individualists. In the novels of Mary Davys and Eliza Haywood, property is precarious for women, often ensnaring rather than empowering them, by which the authors debunk the traditional liberal equation of freedom and property from a gendered perspective.

Sandra Macpherson's *Harm's Way* (2010) turns attention away from contractual property law to legal questions about liability, as she 'addresses the centrality of accident and injury to the realist novel'. Macpherson puts into dialogue the developing law about 'strict liability' and 'eighteenth-century novels that make questions about agency and responsibility central to their formal innovations'.[13] She rejects both parts of Lukács's characterization of the novel as 'untragically exculpatory', arguing that 'the realist novel is a project of blame not exculpation' and that novels make readers 'think of responsible persons as causes rather than agents' (13, 57). This makes the novel a tragic form in a tradition that includes *Roxana, Clarissa,* and Frances Sheridan's *Memoirs of Miss Sidney Bidulph* (1761). Defoe dramatizes 'accidental harm' (29), because the law would render plague victims responsible for infecting others, make Moll guilty for the consequences of her parental neglect, and make Roxana guilty for the murderous actions of her servant. Equally, 'felony murder', an emerging legal category, 'affirms the liability of principals for the unsolicited acts of their agents', making Lovelace responsible not just for the rape of Clarissa, but her death as well, however much he delegates actions to others (65). In an excursus from this line of the novel, Fielding rejects realism's 'logic of strict liability', as his male protagonists settle matters with comic fistfights not legalistic blame (101). Finally, *Sidney Bidulph* raises the legal implications of a man's rape by a woman, which 'transforms the iconology of sentimental fiction, replacing the violated female body with the violated male body' (135). Sheridan's hero, Faulkland, is entrapped into sex by a girl's scheming aunt, then into marriage, and eventually murder when he finds his wife unfaithful. Liability for this chain of events becomes rather diffuse, which Macpherson sees as typical of the novel's inquisition of the law of liability.

A number of critics have re-evaluated the influence of criminal biography on the novel, a subject previously addressed by Richetti (see Chapter 3). For Lincoln Faller, in *Crime and Defoe* (1993), Defoe's fictions represent a 'new kind of writing' because they complicate the formal strategies and ideological messages of conventional criminal biography, 'exploiting, deforming, and in a variety of ways departing from the genre they purported to represent'.[14] Popular crime writing used a simplistic narrative voice, which closes down the interpretive role of the reader, guiding them to an acceptance of a socially sanctioned view of criminality. Conversely, Defoe uses a complexly retrospective, personal, and 'partial' mode that encourages readerly inference and interrogates social mores. However, Hal Gladfelder, in *Criminality and Narrative in Eighteenth-Century England* (2001) finds much of the literary complexity of the novel form as practised by Defoe, Fielding, and Godwin already present in its criminal sources: crime reports and stories, trial proceedings, gallows confessions, and criminal biographies. Gladfelder contends that 'open-ended narrative' in novels and criminal biographies which stage 'the conflict between the transgressive individual and a normative community' produces conflicting effects. Dominant ideologies that figure the criminal as a sexual, ethnic or social deviant are challenged as often as they are endorsed.[15]

Self and society

This section discusses work that returns to the question of the novel's relationship with modern forms of subjectivity and the accommodation of autonomy by the forces of community, a topic that concerned such critics as Ian Watt and Arnold Weinstein, discussed in Chapters 2 and 3, respectively. Betty Schellenberg's *The Conversational Circle* (1996) proposes that mid-eighteenth-century narratives depicting a 'conversational circle', the purpose of which was to curtail selfish action by subsuming it to group consensus, form a short-lived alternative to narratives of masculine individualism.[16] In *David Simple, Pamela II, Sir Charles Grandison, Amelia, Millenium Hall,* and *Humphry Clinker,* Schellenberg suggests that 'conflict, which most commonly supplies the energy of narrative, is replaced by an impulse towards alignment, consensus, and mutual reinforcement' (5). This aspect of the early novel has been overlooked, because such stories are centripetal, static, and lack closure, whereas the paradigms of realism and individualism, which place 'the desirous individual in sustained tension with his or her social environment', privilege linear, eventful, and goal-oriented stories (2). These fictions construct a 'feminized' social self – passive, private, accommodating, affective, and polite – in response to religious and political uncertainties, class conflict, and self-interested economics. However, this social and narrative project was destined for failure, as adventure and courtship powerfully reasserted themselves as dominant narrative arcs. Conversational novels were 'prescriptive and sterile, untrue to the realities of individual and social experience', but their brief flowering offered 'new modes of narration, characterization, and plot' that left an impression on the novel (132).

Foregrounding the individualism that Schellenberg would qualify, John Richetti's *The English Novel in History, 1700–1780* (1999) argues that the novel amounts to 'an unprecedented attempt to project a new sort of particularized presence, and to imagine persons speaking about themselves in their singularity, asserting themselves as unique individuals and thereby breaking with those generalized types and with those communal affiliations that had long served as the primary markers of identity'.[17] However, for Richetti, unlike Watt, novels *interrogate* rather than merely *perpetuate* the principles of individualism, supplying an 'ideological analysis of society' through their depiction of 'the socially constructed self' (8, 4). Society in the eighteenth century 'signified something active and immediate, not an institutionalized totality but a decidedly smaller and specifically connected group of people' (6). This phase of social formation produced the novel as 'part of the process of adapting older social structures to emerging modern conditions', as novels 'render individuals as (potentially) both socially constructed and individually defined' (7, 8). Richetti departs from accounts that foreground the rise of individualism (Watt: see Chapter 2) or the rise of social power (Bender: see Chapter 4), contending that novels 'dramatize an interdependence or even an inseparability between self and society that tends or hopes to nullify the distinction between the two terms' (12). Richetti thus aims to inject humanism into ideological critique, arguing that fiction is not simply the instrument of hegemony, but is 'in a unique position to articulate, if not to understand' how 'individuals and their social surroundings are in a reciprocal process of re-definition and development' (16).

Richetti contends that, at the start of the century, amatory fiction critiques 'the ethos of love and honor that supported the tradition of romance [...] from the Middle Ages to [the] Renaissance' (19). Behn, Manley, and Haywood subvert romance by offering an 'interiorized equivalent of that life of public honor', the focus of which is the passions, and by depicting the emotionality of female vulnerability (20). As in Richetti's earlier discussion of this material (see Chapter 3), the appeal is primarily escapist: 'This fiction offers a pure opportunity for compelling amatory reverie devoid of distracting moral complexity or social knowledge or particularized reference' (42). The pleasures of amatory fiction are private and personal; it marks a stage in the novel's negotiation of individual identity rather than social order. Defoe's fictions, equally embryonic, go the other way, 'offer[ing] rough paradigms for the practice of fiction through most of the century: they both celebrate and deplore an aggressive self-seeking, dramatizing a social context for individual action that inhibits and thereby provokes it' (56). This ranges from *Robinson Crusoe*, which 'reconciles lonely and tortured individualism with confident communal movement and social integration', to *Roxana* – Defoe's 'attempt to imagine a radical individualist who cannot be contained by any totality' (72, 81). Defoe dramatizes the dialectic between self and society characteristic of this period.

Samuel Richardson's originality, for Richetti, consists in his departure from amatory fiction and its presentation of social rank and distinct gender identity as objective realities: 'What *Pamela* offers its readers is not just a *representation* of a world but an *expression* of an individual within it, so that the dynamic and transactional essence of experience within the social as much as the psychosexual realm is to some extent enacted on the page' (87). Richardson supplements the 'psychosexual' world of Haywood – *Fantomina* (1725) is contrasted with *Pamela* – by showing how the social impacts the personal. *Clarissa* is 'a massive rejection of romance' and hence 'a monumental novel without parallel in English or in European fiction', because it does justice to the complexity of social networks and individual being (99). Henry Fielding's novels, reacting to the 'narrative impulse' in Richardson that 'overvalues an isolated and aberrant individuality', are 'affirmations of community and defenders of a neglected sense of connection and tradition' (121). The result in *Joseph Andrews* and *Tom Jones* is 'systematic' fiction, which conservatively contains individuals in social structures. This orderliness wanes in *Amelia*, partly due to artistic shortcomings, partly due to the difficulty of sustaining such a holistic socioethical vision in the wake of social change.

In his discussion of novelists in Richardson and Fielding's wake, Richetti finds that Smollett's heterogeneous narratives aim to 'articulate irreducible diversity rather than to impose unifying form and structure' (168). Satiric purposes are served by the structural looseness of action in those Smollett novels unified only by a protagonist unwilling or unable to extract moral truth from his experience, though *Humphry Clinker* finally switches gears from satire to present a moral and social message of renewal. In his discussion of female-authored 'domestic fiction' by Haywood, Lennox, Sheridan and Burney, Richetti argues that the heroines' resistance to patriarchal forces sees them 'acting out roles that inevitably sustain the very ideology that they oppose' (198). Richetti draws on feminist insights to show how these novels staged the conflict between self and society. Similarly, the sentimental novel sets out to resolve social problems, including poverty and injustice, with mixed degrees of efficacy. Whereas *Sir Charles Grandison* can use the social standing of its hero to suggest a remedy for social ills, the majority of novels attest to the limited efficacy for improving society through the sympathy propounded by moral philosophers like Hume and Smith. The best it can do is to manifest an awareness of its own inutility, and thereby to diminish the potentially exploitative and self-indulgent observation of other people's suffering, as in Mackenzie's *Man of Feeling* and Sterne's *Sentimental Journey*. In *Tristram Shandy*, Richetti discerns 'the definitive comic surrender of narrative's representational project' (276). He asks why the novel focuses on obscure, eccentric, provincial individuals rather than the bigger currents of history, like empire and capitalism; the sentimental novel, it seems, heralds the disengagement of literature from politics.

In *How Novels Think* (2006), Nancy Armstrong extends her earlier work on the novel's production of middle-class ideology (see Chapter 4), arguing that 'the history of the novel and the history of the modern subject are, quite literally, one and the same'. Armstrong says that the British novel came into being 'as writers sought to formulate a kind of subject that had not yet existed in writing', a model of liberal individualism aligned with bourgeois interests. Watt described how the historical phenomenon of individualism was occasioned by intellectual and material developments, and in turn enabled a new form of realistic representation. Armstrong, however, reverses the causality. For her, fiction *produces* individualism rather than just expressing it, and ensures its wider transmission in British cultural life. To produce this individual, novels had to 'think' as if it already existed, which involved making the bourgeois subject both the narrating subject and the narrative object, as well as invalidating 'competing notions of the subject – often proposed by other novels – as idiosyncratic, less than fully human, fantastic, or dangerous'.[18] Armstrong goes on to explain the development whereby novels move from expressing an individualism that exceeds social norms in the eighteenth century to expressing the desirability of social sanctions that paradoxically protect the individualism they curb in the nineteenth century. The history of the novel replicates the history of liberal individualism, whereby excessive selfishness is constrained by self-governance, a process begun in the eighteenth century and completed in the nineteenth.

In the eighteenth century, Armstrong argues, from Defoe and Richardson to the Gothic and sentimental genres, the novel was 'an open-ended political debate about the nature of the individual' (22). Like Watt, Armstrong sees Robinson Crusoe as an archetype of individualism because he exceeds traditional social strictures. However, *Crusoe* is not simply a celebration of individualism, as Watt argued, and as Richetti maintained. Rather Defoe depicts the 'bad subject', as Crusoe is 'naturally disinclined to respond to traditional forms of authority', and must first gain control of himself before compelling others to consent to a 'sacrifice of individualism in return for protection of life, limb, and property' (32–3). This rehabilitative process continues in *Moll Flanders*, *Roxana*, *Pamela*, and *Clarissa*, novels that adumbrate liberalism's social contract. The process culminates in Jane Austen where individual and collective interests happily overlap. In tandem with Austen, the canonization of the eighteenth-century novel in the early nineteenth century marginalized forms like the Gothic and the sentimental that did not conform to the liberal individualist model. Simultaneously, Romantic-period fictions, such as Walter Scott's *Waverley* (1814) and Mary Shelley's *Frankenstein* (1818), purposely attacked excessive individualism on the part of bourgeois morality. In turn, the nineteenth-century novel feminizes 'extreme forms of individualism' and punishes such characters 'so harshly as to persuade a readership that the very excesses that once led to self-fulfillment and the illusion of a more flexible social order now yielded exactly the opposite results' (79). The novels Armstrong places in the main line recapitulate the history of liberal individualism. Defoe and Richardson have the 'bad subject' brought into line with the social contract; Austen shows her readers that social mores exist not for the suppression of freedom but its preservation; Shelley and Scott demonstrate the baneful effects of unbridled wilfulness; and the Brontës, Dickens, and Eliot consolidate nationhood, capitalism, and empire through their production of bourgeois subjectivity with realism.

Conclusion

The work discussed in this chapter is concerned with the various ways in which the early novel represents and produces subjectivity, be that bourgeois consciousness in relation to familial, legal, and social contexts, or a more liberated and enlightened awareness. In criticism, since the 1980s, the novel is conceived as a powerful cultural form, which shaped sexual, legal, and other social practices at the time that it was taking shape as a literary genre. The next chapter extends this discussion, addressing approaches to the early novel through economics, politics, medical discourse, and thing theory.

CHAPTER TEN

Thematic Criticism of the Rise of the Novel (II): Money, Medicine, Politics, and Things

This chapter begins by aiming to answer the question of how critics after Watt have interpreted the rising novel's relationship to economic forces. Next it considers the place of fiction in eighteenth-century political ideology and then in relation to contemporaneous medical ideas. Finally, through the lens of thing theory, it discusses the novel's place in a material culture of objects.

Economics

Ian Watt aligned the rise of the novel with the advent of economic individualism. In *Models of Value* (1996), James Thompson picks up the Marxist 'argument that the rise of the novel is related to the rise of capitalism'.[1] Thompson sees the concurrent rise of political economy and of the novel as interrelated responses to the crisis in the notion of value that resulted from 'the early modern reconceptualization of money from treasure to capital and the consequent refiguration of money from specie to paper' (2). The historical context here is the development of a credit economy, expedited by the foundation of the Bank of England (1694), the institution of a national debt, and the proliferation of paper money with promissory worth, which replaced intrinsic, 'realist' value with nominal, represented value. Amidst this economic restructuring, the novel supplies a means to 'model' social change. Specifically, as the discourses of political economy and the novel developed, the 'doctrine of separate spheres' designated finance masculine and public, romance feminine and private (156). Political economy worked through the public crisis in financial value, as economists like James Steuart and Adam Smith tried to stabilize value; novels work in a complementary way to ascertain what makes heroines valuable in the private sphere.

Defoe and Fielding harbour oppositional views of value, different attitudes towards the new credit mechanisms. Broadly speaking, whereas Defoe is a progressive advocate of the newly-moneyed interest, Fielding is a conservative defender of the landed establishment. Defoe 'predates the full doctrine of separate spheres', the segregation of economic public discourse (political economy) from affective domestic discourse (novels), but in his fictions 'we find the form of capitalist narrative emerging from feudal morality and not yet mystified by novelistic and bourgeois emotion' (13, 131). Defoe's protagonists move from a conception of use value to exchange value, and from bullion and treasure to credit and trade, thereby laying bare the historical development of credit. By contrast, Fielding represents a conservative, late-feudal attempt to 'stabilize' cash and paper credit, to contain currency within 'traditional patterns of property and possession' (133). In Defoe, an individual's worth is diminished if they lose money; in Fielding, loss of money not only does not diminish worth, but may add to it if they have behaved morally: individual morality transcends the cash nexus. In Burney's novels, when the public–private split has taken hold, heroines recurrently fail to handle money, contracting debt that necessitates their enclosure in a domestic space where a husband moderates their spending. The novel was an active agent in 'mystifying' relations between gender and property, which Thompson says is manifest in Austen's fiction where financial relationships often threaten to scupper love relationships: the novel comes to propound the message that money cannot buy love. Nevertheless, because it is hived off from capitalist exchange, the novel is 'a promise of freedom from a realm of purely financial and instrumental social relations' (198). It offers escape from the cash nexus that dehumanizes and alienates people.

Other critical works shed light on economics and the novel. Sandra Sherman's *Finance and Fictionality* (1996) contends that the new system of credit made financial texts (bills of exchange) and fictional texts (novels) 'homologous' – aspects of the same process. Sherman sees fictionality not as a formal property of a genre, the novel, but as an epistemological condition, occasioned by the Financial Revolution in credit initiated in the 1690s.[2] Catherine Ingrassia's *Authorship, Commerce, and Gender* (1998) is a study of the eighteenth-century 'culture of paper credit', which argues that Richardson 'strategically capitalized on the cultural credit Haywood accrued' in writing profitable fiction in order to normalize credit arrangements in the service of Whig politics.[3] She considers Haywood's novels as a gendered critique of restrictions on women's financial activity, and reads Pamela's letters, which secure her marital value, as metaphors for the workings of paper credit. Thompson, Sherman, and Ingrassia all connect the novel to the rise of commerce, including the commercialization of literature (see Chapter 8), and suggest a fundamental similarity between the fictionality of the emergent novel and the new unreality of money.

Like Thompson, Liz Bellamy, in *Commerce, Morality and the Eighteenth-Century Novel* (1998), argues that novels supply models of ethical conduct for people in a newly commercial society, that 'within the novels of the eighteenth century lies an important debate about the relationship between public and private virtue, and the role and nature of each'.[4] The emergent novel, she shows, mediates the conflict between the public-spirited morality of 'civic humanism' and commercial individualism, occasioned most notoriously by Bernard Mandeville's *Fable of the Bees: or, Private Vices, Public Benefits* (1705–14), which scandalously argued that individual immorality, particularly the consumption of luxury commodities, served the common good, because circulation of money increases national wealth. Bellamy traces this ethical debate from Mandeville to David Hume and Adam Smith, and relates economic theory to the novel, which is 'an embodiment of the ethical tensions that conditioned the period, shaped by the artistic consequence of the divide between old civic humanist concepts of the public and more modern, private terms of analysis of moral behaviour' (7). This reformulates McKeon's formulation of the 'questions of virtue' debated in the novel (see Chapter 4). Bellamy, however, sees the novel as reactionary, promoting the traditional view that self-interested behaviour is destructive to the interests of the community.

Bellamy also attempts 'the incorporation of the epic into the story of the rise of the novel', because she sees the epic as the literary form consonant with traditional civic virtue (39). Cultural critics in the eighteenth century lamented the decline of the epic, particularly as the novel 'did not represent the heroic and masculine public virtue that was the essence of epic literature, but instead portrayed a system of morality that was private, domestic and often feminine or feminised' (51). The novel's claim that it could represent modern society was resisted, because it was seen as part of the moral decline: effeminate commercialism. In mid-century – with Richardson, Fielding and Lennox – the novel gradually accommodates itself to the commercial viewpoint, but retains a residual critique of this, drawing on civic humanist ideologies about the decadence of modern society, anti-luxury arguments, and an idealization of the disinterested landed gentleman. The ethical debate continues in three sub-types of the novel in the later century. Novels of circulation, sometimes called 'it-narratives', are told from the point of view of an object or animal, most typically a coin or banknote, as it circulates in commercial society. This genre 'exposed the links within the economic system, denuded of any affective gloss, and satirised the atomisation, alienation and selfishness that were taken to characterise the modern commercial state' (183). Such conservatism is also evident in the sentimental novel, which contrasts the selfish actions of individuals with the collective, sympathetic spirit of communities. Finally, 'Jacobin' novels (Wollstonecraft, Hays, and Godwin), written in the 1790s in support of the French Revolution, sought to resurrect the idea of public virtue, but were less influential than novels of manners (Burney and Austen), which promoted private conduct separable from civic responsibility. Bellamy thus usefully uncovers a retrograde ethical and economic conservatism in the emergent novel.

Deidre Lynch's *Economy of Character* (1998) also addresses the development of a consumerist, commercial culture. Lynch offers a new history of character, 'of Britons' relations to the imaginary people whom they encountered in books', seeking to replace an old history, ascribed to Watt, which maintains that over the course of the eighteenth century 'flat' characters give way to 'rounded' characters with a full inner life as part of the mimetic advance that corresponds with the novel's valorization of private experience.[5] Instead, Lynch argues that characterological changes from the time of Defoe and Haywood to that of Burney and Austen are due to different uses to which readers put characters, and that this change is owing to consumerist culture. Character becomes a construct that enables the reader to 'negotiate the pleasures and dangers of the market-place', a 'coping mechanism' in a new and alienating cash nexus (12, 5). Here, the novel's development is less an improvement in literary craft and more a response to a market-driven change in readers' needs and desires.

Lynch identifies two phases of the history of character. In the first, from about 1720 to 1770, 'character' relates to external not internal features, particularly the typographical 'characters' of print or physical 'characteristics' of a person. This outward conception of character extends beyond fiction, comprehending also the painter William Hogarth's distinctions between character and caricature, the actor David Garrick's use of his body, and Theophrastan 'characteristic writing', which gave taxonomies of character types. 'In the first two-thirds of the eighteenth century', Lynch explains, 'characterization was valued for its usefulness to readers and writers who found themselves dwelling in a new commercial world, one altered by new trade routes and new forms of credit and full of strange commodities that invited the gaze and emptied the pocketbook' (24). Character is a search for legibility in market culture. Lynch uses the example of Smollett's novels, in which picaresque travellers apparently remain bland, transparent and characterless – to fall back on the old binary, they seem 'flat'. This is explained by the fact that such characters are 'supposed to be a means for producing a sense of social context' (87). Here, 'character is the prosthetic device that enables readers to apprehend the comprehensive, impersonal systems that bind them together': circulating protagonists, in Smollett and in it-narratives, 'assuage fears that the social is of unlimited and hence inapprehensible extension', reassuring people that they remain connected (87, 98). To this extent, Lynch shows that this kind of hero can be replaced by a literally *flat* character, a banknote or coin, as they were in it-narratives.

Whereas character in the first two-thirds of the century is a tool for mitigating readers' anxieties about market culture, in the period from around 1770 to 1830 Lynch identifies an 'inward turn' (6). This 'expanded inner life' of characters is 'an artifact of a new form of self-culture', a product of a class-based elevation of taste and increasingly private, domestic reading (126). The reconceptualization of Shakespearean character in the later eighteenth century indicates these changes in reading practices, as critics began to address the interior states of Hamlet and Falstaff (whose portliness makes him literally a *round* character). Readers now wanted identifiable, sympathetic, fictional characters, which (or maybe 'who') manifest a sense of self that transcends commerce. Accordingly, Burney's heroines are young women who are commodified by the marriage market, but who respond by attaining a new sense of self, an inner life, with which the reader can identify as they also deal with the new commercial system. In Austen, heroines have a hidden, inner life, which is enforced by their unsympathetic treatment at the hands of others, and is manifested in their concealment of their feelings. While protective of their own emotional states, these characters are fully sympathetic to others, observing social forms and decorum in ways that help society to function. Inner life and social existence are in interplay now, and the formal expression of this is free indirect discourse. Lynch nullifies the question of why early novelists are 'bad' at rendering the inner life of character; she reconnects transcendent notions of interiority, perpetuated by Romantic ideology, to social processes and practices. She is hostile to Marxist critics of 'prescriptive realism', such as Catherine Belsey, whose *Critical Practice* (1980) had contended that 'inner-life' characterization techniques 'mystify' social relations and impose bourgeois hegemony by giving an illusion of freely-acting individuals (15). Lynch is more optimistic about the way that novels meet readers' emotional needs in a potentially alienating capitalist economy.

James Cruise's *Governing Consumption* (1999) also addresses the relationship between commerce and character. He argues that novelists exploited suspense, deferring the satisfaction of readers' desires through 'suspended characters' in order to maximize profit: both in the financial sense and in the sense of the ethical profit of 'governing consumption' in a needs-and-wants economy.[6] Novels ape credit's system of deferred gratification of stimulated desire. Cruise rejects the search for the novel's 'origins' in the eighteenth century through what he calls 'postdated ideologies' like Marxist dialectics (McKeon: see Chapter 4) or a prehistory of proto-novelistic forms (Hunter: see Chapter 7) (31). Instead of explaining the rise of the novel as a product of capitalism, Cruise considers how nascent capitalist economics impacted fiction. Cruise describes a shift in seventeenth- and eighteenth-century financial writings 'from anthropology to economy, from needs and wants to the narrative of commerce' (66). In an analogous vein, fictions go from relatively simple character to 'suspended characters', whose gradual disclosure sustains readerly interest. 'Defoe, always ready to steal an opportunity or borrow an idea, was the first to exploit such market demands' (72). Thereafter, Richardson and Fielding, 'coax and train [the novel], by investing in its structure and organization in order to address the generic wants that had already been called for' (72). It is not that amatory fiction gave way to high-minded realism, as Warner argues (see Chapter 7), but that the market rewarded a certain type of fiction: amatory subjects remained, but were amplified, indicated for instance by Haywood's accommodation to demand after 1740.

Economic literary critics have shown that the eighteenth-century novel was implicated in the commercialization of culture and worked by kindling the desires of its readers. They have anchored the novel's relationship to capitalism in particular economic developments that one might say are lost in the more abstract treatment of Watt or McKeon.

Politics

The early eighteenth century is the first age of political parties, as Whig and Tory became competing affiliations. For context, the reader may benefit from looking back at the work of McKeon, Davis (see Chapter 4), and Ballaster (see Chapter 5). Critics have considered the ways in which the novel competed in party-political ideological debates and how the subsequent history of the novel displays a distortive political bias.

In *British Fiction and the Production of Social Order* (2000), Miranda Burgess links generic transformations in fiction with political strategies for the legitimation of the British state following the 1688 Revolution.[7] Fiction contributed to political stability after a century of disorder from the outbreak of the English Civil Wars (1642) to the Jacobite Rebellion (1745). Burgess traces three stages of political economy that inform the novel: Lockean liberalism, Humean political economy, and Burkean nationalism. Burgess's three stages are comparable to some extent with those proposed by Carol Kay (see Chapter 4). The first stage is enshrined in the 'classic liberal political theory' of Locke's *Two Treatises* (1689), which rebutted absolutism and vindicated the transition to a constitutional monarchy (19). However, aspects of Lockean Whiggism threatened to perpetuate rather than quell civil strife, leading to its replacement by political economy predicated on natural ties of sentiment, custom, and shared humanity, advocated by Hume and Smith. Richardson's novels move from the first to the second stage. Reacting to 'protofeminist Tory romances' by Haywood and divisions endemic in 1740s Britain, *Pamela* is a 'romance of consensus' that reforms aristocratic corruption with Whiggish appeals to family values (35). However, in response to Scottish Enlightenment thinking on political economy, '*Clarissa* portrays a Britain held together by sentiment and sympathy', rather than the paternal authority sanctioned in *Pamela* (55). Ambivalence about sentimentality as a genre and as a guarantor of social order gains momentum in novels by Sheridan, Burney, and Wollstonecraft, before Scott and Austen use romance to foster national unity in a manner comparable to the affective nationalism represented by Burke's response to the French Revolution (1789). Burgess extends the method of McKeon in assessing the mutuality of generic and social formation, but denies that romance is superseded. Romance remains the 'genre that intervenes between political history and private narrative, social order and family life' (44). Not simply 'aristocratic', romance is ideologically flexible in its mediation of debates about political economy, making it an effective political agent.

In a 2005 article, Nicholas Hudson, drawing on historical studies that argue English society remained hierarchical, agrarian, and aristocratic throughout the period, contends that 'the developing novel of the eighteenth century was, in fact, essentially conservative, anti-capitalist, and, in some cases, even "Tory"'.[8] He argues that Ian Watt typifies 'Whig history', constructing a narrative of historical progress through 'the thesis that the eighteenth-century novel should be regarded as a "progressive," "liberal" genre that signalled a social revolution, connected by Watt with the rising wealth and power of the "middle class"' (563). By contrast, Hudson argues that social change was more feared than actual, and against these anxieties the novel was part of the 'program of stabilizing, not transforming, English society' by upholding traditional, not progressive, values (574). After recovering an overlooked canon of Tory novelists including not just Behn, Manley and Haywood, but also James Howard and Alexander Oldys, Hudson argues that Defoe's novels critique economic individualism and that Richardson backtracked on the radicalism of Pamela's social mobility. As an 'essentially conservative form' the novel remained 'a literary genre fashioned for the work of constraining the energies of amoral capitalism' up to Austen at least (598).

Also targeting Watt's politics, Rachel Carnell's *Partisan Politics, Narrative Realism, and the Rise of the British Novel* (2006) reconsiders formal realism by revealing 'its connection to the partisan political discourses of its time'.[9] She argues that Whig and Tory writers used fiction to intervene in political crises, each seeking to articulate their own partisan vision as universal human 'reality', whilst denying the political nature of such representational strategies. Behn, Manley, and Haywood are Tory novelists, whereas Defoe, Richardson, and Fielding are Whigs. Watt's canon, therefore, excludes female, Tory, and Jacobite writers, and normalizes the Whig version of realism. Watt's formal realism, exemplified by *Robinson Crusoe*, is 'drawn largely from a Protestant, Whig, male, property-owning head of household' (7). By the mid-twentieth century, Carnell says, certain characterization techniques that originated in competing political ideologies were taken to be apolitical and realistic (Whig), whereas others were deemed partisan and non-realistic (Tory). This is the process inaugurated by Hazlitt's Whiggish view of the novel in 1818, detailed in Chapter 1.

Carnell reconstructs Behn and Haywood's 'novelistic Tory realism', defining Behn's fictions as 'narrative attempts to naturalize a different Tory version of reality through formal innovation' (51, 46). In Carnell's reading, Behn discredits Whig attacks on Stuart monarchical absolutism by insisting on the importance of political vows, but she also challenges the anti-feminist line of Tory politics through a promotion of virtue. Haywood's novels are encryptions of Jacobite politics: Tory calls for re-establishing the Stuart kings banished by the Whig Revolution of 1688. Sexual constancy encodes political loyalty to the Stuart cause; weak parenting that sees daughters abscond with their lovers promotes a less liberal political patriarchy; and figurations of the Jacobite Pretender abound in Haywood's fictions, which retain romance elements associated with Tory values. Defoe and Richardson, meanwhile, are on the Whig side. Defoe's much-vaunted realism, however, sees him 'subject[ing] his characters to ironic narrative inversions, thereby challenging political caricatures, both Whig and Tory' (83). Though it sits uncomfortably with her claim that critics down to Watt naively bought into a Whig version of realism, Carnell says that Defoe offers an interrogative, rather than prescriptive version of Whig realism, exposing the ideological contradictions of possessive individualism. Richardson also emerges as more misunderstood than partisan: his novels moderate political debate and only inadvertently 'reinforce a moral humanism that would encourage later generations of readers to conflate realism with a representation of apolitical universal selfhood' (105). Pamela goes from espousing a Whig right to resistance to personifying a wifely Tory passive obedience; Mr. B. goes from an absolute to a contractarian ruler – however, the overall effect is to 'humanize' the characters in ways that eschew simplistic political identifications. Epistolary exchange in Clarissa offers a model for bipartisanship, 'with Clarissa representing virtuous Tory selfhood and Anna virtuous Whig selfhood' (114). And in *Grandison*, narrative realism emerges from an ostensible avoidance of partisan debate through a humanizing domestic morality and individual psychology. Carnell's main point is that partisan strategies were later interpreted solely in aesthetic terms which favoured Whiggish authors. She therefore locates the origins of the novel in political interventions rather than formal innovations.

Medical discourse

Several recent studies have connected the rise of the novel to developments in medicine. As early as 1986, Robert Erickson's *Mother Midnight* (see Chapter 4) related the novel to intersecting concepts of birth, death, and fate, comparing fiction to early modern midwifery manuals. In *The Language of the Heart* (1997), Erickson pursues the relationship of prose fiction to medical discourse, providing a model of the emergent novel based on William Harvey's discovery of the circulation of the blood.[10] In Erickson's reading, *The Motion of the Heart* (1653), the translation of Harvey's *De motu cordis* (1628), is an archetype for the novel. Harvey's anatomical treatise pioneers the circumstantial, descriptive language that would become characteristic of fiction, and it adopts a narrative of outgoing and homecoming subsequently employed by writers from Behn and Defoe to Fielding and Burney. Furthermore, Erickson outlines the vast accumulation of meanings that attach to the heart between the publications of the King James Bible (1611) and Richardson's *Clarissa*, as the heart became the seat of feeling, of sincerity, and of love, was tied into a host of theological discourses, and was associated with writing, thought, and desire. Cardiology is thus a part of 'the multifaceted birth of the novel', as the metaphorical conception of the heart is developed from Harvey's masculine, 'phallic' model of the heart – involving dilation and constriction, pumping and ejaculation – to a more feminized model of softness, reception, impression, and circulatory exchange in Richardson's melodrama (163).

In a comparable vein, Geoffrey Sill, in *The Cure of the Passions* (2001), connects the rise of the novel to developments between the sixteenth and eighteenth centuries in the medical theory of 'the passions', which were widely believed to determine human behaviour. In Chapter 1, I quoted James Beattie, writing in the 1780s, to the effect that novels stimulated the passions in harmful ways. On the contrary, Sill argues, novelists like Defoe, Fielding, Richardson, Burney, Smollett, and Edgeworth joined physicians, philosophers, theologians, and conduct writers in the effort to *cure* the passions through the means of narrative.[11] This is the emergent novel's occasion and its agenda. The gradual decline of Galenist anatomical theory, based on the balance of the four humours of Hippocratic medicine, was expedited by Harvey's discovery of the circulation of the blood – until it was disturbingly recalled in the 1690s that the sixteenth-century Spanish physician and heretic, Michael Servetus, burned for antitrinitarian heresy in 1553, had pre-empted Harvey's discovery. Sill argues that a fuller understanding of the interplay between body and mind was possible with circulation theory, but the 'ghost of Servetus', the threat of religious heterodoxy, civic unrest, and ungovernable passions, haunts early modern medical discourse. Sill contends that 'eighteenth-century references to Servetus [...] invoke[e] this problematic tension between individual passion and institutional authority which lay at the origins of the novel' (6–7). Sill thus adds the 'question' of the passions to the 'questions' of virtue and truth outlined by McKeon (see Chapter 4). For Sill, the 'categorical instability' at the heart of the novel is not primarily social or epistemological, but psychological.

Sill reads Defoe's novels as 'natural histories of the passions' or 'illness narratives' – they are 'case studies of the perturbation of human nature by desires of various sorts, including youthful lusts for selfhood, irrational curiosities about death in the midst of plague, and ambitions for a place in society to which one has no legitimate claim' (10). This is how he characterizes, successively, *Robinson Crusoe*, *A Journal of the Plague Year*, and *Moll Flanders*. Focusing on the prototypical *Crusoe*, Sill shows that in the midst of a heated theological controversy about the Trinity that recalled Servetus in 1719, Defoe sought to moderate unruly religious and civic passions. *Crusoe* thus dramatizes the cure of the passions, the protagonist's struggle towards a rational self-mastery after being initially swayed by emotion. Crucial to the cures of the passions proposed in novels is restorative dialogue with a 'physician of the mind', a philosopher, counsellor and friend, typified by figures like Dr. Lewis in *Humphry Clinker*, the counsellor who helps cure Arabella in *The Female Quixote*, and Dr. Harrison in *Amelia*. The cure is also tied to neural theory typified by the work on vitalism of Alexander Monro and the moral philosophy of Francis Hutcheson. Both moral philosophy and vitalism reject the 'mechanistic' physiology propounded by Descartes, Hobbes, and Mandeville. Fielding's hero Tom Jones possesses the Hutchesonian 'moral sense' which helps him to redirect his passions and 'prompts him to act not only in his own interest but also in the interests of others, an "active principle" in the pursuit of good' (162). The novels of Richardson and Burney work to 'extirpate' the passions in narratives about the trials of young women who must first control their own passions, and then counsel others or lead by example. Sill concludes by reflecting that the theory of the passions had given way by the end of the eighteenth century to 'the more malleable psychology of the emotions', stating that 'the replacement of the passions by the emotions as the primary subject of fiction in the new century effectively marks the ends of the "origins" phase of the genre of the novel' (187). The woman in control of her passions, like Edgeworth's Belinda or Austen's heroines, becomes the appropriate heroine of the nineteenth-century novel.

In her original and persuasive *Reading the Body in the Eighteenth-Century Novel* (2004), Juliet McMaster touches on some similar issues to Sill. McMaster examines 'contemporary discourses on the body that fed into fictional practice', including treatises on the passions, actors' manuals, pathological theory, and scientific writing on reading faces.[12] McMaster argues for 'a growing awareness on the part of the novelists that they were catering to a readership that was [...] increasingly alert to the possibility of interpreting character from body' (xiv). Somatic theory was a useful aesthetic tool for the budding novel, but fiction also participated in debates about the body at a time of transition when 'moderns' like Harvey and Descartes started to challenge 'ancients' like Aristotle, Hippocrates, and Galen.

McMaster outlines a number of areas of debate about the body and illustrates how novels interacted with the topic. First is the inner operations of the diseased body: the medical practice was to follow Aristotelian methods of cathartic extraction, rather than invasive surgery, and 'moral purgation that coincides with a physical one becomes a standard storyline' in the period's fiction, as in Mr. B.'s illness in *Pamela* (10). Second is the relationship of body to mind, approached enigmatically by Sterne in *Tristram Shandy*, but tending towards the view that the mind can be read through the body. This assumption underlines the popular practices of physiognomy (reading personality through facial features) and pathognomy (reading facial expressions and gestures as revealers of states of mind). Physiognomy was a contentious science, and eighteenth-century novels are 'documents in the ongoing debate on physiognomy' (45). The contempt registered by Fielding is offset by the approval of Brooke and Radcliffe, as novels came under the influence of Johann Caspar Lavater's *Essays on Physiognomy* (1772). Pathognomy and gesture were less contentious, as eighteenth-century culture became interested in the outward expression of interior passions in the mutually influencing fields of painting (Hogarth, Le Brun, Reynolds), acting (Garrick), and the novel. In an intensive close reading, McMaster uses *Clarissa* to illustrate the ethical significance novels gave to gesture: appearances should express interior states. The reader's knowledge of character is frequently restricted to their body signs, so reading these becomes an important skill, especially when insincerity renders the body an unreliable signifier; indeed, as a verbal form, the novel was well placed to 'authoritatively *declare* that the expression is legible, without having to make it so' (167). The novel also stages the reading of bodies, as characters assess one another with varying results. McMaster reads Burney's *Camilla* as 'a sustained meditation on the relation of mind to body', which utilizes bodies as things to be interpreted and trains the reader in interpretation (148). In terms of literary-historical development, McMaster claims that the novel moves from displaying its expertise in reading the body to a greater awareness of 'the pleasures, problems, and varying skills in reading them [bodies]' (173).

Finally here, Katherine Kickel, in *Novel Notions* (2007), links the early novel with 'the seventeenth-century movement to reformulate, challenge, and revise Galenic principles', identifying its 'indebtedness to the medical discourse on the imagination'.[13] Kickel connects Thomas Willis's seventeenth-century assertion that he had discovered the part of the brain responsible for the imagination with novelistic practices by Defoe, Fielding, Sterne, and Radcliffe. She argues that novelists extended early modern medicine's interest in perception and cognition by 'mapping the imagination'; they do so by reflecting on the process of authorship in light of medical ideas. The application of medical contexts to eighteenth-century narratives has thus added to our understanding of the meaning of fiction at the time. The subject of the following section, thing theory, is a critical method that has been applied retrospectively to elucidate the formal properties and cultural significance of early novels.

Thing theory

Thing theory is a relatively new branch of critical theory concerned with the role of physical objects in literature and culture. Recent studies have productively applied its insights to the stylistic development and thematic concerns of the emergent novel. Cynthia Wall's pioneering *The Prose of Things* (2006) tracks developments in prose description during the eighteenth century, accounting for the (perceived) paucity of description in pre-Victorian novels:

> ■ Instead of presenting us with settings, with fully visualized spaces, the early novel describes things. Or, rather, it *presents* things. [...] To the post-nineteenth-century reader, these "things" seem disconcerting, contextless, isolated in otherwise empty space, not part of the properly furnished homes with Dickensian detail and Jamesian significance.[14] □

Things *stand in for* description in eighteenth-century novels, whereas they *are described* in accretive detail in nineteenth-century novels. Wall re-attunes our stylistic expectations of early novels and extends Watt's point that realism is achieved through the particularized narrative description of the empirically observed world. Wall contends that transformations of description over the course of the century were related to four cultural changes: the appearance of new visual technologies, such as microscopes and telescopes; the expansion of commercial culture and commodification; changing epistemological attitudes towards the 'general' and the 'particular', the universal and individual; and changes in domestic space and its narrative representation. A classical demand for the ideal and universal was preponderant until the mid-century, at which time the new empiricist epistemology of Locke and Hume turned attention to the real and the everyday.

Wall outlines 'the techniques of early fiction in stuffing objects with meaning, in poising objects in space, in generating space through movement' (40). Her point is that things exist in a relatively 'unvisualized' space, as 'early fiction tends to use detail emblematically, but it frequently invests those emblems with a rich ordinariness, a telling local concreteness, that seems to bolt them more firmly to the here and now than the hereafter' (3). This manifests earlier in the cartographical work of Stow, Strype, and Ogilby; in personal diaries like those of Evelyn and Pepys; in the scientific treatises of the Royal Society; and in the Puritan habit of imbuing everyday objects with spiritual meaning. However, space and things were undergoing a gradual change from having emblematic significance to having particularized quality. As a gauge of this change, Wall reads the transition in *The Pilgrim's Progress* from allegorical generality in Part 1 to the germs of domestic specificity in Part 2. In turn, things in Defoe are 'reconstituted emblems' – items that attain a particular quality but retain an emblematic significance (112).

Things appear in early novels to stimulate action, and expecting 'rich' description for its own sake is anachronistic. In Behn, Haywood, Aubin, and Davys, Wall shows that spatial detail is rendered only as and when it is called for by narrative incident. In the later-century, *The Castle of Otranto*, a novel populated with absurdly overdetermined and oversized things, satirizes the placement of objects outside of appropriate spatial contexts. Wall claims that *Pamela* predominantly operates in the 'old' way, using space to fulfil narrative need and utilizing emblematic items, whereas 'Richardson employs full-scale description in a few rare moments in *Clarissa*' (142). In the later eighteenth century, 'the things of the house – china, laces, caps, "everything in the world" [says Mrs Larolles to Burney's heroine, Cecilia], began to emerge as visible, connected objects within novelistic spaces, in part because of a new profusion of things, of ways and means to collect and arrange as well as to disperse and disassemble them' (149). Interior space was too diversified by such consumer goods for it to remain implicit, and *Grandison* reflects this, absorbing 'the kind of spatial detail that by midcentury was permeating public consciousness in the advertisements, shopwindows, newspapers, satires, auction catalogs, and country house guides' (199). Wall sets moments of narrative description in novels of manners, Gothic fictions, and the historical romances of Scott alongside the rise of fixed shops with display windows, auction catalogues giving extensive inventories of *objets d'art* like Wedgwood pottery, the new fashion for taking domestic tours of country houses, and customized furniture by Chippendale. She says that 'by the end of the eighteenth century and the beginning of the nineteenth, Radcliffe and then Scott present us with a fully visualized *setting* in which events will occur. We are given the visual world; we no longer extrapolate it' (5). Wall thus explains how 'unvisualized', apparently empty, novelistic space was transformed into the detailed landscapes and upholstered interiors of Victorian fiction.

Thing theory has, unsurprisingly, taken an interest in 'it-narratives', the 'novels of circulation', discussed in the context of the commercialization of culture by Deidre Lynch and Liz Bellamy. Jonathan Lamb's *The Things Things Say* (2011), which was published too late for consideration in this guide, promises a full study of this subgenre.[15] Meanwhile, Mark Blackwell has edited a collection of essays on this topic, *The Secret Life of Things* (2007). The it-narrative is characterized by Blackwell as 'an odd subgenre of the novel, a type of prose fiction in which inanimate objects (coins, waist-coats, pins, corkscrews, coaches) or animals (dogs, fleas, cats, ponies) serve as the central characters'. Blackwell argues that this subgenre is typically 'overlooked by studies that emphasize richly characterized, psychologically complex novels as the terminus ad quem of eighteenth-century narrative evolution'. However, because it fits between Richardson and Fielding and the institutionalization of the novel in the Romantic period, attention to this genre can 'enrich and complicate the history of prose fiction'.[16] The collected essays reflect on the relationship between this genre and commercial culture, authors' anxieties about the circulation of their novels as commodities in the public sphere, the tastes of middle-class readerships, and political debates, from the Jewish Naturalization Act (1753) to abolitionism. Moreover, Bellamy's contribution provides a bibliography of the genre, which shows that it-narratives endured throughout the nineteenth century.[17]

Finally here, Julie Park's *The Self and It* (2010) connects the rise of the novel and the proliferation of *things* in a burgeoning, elite metropolitan consumer culture as parallel determinants of a model of selfhood that effaced the 'boundaries between person and thing, subject and object'.[18] Park discusses two kinds of object. Firstly, there are those that seem like an *appendage* to the human, such as clothing and jewellery, but which frequently constitute selfhood. So, for example,

Sophia Western's muff in *Tom Jones* stands in for the heroine, and the heroine's dress in *Roxana* supplies her with an identity. Secondly, there are those animate and inanimate anthropomorphized objects that *replicate* the human, such as dolls, automata, puppets, and waxworks. These items, like prose fictions, were 'new tools for devising novel versions of the self', so that, for example, the novel is like a puppet show or exhibition of automata because it reproduces the illusion of real human behaviour, 'counterfeiting' human subjectivity and allowing readers to model identity (xiii, 47). As Park explains: 'Just as prose fiction, with its innovations in constructing character, conceived the self as a malleable subject, susceptible to factors in its immediate environment, so too did the waxwork shows of eighteenth-century London' (97). What is more, no less than puppets or dolls, the novel was an object, 'a thing that binds printed paper, [...] a purported "container" of an individual subjectivity and the objects that chart and surround it' (xvii). Park argues that the eighteenth-century novel 'produced the self not only as a textual construct, but as a deeply material and even mechanical one' (xix).

As well as supplying an image of the self as a 'made' thing – an object – the novel was a commodity, stimulating and satisfying a cultural desire for novelty. Park draws on Marx's idea of commodity fetishism, whereby an object is invested with value abstracted from its material production and appears to possess its own agency – much like novelistic characters who behave apparently without the manipulation of a creator, or a puppet whose strings cannot be seen. Fetishism also invokes Freud, as Park makes the connection between the libertine fetishist, Lovelace, who zeroes in on a missing 'thing' (absent female genitalia) and the novelist, Richardson, who reflects the male perception of woman as a doll, a painted figure in need of male mechanical animation. As 'male constructivists of female subjectivity', both novelist and libertine 'demonstrate that male subjectivity insists on objectifying feminine subjectivity in terms of its body parts in order to overcome the anxiety of affective as well as anatomical lack' (76). After Richardson, Park assesses strategies of female self-representation through puppetry in Charlotte Charke's *Narrative* (1755) as analogous to the novel's 'attempt to embody [...] the voice and heart of the human being in its own absence', in particular Burney's challenge to the male perception of women as automata (165).

Conclusion

The final two chapters of this guide have attested to the wide range of cultural contexts and theoretical understandings that have been adduced to explain the novel's emergence and its early development. These chapters demonstrate the attempt to explain the provenance of the novel through the history of ideas (medicine, for example) and in relation to material history (including actual objects). This scholarship also attends to formal techniques, including narrative description and characterization. In the Conclusion I will discuss some recent work that has returned to questions of novelistic form as well as questions of history.

Conclusion: Recent and Future Directions

'Beginning a story of the novel with the beginning of the eighteenth century is an arbitrary choice', declares Patricia Meyer Spacks.[1] The criticism that I have organized into a narrative about the developing idea of the rise of the novel validates this point. However, the connection between this historical period and this literary genre is hard to sever, and given the weight of criticism behind it I would question the usefulness of doing so. Perhaps Watt's account seems so enduringly satisfying because it is a simplification. As far as simplifications go, it is remarkably capacious, but simplifications always need to be complicated. I want to conclude this book not with summary, but with a comparison of two recent books, each generously offered as resources for non-specialists and students, which take different, but I would argue complementary, approaches to the development of the novel, indicating the current state of critical understanding.

Spacks, in *Novel Beginnings* (2006), proposes 'a fresh story about the eighteenth-century novel' to be gained through looking closely at the texts themselves (4). The result, despite her acknowledgement that 'social changes impinged upon, even helped to determine, the shape of narrative' and that 'the early novel paid attention to the problems of the society that generated it', is primarily a formalist analysis that emphasizes the 'multiplicity of narrative experiments' at a time when 'the novel in its newness enjoyed few rules of composition' (5, 12, 18). Spacks shifts attention away from historical context and literary history and towards particular novels' formal workings: she 'focuses not on where the novel comes from but on what the novel in its varied early manifestations *is*, not on how the novel reflects or comments on social conditions but on how it shapes itself to engage interest and provide enlightenment' (25). She insistently resists attempts at summary characterization that would 'fit the variety of eighteenth-century fiction under a single rubric', because 'no formal taxonomy can comprehend the richness and variety of the period's fiction' (24, 26).

Spacks organizes a broad range of texts into seven subgenres, which she terms 'systems of convention'. The subgenres are: novels of adventure, novels of development, novels of consciousness, novels of sentiment, novels of manners, Gothic novels, and political novels. The point behind the title, *Novel Beginnings*, is that these are each points of departure for the new form, as conventions were still in flux. The subgenres are distinct, but overlap, and there is variety 'within as well as amongst novels', as many works prove multiform (273). If one thing connects Spacks's discussion, it is that eighteenth-century novels are 'deviations from realism' (2). This is interestingly expressed, because deviance implies a norm. Watt clearly looms large, but Spacks's discussion allows for texts that conform to realist paradigms and those that do not. Spacks thinks of 'possibilities along an axis extending between the imagined poles of realism and fantasy' (23). The novel is no one thing; its conventions had not yet been stabilized.

Novels of adventure, ranging from Barker, Haywood, and Defoe to mid-century it-narratives, work through 'narrative multiplicity rather than detailed development', as 'the reader is invited to take pleasure in a collection of happenings linked more by sequence than by logic and to register the excitement of sheer event' (30, 34). Novels of development, like *Tom Jones*, *Betsy Thoughtless*, and *The Female Quixote*, are interested in 'the moral implications of characters' actions'. They are non-individualistic, because they present 'fictional personages abstracted and generalized from direct experience, rather than equivalents for individualized human beings' (61). Novels of consciousness, in epistolary form, vary from focusing 'more intensely on internal than on external event', in Richardson, to attention to the 'social world', in *Humphry Clinker* (92, 114). Experimental versions attempt to render consciousness in narrative, such as *The Cry*, or attest to the impossibility of doing so, like *A Sentimental Journey*. Spacks finds that sentimental novels are deliberately non-realistic and elevate feeling over reason as the foundation of morality. Structurally, they incorporate 'multiplied brief narratives' and exhibit a 'refusal of narrative completion' that 'duplicates the refusal of psychological detail' (137). The novel of manners, from Burney to Austen, turns from personal ethics to public codes, investigating social customs. Gothic fiction after Walpole provides a particular take on novelistic psychology by utilizing the supernatural and the sublime. Finally, political novels in the 1790s offer 'visions of ideal political possibility or, more daringly, indictments of society as it currently existed' in direct response to the French Revolution (222). All of these subgenres proceed with a provisional set of rules that are continually subverted and only slowly solidified.

Spacks reserves a special category for *Tristram Shandy*, which draws on many of these subgenres but fits into none. Being atypical paradoxically makes Sterne's novel typical (as Viktor Shklovsky remarked many years earlier). For Spacks, 'the most eccentric novel of the eighteenth century best exemplifies the genre's developing resources and the sense of wide possibility that had accrued to it' (254). *Tristram Shandy*, although it is 'a diverting, willful, rule-breaking work that bears few obvious similarities to other fiction of its own period or to anything else before postmodern inventions, nonetheless reveals much about what had happened to the novel in less than fifty years of its early evolution' (254). Spacks concludes by arguing that the eighteenth-century novel laid the groundwork for later fiction, but that it also opened up narrative possibilities that were not taken up. To avoid misplaced evaluation and to do justice to the formal diversity of the emergent novel, she proposes practicing 'literary history as a record of reading literary works', building up classification afresh by re-engaging with texts (282).

Brean Hammond and Shaun Regan's *Making the Novel* is in some respects a more traditional literary history, surveying fiction from 1660 to 1790 chronologically. Whereas Spacks sorted into subgenres, Hammond and Regan periodize; and whereas Spacks stresses formal multiplicity, they stress contextual multiplicity, addressing the manifold 'artistic, social and economic forces that first brought the novel into being'.[2] They concentrate on issues of content rather than form, identifying 'certain kinds of discourse with particular ideological agendas', rather than the 'specific formal features associated with genre' (25). They make it clear that the novel is not a genre that can be closed off from social history; nor can its fortunes be severed from drama or poetry in a period which saw the broader 'novelization' of culture.[3] Hammond and Regan state:

> ■ We [...] want to resist the idea that the novel itself progressed inexorably, onwards and upwards, from uncertain beginnings in the early eighteenth century to the works of the great Victorian novelists and beyond. Rather, our readings seek to show how the early novelists operated in contested fields of discourse, grappling with a verbal, printed medium whose rules and conventions existed in an ongoing process of formation and modulation. (xi) □

Smooth teleology is replaced with 'considerable evidence of contestation and struggle' in several stages of the novel's development (5). This struggle is between novels and their cultural contexts, but also subsists in 'local competition' between novels and novelists (124). In the early years, this is the wrangling between the representational claims of romance and realism in Congreve, Behn, and Manley. Then there is 'a market-driven competition to locate a successful fictional product' between Defoe and Haywood in the 1720s, a process in which the former emerges as posterity's victor, with 'the invention of a psychological "depth model" for novelistic characterization' lacking in Haywood (85, 61). In turn, there is the contest between Defoe and Swift over the value of modernity and novelty. *Robinson Crusoe* is 'a new kind of serious realist fiction' and 'a new account of subjectivity; a representation of selfhood that is recognizably "modern"' (64–5). *Gulliver's Travels*, by contrast, 'is ideologically opposed to the set of attitudes and beliefs that was fuelling the development of the genre' (79). And of course there is the dispute between Richardson and Fielding about how and what the novel should teach readers.

Making the Novel restates the importance of doing literary history synchronically as well as (like Spacks) diachronically. For instance, Hammond and Regan see the 1730s as a 'nodal point', at which the novel's history could have developed differently (85). Defoe and Haywood's moment had passed and drama and poetry were in the ascendancy. The 1740s was, however, a crucial formative decade, because, at a time when social standards seemed in decline, *Pamela* was borne out of 'Richardson's perception that the novel could become a potent vehicle for ethical instruction' (91). The Licensing Act (1737) pushed Fielding away from writing drama and he was impelled to respond to Richardson. The 1750s are no less pivotal: although some rules had been established, it was at this time that the novel became 'a discrete literary genre that was nevertheless defined by a continual process of renewal' (124). This necessity for renewal manifests in multiform experimentation: erotic fiction (*Fanny Hill*), novels of circulation (*Pompey the Little*), quixotic novels (*The Female Quixote*), the Gothic (*The Castle of Otranto*), utopian fiction (*Millenium Hall*), and sentimental fiction (*The Man of Feeling*). For Hammond and Regan, as for Spacks, this 'precarious moment' of manifold experimentation' is represented by the unclassifiable *Tristram Shandy*, which 'was responsible for revitalizing the genre' (165). Thanks to this activity, by the 1770s, 'the novel had established itself as one of the most important media for examining contemporary social developments and cultural concerns' (201). The interventions of *Humphry Clinker* and *Evelina* on debates about national identity – was Britain a polite or a luxurious nation? – give a sense of the novel's cultural prestige, making the novel 'one of the most successful products to have been manufactured within Britain's new, commercial economy' (241).

What conclusions are there to draw from these two books and how might future contributors find a way in to the challenge of accounting for the cultural status and the aesthetic power the novel had achieved by the turn of the nineteenth century? Unlike Watt and McKeon, both *Novel Beginnings* and *Making the Novel* take their accounts well past mid-century and stress the diffuseness of both the novel's form and its social preoccupations. Some critical work that was published too late for inclusion in this book attests to the range of the early novel's concerns.[4] Both *Novel Beginnings* and *Making the Novel* challenge the view that the novel's rise was tidy and culminatory by showing that it was gradual and uneven, proceeding by formal experimentation and historical accidentals. However, both maintain that the novel *was not* yet in place at the start of the eighteenth century but *was* established by its end. In terms of the canon, which I have tracked throughout this book, we are finally achieving an appropriate level of inclusivity.

Hammond and Regan and Spacks continually remind us that singular accounts of the novel's rise are often untrustworthy. This goes for general statements about *The Rise of the Novel* as well: I urge the reader new to this field to test against the original *all* claims made about what Ian Watt argues, because, although I forbear from naming names (because each critic's argument should be assessed first and foremost on its own terms), in the course of my reading for this study I have found a considerable extent of misprision and, what is worse, misrepresentation of *The Rise of the Novel*. It has unfortunately become a book more often caricatured than consulted. Watt remains the voice in this field to be contended with, as indicated by a special issue of the journal *The Eighteenth Century: Theory and Interpretation*, called *The Drift of Fiction: Reconsidering the Rise of the Novel*, edited by Julie Park, published in late 2011 (appearing too late for consideration in this book). Finally, I would like to stress the complementary rather than adversarial approaches of formal and cultural analysis, represented here by Spacks and by Hammond and Regan. We have seen these approaches take trenchantly opposed positions at key stages throughout this study, but the challenge of the coming years is to see the novel's historical significance and its formal strategies as parts of the same story by paying historical attention to features of form as well as content and by eschewing generic assumptions derived from later periods. The eighteenth-century novel needs to be read on its own terms, and there is still critical work to be done to delineate what exactly those terms are.

Notes

INTRODUCTION

1. Lennard J. Davis, 'Who Put the *The* in *the Novel*: Identity Politics and Disability in Novel Studies', *Novel*, 31 (1998), 79–101 (80).
2. See John Skinner, *An Introduction to Eighteenth-Century Fiction: Raising the Novel* (Basingstoke: Palgrave Macmillan, 2001) for 'as reader-friendly a survey as possible' (p. x).
3. The Gothic has received separate treatment in this series, in Angela Wright, *Gothic Fiction: A Reader's Guide to Essential Criticism* (Basingstoke: Palgrave Macmillan, 2007).

CHAPTER ONE: EIGHTEENTH- AND NINETEENTH-CENTURY ACCOUNTS OF THE RISE OF THE NOVEL

1. Ioan Williams (ed.), *Novel and Romance, 1700–1800: A Documentary Record* (London: Routledge and Kegan Paul, 1970), p. 75. Hereafter referenced as *N&R*.
2. Pierre-Daniel Huet, *The History of Romances: An Enquiry into their Original*, trans. Stephen Lewis (London: J. Hooke and T. Caldecott, 1715), p. 6.
3. Clara Reeve, *The Progress of Romance* [...], 2 vols (Colchester: W. Keymer, 1785), I: 111.
4. *Selected Letters of Samuel Richardson*, ed. John Carroll (Oxford: Clarendon, 1964), p. 41.
5. Henry Fielding, *Tom Jones* (1749), ed. R. P. C. Mutter (London: Penguin, 1985), p. 60.
6. Allen Michie, *Richardson and Fielding: The Dynamics of a Critical Rivalry* (Lewisburg, PA: Bucknell University Press, 1999).
7. See John Tinnon Taylor, *The Early Opposition to the English Novel: The Popular Reaction from 1760 to 1830* (New York: King's Crown Press, 1943).
8. James Beattie, *Dissertations Moral and Critical* (London and Edinburgh: W. Strahan, T. Cadell, and W. Creech, 1783), p. 508.
9. Reeve (1785), I: 8.
10. Hugh Murray, *The Morality of Fiction; or, An Inquiry into the Tendency of Fictitious Narratives* (Edinburgh: Mundell and Son, 1805), pp. 94–112.
11. Anna Laetitia Barbauld, 'On the Origin and Progress of Romance' (1810), in *Selected Poetry and Prose*, ed. William McCarthy and Elizabeth Kraft (Peterborough, Ont.: Broadview, 2002), pp. 377–417.
12. Ioan Williams (ed.), *Sir Walter Scott on Novelists and Fiction* (London: Routledge and Kegan Paul, 1968), pp. 40, 21, 47.
13. John Dunlop, *The History of Fiction: Being a Critical Account of the most Celebrated Prose Works of Fiction from the Earliest Greek Romances to the Novels of the Present Age* (1814), 2 vols (New York: Franklin, 1970), II: 569, 566.
14. William Hazlitt, 'Lecture VI: On the English Novelists', in *Lectures on the English Comic Writers* (1818), intro. R. B. Johnson (London: Oxford University Press, 1908), pp. 138–74.
15. Wilbur Cross, *The Development of the English Novel* (1899; reprinted New York: Greenwood, 1969), p. xv.
16. Richard Burton, *Masters of the English Novel: A Study of Principles and Personalities* (New York: Henry Holt, 1909), p. 32.
17. Burton (1909), p. 18.
18. Edmund Gosse, *A History of Eighteenth-Century Literature* (1889; reprinted London, 1909), pp. 242–3.
19. *The Spectator*, no. 484, 22 April 1871.

20. Two studies that look earlier than the eighteenth century are Bayard Tuckerman, *A History of English Prose Fiction: From Sir Thomas Malory to George Eliot* (New York: Putnam, 1882) and Carl Holliday, *English Fiction from the Fifth to the Twentieth Century* (New York: Century, 1912).
21. Lord Ernle, *The Light Reading of Our Ancestors: Chapters in the Growth of the English Novel* (London: English Association, 1921), pp. 2, 189.
22. Hippolyte Taine, *History of English Literature* (1863–9), trans. H. van Laun, 4 vols (London: Chatto and Windus, 1890), III: 257.
23. W. J. Dawson, *The Makers of English Fiction* (New York: Fleming H. Revell, 1905), p. 8.
24. Burton (1909), pp. 25, 18.
25. Cross (1899, 1969), p. xii.
26. George Saintsbury, *The English Novel* (1913; reprinted London: Dent, 1927), pp. 7, 91.
27. Percy Russell, *A Guide to British and American Novels [...] from its Commencement down to 1894* (London: Digby, Long & co., 1895), p. 5.
28. William Forsyth, *The Novels and Novelists of the Eighteenth Century, in Illustration of the Manners and Morals of the Age* (London: Murray, 1871), p. 7.
29. Burton (1909), pp. 55–6.
30. Sidney Lanier, *The English Novel and the Principle of Its Development* (1892), Clarence Gohdes and Kemp Malone (eds), in *The Centennial Edition of the Works of Sidney Lanier*, ed. Charles R. Anderson, 10 vols (Baltimore, MD: Johns Hopkins University Press, 1945), IV: 3–251 (146–59).
31. William Lyon Phelps, *The Advance of the English Novel* (1915; reprinted London: Murray, 1919), p. 79.
32. Forsyth (1871), p. 1.
33. Taine (1863–9, 1890), p. 257.
34. Sir Walter Raleigh, *The English Novel: Being a Short Sketch of its History from the Earliest Times to the Appearance of 'Waverley'* (London: Murray, 1894), p. 1.
35. See also Cross (1899, 1969), pp. 22–5 and Phelps (1915, 1919), pp. 30–3.
36. Gosse (1889, 1909), p. 243; Cross (1899, 1969), pp. 57–63; Dawson (1905), p. 1.
37. Saintsbury (1913, 1927), p. 132.
38. Dawson (1905), p. 20; Burton (1909), p. 42.

CHAPTER TWO: NEW CRITICISM TO *THE RISE OF THE NOVEL*, 1924–57

1. Ernest A. Baker, *The History of the English Novel*, 10 vols (1924–39; reprinted New York: Barnes and Noble, 1950), I: 15.
2. Frances Hovey Stoddard, *The Evolution of the English Novel* (New York: Macmillan, 1900).
3. J. M. S. Tompkins, *The Popular Novel in England, 1770–1800* (1932; reprinted London: Methuen, 1969), pp. v, 1.
4. F. R. Leavis, *The Great Tradition: George Eliot, Henry James, Joseph Conrad* (London: Chatto and Windus, 1948), p. 11.
5. Arnold Kettle, *An Introduction to the English Novel*, 2 vols (London: Hutchinson, 1951–3), I: 9, 27.
6. Richard Church, *The Growth of the English Novel* (London: Methuen, 1951), pp. 65, 50–1.
7. Dorothy Van Ghent, *The English Novel: Form and Function* (New York: Rhinehart, 1953), p. 4.
8. Walter Allen, *The English Novel: A Short Critical History* (1954; reprinted London: Penguin, 1958), pp. 16–17.
9. Alan Dugald McKillop, *The Early Masters of English Fiction* (Lawrence, KS: University of Kansas Press, 1956), p. vii.
10. Northrop Frye, *Anatomy of Criticism: Four Essays* (1957; reprinted Princeton, NJ: Princeton University Press, 2000), pp. 303–4.
11. Northrop Frye, *The Secular Scripture: A Study of the Structure of Romance* (Cambridge, MA: Harvard University Press, 1976), p. 59.

12. J. Paul Hunter, 'Novels and History and Northrop Frye', *Eighteenth-Century Studies,* 24 (1990–1), 225–41 (231).
13. Ian Watt, *The Rise of the Novel: Studies in Defoe, Richardson and Fielding* (London: Chatto and Windus, 1957).

CHAPTER THREE: RESTRUCTURING THE RISE OF THE NOVEL, 1958–85

1. Northrop Frye, *The Secular Scripture: A Study of the Structure of Romance* (Cambridge, MA: Harvard University Press, 1976), pp. 38, 43.
2. E. M. W. Tillyard, *The Epic Strain in the English Novel* (London: Chatto and Windus, 1958), pp. 16–17.
3. Robert Scholes and Robert Kellogg, *The Nature of Narrative* (New York: Oxford University Press, 1966), p. 1.
4. J. Paul Hunter, *The Reluctant Pilgrim: Defoe's Emblematic Method and Quest for Form in 'Robinson Crusoe'* (Baltimore, MD: Johns Hopkins University Press, 1966), p. ix.
5. John J. Richetti, *Popular Fiction Before Richardson: Narrative Patterns, 1700–1739* (Oxford: Clarendon, 1969), p. 4.
6. English Showalter, Jr., *The Evolution of the French Novel, 1641–1782* (Princeton, NJ: Princeton University Press, 1972), pp. 3–8, 69, 72, 5. David H. Hirsch, 'The Reality of Ian Watt', *Critical Quarterly,* 11 (1969), 164–79.
7. Wayne C. Booth, *The Rhetoric of Fiction* (Chicago, IL: University of Chicago Press, 1961), p. 41.
8. Ian Watt, 'Serious Reflections on *The Rise of the Novel*', *Novel,* 1 (1968), 205–18.
9. Ian Watt, 'The Recent Critical Fortunes of *Moll Flanders*', *Eighteenth-Century Studies,* 1 (1967), 109–26.
10. Barbara Hardy, *The Appropriate Form: An Essay on the Novel* (New York: Oxford University Press, 1964), pp. 4, 54.
11. Maximillian E. Novak, *Economics and the Fiction of Daniel Defoe* (Berkeley, CA: University of California Press, 1962); *Defoe and the Nature of Man* (Oxford: Oxford University Press, 1963), p. 159.
12. Martin C. Battestin, *The Moral Basis of Fielding's Art: A Study of 'Joseph Andrews'* (Middletown, CT: Wesleyan University Press, 1959).
13. Maurice O. Johnson, *Fielding's Art of Fiction* (Philadelphia, PA: University of Pennsylvania Press, 1961).
14. Michael Irwin, *Henry Fielding: The Tentative Realist* (Oxford: Clarendon, 1967).
15. Andrew H. Wright, *Henry Fielding: Mask and Feast* (Berkeley, CA: University of California Press, 1965); Glenn W. Hatfield, *Henry Fielding and the Language of Irony* (Chicago, IL: University of Chicago Press, 1968).
16. Robert Alter, *Fielding and the Nature of the Novel* (Cambridge, MA: Harvard University Press, 1968).
17. Homer Goldberg, *The Art of 'Joseph Andrews'* (Chicago, IL: University of Chicago Press, 1969), p. 286.
18. Sheldon Sacks, *Fiction and the Shape of Belief: A Study of Henry Fielding with Glances at Swift, Johnson and Richardson* (Berkeley, CA: University of California Press, 1966), p. 25.
19. Robert Alan Donovan, *The Shaping Vision: Imagination in the English Novel from Defoe to Dickens* (Ithaca, NY: Cornell University Press, 1966), pp. 4–5, 11.
20. Douglas Brooks, *Number and Pattern in the Eighteenth-Century Novel* (London: Routledge and Kegan Paul, 1973), p. 2.
21. Donald Ball, *Samuel Richardson's Theory of Fiction* (The Hague: Mouton, 1971); Elizabeth Bergen Brophy, *Samuel Richardson: The Triumph of Craft* (Knoxville, TN: University of Tennessee Press, 1974).
22. Robert Adams Day, *Told in Letters: Epistolary Fiction Before Richardson* (Ann Arbor, MI: University of Michigan Press, 1966), p. 2.

23. Richetti (1969), p. 22.
24. Jerry C. Beasley, *Novels of the 1740s* (Athens, GA: University of Georgia Press, 1982), p. xii.
25. Margaret Anne Doody, *A Natural Passion: A Study of the Novels of Samuel Richardson* (Oxford: Clarendon, 1974), p. 24.
26. Mark Kinkead-Weekes, *Samuel Richardson: Dramatic Novelist* (London: Methuen, 1973), pp. 395–502.
27. Ira Konigsberg, *Samuel Richardson and the Dramatic Novel* (Lexington, KY: University Press of Kentucky, 1968), p. 4.
28. Laura Brown, *English Dramatic Form, 1660–1760: An Essay in Generic History* (New Haven, CT: Yale University Press, 1981), pp. 185–209.
29. G. A. Starr, *Defoe and Spiritual Autobiography* (Princeton, NJ: Princeton University Press, 1965).
30. Hunter (1966), p. 202.
31. Ronald Paulson, *Satire and the Novel in Eighteenth-Century England* (New Haven, CT: Yale University Press, 1967).
32. Robert Alter, *Rogue's Progress: Studies in the Picaresque Novel* (Cambridge, MA: Harvard University Press, 1964).
33. Alexander Blackburn, *The Myth of the Picaro: Continuity and Transformation of the Picaresque Novel, 1554–1954* (Chapel Hill, NC: University of North Carolina Press, 1979), pp. 25, 95, 147.
34. Walter L. Reed, *An Exemplary History of the Novel: The Quixotic versus the Picaresque* (Chicago, IL: University of Chicago Press, 1981), pp. 93, 22–3.
35. Henry Knight Miller, *Henry Fielding's 'Tom Jones' and the Romance Tradition* (Victoria: University of Victoria Press, 1976); James J. Lynch, *Henry Fielding and the Heliodoran Novel: Romance, Epic, and Fielding's New Province of Writing* (Cranbury, NJ: Associated University Presses, 1986).
36. J. Paul Hunter, *Occasional Form: Henry Fielding and the Chains of Circumstance* (Baltimore, MD: Johns Hopkins University Press, 1975), p. 186.
37. Leo Braudy, *Narrative Form in Fiction and History: Hume, Fielding and Gibbon* (Princeton, NJ: Princeton University Press, 1970), p. 4.
38. Percy G. Adams, *Travel Literature and the Evolution of the Novel* (Lexington, KY: University Press of Kentucky, 1983).
39. Patricia Meyer Spacks, *Imagining a Self: Autobiography and Novel in Eighteenth-Century England* (Cambridge, MA: Harvard University Press, 1976), p. 20.
40. Frederick R. Karl, *The Adversary Literature: The English Novel in the Eighteenth Century. A Study in Genre* (New York: Farrar, 1974), p. 36.
41. John Preston, *The Created Self: The Reader's Role in Eighteenth-Century Fiction* (London: Heinemann, 1970).
42. Wolfgang Iser, *The Implied Reader: Patterns of Communication in Prose Fiction from Bunyan to Beckett* (Baltimore, MD: Johns Hopkins University Press, 1972), p. xi.
43. Paula R. Backscheider, *A Being More Intense: A Study of the Prose Works of Bunyan, Swift, and Defoe* (New York: AMS Press, 1984), pp. xi–xii.
44. Arnold L. Weinstein, *Fictions of the Self, 1550–1800* (Princeton, NJ: Princeton University Press, 1981), p. 7.
45. Ira Konigsberg, *Narrative Technique in the English Novel: Defoe to Austen* (London: Archon, 1985), p. 17.
46. Marthe Robert, *Origins of the Novel* (1972), trans. Sacha Rabinovitch (Brighton: Harvester Wheatsheaf, 1980), p. 31.

CHAPTER FOUR: CULTURAL HISTORY AND THE RISE OF THE NOVEL, 1980–9

1. Daniel R. Schwarz, 'The Importance of Ian Watt's *The Rise of the Novel*', *Journal of Narrative Technique*, 13 (1983), 61–73 (61).

2. Lennard J. Davis, *Factual Fictions: The Origins of the English Novel* (1983; reprinted Philadelphia, PA: University of Pennsylvania Press, 1996), p. xii.
3. For a critique of Davis, see Michael McKeon, 'The Origins of the English Novel', *Modern Philology*, 82 (1984), 76–86.
4. John Bender, *Imagining the Penitentiary: Fiction and the Architecture of Mind in Eighteenth-Century England* (Chicago, IL: University of Chicago Press, 1987), p. 1.
5. Also on the ideological use of space in early fiction, see Simon Varey, *Space and the Eighteenth-Century English Novel* (Cambridge: Cambridge University Press, 1990).
6. Nancy Armstrong, *Desire and Domestic Fiction: A Political History of the Novel* (New York: Oxford University Press, 1987), p. 3.
7. William Beatty Warner, 'Social Power and the Eighteenth-Century Novel: Foucault and Transparent Literary History', *Eighteenth-Century Fiction*, 3 (1991), 185–203.
8. W. Austin Flanders, *Structures of Experience: History, Society, and Personal Life in the Eighteenth-Century British Novel* (Columbia, SC: University of South Carolina Press, 1984), p. ix.
9. Leopold Damrosch, Jr., *God's Plot and Man's Stories: Studies in the Fictional Imagination from Milton to Fielding* (Chicago, IL: University of Chicago Press, 1985).
10. Stuart Sim, *Negotiations with Paradox: Narrative Practice and Narrative Form in Bunyan and Defoe* (London: Harvester Wheatsheaf, 1990), pp. 2–3.
11. Robert A. Erickson, *Mother Midnight: Birth, Sex, and Fate in Eighteenth-Century Fiction* (New York: AMS Press, 1986), p. x.
12. Eve Tavor, *Scepticism, Society, and the Eighteenth-Century Novel* (Basingstoke: Macmillan, 1987), p. 110.
13. Carol Kay, *Political Constructions: Defoe, Richardson, and Sterne in Relation to Hobbes, Hume, and Burke* (Ithaca, NY: Cornell University Press, 1988).
14. M. M. Bakhtin, *The Dialogic Imagination: Four Essays* (1975), ed. Michael Holquist, trans. Caryl Emerson and Michael Holquist (Austin, TX: University of Texas Press, 1981), p. 3.
15. Terry Castle, *Masquerade and Civilization: The Carnivalesque in Eighteenth-Century English Culture and Fiction* (London: Methuen, 1986), p. 125.
16. Michael McKeon, *The Origins of the English Novel, 1600–1740* (1987; reprinted Baltimore, MD: Johns Hopkins University Press, 2002).
17. Michael McKeon, 'A Defense of Dialectical Method in Literary History', *Diacritics*, 19 (1989), 82–96 (89).
18. Compare McKeon's dialectic approach to the view of 'narrative as a socially symbolic act' with 'the function of inventing imaginary or formal "solutions" to unresolvable social contradictions', adopted by Fredric Jameson, *The Political Unconscious* (London: Methuen, 1981), p. 79.
19. For a taxonomy and history of pre-eighteenth-century fiction, see Paul Salzman, *English Prose Fiction 1558–1700: A Critical History* (Oxford: Clarendon, 1985). Salzman affirms the view that the 1740s represent something new (p. 339).
20. William Warner, 'Realist Literary History: McKeon's New Origins of the Novel', *Diacritics*, 19 (1989), 62–81. See McKeon (1989).
21. Alastair Duckworth, 'Michael McKeon and Some Recent Studies of Eighteenth-Century Fiction', *Eighteenth-Century Fiction*, 1 (1988), 53–66.
22. Homer Obed Brown, 'Of the Title to Things Real: Conflicting Stories', *English Literary History*, 55 (1988), 917–54.
23. Ralph W. Rader, 'The Emergence of the Novel in England: Genre in History vs. History of Genre', *Narrative*, 1 (1993), 69–83.
24. Michael McKeon, 'Reply to Ralph Rader', *Narrative*, 1 (1993), 84–90 (89, 87).
25. Robert Folkenflik, 'The Heirs of Ian Watt', *Eighteenth-Century Studies*, 25 (1991–2), 203–17 (211).
26. John Richetti, 'The Legacy of Ian Watt's *The Rise of the Novel*', in *The Profession of Literature: Reflections on an Institution*, ed. Leo Damrosch (Madison, WI: University of Wisconsin Press, 1992), pp. 95–112 (p. 97).

CHAPTER FIVE: FEMINISM AND THE RISE OF THE NOVEL

1. Brian Corman, *Women Novelists Before Jane Austen: The Critics and Their Canons* (Toronto: University of Toronto Press, 2009).
2. Joyce Horner, *The English Women Novelists and their Connection with the Feminist Movement, 1699–1797* (Northampton, MA: Smith College, 1930); B. G. MacCarthy, *The Female Pen: Women and Novelists, 1621–1818* (1944–7; reprinted Cork: Cork University Press, 1994).
3. Ellen Moers, *Literary Women: The Great Writers* (New York: Doubleday & Co., 1976), pp. 116–18. Elaine Showalter, *A Literature of Their Own: British Women Novelists from Brontë to Lessing* (Princeton, NJ: Princeton University Press, 1977), p. 16. Eva Figes, *Sex and Subterfuge: Women Writers to 1850* (London: Pandora, 1982), pp. 1–32.
4. Jane Spencer, *The Rise of the Woman Novelist: From Aphra Behn to Jane Austen* (Oxford: Blackwell, 1986), p. viii.
5. Janet Todd, *The Sign of Angelica: Women, Writing and Fiction, 1660–1800* (London: Virago, 1989), p. 2.
6. Dale Spender, *Mothers of the Novel: 100 Good Women Writers Before Jane Austen* (London: Pandora, 1986), p. 4.
7. Spender (1986), pp. 64–6 (Behn), pp. 80–1 (Manley), pp. 108–11 (Haywood), pp. 119–37 (106 other female novelists).
8. Spencer (1986), p. ix.
9. Todd (1989), p. 2.
10. Mary Anne Schofield and Cecilia Macheski (eds), *Fetter'd or Free? British Women Novelists, 1670–1815* (Athens, OH: Ohio University Press, 1986).
11. Ruth Perry, *Women, Letters, and the Novel* (New York: AMS Press, 1980), pp. ix–x.
12. Terry Lovell, *Consuming Fictions* (London: Verso, 1987), pp. 19–24, 5.
13. Judith Kegan Gardiner, 'The First English Novel: Aphra Behn's *Love Letters*, The Canon, and Women's Tastes', *Tulsa Studies in Women's Literature*, 8 (1985), 201–22.
14. Kristina Straub, *Divided Fictions: Fanny Burney and Feminine Strategy* (Lexington, KY: University Press of Kentucky, 1987); Julia Epstein, *The Iron Pen: Frances Burney and the Politics of Women's Writing* (Madison, WI: University of Wisconsin Press, 1989); Katherine M. Rogers, *Frances Burney: The World of 'Female Difficulties'* (Brighton: Harvester Wheatsheaf, 1990); Joanne Cutting-Gray, *Woman as 'Nobody' and the Novels of Frances Burney* (Gainesville, FL: University Press of Florida, 1992); Barbara Zonitch, *Familiar Violence: Gender and Social Upheaval in the Novels of Frances Burney* (Newark, DE: University of Delaware Press, 1997).
15. Elizabeth Bergen Brophy, *Women's Lives and the Eighteenth-Century English Novel* (Tampa, FL: University of South Florida Press, 1991).
16. Mona Scheuermann, *Her Bread to Earn: Women, Money, and Society from Defoe to Austen* (Lexington, KY: University Press of Kentucky, 1993), p. 1.
17. Deborah Ross, *The Excellence of Falsehood: Romance, Realism, and Women's Contribution to the Novel* (Lexington, KY: University Press of Kentucky, 1991), p. 14.
18. Laurie Langbauer, *Women and Romance: The Consolations of Gender in the English Novel* (Ithaca, NY: Cornell University Press, 1990), p. 4.
19. Katherine Sobba Green, *The Courtship Novel, 1740–1820: A Feminized Genre* (Lexington, KY: University Press of Kentucky, 1991), p. 2.
20. Ruth Bernard Yeazell, *Fictions of Modesty: Women and Courtship in the English Novel* (Chicago, IL: University of Chicago Press, 1991), p. 4.
21. Patricia Meyer Spacks, *Desire and Truth: Functions of Plot in Eighteenth-Century English Novels* (Chicago, IL: University of Chicago Press, 1990), p. 240.
22. Ros Ballaster, *Seductive Forms: Women's Amatory Fiction, 1684–1740* (Oxford: Clarendon, 1992), pp. 18–19.
23. For more on these genres and an account that locates the origins of the novel in seventeenth-century French women's writing, not eighteenth-century English male writing, see Joan DeJean, *Tender Geographies: Women and the Origins of the Novel in France* (New York: Columbia University Press, 1993).

24. Mary Anne Schofield, *Masking and Unmasking the Female Mind: Disguising Romances in Feminine Fiction, 1713–1799* (Cranberry, NJ: Associated University Presses, 1990), pp. 24, 9.
25. Elizabeth Craft-Fairchild, *Masquerade and Gender: Disguise and Female Identity in Eighteenth-Century Fictions by Women* (University Park, PA: Pennsylvania State University Press, 1993), p. 173.
26. Josephine Donovan, *Women and the Rise of the Novel, 1405–1726* (New York: St. Martin's Press, 1999), p. 12.
27. William Beatty Warner, *Reading 'Clarissa': The Struggles of Interpretation* (New Haven, CT: Yale University Press, 1979).
28. Terry Castle, *Clarissa's Ciphers: Meaning and Disruption in Richardson's 'Clarissa'* (Ithaca, NY: Cornell University Press, 1982), pp. 116–17.
29. Terry Eagleton, *The Rape of Clarissa: Writing, Sexuality, and Class Struggle in Samuel Richardson* (Oxford: Blackwell, 1982), pp. 65–8.
30. Sue Warrick Doederlein, 'Clarissa in the Hands of the Critics', *Eighteenth-Century Studies*, 16 (1983), 401–14 (405, 412).
31. Frances Ferguson, 'Rape and the Rise of the Novel', *Representations*, 20 (1987), 88–112 (109).
32. A study of seduction and rape in the emergent novel that appeared too late for consideration here is Toni Bowers, *Force or Fraud: British Seduction Stories and the Problem of Resistance, 1660–1760* (Oxford: Oxford University Press, 2011).
33. Tassie Gwilliam, *Samuel Richardson's Fictions of Gender* (Stanford, CA: Stanford University Press, 1993); Robert Spector, *Smollett's Women: A Study in an Eighteenth-Century Masculine Sensibility* (Westport, CT: Greenwood Press, 1994); Jill Campbell, *Natural Masques: Gender and Identity in Fielding's Plays and Novels* (Stanford, CA: Stanford University Press, 1995).
34. Madeleine Kahn, *Narrative Transvestism: Rhetoric and Gender in the Eighteenth-Century English Novel* (Ithaca, N.Y.: Cornell University Press, 1994), p. 2.
35. Helene Moglen, *The Trauma of Gender: A Feminist Theory of the English Novel* (Berkeley, CA: University of California Press, 2001), p. 1.
36. Lisa Moore, *Dangerous Intimacies: Toward a Sapphic History of the British Novel* (Durham, NC: Duke University Press, 1997), p. 13.
37. Eve Tavor Bannet, *The Domestic Revolution: Enlightenment Feminisms and the Novel* (Baltimore, MD: Johns Hopkins University Press, 2000), p. 2.
38. Helen Thompson, *Ingenuous Subjection: Compliance and Power in the Eighteenth-Century Domestic Novel* (Philadelphia, PA: University of Pennsylvania Press, 2005), p. 20.
39. Jürgen Habermas, *The Structural Transformation of the Public Sphere* (1962), trans. Thomas Burger (Cambridge: Polity Press, 1989), pp. 43, 49–50.
40. Michael McKeon, *The Secret History of Domesticity: Public, Private, and the Division of Knowledge* (Baltimore, MD: Johns Hopkins University Press, 2005).
41. Helen Thompson, 'The Personal is Political: Domesticity's Domestic Contents', *Eighteenth Century: Theory and Interpretation*, 50 (2010), 355–70 (358, 367).

CHAPTER SIX: POSTCOLONIALISM, POSTNATIONALISM, AND THE RISE OF THE NOVEL

1. Martin Green, *Dreams of Adventure, Deeds of Empire* (London: Routledge, 1980), p. 83.
2. Peter Hulme, *Colonial Encounters: Europe and the Native Caribbean, 1492–1797* (London: Methuen, 1986), p. 208.
3. Edward W. Said, *Culture and Imperialism* (London: Vintage, 1993), pp. 83–4.
4. Firdous Azim, *The Colonial Rise of the Novel* (London: Routledge, 1993), p. 30.
5. Mike Marais, 'Colonialism and the Epistemological Underpinnings of the Early English Novel', *English in Africa*, 23 (1996), 47–66.
6. Laura Brown, *Ends of Empire: Women and Ideology in Early Eighteenth-Century English Literature* (Ithaca, NY: Cornell University Press, 1993).

7. Felicity A. Nussbaum, *Torrid Zones: Maternity, Sexuality, and Empire in Eighteenth-Century English Narratives* (Baltimore, MD: Johns Hopkins University Press, 1995).
8. Maaja A. Stewart, *Domestic Realities and Imperial Fictions: Jane Austen's Novels in Eighteenth-Century Contexts* (Athens, GA: University of Georgia Press, 1993), p. ix.
9. Brett C. McInelly, 'Expanding Empires, Expanding Selves: Colonialism, the Novel, and *Robinson Crusoe*', *Studies in the Novel*, 35 (2003), 1–21 (2, 6, 19).
10. Robert Markley, *The Far East and the English Imagination, 1600–1730* (Cambridge: Cambridge University Press, 2006), pp. 203–4.
11. Roxann Wheeler, *The Complexion of Race: Categories of Difference in Eighteenth-Century English Culture* (Philadelphia, PA: University of Pennsylvania Press, 2000), pp. 77, 115.
12. Srinivas Aravamudan, *Tropicopolitans: Colonialism and Agency, 1688–1804* (Durham, NC: Duke University Press, 1999), p. 4.
13. Srinivas Aravamudan, 'Fiction/Translation/Transnation: The Secret History of the Eighteenth-Century Novel', in *A Companion to the Eighteenth-Century English Novel and Culture*, ed. Paula R. Backscheider and Catherine Ingrassia (Oxford: Blackwell, 2005), pp. 48–74 (49–50, 54, 70). Aravamudan's subsequent study appeared too late for consideration here: *Enlightenment Orientalism: Resisting the Rise of the Novel* (Chicago, IL: University of Chicago Press, 2011).
14. Benedict Anderson, *Imagined Communities: Reflections on the Origin and Spread of Nationalism* (1983), 2nd rev. edn (London: Verso, 1991), pp. 24–5.
15. Benedict Anderson, *The Spectre of Comparisons: Nationalism, Southeast Asia, and the World* (London: Verso, 1988), p. 334.
16. Jonathan Culler, 'Anderson and the Novel', *Diacritics*, 29 (1999), 20–39.
17. Patrick Parrinder, *Nation and Novel: The English Novel From Its Origins to the Present Day* (Oxford: Oxford University Press, 2006), p. 18.
18. Janet Sorensen, 'Internal Colonialism and the British Novel', *Eighteenth-Century Fiction*, 15 (2002), 53–8 (55).
19. Leith Davis, *Acts of Union: Scotland and the Literary Negotiation of the British Nation, 1707–1830* (Stanford, CA: Stanford University Press, 1998), p. 47.
20. Alexander Cowie, *The Rise of the American Novel* (New York: American Book Co., 1948).
21. Cathy N. Davidson, *Revolution and the Word: The Rise of the Novel in America* (Oxford: Oxford University Press, 1986), pp. 10–11.
22. William C. Spengeman, 'The Earliest American Novel: Aphra Behn's *Oroonoko*', *Nineteenth-Century Fiction*, 38 (1984), 384–414.
23. Nancy Armstrong and Lennard Tennenhouse, 'The American Origins of the English Novel', *American Literary History*, 4 (1992), 386–410 (386).
24. Nancy Armstrong and Leonard Tennenhouse, *The Imaginary Puritan: Literature, Intellectual Labor, and the Origins of Personal Life* (Berkeley, CA: University of California Press, 1992).
25. Ed White, 'Captaine Smith, Colonial Novelist', *American Literature*, 75 (2003), 487–513 (489, 490, 509).
26. Elizabeth Maddock Dillon, 'The Original American Novel, or, The American Origin of the Novel', in Backscheider and Ingrassia (2005), pp. 235–60 (256, 236).
27. Laura Doyle, *Freedom's Empire: Race and the Rise of the Novel in Atlantic Modernity, 1640–1940* (Durham, NC: Duke University Press, 2008).
28. Andrew Hadfield, 'When was the First English Novel and What does it Tell us?', in *Remapping the Rise of the European Novel*, ed. Jenny Mander (Oxford: Voltaire Foundation, 2007), pp. 23–34 (27).
29. Diana de Armas Wilson, 'Of Pilgrims and Polyglots: Heliodorus, Cervantes and Defoe', in Mander (2007), pp. 47–57 (47).
30. Kate Williams, 'Passion in Translation: Translating and the Development of the Novel in Early-Eighteenth-Century England', in Mander (2007), pp. 157–69.
31. Mary Helen McMurran, *The Spread of Novels: Translation and Prose Fiction in the Eighteenth Century* (Princeton, NJ: Princeton University Press, 2010), p. 51.

32. Margaret Cohen and Carolyn Dever (eds), *The Literary Channel: The Inter-National Invention of the Novel* (Princeton, NJ: Princeton University Press, 2002), p. 17.
33. Margaret Cohen, *The Novel and the Sea* (Princeton, NJ: Princeton University Press, 2010), pp. 9, 4.

CHAPTER SEVEN: RETHINKING THE RISE OF THE NOVEL, 1990–2000

1. J. Paul Hunter, *Before Novels: The Cultural Contexts of Eighteenth-Century English Fiction* (New York: Norton, 1990), p. 9.
2. Margaret Anne Doody, review of J. Paul Hunter, *Before Novels, South Atlantic Review*, 57 (1992), 123–6 (125–6).
3. Margaret Anne Doody, *The True Story of the Novel* (1996; reprinted London: Fortuna Press, 1998), p. 1.
4. Hunter (1990), p. 7.
5. William Ray, *Story and History: Narrative Authority and Social Identity in the Eighteenth-Century French and English Novels* (Oxford: Blackwell, 1990), p. 9.
6. Everett Zimmerman, *The Boundaries of Fiction: History and the Eighteenth-Century British Novel* (Ithaca, NY: Cornell University Press, 1996), p. 206.
7. Robert Mayer, *History and the Early English Novel: Matters of Fact from Bacon to Defoe* (Cambridge: Cambridge University Press, 1997), pp. 235–6.
8. Frank Palmeri, *Satire, History, Novel: Narrative Forms, 1665–1815* (Newark, DE: University of Delaware Press, 2003), p. 12.
9. Karen O'Brien, 'History and the Novel in Eighteenth-Century Britain', *Huntington Library Quarterly*, 68 (2005), 397–413.
10. Joseph F. Bartolomeo, *A New Species of Criticism: Eighteenth-Century Discourse on the Novel* (Newark, DE: University of Delaware Press, 1994), p. 10.
11. William B. Warner, *Licensing Entertainment: The Elevation of Novel Reading in Britain, 1684–1750* (Berkeley, CA: University of California Press, 1998), p. xi.
12. Bradford K. Mudge, *The Whore's Story: Women, Pornography, and the British Novel, 1684–1830* (Oxford: Oxford University Press, 2000), p. 28.
13. Homer Obed Brown, *The Institutions of the English Novel: From Defoe to Scott* (Philadelphia, PA: University of Pennsylvania Press, 1997), p. 183.
14. Clifford Siskin, *The Work of Writing: Literature and Social Change in Britain, 1700–1830* (Baltimore, MD: Johns Hopkins University Press, 1999), p. 183.
15. John Richetti (ed.), *The Cambridge Companion to the Eighteenth-Century Novel* (Cambridge: Cambridge University Press, 1996); John Richetti et al. (eds), *The Columbia History of the British Novel* (New York: Columbia University Press, 1994).
16. David Blewett, 'Introduction', *Reconsidering the Rise of the Novel*, ed. David Blewett, special issue of *Eighteenth-Century Fiction*, 12 (2000), 141–5 (141). Hereafter *Reconsidering*.
17. Ian Watt, 'Flat-Footed and Fly-Blown: The Realities of Realism' (1978), *Reconsidering*, 147–66.
18. Maximillian E. Novak, 'Gendered Cultural Criticism and the Rise of the Novel: The Case of Defoe', *Reconsidering*, 239–52.
19. W. B. Carnochan, '"A Matter *Discutable*": *The Rise of the Novel*', *Reconsidering*, 167–84.
20. Michael McKeon, 'Watt's *Rise of the Novel* within the Tradition of the Rise of the Novel', *Reconsidering*, 253–76.
21. Lennard J. Davis, 'Reconsidering Origins: How Novel Are Theories of the Novel?', *Reconsidering*, 479–99.
22. J. Paul Hunter, Serious Reflections on Daniel Defoe (with an Excursus on the Farther Adventures of Ian Watt and Two Notes on the Present State of Literary Studies', *Reconsidering*, 227–37.
23. Max Byrd, 'Two or Three Things I Know about Setting', *Reconsidering*, 185–91; Michael Seidel, 'The Man Who Came to Dinner: Ian Watt and the Theory of Formal Realism', *Reconsidering*, 193–212.

24. Novak (2000), 242.
25. John Richetti, 'Ideas and Voices: The New Novel in Eighteenth-Century England', *Reconsidering*, 327–44 (329).
26. Janet Todd, 'Fatal Fluency: Behn's Fiction and the Restoration Letter', *Reconsidering*, 417–34 (419).
27. J. A. Downie, 'Mary Davys's "Probable Feign'd Stories" and Critical Shibboleths about "The Rise of the Novel"', *Reconsidering*, 309–26.
28. Robert D. Hume, *Reconstructing Contexts: The Aims and Principles of Archaeo-Historicism* (Oxford: Oxford University Press, 1999), pp. 50, 110.

CHAPTER EIGHT: PRINT CULTURE AND THE RISE OF THE NOVEL, 1990–2010

1. John Feather, *A History of British Publishing*, 2nd edn (London: Routledge, 2006).
2. William H. McBurney, *A Check List of Prose Fiction Published in England, 1700–1739* (Cambridge, MA: Harvard University Press, 1960); Jerry C. Beasley, *A Check List of Prose Fiction Published in England, 1740–1749* (Charlottesville, VA: University of Virginia Press, 1972).
3. James Raven, *British Fiction 1750–1770: A Chronological Checklist of Prose Fiction Printed in Britain and Ireland* (Newark, DE: University of Delaware Press, 1987); James Raven and Antonia Forster, *British Fiction 1770–1829: A Bibliographical Survey of Prose Fiction Published in the Britain Isles, Volume 1: 1770–1799* (Oxford: Oxford University Press, 2000).
4. J. A. Downie, 'The Making of the English Novel', *Eighteenth-Century Fiction*, 9 (1997), 249–66.
5. Walter Benjamin, 'The Storyteller: Reflections on the Work of Nikolai Leskov' (1936), in *Illuminations*, ed. Hannah Arendt, trans. Harry Zohn (New York: Schocken Books, 1969), pp. 83–109 (87).
6. Maurice Couturier, *Textual Communication: A Print-based Theory of the Novel* (London: Routledge, 1991), p. 77.
7. Walter J. Ong, *Orality and Literacy* (London: Methuen, 1982), pp. 148–9.
8. Stephanie Fysh, *The Work(s) of Samuel Richardson* (Newark, DE: University of Delaware Press, 1997), p. 16.
9. Thomas Keymer, *Sterne, the Moderns, and the Novel* (Oxford: Oxford University Press, 2002), pp. 8, 5, 1.
10. Leah Price, *The Anthology and the Rise of the Novel: From Richardson to George Eliot* (Cambridge: Cambridge University Press, 2000), p. 13.
11. Janine Barchas, *Graphic Design, Print Culture, and the Eighteenth-Century Novel* (Cambridge: Cambridge University Press, 2003).
12. A relevant study that appeared too late for consideration here is Christopher Flint, *The Appearance of Print in Eighteenth-Century Fiction* (Cambridge: Cambridge University Press, 2011).
13. Brean S. Hammond, *Professional Imaginative Writing in England, 1670–1740: 'Hackney for Bread'* (Oxford: Clarendon, 1997), p. 232.
14. George Justice, *The Manufacturers of Literature: Writing and the Literary Marketplace in Eighteenth-Century England* (Newark, DE: University of Delaware Press, 2002), p. 147.
15. Frank Donoghue, *The Fame Machine: Book Reviewing and Eighteenth-Century Literary Careers* (Stanford, CA: Stanford University Press, 1996), pp. 16–17.
16. Catherine Gallagher, *Nobody's Story: The Vanishing Acts of Women Writers in the Market-place, 1670–1820* (Berkeley, CA: University of California Press, 1994), p. xiv.
17. Thomas Keymer and Peter Sabor, *'Pamela' in the Marketplace: Literary Controversy and Print Culture in Eighteenth-Century Britain and Ireland* (Cambridge: Cambridge University Press, 2005), pp. 4–5.
18. Robert Mayer, 'Did You Say Middle Class? The Question of Taste and the Rise of the Novel', *Reconsidering the Rise of the Novel*, ed. David Blewett, special issue of *Eighteenth-Century Fiction*, 12 (2000), 277–307. Hereafter *Reconsidering*.

19. On the early modern transition from *intensive* reading, where readers thoroughly study a few usually religious texts, to *extensive* reading, where they rapidly cover a variety of material, see Rolf Engelsing, *Der Bürger als Leser: Lesergeschichte in Deutschland, 1500–1800* (Stuttgart: Metzlersche, 1974).
20. Patricia Meyer Spacks, *Privacy: Concealing the Eighteenth-Century Self* (Chicago, IL: University of Chicago Press, 2003), pp. 27–54.
21. William Beatty Warner, 'Staging Readers Reading', *Reconsidering*, 391–416.
22. Tom Keymer, *Richardson's 'Clarissa' and the Eighteenth-Century Reader* (Cambridge: Cambridge University Press, 1992), p. xviii.
23. Ellen Gardiner, *Regulating Readers: Gender and Literary Criticism in the Eighteenth-Century Novel* (Newark, DE: University of Delaware Press, 1999), p. 11.
24. Elspeth Jajdelska, *Silent Reading and the Birth of the Narrator* (Toronto: University of Toronto Press, 2007), p. 3.
25. Susan E. Whyman, 'Letter Writing and the Rise of the Novel: The Epistolary Literacy of Jane Johnson and Samuel Richardson', *Huntington Library Quarterly*, 70 (2007), 577–606.
26. David Allan, *Commonplace Books and Reading in Georgian England* (Cambridge: Cambridge University Press, 2010), p. 260.
27. Kate Loveman, *Reading Fictions, 1660–1740: Deception in English Literary and Political Culture* (Aldershot: Ashgate, 2008), p. 2.

CHAPTER NINE: THEMATIC CRITICISM OF THE RISE OF THE NOVEL (I): FAMILY, LAW, SEX, AND SOCIETY

1. T. G. A. Nelson, *Children, Parents, and the Rise of the Novel* (Newark, DE: University of Delaware Press, 1995), p. 221.
2. Toni Bowers, *The Politics of Motherhood: British Writing and Culture, 1680–1760* (Cambridge: Cambridge University Press, 1996).
3. Christopher Flint, *Family Fictions: Narrative and Domestic Relations in Britain, 1688–1798* (Stanford, CA: Stanford University Press, 1998), p. 37.
4. Richard A. Barney, *Plots of Enlightenment: Education and the Novel in the Eighteenth Century* (Stanford, CA: Stanford University Press, 1999), p. 2.
5. Brian McCrea, *Impotent Fathers: Patriarchy and Demographic Crisis in the Eighteenth-Century Novel* (Newark, DE: University of Delaware Press, 1998), p. 15.
6. Caroline Gonda, *Reading Daughters' Fictions 1709–1834* (Cambridge: Cambridge University Press, 1996), p. xv.
7. Eleanor Wikborg, *The Lover as Father Figure in Eighteenth-Century Women's Fiction* (Gainesville, FL: University Press of Florida, 2002).
8. Ellen Pollak, *Incest and the English Novel, 1684–1814* (Baltimore, MD: Johns Hopkins University Press, 2003), p. 25.
9. Ruth Perry, *Novel Relations: The Transformation of Kinship in Eighteenth-Century Literature and Culture, 1748–1818* (Cambridge: Cambridge University Press, 2004), p. 6.
10. John P. Zomchick, *Family and the Law in Eighteenth-Century Fiction: The Public Conscience in the Private Sphere* (Cambridge: Cambridge University Press, 1993), p. 2.
11. Wolfram Schmidgen, *Eighteenth-Century Fiction and the Law of Property* (Cambridge: Cambridge University Press, 2002), p. 1.
12. Susan Paterson Glover, *Engendering Legitimacy: Law, Property, and Early Eighteenth-Century Fiction* (Lewisburg, PA: Bucknell University Press, 2006), pp. 20–1.
13. Sandra Macpherson, *Harm's Way: Tragic Responsibility and the Novel Form* (Baltimore, MD: Johns Hopkins University Press, 2010), p. 4.
14. Lincoln B. Faller, *Crime and Defoe: A New Kind of Writing* (Cambridge: Cambridge University Press, 1993), p. xiii.
15. Hal Gladfelder, *Criminality and Narrative in Eighteenth-Century England: Beyond the Law* (Baltimore, MD: Johns Hopkins University Press, 2001), p. 71.

16. Betty A. Schellenberg, *The Conversational Circle: Rereading the English Novel, 1740–1775* (Lexington, KY: University Press of Kentucky, 1996).
17. John Richetti, *The English Novel in History, 1700–1780* (London: Routledge, 1999), p. 1.
18. Nancy Armstrong, *How Novels Think: The Limits of Individualism from 1719–1900* (New York: Columbia University Press, 2006), p. 3.

CHAPTER TEN: THEMATIC CRITICISM OF THE RISE OF THE NOVEL (II): MONEY, MEDICINE, POLITICS, AND THINGS

1. James Thompson, *Models of Value: Eighteenth-Century Political Economy and the Novel* (Durham, NC: Duke University Press, 1996), p. 187.
2. Sandra Sherman, *Finance and Fictionality in the Early Eighteenth Century: Accounting for Defoe* (Cambridge: Cambridge University Press, 1996).
3. Catherine Ingrassia, *Authorship, Commerce, and Gender in Early Eighteenth-Century England: A Culture of Paper Credit* (Cambridge: Cambridge University Press, 1998), p. 14.
4. Liz Bellamy, *Commerce, Morality and the Eighteenth-Century Novel* (Cambridge: Cambridge University Press, 1998), p. 182.
5. Deidre Shauna Lynch, *The Economy of Character: Novels, Market Culture, and the Business of Inner Meaning* (Chicago, IL: University of Chicago Press, 1998), p. 4.
6. James Cruise, *Governing Consumption: Needs and Wants, Suspended Characters, and the 'Origins' of Eighteenth-Century English Novels* (Lewisburg, PA: Bucknell University Press, 1999), p. 15.
7. Miranda J. Burgess, *British Fiction and the Production of Social Order, 1740–1830* (Cambridge: Cambridge University Press, 2000).
8. Nicholas Hudson, 'Social Rank, "The Rise of the Novel", and Whig Histories of Eighteenth-Century Fiction', *Eighteenth-Century Fiction*, 17 (2005), 563–98 (563).
9. Rachel Carnell, *Partisan Politics, Narrative Realism, and the Rise of the British Novel* (Basingstoke: Palgrave Macmillan, 2006), p. 1.
10. Robert A. Erickson, *The Language of the Heart, 1600–1750* (Philadelphia, PA: University of Pennsylvania Press, 1997).
11. Geoffrey Sill, *The Cure of the Passions and the Rise of the Novel* (Cambridge: Cambridge University Press, 2001).
12. Juliet McMaster, *Reading the Body in the Eighteenth-Century Novel* (Basingstoke: Palgrave Macmillan, 2004), p. xi.
13. Katherine E. Kickel, *Novel Notions: Medical Discourse and the Mapping of the Imagination in Eighteenth-Century English Fiction* (London: Routledge, 2007), p. 13.
14. Cynthia Sundberg Wall, *The Prose of Things: Transformations of Description in the Eighteenth Century* (Chicago, IL: University of Chicago Press, 2006), p. 1.
15. Jonathan Lamb, *The Things Things Say* (Princeton, NJ: Princeton University Press, 2011).
16. Mark Blackwell (ed.), *The Secret Life of Things: Animals, Objects, and It-Narratives in Eighteenth-Century England* (Lewisburg, PA: Bucknell University Press, 2007), pp. 10, 14.
17. Liz Bellamy, 'It-Narrators and Circulation: Defining a Subgenre', in Blackwell (2007), pp. 117–46.
18. Julie Park, *The Self and It: Novel Objects in Eighteenth-Century England* (Stanford, CA: Stanford University Press, 2010), p. 38.

CONCLUSION: RECENT AND FUTURE DIRECTIONS

1. Patricia Meyer Spacks, *Novel Beginnings: Experiments in Eighteenth-Century English Fiction* (New Haven, CT: Yale University Press, 2006), p. 2.
2. Brean Hammond and Shaun Regan, *Making the Novel: Fiction and Society in Britain, 1660–1789* (Basingstoke: Palgrave Macmillan, 2006), p. x.

3. G. Gabrielle Starr, *Lyric Generations: Poetry and the Novel in the Long Eighteenth Century* (Baltimore, MD: Johns Hopkins University Press, 2004) offers a generic history that switches from the causes to the effects of the rise of the novel, tracing the transformation of lyric poetry wrought by its appropriation in prose fictions.
4. Scarlet Brown, *The Politics of Custom in Eighteenth-Century British Fiction* (Basingstoke: Palgrave Macmillan, 2010); Jesse Molesworth, *Chance and the Eighteenth-Century Novel: Realism, Probability, Magic* (Cambridge: Cambridge University Press, 2010); Carol Stewart, *The Eighteenth-Century Novel and the Secularization of Ethics* (Aldershot: Ashgate, 2010). See also Paula R. Backscheider and Catherine Ingrassia (eds), *A Companion to the Eighteenth-Century English Novel and Culture* (Oxford: Blackwell, 2005) for a collection of essays that cover several critical approaches and a wide range of texts and contexts.

Bibliography

INTRODUCTION

Lennard J. Davis, 'Who Put the *The* in *the Novel*: Identity Politics and Disability in Novel Studies', *Novel*, 31 (1998), 79–101.

John Skinner, *An Introduction to Eighteenth-Century Fiction: Raising the Novel* (Basingstoke: Palgrave Macmillan, 2001).

Angela Wright, *Gothic Fiction: A Reader's Guide to Essential Criticism* (Basingstoke: Palgrave Macmillan, 2007).

CHAPTER ONE: EIGHTEENTH- AND NINETEENTH-CENTURY ACCOUNTS OF THE RISE OF THE NOVEL

Anna Laetitia Barbauld, 'On the Origin and Progress of Romance' (1810), in *Selected Poetry and Prose*, ed. William McCarthy and Elizabeth Kraft (Peterborough, Ont.: Broadview, 2002), pp. 377–417.

James Beattie, *Dissertations Moral and Critical* (London and Edinburgh: W. Strahan, T. Cadell, and W. Creech, 1783).

Richard Burton, *Masters of the English Novel: A Study of Principles and Personalities* (New York: Henry Holt, 1909).

Wilbur Cross, *The Development of the English Novel* (1899; reprinted New York: Greenwood, 1969).

W. J. Dawson, *The Makers of English Fiction* (New York: Fleming H. Revell, 1905).

John Dunlop, *The History of Fiction: Being a Critical Account of the most Celebrated Prose Works of Fiction from the Earliest Greek Romances to the Novels of the Present Age* (1814), 2 vols (New York: Franklin, 1970).

Lord Ernle, *The Light Reading of Our Ancestors: Chapters in the Growth of the English Novel* (London: English Association, 1921).

Henry Fielding, *Tom Jones* (1749), ed. R. P. C. Mutter (London: Penguin, 1985).

William Forsyth, *The Novels and Novelists of the Eighteenth Century, in Illustration of the Manners and Morals of the Age* (London: Murray, 1871).

Edmund Gosse, *A History of Eighteenth-Century Literature* (1889; reprinted London, 1909).

William Hazlitt, 'Lecture VI: On the English Novelists', in *Lectures on the English Comic Writers* (1818), intro. R. B. Johnson (London: Oxford University Press, 1908), pp. 138–74.

Carl Holliday, *English Fiction from the Fifth to the Twentieth Century* (New York: Century, 1912).

Pierre-Daniel Huet, *The History of Romances. An Enquiry into their Original*, trans. Stephen Lewis (London: J. Hooke and T. Caldecott, 1715).

Sidney Lanier, *The English Novel and the Principle of Its Development* (1892), ed. Clarence Gohdes and Kemp Malone, in *The Centennial Edition of the Works of Sidney Lanier*, ed. Charles R. Anderson, 10 vols (Baltimore, MD: Johns Hopkins University Press, 1945), IV: 3–251.

Allen Michie, *Richardson and Fielding: The Dynamics of a Critical Rivalry* (Lewisburg, PA: Bucknell University Press, 1999).

Hugh Murray, *The Morality of Fiction; or, An Inquiry into the Tendency of Fictitious Narratives* (Edinburgh: Mundell and Son, 1805).

William Lyon Phelps, *The Advance of the English Novel* (1915; reprinted London: Murray, 1919).

Sir Walter Raleigh, *The English Novel: Being a Short Sketch of its History from the Earliest Times to the Appearance of 'Waverley'* (London: Murray, 1894).

Clara Reeve, *The Progress of Romance* [...], 2 vols (Colchester: W. Keymer, 1785).
Samuel Richardson, *Selected Letters of Samuel Richardson*, ed. John Carroll (Oxford: Clarendon, 1964).
Percy Russell, *A Guide to British and American Novels [...] from its Commencement down to 1894* (London: Digby, Long & co., 1895).
George Saintsbury, *The English Novel* (1913; reprinted London: Dent, 1927).
The Spectator, no. 484, 22 April 1871.
Hippolyte Taine, *History of English Literature* (1863–9), trans. H. van Laun, 4 vols (London: Chatto and Windus, 1890).
John Tinnon Taylor, *The Early Opposition to the English Novel: The Popular Reaction from 1760 to 1830* (New York: King's Crown Press, 1943).
Bayard Tuckerman, *A History of English Prose Fiction: From Sir Thomas Malory to George Eliot* (New York: Putnam, 1882).
Ioan Williams (ed.), *Novel and Romance, 1700–1800: A Documentary Record* (London: Routledge and Kegan Paul, 1970).
Ioan Williams (ed.), *Sir Walter Scott on Novelists and Fiction* (London: Routledge and Kegan Paul, 1968).

CHAPTER TWO: NEW CRITICISM TO *THE RISE OF THE NOVEL*, 1924–57

Walter Allen, *The English Novel: A Short Critical History* (1954; reprinted London: Penguin, 1958).
Ernest A. Baker, *The History of the English Novel*, 10 vols (1924–39; reprinted New York: Barnes and Noble, 1950).
Richard Church, *The Growth of the English Novel* (London: Methuen, 1951).
Northrop Frye, *Anatomy of Criticism: Four Essays* (1957; reprinted Princeton, NJ: Princeton University Press, 2000).
Northrop Frye, *The Secular Scripture: A Study of the Structure of Romance* (Cambridge, MA: Harvard University Press, 1976).
J. Paul Hunter, 'Novels and History and Northrop Frye', *Eighteenth-Century Studies*, 24 (1990–1), 225–41.
Arnold Kettle, *An Introduction to the English Novel*, 2 vols (London: Hutchinson, 1951–3).
F. R. Leavis, *The Great Tradition: George Eliot, Henry James, Joseph Conrad* (London: Chatto and Windus, 1948).
Q. D. Leavis, *Fiction and the Reading Public* (London: Chatto and Windus, 1932).
Alan Dugald McKillop, *The Early Masters of English Fiction* (Lawrence, KS: University of Kansas Press, 1956).
Frances Hovey Stoddard, *The Evolution of the English Novel* (New York: Macmillan, 1900).
R. H. Tawney, *Religion and the Rise of Capitalism: A Historical Study* (London: Murray, 1926).
J. M. S. Tompkins, *The Popular Novel in England, 1770–1800* (1932; reprinted London: Methuen, 1969).
Dorothy Van Ghent, *The English Novel: Form and Function* (New York: Rhinehart, 1953).
Ian Watt, *The Rise of the Novel: Studies in Defoe, Richardson and Fielding* (London: Chatto and Windus, 1957).
Max Weber, *The Protestant Ethic and the Spirit of Capitalism* (1905), trans. T. Parsons (London: Allen and Unwin, 1930).

CHAPTER THREE: RESTRUCTURING THE RISE OF THE NOVEL, 1958–85

Percy G. Adams, *Travel Literature and the Evolution of the Novel* (Lexington, KY: University Press of Kentucky, 1983).

Robert Alter, *Fielding and the Nature of the Novel* (Cambridge, MA: Harvard University Press, 1968).
Robert Alter, *Rogue's Progress: Studies in the Picaresque Novel* (Cambridge, MA: Harvard University Press, 1964).
Erich Auerbach, *Mimesis: The Representation of Reality in Western Literature* (1946), trans. Willard R. Trask (Princeton, NJ: Princeton University Press, 1953).
Paula R. Backscheider, *A Being More Intense: A Study of the Prose Works of Bunyan, Swift, and Defoe* (New York: AMS Press, 1984).
Donald Ball, *Samuel Richardson's Theory of Fiction* (The Hague: Mouton, 1971).
Martin C. Battestin, *The Moral Basis of Fielding's Art: A Study of 'Joseph Andrews'* (Middletown, CT: Wesleyan University Press, 1959).
Jerry C. Beasley, *Novels of the 1740s* (Athens, GA: University of Georgia Press, 1982).
Alexander Blackburn, *The Myth of the Picaro: Continuity and Transformation of the Picaresque Novel, 1554–1954* (Chapel Hill, NC: University of North Carolina Press, 1979).
Wayne C. Booth, *The Rhetoric of Fiction* (Chicago, IL: University of Chicago Press, 1961).
Leo Braudy, *Narrative Form in Fiction and History: Hume, Fielding and Gibbon* (Princeton, NJ: Princeton University Press, 1970).
Douglas Brooks, *Number and Pattern in the Eighteenth-Century Novel* (London: Routledge and Kegan Paul, 1973).
Elizabeth Bergen Brophy, *Samuel Richardson: The Triumph of Craft* (Knoxville, TN: University of Tennessee Press, 1974).
Laura Brown, *English Dramatic Form, 1660–1760: An Essay in Generic History* (New Haven, CT: Yale University Press, 1981).
Robert Adams Day, *Told in Letters: Epistolary Fiction Before Richardson* (Ann Arbor, MI: University of Michigan Press, 1966).
Robert Alan Donovan, *The Shaping Vision: Imagination in the English Novel from Defoe to Dickens* (Ithaca, NY: Cornell University Press, 1966).
Margaret Anne Doody, *A Natural Passion: A Study of the Novels of Samuel Richardson* (Oxford: Clarendon, 1974).
Homer Goldberg, *The Art of 'Joseph Andrews'* (Chicago, IL: University of Chicago Press, 1969).
Lucien Goldmann, *Towards a Sociology of the Novel* (1963), trans. Alan Sheridan (London: Tavistock, 1975).
Barbara Hardy, *The Appropriate Form: An Essay on the Novel* (New York: Oxford University Press, 1964).
Glenn W. Hatfield, *Henry Fielding and the Language of Irony* (Chicago, IL: University of Chicago Press, 1968).
David H. Hirsch, 'The Reality of Ian Watt', *Critical Quarterly*, 11 (1969), 164–79.
J. Paul Hunter, *Occasional Form: Henry Fielding and the Chains of Circumstance* (Baltimore, MD: Johns Hopkins University Press, 1975).
J. Paul Hunter, *The Reluctant Pilgrim: Defoe's Emblematic Method and Quest for Form in 'Robinson Crusoe'* (Baltimore, MD: Johns Hopkins University Press, 1966).
Michael Irwin, *Henry Fielding: The Tentative Realist* (Oxford: Clarendon, 1967).
Wolfgang Iser, *The Implied Reader: Patterns of Communication in Prose Fiction from Bunyan to Beckett* (Baltimore, MD: Johns Hopkins University Press, 1972).
Maurice O. Johnson, *Fielding's Art of Fiction* (Philadelphia, PA: University of Pennsylvania Press, 1961).
Erich Kahler, *The Inward Turn of Narrative*, trans. Richard and Clara Winston (Princeton, NJ: Princeton University Press, 1973).
Frederick R. Karl, *The Adversary Literature: The English Novel in the Eighteenth Century. A Study in Genre* (New York: Farrar, 1974).
Mark Kinkead-Weekes, *Samuel Richardson: Dramatic Novelist* (London: Methuen, 1973).
Ira Konigsberg, *Narrative Technique in the English Novel: Defoe to Austen* (London: Archon, 1985).

Ira Konigsberg, *Samuel Richardson and the Dramatic Novel* (Lexington, KY: University Press of Kentucky, 1968).

György Lukács, *The Theory of the Novel: A Historico-Philosophic Essay on the Forms of Great Epic Literature* (1916), trans. Anna Bostock (London: MIT Press, 1971).

James J. Lynch, *Henry Fielding and the Heliodoran Novel: Romance, Epic, and Fielding's New Province of Writing* (Cranbury, NJ: Associated University Presses, 1986).

Henry Knight Miller, *Henry Fielding's 'Tom Jones' and the Romance Tradition* (Victoria: University of Victoria Press, 1976).

Maximillian E. Novak, *Defoe and the Nature of Man* (Oxford: Oxford University Press, 1963).

Maximillian E. Novak, *Economics and the Fiction of Daniel Defoe* (Berkeley, CA: University of California Press, 1962).

Ronald Paulson, *Satire and the Novel in Eighteenth-Century England* (New Haven, CT: Yale University Press, 1967).

John Preston, *The Created Self: The Reader's Role in Eighteenth-Century Fiction* (London: Heinemann, 1970).

Walter L. Reed, *An Exemplary History of the Novel: The Quixotic versus the Picaresque* (Chicago, IL: University of Chicago Press, 1981).

John J. Richetti, *Popular Fiction Before Richardson: Narrative Patterns, 1700–1739* (Oxford: Clarendon, 1969).

Marthe Robert, *Origins of the Novel* (1972), trans. Sacha Rabinovitch (Brighton: Harvester Wheatsheaf, 1980).

Sheldon Sacks, *Fiction and the Shape of Belief: A Study of Henry Fielding with Glances at Swift, Johnson and Richardson* (Berkeley, CA: University of California Press, 1966).

Robert Scholes and Robert Kellogg, *The Nature of Narrative* (New York: Oxford University Press, 1966).

English Showalter, Jr., *The Evolution of the French Novel, 1641–1782* (Princeton, NJ: Princeton University Press, 1972).

Patricia Meyer Spacks, *Imagining a Self: Autobiography and Novel in Eighteenth-Century England* (Cambridge, MA: Harvard University Press, 1976).

G. A. Starr, *Defoe and Spiritual Autobiography* (Princeton, NJ: Princeton University Press, 1965).

E. M. W. Tillyard, *The Epic Strain in the English Novel* (London: Chatto and Windus, 1958).

Ian Watt, 'The Recent Critical Fortunes of *Moll Flanders*', *Eighteenth-Century Studies*, 1 (1967), 109–26.

Ian Watt, 'Serious Reflections on *The Rise of the Novel*', *Novel*, 1 (1968), 205–18.

Arnold L. Weinstein, *Fictions of the Self, 1550–1800* (Princeton, NJ: Princeton University Press, 1981).

Ioan Williams, *The Idea of the Novel in Europe, 1600–1800* (London: Macmillan, 1978).

Andrew H. Wright, *Henry Fielding: Mask and Feast* (Berkeley, CA: University of California Press, 1965).

CHAPTER FOUR: CULTURAL HISTORY AND THE RISE OF THE NOVEL, 1980–9

Nancy Armstrong, *Desire and Domestic Fiction: A Political History of the Novel* (New York: Oxford University Press, 1987).

M. M. Bakhtin, *The Dialogic Imagination: Four Essays* (1975), ed. Michael Holquist, trans. Caryl Emerson and Michael Holquist (Austin, TX: University of Texas Press, 1981).

M. M. Bakhtin, *Rabelais and His World* (1965), trans. Hélène Iswolsky (Bloomington, IN: Indiana University Press, 1984).

John Bender, *Imagining the Penitentiary: Fiction and the Architecture of Mind in Eighteenth-Century England* (Chicago, IL: University of Chicago Press, 1987).

Homer Obed Brown, 'Of the Title to Things Real: Conflicting Stories', *English Literary History*, 55 (1988), 917–54.

Terry Castle, *Masquerade and Civilization: The Carnivalesque in Eighteenth-Century English Culture and Fiction* (London: Methuen, 1986).

Leopold Damrosch, Jr., *God's Plot and Man's Stories: Studies in the Fictional Imagination from Milton to Fielding* (Chicago, IL: University of Chicago Press, 1985).

Lennard J. Davis, *Factual Fictions: The Origins of the English Novel* (1983; reprinted Philadelphia, PA: University of Pennsylvania Press, 1996).

Lennard J. Davis, *Resisting Novels: Ideology and Fiction* (London: Methuen, 1987).

Alastair Duckworth, 'Michael McKeon and Some Recent Studies of Eighteenth-Century Fiction', *Eighteenth-Century Fiction*, 1 (1988), 53–66.

Robert A. Erickson, *Mother Midnight: Birth, Sex, and Fate in Eighteenth-Century Fiction* (New York: AMS Press, 1986).

W. Austin Flanders, *Structures of Experience: History, Society, and Personal Life in the Eighteenth-Century British Novel* (Columbia, SC: University of South Carolina Press, 1984).

Robert Folkenflik, 'The Heirs of Ian Watt', *Eighteenth-Century Studies*, 25 (1991–2), 203–17.

Michel Foucault, *Discipline and Punish* (1975), trans. Alan Sheridan (London: Allen Lane, 1977).

Michel Foucault, *The History of Sexuality*, 3 vols (1976–84), trans. Robert Hurley (London: Penguin, 1979–91).

Fredric Jameson, *The Political Unconscious* (London: Methuen, 1981).

Carol Kay, *Political Constructions: Defoe, Richardson, and Sterne in Relation to Hobbes, Hume, and Burke* (Ithaca, NY: Cornell University Press, 1988).

Michael McKeon, 'A Defense of Dialectical Method in Literary History', *Diacritics*, 19 (1989), 82–96.

Michael McKeon, 'The Origins of the English Novel', *Modern Philology*, 82 (1984), 76–86.

Michael McKeon, *The Origins of the English Novel, 1600–1740* (1987; reprinted Baltimore, MD: Johns Hopkins University Press, 2002).

Michael McKeon, 'Reply to Ralph Rader', *Narrative*, 1 (1993), 84–90.

Ralph W. Rader, 'The Emergence of the Novel in England: Genre in History vs. History of Genre', *Narrative*, 1 (1993), 69–83.

John Richetti, 'The Legacy of Ian Watt's *The Rise of the Novel*', in *The Profession of Literature: Reflections on an Institution*, ed. Leo Damrosch (Madison, WI: University of Wisconsin Press, 1992), pp. 95–112.

Paul Salzman, *English Prose Fiction 1558–1700: A Critical History* (Oxford: Clarendon, 1985).

Daniel R. Schwarz, 'The Importance of Ian Watt's *The Rise of the Novel*', *Journal of Narrative Technique*, 13 (1983), 61–73.

Stuart Sim, *Negotiations with Paradox: Narrative Practice and Narrative Form in Bunyan and Defoe* (London: Harvester Wheatsheaf, 1990).

Eve Tavor, *Scepticism, Society, and the Eighteenth-Century Novel* (Basingstoke: Macmillan, 1987).

Simon Varey, *Space and the Eighteenth-Century English Novel* (Cambridge; Cambridge University Press, 1990).

William B. Warner, 'Realist Literary History: McKeon's New Origins of the Novel', *Diacritics*, 19 (1989), 62–81.

William Beatty Warner, 'Social Power and the Eighteenth-Century Novel: Foucault and Transparent Literary History', *Eighteenth-Century Fiction*, 3 (1991), 185–203.

CHAPTER FIVE: FEMINISM AND THE RISE OF THE NOVEL

Ros Ballaster, *Seductive Forms: Women's Amatory Fiction, 1684–1740* (Oxford: Clarendon, 1992).

Elizabeth Bergen Brophy, *Women's Lives and the Eighteenth-Century English Novel* (Tampa, FL: University of South Florida Press, 1991).

Toni Bowers, *Force or Fraud: British Seduction Stories and the Problem of Resistance, 1660–1760* (Oxford: Oxford University Press, 2011).

Jill Campbell, *Natural Masques: Gender and Identity in Fielding's Plays and Novels* (Stanford, CA: Stanford University Press, 1995).

Terry Castle, *Clarissa's Ciphers: Meaning and Disruption in Richardson's 'Clarissa'* (Ithaca, NY: Cornell University Press, 1982).

Brian Corman, *Women Novelists Before Jane Austen: The Critics and Their Canons* (Toronto: University of Toronto Press, 2009).

Elizabeth Craft-Fairchild, *Masquerade and Gender: Disguise and Female Identity in Eighteenth-Century Fictions by Women* (University Park, PA: Pennsylvania State University Press, 1993).

Joanne Cutting-Gray, *Woman as 'Nobody' and the Novels of Frances Burney* (Gainesville, FL: University Press of Florida, 1992).

Joan DeJean, *Tender Geographies: Women and the Origins of the Novel in France* (New York: Columbia University Press, 1993).

Josephine Donovan, *Women and the Rise of the Novel, 1405–1726* (New York: St. Martin's Press, 1999).

Terry Eagleton, *The Rape of Clarissa: Writing, Sexuality, and Class Struggle in Samuel Richardson* (Oxford: Blackwell, 1982).

Julia Epstein, *The Iron Pen: Frances Burney and the Politics of Women's Writing* (Madison, WI: University of Wisconsin Press, 1989).

Frances Ferguson, 'Rape and the Rise of the Novel', *Representations*, 20 (1987), 88–112.

Eva Figes, *Sex and Subterfuge: Women Writers to 1850* (London: Pandora, 1982).

Judith Kegan Gardiner, 'The First English Novel: Aphra Behn's *Love Letters*, The Canon, and Women's Tastes', *Tulsa Studies in Women's Literature*, 8 (1985), 201–22.

Katherine Sobba Green, *The Courtship Novel, 1740–1820: A Feminized Genre* (Lexington, KY: University Press of Kentucky, 1991).

Tassie Gwilliam, *Samuel Richardson's Fictions of Gender* (Stanford, CA: Stanford University Press, 1993).

Jürgen Habermas, *The Structural Transformation of the Public Sphere* (1962), trans. Thomas Burger (Cambridge: Polity Press, 1989).

Joyce Horner, *The English Women Novelists and their Connection with the Feminist Movement, 1699–1797* (Northampton, MA: Smith College, 1930).

Madeleine Kahn, *Narrative Transvestism: Rhetoric and Gender in the Eighteenth-Century English Novel* (Ithaca, NY: Cornell University Press, 1994).

Laurie Langbauer, *Women and Romance: The Consolations of Gender in the English Novel* (Ithaca, NY: Cornell University Press, 1990).

Terry Lovell, *Consuming Fictions* (London: Verso, 1987).

György Lukács, *History and Class Consciousness: Studies in Marxist Dialectics* (1923), trans. Rodney Livingstone (London: Merlin Press, 1971).

B. G. MacCarthy, *The Female Pen: Women and Novelists, 1621–1818* (1944–7; reprinted Cork: Cork University Press, 1994).

Michael McKeon, *The Secret History of Domesticity: Public, Private, and the Division of Knowledge* (Baltimore, MD: Johns Hopkins University Press, 2005).

Ellen Moers, *Literary Women: The Great Writers* (New York: Doubleday & Co., 1976).

Helene Moglen, *The Trauma of Gender: A Feminist Theory of the English Novel* (Berkeley, CA: University of California Press, 2001).

Lisa Moore, *Dangerous Intimacies: Toward a Sapphic History of the British Novel* (Durham, NC: Duke University Press, 1997).

Carole Pateman, *The Sexual Contract* (London: Polity Press, 1988).

Ruth Perry, *Women, Letters, and the Novel* (New York: AMS Press, 1980).

Katherine M. Rogers, *Frances Burney: The World of 'Female Difficulties'* (Brighton: Harvester Wheatsheaf, 1990).

Deborah Ross, *The Excellence of Falsehood: Romance, Realism, and Women's Contribution to the Novel* (Lexington, KY: University Press of Kentucky, 1991).

Mona Scheuermann, *Her Bread to Earn: Women, Money, and Society from Defoe to Austen* (Lexington, KY: University Press of Kentucky, 1993).

Mary Anne Schofield and Cecilia Macheski (eds), *Fetter'd or Free? British Women Novelists, 1670–1815* (Athens, OH: Ohio University Press, 1986).

Mary Anne Schofield, *Masking and Unmasking the Female Mind: Disguising Romances in Feminine Fiction, 1713–1799* (Cranberry, NJ: Associated University Presses, 1990).

Viktor Shklovsky, *Theory of Prose* (1925), trans. Benjamin Sher, intro. Gerald L. Bruns (Elmwood Park, IL: Dalkey Archive Press, 1990).

Elaine Showalter, *A Literature of Their Own: British Women Novelists from Brontë to Lessing* (Princeton, NJ: Princeton University Press, 1977).

Patricia Meyer Spacks, *Desire and Truth: Functions of Plot in Eighteenth-Century English Novels* (Chicago, IL: University of Chicago Press, 1990).

Robert Spector, *Smollett's Women: A Study in an Eighteenth-Century Masculine Sensibility* (Westport, CT: Greenwood Press, 1994).

Jane Spencer, *The Rise of the Woman Novelist: From Aphra Behn to Jane Austen* (Oxford: Blackwell, 1986).

Dale Spender, *Mothers of the Novel: 100 Good Women Writers Before Jane Austen* (London: Pandora, 1986).

Kristina Straub, *Divided Fictions: Fanny Burney and Feminine Strategy* (Lexington, KY: University Press of Kentucky, 1987).

Eve Tavor Bannet, *The Domestic Revolution: Enlightenment Feminisms and the Novel* (Baltimore, MD: Johns Hopkins University Press, 2000).

Helen Thompson, *Ingenuous Subjection: Compliance and Power in the Eighteenth-Century Domestic Novel* (Philadelphia, PA: University of Pennsylvania Press, 2005).

Helen Thompson, 'The Personal is Political: Domesticity's Domestic Contents', *Eighteenth Century: Theory and Interpretation*, 50 (2010), 355–70.

Janet Todd, *The Sign of Angelica: Women, Writing and Fiction, 1660–1800* (London: Virago, 1989).

William Beatty Warner, *Reading 'Clarissa': The Struggles of Interpretation* (New Haven, CT: Yale University Press, 1979).

Sue Warrick Doederlein, 'Clarissa in the Hands of the Critics', *Eighteenth-Century Studies*, 16 (1983), 401–14.

Ruth Bernard Yeazell, *Fictions of Modesty: Women and Courtship in the English Novel* (Chicago, IL: University of Chicago Press, 1991).

Barbara Zonitch, *Familiar Violence: Gender and Social Upheaval in the Novels of Frances Burney* (Newark, DE: University of Delaware Press, 1997).

CHAPTER SIX: POSTCOLONIALISM, POSTNATIONALISM, AND THE RISE OF THE NOVEL

Benedict Anderson, *Imagined Communities: Reflections on the Origin and Spread of Nationalism* (1983), 2nd rev. edn (London: Verso, 1991).

Benedict Anderson, *The Spectre of Comparisons: Nationalism, Southeast Asia, and the World* (London: Verso, 1988).

Srinivas Aravamudan, *Enlightenment Orientalism: Resisting the Rise of the Novel* (Chicago, IL: University of Chicago Press, 2011).

Srinivas Aravamudan, 'Fiction/Translation/Transnation: The Secret History of the Eighteenth-Century Novel', in *A Companion to the Eighteenth-Century English Novel and Culture*, ed. Paula R. Backscheider and Catherine Ingrassia (Oxford: Blackwell, 2005), pp. 48–74.

Srinivas Aravamudan, *Tropicopolitans: Colonialism and Agency, 1688–1804* (Durham, N.C.: Duke University Press, 1999).

Diana de Armas Wilson, 'Of Pilgrims and Polyglots: Heliodorus, Cervantes and Defoe', in Mander (2007), pp. 47–57.

Nancy Armstrong and Lennard Tennenhouse, 'The American Origins of the English Novel', *American Literary History*, 4 (1992), 386–410.

Nancy Armstrong and Leonard Tennenhouse, *The Imaginary Puritan: Literature, Intellectual Labor, and the Origins of Personal Life* (Berkeley, CA: University of California Press, 1992).

Firdous Azim, *The Colonial Rise of the Novel* (London: Routledge, 1993).

Laura Brown, *Ends of Empire: Women and Ideology in Early Eighteenth-Century English Literature* (Ithaca, NY: Cornell University Press, 1993).

Margaret Cohen, *The Novel and the Sea* (Princeton, NJ: Princeton University Press, 2010).

Margaret Cohen and Carolyn Dever (eds), *The Literary Channel: The Inter-National Invention of the Novel* (Princeton, NJ: Princeton University Press, 2002).

Alexander Cowie, *The Rise of the American Novel* (New York: American Book Co., 1948).

Jonathan Culler, 'Anderson and the Novel', *Diacritics*, 29 (1999), 20–39.

Cathy N. Davidson, *Revolution and the Word: The Rise of the Novel in America* (Oxford: Oxford University Press, 1986).

Leith Davis, *Acts of Union: Scotland and the Literary Negotiation of the British Nation, 1707–1830* (Stanford, CA: Stanford University Press, 1998).

Elizabeth Maddock Dillon, 'The Original American Novel, or, The American Origin of the Novel', in Backscheider and Ingrassia (2005), pp. 235–60.

Laura Doyle, *Freedom's Empire: Race and the Rise of the Novel in Atlantic Modernity, 1640–1940* (Durham, NC: Duke University Press, 2008).

Martin Green, *Dreams of Adventure, Deeds of Empire* (London: Routledge, 1980).

Andrew Hadfield, 'When was the First English Novel and What Does it Tell us?', in Mander (2007), pp. 23–34.

Peter Hulme, *Colonial Encounters: Europe and the Native Caribbean, 1492–1797* (London: Methuen, 1986).

Jenny Mander (ed.), *Remapping the Rise of the European Novel* (Oxford: Voltaire Foundation, 2007).

Mike Marais, 'Colonialism and the Epistemological Underpinnings of the Early English Novel', *English in Africa*, 23 (1996), 47–66.

Robert Markley, *The Far East and the English Imagination, 1600–1730* (Cambridge: Cambridge University Press, 2006).

Brett C. McInelly, 'Expanding Empires, Expanding Selves: Colonialism, the Novel, and *Robinson Crusoe*', *Studies in the Novel*, 35 (2003), 1–21.

Mary Helen McMurran, *The Spread of Novels: Translation and Prose Fiction in the Eighteenth Century* (Princeton, NJ: Princeton University Press, 2010).

Felicity A. Nussbaum, *Torrid Zones: Maternity, Sexuality, and Empire in Eighteenth-Century English Narratives* (Baltimore, MD: Johns Hopkins University Press, 1995).

Patrick Parrinder, *Nation and Novel: The English Novel From Its Origins to the Present Day* (Oxford: Oxford University Press, 2006).

Edward W. Said, *Culture and Imperialism* (London: Vintage, 1993).

Janet Sorensen, 'Internal Colonialism and the British Novel', *Eighteenth-Century Fiction*, 15 (2002), 53–8.

William C. Spengeman, 'The Earliest American Novel: Aphra Behn's *Oroonoko*', *Nineteenth-Century Fiction*, 38 (1984), 384–414.

Maaja A. Stewart, *Domestic Realities and Imperial Fictions: Jane Austen's Novels in Eighteenth-Century Contexts* (Athens, GA: University of Georgia Press, 1993).

Roxann Wheeler, *The Complexion of Race: Categories of Difference in Eighteenth-Century English Culture* (Philadelphia, PA: University of Pennsylvania Press, 2000).

Ed White, 'Captaine Smith, Colonial Novelist', *American Literature*, 75 (2003), 487–513.

Kate Williams, 'Passion in Translation: Translating and the Development of the Novel in Early-Eighteenth-Century England', in Mander (2007), pp. 157–69.

CHAPTER SEVEN: RETHINKING THE RISE OF THE NOVEL, 1990–2000

Joseph F. Bartolomeo, *A New Species of Criticism: Eighteenth-Century Discourse on the Novel* (Newark, DE: University of Delaware Press, 1994).

David Blewett (ed.), *Reconsidering the Rise of the Novel*, special issue of *Eighteenth-Century Fiction*, 12 (2000).

Homer Obed Brown, *The Institutions of the English Novel: From Defoe to Scott* (Philadelphia, PA: University of Pennsylvania Press, 1997).

Max Byrd, 'Two or Three Things I Know about Setting', in Blewett (2000), 185–91.

W. B. Carnochan, '"A Matter *Discutable*": *The Rise of the Novel*', in Blewett (2000), 167–84.

Lennard J. Davis, 'Reconsidering Origins: How Novel Are Theories of the Novel?', in Blewett (2000), 479–99.

Margaret Anne Doody, review of J. Paul Hunter, *Before Novels*, *South Atlantic Review*, 57 (1992), 123–6.

Margaret Anne Doody, *The True Story of the Novel* (1996; reprinted London: Fortuna Press, 1998).

J. A. Downie, 'Mary Davys's "Probable Feign'd Stories" and Critical Shibboleths about "The Rise of the Novel"', in Blewett (2000), 309–26.

José Ortega y Gasset, *Meditations on Quixote* (1914), trans. Evelyn Rugg and Diego Martin, intro. Julian Marias (New York: Norton, 1961).

Robert D. Hume, *Reconstructing Contexts: The Aims and Principles of Archaeo-Historicism* (Oxford: Oxford University Press, 1999).

J. Paul Hunter, *Before Novels: The Cultural Contexts of Eighteenth-Century English Fiction* (New York: Norton, 1990).

J. Paul Hunter, Serious Reflections on Daniel Defoe (with an Excursus on the Farther Adventures of Ian Watt and Two Notes on the Present State of Literary Studies', in Blewett (2000), 227–37.

Robert Mayer, *History and the Early English Novel: Matters of Fact from Bacon to Defoe* (Cambridge: Cambridge University Press, 1997).

Michael McKeon, 'Watt's *Rise of the Novel* within the Tradition of the Rise of the Novel', in Blewett (2000), 253–76.

Bradford K. Mudge, *The Whore's Story: Women, Pornography, and the British Novel, 1684–1830* (Oxford: Oxford University Press, 2000).

Maximillian E. Novak, 'Gendered Cultural Criticism and the Rise of the Novel: The Case of Defoe', in Blewett (2000), 239–52.

Karen O'Brien, 'History and the Novel in Eighteenth-Century Britain', *Huntington Library Quarterly*, 68 (2005), 397–413.

Frank Palmeri, *Satire, History, Novel: Narrative Forms, 1665–1815* (Newark, DE: University of Delaware Press, 2003).

William Ray, *Story and History: Narrative Authority and Social Identity in the Eighteenth-Century French and English Novels* (Oxford: Blackwell, 1990).

John Richetti (ed.), *The Cambridge Companion to the Eighteenth-Century Novel* (Cambridge: Cambridge University Press, 1996).

John Richetti et al. (eds), *The Columbia History of the British Novel* (New York: Columbia University Press, 1994).

John Richetti, 'Ideas and Voices: The New Novel in Eighteenth-Century England', in Blewett (2000), 327–44.

Michael Seidel, 'The Man Who Came to Dinner: Ian Watt and the Theory of Formal Realism', in Blewett (2000), 193–212.

Clifford Siskin, *The Work of Writing: Literature and Social Change in Britain, 1700–1830* (Baltimore, MD: Johns Hopkins University Press, 1999).

Janet Todd, 'Fatal Fluency: Behn's Fiction and the Restoration Letter', in Blewett (2000), 417–34.

William B. Warner, *Licensing Entertainment: The Elevation of Novel Reading in Britain, 1684–1750* (Berkeley, CA: University of California Press, 1998).

Ian Watt, 'Flat-Footed and Fly-Blown: The Realities of Realism' (1978), in Blewett (2000), 147–66.

Everett Zimmerman, *The Boundaries of Fiction: History and the Eighteenth-Century British Novel* (Ithaca, NY: Cornell University Press, 1996).

CHAPTER EIGHT: PRINT CULTURE AND THE RISE OF THE NOVEL, 1990–2010

David Allan, *Commonplace Books and Reading in Georgian England* (Cambridge: Cambridge University Press, 2010).

Janine Barchas, *Graphic Design, Print Culture, and the Eighteenth-Century Novel* (Cambridge: Cambridge University Press, 2003).

Jerry C. Beasley, *A Check List of Prose Fiction Published in England, 1740–1749* (Charlottesville, VA: University of Virginia Press, 1972).

Walter Benjamin, 'The Storyteller: Reflections on the Work of Nikolai Leskov' (1936), in *Illuminations*, ed. Hannah Arendt, trans. Harry Zohn (New York: Schocken Books, 1969), pp. 83–109.

Maurice Couturier, *Textual Communication: A Print-Based Theory of the Novel* (London: Routledge, 1991).

Frank Donoghue, *The Fame Machine: Book Reviewing and Eighteenth-Century Literary Careers* (Stanford, CA: Stanford University Press, 1996).

J. A. Downie, 'The Making of the English Novel', *Eighteenth-Century Fiction*, 9 (1997), 249–66.

Elizabeth Eisenstein, *The Printing Press as an Agent of Change*, 2 vols (Cambridge: Cambridge University Press, 1979).

Rolf Engelsing, *Der Bürger als Leser: Lesergeschichte in Deutschland, 1500–1800* (Stuttgart: Metzlersche, 1974).

John Feather, *A History of British Publishing*, 2nd edn (London: Routledge, 2006).

Christopher Flint, *The Appearance of Print in Eighteenth-Century Fiction* (Cambridge: Cambridge University Press, 2011).

Stephanie Fysh, *The Work(s) of Samuel Richardson* (Newark, DE: University of Delaware Press, 1997).

Catherine Gallagher, *Nobody's Story: The Vanishing Acts of Women Writers in the Marketplace, 1670–1820* (Berkeley, CA: University of California Press, 1994).

Ellen Gardiner, *Regulating Readers: Gender and Literary Criticism in the Eighteenth-Century Novel* (Newark, DE: University of Delaware Press, 1999).

Brean S. Hammond, *Professional Imaginative Writing in England, 1670–1740: 'Hackney for Bread'* (Oxford: Clarendon, 1997).

Elspeth Jajdelska, *Silent Reading and the Birth of the Narrator* (Toronto: University of Toronto Press, 2007).

George Justice, *The Manufacturers of Literature: Writing and the Literary Marketplace in Eighteenth-Century England* (Newark, DE: University of Delaware Press, 2002).

Tom Keymer, *Richardson's 'Clarissa' and the Eighteenth-Century Reader* (Cambridge: Cambridge University Press, 1992).

Thomas Keymer, *Sterne, the Moderns, and the Novel* (Oxford: Oxford University Press, 2002).

Thomas Keymer and Peter Sabor, *'Pamela' in the Marketplace: Literary Controversy and Print Culture in Eighteenth-Century Britain and Ireland* (Cambridge: Cambridge University Press, 2005).

Kate Loveman, *Reading Fictions, 1660–1740: Deception in English Literary and Political Culture* (Aldershot: Ashgate, 2008).

Robert Mayer, 'Did You Say Middle Class? The Question of Taste and the Rise of the Novel', in *Reconsidering the Rise of the Novel*, ed. David Blewett, special issue of *Eighteenth-Century Fiction*, 12 (2000), 277–307.

William H. McBurney, *A Check List of Prose Fiction Published in England, 1700–1739* (Cambridge, MA: Harvard University Press, 1960).

Walter J. Ong, *Orality and Literacy* (London: Methuen, 1982).
Leah Price, *The Anthology and the Rise of the Novel: From Richardson to George Eliot* (Cambridge: Cambridge University Press, 2000).
James Raven, *British Fiction 1750–1770: A Chronological Checklist of Prose Fiction Printed in Britain and Ireland* (Newark, DE: University of Delaware Press, 1987).
James Raven and Antonia Forster, *British Fiction 1770–1829: A Bibliographical Survey of Prose Fiction Published in the Britain Isles, Volume 1: 1770–1799* (Oxford: Oxford University Press, 2000).
Patricia Meyer Spacks, *Privacy: Concealing the Eighteenth-Century Self* (Chicago, IL: University of Chicago Press, 2003).
William Beatty Warner, 'Staging Readers Reading', in *Reconsidering the Rise of the Novel*, ed. David Blewett, special issue of *Eighteenth-Century Fiction*, 12 (2000), 391–416.
Susan E. Whyman, 'Letter Writing and the Rise of the Novel: The Epistolary Literacy of Jane Johnson and Samuel Richardson', *Huntington Library Quarterly*, 70 (2007), 577–606.

CHAPTER NINE: THEMATIC CRITICISM OF THE RISE OF THE NOVEL (I): FAMILY, LAW, SEX, AND SOCIETY

Nancy Armstrong, *How Novels Think: The Limits of Individualism from 1719–1900* (New York: Columbia University Press, 2006).
Richard A. Barney, *Plots of Enlightenment: Education and the Novel in the Eighteenth Century* (Stanford, CA: Stanford University Press, 1999).
Toni Bowers, *The Politics of Motherhood: British Writing and Culture, 1680–1760* (Cambridge: Cambridge University Press, 1996).
Lincoln B. Faller, *Crime and Defoe: A New Kind of Writing* (Cambridge: Cambridge University Press, 1993).
Christopher Flint, *Family Fictions: Narrative and Domestic Relations in Britain, 1688–1798* (Stanford, CA: Stanford University Press, 1998).
Hal Gladfelder, *Criminality and Narrative in Eighteenth-Century England: Beyond the Law* (Baltimore, MD: Johns Hopkins University Press, 2001).
Susan Paterson Glover, *Engendering Legitimacy: Law, Property, and Early Eighteenth-Century Fiction* (Lewisburg, PA: Bucknell University Press, 2006).
Caroline Gonda, *Reading Daughters' Fictions 1709–1834* (Cambridge: Cambridge University Press, 1996).
Sandra Macpherson, *Harm's Way: Tragic Responsibility and the Novel Form* (Baltimore, MD: Johns Hopkins University Press, 2010).
Brian McCrea, *Impotent Fathers: Patriarchy and Demographic Crisis in the Eighteenth-Century Novel* (Newark, DE: University of Delaware Press, 1998).
T. G. A. Nelson, *Children, Parents, and the Rise of the Novel* (Newark, DE: University of Delaware Press, 1995).
Ruth Perry, *Novel Relations: The Transformation of Kinship in Eighteenth-Century Literature and Culture, 1748–1818* (Cambridge: Cambridge University Press, 2004).
Ellen Pollak, *Incest and the English Novel, 1684–1814* (Baltimore, MD: Johns Hopkins University Press, 2003).
John Richetti, *The English Novel in History, 1700–1780* (London: Routledge, 1999).
Betty A. Schellenberg, *The Conversational Circle: Rereading the English Novel, 1740–1775* (Lexington, KY: University Press of Kentucky, 1996).
Wolfram Schmidgen, *Eighteenth-Century Fiction and the Law of Property* (Cambridge: Cambridge University Press, 2002).
Lawrence Stone, *The Family, Sex, and Marriage in England 1500–1800* (London: Weidenfelf and Nicolson, 1977).
Eleanor Wikborg, *The Lover as Father Figure in Eighteenth-Century Women's Fiction* (Gainesville, FL: University Press of Florida, 2002).

John P. Zomchick, *Family and the Law in Eighteenth-Century Fiction: The Public Conscience in the Private Sphere* (Cambridge: Cambridge University Press, 1993).

CHAPTER TEN: THEMATIC CRITICISM OF THE RISE OF THE NOVEL (II): MONEY, MEDICINE, POLITICS, AND THINGS

Liz Bellamy, *Commerce, Morality and the Eighteenth-Century Novel* (Cambridge: Cambridge University Press, 1998).

Liz Bellamy, 'It-Narrators and Circulation: Defining a Subgenre', in Blackwell (2007), pp. 117–46.

Catherine Belsey, *Critical Practice* (London: Methuen, 1980).

Mark Blackwell (ed.), *The Secret Life of Things: Animals, Objects, and It-Narratives in Eighteenth-Century England* (Lewisburg, PA: Bucknell University Press, 2007).

Miranda J. Burgess, *British Fiction and the Production of Social Order, 1740–1830* (Cambridge: Cambridge University Press, 2000).

Rachel Carnell, *Partisan Politics, Narrative Realism, and the Rise of the British Novel* (Basingstoke: Palgrave Macmillan, 2006).

James Cruise, *Governing Consumption: Needs and Wants, Suspended Characters, and the 'Origins' of Eighteenth-Century English Novels* (Lewisburg, PA: Bucknell University Press, 1999).

Robert A. Erickson, *The Language of the Heart, 1600–1750* (Philadelphia, PA: University of Pennsylvania Press, 1997).

Nicholas Hudson, 'Social Rank, "The Rise of the Novel", and Whig Histories of Eighteenth-Century Fiction', *Eighteenth-Century Fiction*, 17 (2005), 563–98.

Catherine Ingrassia, *Authorship, Commerce, and Gender in Early Eighteenth-Century England: A Culture of Paper Credit* (Cambridge: Cambridge University Press, 1998).

Katherine E. Kickel, *Novel Notions: Medical Discourse and the Mapping of the Imagination in Eighteenth-Century English Fiction* (London: Routledge, 2007).

Jonathan Lamb, *The Things Things Say* (Princeton, NJ: Princeton University Press, 2011).

Deidre Shauna Lynch, *The Economy of Character: Novels, Market Culture, and the Business of Inner Meaning* (Chicago, IL: University of Chicago Press, 1998).

Juliet McMaster, *Reading the Body in the Eighteenth-Century Novel* (Basingstoke: Palgrave Macmillan, 2004).

Julie Park, *The Self and It: Novel Objects in Eighteenth-Century England* (Stanford, CA: Stanford University Press, 2010).

Sandra Sherman, *Finance and Fictionality in the Early Eighteenth Century: Accounting for Defoe* (Cambridge: Cambridge University Press, 1996).

Geoffrey Sill, *The Cure of the Passions and the Rise of the Novel* (Cambridge: Cambridge University Press, 2001).

James Thompson, *Models of Value: Eighteenth-Century Political Economy and the Novel* (Durham, NC: Duke University Press, 1996).

Cynthia Sundberg Wall, *The Prose of Things: Transformations of Description in the Eighteenth Century* (Chicago, IL: University of Chicago Press, 2006).

CONCLUSION: RECENT AND FUTURE DIRECTIONS

Paula R. Backscheider and Catherine Ingrassia (eds), *A Companion to the Eighteenth-Century English Novel and Culture* (Oxford: Blackwell, 2005).

Scarlet Brown, *The Politics of Custom in Eighteenth-Century British Fiction* (Basingstoke: Palgrave Macmillan, 2010).

Brean Hammond and Shaun Regan, *Making the Novel: Fiction and Society in Britain, 1660–1789* (Basingstoke: Palgrave Macmillan, 2006).

Jesse Molesworth, *Chance and the Eighteenth-Century Novel: Realism, Probability, Magic* (Cambridge: Cambridge University Press, 2010).

Julie Park (ed), *The Drift of Fiction: Reconsidering the Rise of the Novel*, special issue of *Eighteenth Century: Theory and Interpretation*, 52 (2011).

Patricia Meyer Spacks, *Novel Beginnings: Experiments in Eighteenth-Century English Fiction* (New Haven, CT: Yale University Press, 2006).

G. Gabrielle Starr, *Lyric Generations: Poetry and the Novel in the Long Eighteenth Century* (Baltimore, MD: Johns Hopkins University Press, 2004).

Carol Stewart, *The Eighteenth-Century Novel and the Secularization of Ethics* (Aldershot: Ashgate, 2010).

Index